INTRINSIC

THE TERRAN CYCLE: BOOK ONE

PHILIP C. QUAINTRELL

Copyright © 2016 by Philip C. Quaintrell
First edition published 2016.
Second edition published 2021.

Cover Illustration by Tom Edwards
Book design by BodiDog Design
Edited by David Bradley

ISBN: 978-1-916610-24-8 (paperback)
ASIN: B08Y4R8YD9 (ebook)

Published by Quaintrell Publishings

ALSO BY PHILIP C. QUAINTRELL

"It is not in the stars to hold our destiny but in ourselves."

William Shakespeare

PROLOGUE

Keep running. It was the only thought Savrick had anymore. If he ever stopped running they would find Esabelle and take her from him. The Terran would most certainly kill him for breaking the law and having a child in the first place, but he wouldn't let them take his daughter. Esabelle was all he had left of his wife and, with only three standard years of life, Esabelle's blue eyes already reflected her mother's.

Keep running!

"He went this way!" a deep Terran voice echoed through the cave.

Savrick tried to ignore the pain in his lungs and push on. He had to put as much distance between them and Esabelle as possible. Just thinking of the toddler, hidden away in their makeshift home of a cave, renewed Savrick's efforts to keep running. The torches mounted on his chest strap struggled to highlight the safest path through the tunnels as he sprinted through the dark.

The pitch-black was momentarily illuminated by a *crack* of lightning when a ball of organic plasma shot through the cave and exploded against the stone wall. The super-heated energy skimmed Savrick's shoulder, scorching his flesh down to the muscle. His scream of pain couldn't be helped. His pain receptors begged him to stop running and nurse the burn, but the Terran were faster and stronger than him; he couldn't afford to stop. Savrick had always known that death was coming for him: it became a certainty the moment he was detected outside the mountain.

The gleaming city of Kaldor lay several kilometres away from the base of the mountain, the only city on the relatively uninhabited planet. The Terran had settled here mostly out of curiosity for the ancient warships that littered the surface of this world like a graveyard, the remnants of their ancestors. Savrick had only survived this long by salvaging parts. He was good with his hands - resourceful his wife had always said.

Esabelle... Keep running you fool!

Hunger has a way of driving people to be reckless. Hunting the Rorstack outside the protective walls of the mountain had been his mistake, one that would now cost him his life and probably that of his daughter. Kaldor's sensor sweep had only required seconds to detect his presence and alert the inhabitants to the fugitive. It had taken many months to smuggle both Esabelle and himself onto the deserted planet, away from the empire's capital world, Albadar. Savrick had underestimated Kaldor's growing population and how quickly the Terran would flock to the dead planet.

Running footsteps gained on him. The Terran had no need for torches or scanning equipment to find him. Their higher state of evolution made them perfect hunters in the dark, able to feel his very existence emanating in the soup of the universe. Every movement he made exerted pressure on the molecules in the atmosphere around him, and those molecules, in turn, vibrated all the way back to the Terran's heightened senses, giving away his exact location. Even if he stayed perfectly still, they would smell his pheromones in the air or hear his heart pounding in his chest.

Savrick was forced to release another *yelp* of pain when he miscalculated the size of a rock on the ground and tripped. The spiky rock cut his knees and hands, spreading more pain throughout his body. Exhaustion was becoming harder to fight off in the damp cave and he only made it a few more metres before his next mistake proved to be his last. Running as fast as he could, the torches failed to reveal the abyss-like hole before him. A sharp scream was all Savrick gave until he continued to fall in silence. It was a short drop with a sudden stop that left him reeling in more pain, face down in a shallow stream.

The thought of what they would do if they found Esabelle was the only thing that gave him strength. Savrick pushed himself up, blinking the ice-cold water from his eyes, and tried to stand. His left leg buckled under the pain in his ankle, causing him to instantly collapse back into the stream. Muffled voices and heavy footsteps could be heard through the small opening in the roof of the cave.

They had found him.

Savrick gripped his spear tightly. The crude weapon had been made from old piping salvaged from one of the buried ships, entombed within the mountain. Had he used any kind of energy weapon, the Terran would have discovered them sooner.

If they were going to kill him he wouldn't go out without a fight. They all deserved to die anyway for what they had done to his wife. He only wished he could make them suffer as she had.

On his hands and one good knee, Savrick dragged his body through the stream. Looking around the small cave, he realised there was nowhere to escape; the stream entered and left the cave via a small tunnel that he couldn't fit through. Three heavy *thuds* and a splash of water was all that preceded the Terran.

Savrick slowly turned around, his pain forgotten in the final moments of his life. The dark plated armour allowed the Terran to blend into the inky shadows of the cave, for Savrick's torchlight was the only source of illumination. The central Terran stepped forward as a small light appeared on his waistline, creating a holographic image of an old man. Savrick knew who he was of course; there was only one old-looking man amongst the immortal Terran.

"Hello, Savrick." The hologram greeted him as an old friend, long missed.

3

"ALF..." Savrick hated the artificial life form. Everything that had happened to him could be laid at the AI's feet.

"It's time to stop running," ALF continued.

"I'll never give her to you!" Savrick knew what ALF really wanted.

"She was never meant to exist, Savrick. There's a reason I created that law, and it wasn't out of malice. Many Terran have died because of her."

"And that's all you care about, isn't it? The precious Terran! What about us? What about the Gomar? Aren't we your children as well?" Savrick could see that he wasn't going to change the AI's mind. But when it came to his daughter, he would do anything, even beg. "Please, ALF... she's just a child."

"Esabelle is dangerous and-" ALF's image flickered before going out completely.

What was happening? Savrick had never seen an image of ALF be disrupted before. Had the Terran ended the communication to get straight to killing him? He angled the spear towards them, prepared to die fighting if that was the way it had to be. There was no movement from his three would-be-killers in the dark. What were they waiting for? He would beg for Esabelle's life but not his own.

Savrick adjusted his position on the floor and directed his torches at the Terran. All of them were frozen in agony, silently screaming, with what appeared to be black liquid sinking into every orifice of their faces. Almost as one, they dropped to their knees clutching at their throats, desperate to breathe. As suddenly as their agony started, it stopped. The Terran dropped face-first onto the hard ground, as lifeless as the rock around them. In the torchlight, Savrick watched in horror as the black liquid wormed out of their bodies and returned to the source, *behind* him.

With an abundance of splashing, Savrick rolled over in the stream and used his elbows to get as far away from the cave wall as possible. In his desperate thrashing, torchlight flashed across something metallic and shiny embedded in the wall. Uttering a deep grunt of pain, Savrick stood on one leg and slowly hopped towards the mysterious object. He moved his hand across the jagged, slippery surface, unsure of what he was feeling. Some of the object was coated in dense rock while other sections of the shiny metal were visible in between. Had he not reached out and touched the object, it would have been impossible to distinguish its smooth surface from the surrounding rock.

"What are *you*?" Savrick stood back, taking it all in.

He could see the rough outline of the embedded object and decided it was one side of a cube, at least six-feet wide. Wielding the tip of his spear as if it were a knife, he began to prise the sharp rock away from the flat surface. Wiping away the mud and sludge revealed strange markings and engravings on the cube. To be so deep within the cavern the object must be ancient. This was the sort of find the Terran were searching for, a relic of the old wars. Like all recorded history of that time, knowledge was sketchy; so much had been lost in those violent times. He knew a great battle had been fought in this system, but he couldn't remember over what or exactly when.

Savrick took a moment to look over the hieroglyphs and symbols that ran in interlacing circles across the cube. The writing was unrecognisable - if it was indeed writing - but it could have been a pre-Criterion text. He suddenly withdrew his hand as he cut the pad of his thumb and index finger on the razor edge of a rock. Savrick grimaced at the blood he saw dripping down between the circling hieroglyphs. There were other predators inside the mountain that would be drawn to that smell. He moved to wipe it away when the surrounding rock cracked from an unseen pressure.

Instinctively, Savrick jumped back and landed in the stream again, gripping his spear with white knuckles. Fissures split the wall, causing a waterfall effect as rocks crumbled across the smooth surface. The cube came to life when openings appeared along the edges and the circled markings began to rotate like the cogs in a clock. Savrick held his breath somewhere between curiosity and fear. All at once the activity stopped, leaving a hand-sized hole just above the centre. There was nothing but darkness inside.

Savrick rose from the wet ground and tentatively approached the cube. He may have been labelled a Gomar but he *was* Terran in nature. His species had advanced so far because of their curiosity and exploration of the unknown after all.

Hesitantly, Savrick placed his hand inside... and felt only pain.

ONE

200,000 years later

Kalian woke up to the sound of the mag-train gliding past his apartment. It took him a moment to shake off the after-effects of sleep, and realise he was supposed to be walking out through the door when the 08:30 train passed by. He shot out of bed with the kind of start only someone late for work could have. Checking his wrist for the time proved fruitless, as the emitters inside his skin had frozen the holographic time at 03:10. Frustrated, Kalian tapped his arm until the display flickered and disappeared completely. Groaning, he wondered why he had even bothered having it implanted in the first place; technology always disagreed with him.

He checked his hair quickly in the mirror, thankful there was still some of yesterday's gel in it to keep it fairly styled. He threw on the first items of clothing the wardrobe presented him with, hoping the dark blue shirt would match his cargo trousers. The open-plan living space made it easy to run around collecting everything he needed while shoving a toothbrush in his mouth and wishing it would do the work for him. Kalian hopped into the kitchen space with one trouser leg refusing to cooperate while he ignored the odd socks.

That was when he stopped in the most unorthodox position.

His apartment was a mess, but it hadn't been when he fell asleep last night. It had been a part of his routine to tidy his home every Sunday night before the start of a new week. The first thing he noticed was his cream coloured toaster stuck unnaturally halfway up the kitchen wall. He tapped it lightly on the side and the machine crashed back onto the counter. Almost every cupboard was open, exposing the disorganised contents within. The chopping board stood on one of its corners, slowly turning by itself at an impossible angle. His favourite spotted teacups had been removed from their rack and were each stuck at a different angle to the underside of the cupboard above.

Looking around the apartment it was clear to see the same had happened everywhere. The bedside table was standing on only one leg, though somehow the contents had failed to slide off, leaving the lamp lopsided. The central rug had simply turned upside down, hiding the pattern from view. Kalian verbally commanded the TV, embedded in the wall, to switch on but received nothing but silence.

"Not again..." The words were garbled by the impeding toothbrush.

He pulled it out and saw that he had forgotten to put any paste on it. Groaning again, he threw the toothbrush into the bathroom, the only other room in the apartment. Kalian finally adjusted his trousers and rolled his Datapad up, shoving it into his satchel for work. He didn't have time to deal with yet another unexplainable event. If he didn't leave immediately he would be unforgivably late, and he didn't want to set a precedent with the freshers.

He took one last look out of the window which made up one of his four walls, and narrowed his vision between the buildings. Kalian could just make out the sun rising steadily over the San Francisco horizon, its light bringing life to the city.

The walk to the university was long, or at least it felt that way in the summer heat the Weather-Net had created. Kalian was thankful for the towering height of the surrounding skyscrapers for they provided much-needed shade. It was easy to feel small living amongst such colossal structures; he admired the height of them though, with the central buildings able to touch the cloud bank most days. The majority had been built centuries ago for housing purposes and, as a history lecturer, Kalian was well aware of the population crisis before the construction of habitats on the Moon and the mega structures built on Mars. Earth had been running out of land at the time and there was only one way to build - up.

After some of the pressure was relieved, Central Parliament had cities all over the world re-designed to bring back their beauty and restore a dwindling economy. With housing no longer an issue, Central Parliament was even able to rescind the population laws, allowing for families to have two children instead of one. It had never concerned Kalian much since he was an only child, like his parents.

Kalian liked his part of the city. He had moved here after taking his job at the university four years ago. Being closer to the bay it wasn't as dense, allowing more space for parks and trees. In some of the denser areas, it was hard to even see the clouds through all the sky-bridges and advertising holo-boards.

The sight always amused him, making him think of his ancestors, centuries before. They had thought everyone would be flown by automated cars across the galaxy, to one of the many worlds they had no doubt terraformed, and that the human race would conquer death with futuristic medicine; all diseases cured. Well, they had succeeded at a great many feats, including the habitation of the solar system and beyond, as well as expanding the human lifespan, but the sights surrounding him only proved that technology could only progress so fast.

The streets were as hectic as normal. Kalian saw dozens of auto-mated transports crammed with people. Hundreds of people hurried about in every direction, each just as late for work as he was, judging by the general rush. He couldn't quite make out the university through all the mag-transports that glided between the buildings on the traverse ways above.

In his hurried flight, Kalian walked straight into the back of a woman standing still in the moving crowds. With a quick apology, he stole a cursory glance at the screen on her Datapad, wondering what could possibly make someone brave enough to stop in the flow of human traffic. He recognised one of the better-known news reporters, but he didn't have time for the headlines now - he was *really* late. Kalian silently cursed his info band at failing to wake him, then he cursed himself for expecting it to after all the others that had spontaneously broken.

He heard the magnetic hum as someone drove past him at high speed in their mag-car. Some idiot had obviously hacked the safety protocols to put it into manual drive - a feature that was not supposed to be available in the city. He felt his grip tighten around the strap on his satchel.

Focus, think of something else.

Kalian's emotions slowly spun out of control. The unusual speed of the mag-car brought back the memory. There wasn't time to push it to the back of his mind like he had practised so many times before. He felt the static on his arms as the hairs stood on end. The usual tingling sensation in his spine left his hands feeling numb. The noise above his head had him looking up; the sound of some machine malfunctioning was all too familiar. This time it was one of the servo lamps that hovered above street level. Sparks erupted out of the top before it spun end-over-end. The noise didn't go unnoticed by the people that surrounded Kalian either. *He* knew what was coming though. Jumping to the side, he pushed the person in front to create space as it plummeted to the ground, shattering the glass encasing it. Only moments later, a cleaning mech hovered out of its housing unit and began clearing up the glass and debris into its body for recycling.

The sight of a Mag-car didn't usually bother him so much; in fact, he barely noticed them among the usual activities of the street. It was the out of control driving that had done it. Kalian was suddenly aware of the disgruntled people around him. The servo lamp could have seriously injured any one of them. The guilt was already setting in, along with some paranoia. Thinking logically, he wasn't sure what he was worried about; to the casual observer, he hadn't even touched the servo lamp. His real worry was that he had no idea *how* he had broken it but, like all the other unexplainable incidents in his life, he knew he was responsible.

Blending back into the crowd, Kalian moved on, keeping his head down until he didn't recognise the people around him anymore. He could see the reflection of the sun on the domed university exterior now. His lecture theatre was a refuge where he could focus his mind on Earth's history rather than his own.

The campus was teeming with students and lecturers as usual. He found himself checking the time on the Info-band again. His wrist was, naturally, blank.

Technology hates me...

He regretted not having the time to take in the beauty of the campus and its surroundings. The position of the university allowed for a clear view of the Golden Gate Bridge.

What I wouldn't give to see the old one. To think that bridges used to stand in the water...

Embarrassingly, Kalian failed to navigate the group of children touring the campus with their school teacher. He tried to slip through the minors, but he ended up tangled amid the throng. Keeping calm, Kalian let them pass by, flashing a fake smile to the teacher as she silently apologised. After breaking into a quick march, he found the corridors were fairly clear of students and teachers, with the occasional cleaning mech wiping the floors. The automatic door, made to look like oak, parted in the middle as he approached. He walked straight to his desk while rummaging through his bag in search of his Datapad, where he had stored all the sessions for the day.

"Sorry, I'm late everyone. Let's get started, shall we?" The general chatter of the first-year class began to die down immediately. "As I told you yesterday, today we're going back four hundred and twenty-one years to look at the history of Solar Drive technology." He took a breath, rolling out his Datapad until it became rigid like a tablet. "Now, who can tell me the significance of this event?" Kalian looked up for the first time since entering the room.

The lecture theatre was full up to its thirtieth row with eager new starters. It always amused Kalian that history had been a rather dull subject in ancient times. The birth of Solar Drive had changed that. Before Solar Drive, history had comprised of the corporate takeover in the twenty-third century and, of course, the rise of Central Parliament, which waged war against the corporations in the twenty-fifth century.

Kalian always wondered what the world would have been like if the corporations had won that war and discovered the Solar Drive in the next century. It was common knowledge that the corporate wars had stunted the growth of technology. However, Central Parliament had done everything it could to get the future back on track.

The glass board behind him lit up with information on the Solar Drive when it connected with his Datapad. The board showed a quick image of a chunky-looking ship flying towards the sun, before it streaked across the stars, out of sight.

The glare off the board reflected his image back at him. His dark hair was getting long again, at least by Kalian's standards. He had strong cheekbones thanks to his father but, from the images stored at home of his parents, he knew he had his mother's dark eyes.

Most of his students teased him for his youthful looks but he *was* young; he had at least two hundred years left. At twenty-eight he had done well to secure his position at the university but his passion for history had driven him academically. Sometimes though, he wished he'd been born centuries earlier, just so he could experience life without all the technology. Doing the maths, however, he realised that he would have to go back a thousand years to experience life with minimal technology.

A student in the middle row spoke up. "That was the year everything changed."

A good answer, but Kalian was looking for something more than that. "Care to elaborate?"

The student hesitated in front of his classmates. "It was the year we discovered faster-than-light-travel."

Again, a very accurate answer, but he was only getting snippets from them. Kalian could see he would have to coax them a bit. "True, very true. And *discover* is probably the right word for it. As I'm sure you all learnt growing up, faster-than-light-travel was discovered on an *alien* ship on the edge of our solar system."

With his Datapad, Kalian used the eyetrak to connect an old video log to the glass board. It showed a huge meteor shower flying through the solar system.

"Records taken at the time show that the meteors ranged in size from that of your hand to entire cities. Two of the asteroids on a collision course for Earth were said to have been world enders. Thanks to the United Defence Corps, the asteroids were knocked off course. The majority of the shower found its way to the surrounding planets and moons. Any meteors that didn't, began a new journey orbiting the sun." Kalian knew the footage he was showing them wasn't new; in fact, every human alive would have seen this footage on the news and in documentaries and even in a few movies.

"It didn't take long before exploration and mining began on the rocky remains. The trajectory of the shower indicates that it all came from the same point in space, though it has proved to be too far to reach. Now I find geology to be as exciting as the next guy, but the unknown mineral in these alien rocks was a catalyst for the turning point in human history." He turned to the next file on his Datapad with a flick of his eyes.

The images were clearly being shot from a vessel flying over Pluto on the edge of the solar system. The camera moved to focus on Charon, Pluto's largest moon, where a dark trail could be seen stretching several miles across the crystalline surface. The zooming increased until it found the point of the trail, where the alien ship had found its end.

"After the video log had been spread across the globe, human beings looked up to the stars for the first time and knew they were not alone." That was his favourite line. He always used it on the freshers. "However, four hundred and twenty-one years has gone by with no further evidence of other life. Even the ship itself was devoid of any beings to study. But in time, humanity came to terms with this revelation. It then turned its attention to the wonders the ship had to offer."

He pulled up some side images of various scientists examining the ship's engine. Kalian had no real idea how they replicated the technology or figured out that the meteorites contained the necessary fuel, Solarcite, as it was later named. He remembered the mechanics had been somewhat overwhelming in his own years at school. In his lectures, he simply used the term re-engineered. This seemed to suffice.

"However technical, it was this discovery that led to the creation of the Solar Drive and humanity's eventual exploration of space beyond our sun's light."

Even though the discovery was primarily scientific, it was still considered to be the most significant event in human history. For this reason, it was one of Kalian's biggest teaching subjects.

Damn, he was starting to lose them. To his dismay, the majority of students appeared to have become distracted by their own Datapads.

"Ok guys, let's try and stay focused."

A girl with frizzy dark hair near the front looked up from her Datapad like she had seen a ghost. "Mr Gaines, you need to see this."

He was hesitant, on the brink of reprimanding them, but her face was the same as everyone else's. Kalian walked over as she turned the screen around for him. He couldn't believe what was on the screen; it was too much of a coincidence.

"Is this live?" Kalian couldn't take his eyes away.

The girl gave a silent nod.

"Connect it to the glass board."

A couple of quick movements of her eyes and the old video log was replaced by the Central News. The larger image caught everyone's attention. It was clearly being shot from a lens on Earth somewhere, as the backdrop was blue skies. In the centre of the image was some kind of ship. Kalian had seen plenty of UDC ships before, as they were always in the news for something, but this was definitely not UDC. To be seen in such detail from the ground it must be massive in size. The news headline simply read: **Unknown Alien Ship Slips Past United Defence Corps. Have They Returned?**

It had to be alien. It was just too, well... alien. Kalian couldn't quite make out any defining features from this distance, but it looked to be purple. A smaller headline appeared at the bottom of the screen explaining that the ship was directly over San Francisco. He had to stop his jaw from dropping. It was above this very city. En masse, all thirty rows jumped up from their seats and crowded around the panoramic window next to Kalian's desk. People were pushing past each other to try and catch a glimpse of the alien visitors.

Kalian looked back at the ship on the screen. Alien? Yes. Returned? He wasn't so sure. He was no expert in ship design but this one looked nothing like the crashed ship on Charon. It was much bigger for starters. The other one had been bulkier and not so smooth in appearance. The door to the lecture theatre opened, stopping his train of thought. Four men in black and grey UDC uniforms entered the lecture theatre.

"Sir, we're with the UDC. Are you Kalian Gaines?"

Kalian was speechless.

What the hell do they want with me?

"Sir?" The soldier had a feeling of urgency about him.

Kalian hesitated. "Yes, I'm Kalian Gaines."

Before he had even finished the sentence one of the soldiers broke away and approached him. He held up a small transparent square to Kalian's eye and the glass lit up with a picture of his face and several personal details about his life.

"ID's confirmed, sir. This is him."

A small nod from their commanding officer was all they needed to proceed. As one, they surrounded Kalian and grabbed him by the arms, not roughly but firmly. A couple of the students looked to protest, but Kalian held up a hand to calm them.

"Mr Gaines, my men and I have orders to escort you off campus." Before Kalian could ask any questions, the commanding officer simply stated, "As you can see..." He pointed to the soldiers either side of the lecturer. "This isn't optional."

As Kalian was forced out of the room, he noticed one of the soldiers packing his Datapad into a bag. He didn't know why since there was nothing but lecture material on it. Waiting outside on one of the campus lawns was a large UDC craft, bigger than any Mag-transport. Everyone around them was almost oblivious to his predicament, completely distracted by the looming alien ship. Only the group of touring children stopped to look at him before returning to the view above.

"Where *off campus* are we going exactly?" Kalian could see the thrusters underneath; this was designed for flying not driving.

Only the UDC had permission to use air-space for travel. Kalian could see the logic in it; this way they could respond to emergency situations without worrying about mid-air collisions, as well as ensuring air superiority. That's why the Mag Hyperways had been built across the oceans five hundred years ago.

The commanding officer didn't halt his stride. "It's a matter of planetary security, sir."

That was a phrase Kalian had only ever heard in movies. It occurred to Kalian that he had only flown once before, as a child. It was on a school trip to Armstrong, the capital city of The Moon. At least on that trip, he knew what awaited him on the other side. This was somewhat scarier.

Kalian was directed to his seat and the soldiers took their positions either side of him.

Am I a prisoner?

The craft rose vertically into the sky, creating a strange sense of pressure that passed from head to toe.

One of the soldiers in front of Kalian noticed his expression of discomfort. "It's just the Grav Enforcers." He looked down to the floor. "It stops us from sliding all over the place."

The lecturer nodded in understanding, well at least the theory of it.

It felt to Kalian as if they had been travelling for a lifetime, but he realised it had probably been less than an hour. Anxiety could do that. He had bombarded the soldiers with questions about where they were taking him and why, but their expressions never changed. There was always the chance that the soldiers didn't even know why they had been ordered to retrieve him.

Just keep calm and stay in control.

Kalian kept thinking it like a mantra, over and over in his head. The craft shuddered and a loud *thud* came from underneath.

"Clear to disembark." The pilot's voice came through the speakers above them.

The heavy side door slid open and sunlight flooded the cabin. Walking into the shadow of the ship were two more soldiers wearing UDC uniforms, each bearing a rifle that looked too heavy to hold.

They instantly noticed Kalian. "Who's the civilian?" The lack of uniform was a dead giveaway.

The commanding officer stepped out first. "Orders from the Chief Commander himself. He's a Priority One."

The guard checked his Info-band to confirm the orders were legitimate. The spherical emitters inside produced a miniature holographic image above his wrist.

"Order confirmed. Proceed." The guard pointed somewhere out of sight.

Kalian stepped out of the craft and instantly felt the heat of the sun engulf him. The air was dry, making it initially hard to breathe.

I'm definitely not in San Francisco.

Taking in the view, Kalian felt his lips part involuntarily. It couldn't be what he thought it was. It looked as if he had been brought to a UDC base and, judging from its size, it couldn't be just any base; this was central command.

"The Hub..." The words barely left his dry lips.

The name had always seemed appropriate to Kalian since this was the base from which all security protocols were sent. From security patrols in the cities to orbital defence ships in space - all orders came from here. Kalian had heard it mentioned on the news whenever a new security act had been passed through Central Parliament. He could see why they didn't need to keep the place a secret - it was a fortress.

The base was surrounded by landing pads that stretched out into the desert, further than he could see. Considering there hadn't been a war for nearly five hundred years, they were certainly prepared for one. Kalian had heard of the occasional separatist faction here and there, but nothing that required this level of security. At several points on the wall were groups of soldiers manning high powered rail-guns. All of them were watching Kalian. The high walls blocked any view from the ground of what might lie on the other side. It all felt so disorientating.

Kalian recalled a segment in a documentary, stating it had been built in the Nevada desert. It was the perfect location when they were building The Hub, centuries ago, for this particular desert was one of the few that had never been altered for living space.

The only visible door, at least two-feet thick, parted upon their approach. Before entering, Kalian took one last look at the sky, trying to spot the massive ship. The vista of blue was completely devoid of clouds, but he couldn't see the massive ship from here. Why was it above San Francisco?

The soldier tugged on his arm a little harder. "Come on. The Chief Commander is waiting for you."

Kalian remembered hearing that name; something about new security measures the UDC was taking on Mars. The man he had seen on the news looked like a man of power. He had been wearing his uniform with several medals on his chest, but his most striking feature had been a scar that ran from his jaw up to a point below his right eye.

Surely I'm not about to meet him. He's in charge of the entire UDC!

The only people above the Chief Commander were the council members in Central Parliament.

Kalian was ushered into a lift at the end of a large square foyer. The commanding officer entered with him, but the remaining soldiers took their stations surrounding the doors. Kalian may have been a priority, but he obviously wasn't considered a threat to be left with just one guard.

He felt the jolt as the lift began to move. "Are we going up or down?"

The ride was so smooth he couldn't tell. The commanding officer didn't move, oblivious to Kalian's existence.

"You guys don't talk much, huh?"

The doors parted, revealing a wide room filled with lots of monitors, surrounded by glowing holographics. Behind each monitor sat men and women in technical headgear with microphones. They all appeared to be talking at once. At the end of the room was the largest monitor, at least twenty feet across. Spread from edge to edge was a much clearer image of the massive unknown ship.

"Welcome to The Hub, Mr Gaines." A tall woman, with cropped black hair and dressed in UDC uniform, was stood by the entrance to the lift, obviously awaiting his arrival.

"I'm Lieutenant Walsh. If you would like to follow me." The lieutenant extended her hand towards a door at the far side of the room.

Her smile eased some of Kalian's tension. The lieutenant made him feel like he had come here of his own accord, rather than having been man-handled out of his lecture theatre.

The room he was shown to was long and rectangular, with the majority of it taken up by a table and large chairs made of synthetic leather. Two men were sitting near the far end, pouring over Datapads and holo-projections. Despite the air conditioning, both men were sweating and had frustrated looks on their faces. Kalian couldn't see the face of the man behind them; he had his back to the door and his hands clasped behind his back. Lieutenant Walsh pulled out a seat halfway up the table and gestured for Kalian to sit down. Before he had taken the seat, the lieutenant had already left the room.

The man turned to face Kalian. "Thank you for joining us, Mr Gaines."

A small pit opened in his stomach. Perhaps the most insignificant man in the world was being addressed by the most powerful, and he had no idea why.

"I realise the way you were brought here wasn't... ideal." His voice was rough and full of authority. It commanded attention immediately.

It was this voice that ordered thousands of men and women across the stars on a daily basis. The Chief Commander appeared less composed in comparison to his public interviews. He had the face of a man who hadn't been sleeping well for years. Who could with all that responsibility? The scar across his cheek was paler in the flesh. Kalian wondered why he had never had it removed. The Chief no longer had the look of a soldier; his hair had grown out, along with his stomach. Cold grey eyes rested on the history lecturer. It was as if he was being inspected from the inside out. The tension crept back into his muscles.

"I am Chief Commander Hendricks."

Kalian stole a quick glance at the other men, but the Chief Commander apparently had no intention of introducing them.

"Do you know why you're here, Mr Gaines?" The Chief moved around the table until he was standing opposite Kalian.

The spotlight above them shadowed his eyes and accentuated his scar. A lump formed inside Kalian's throat preventing him from answering.

The Chief continued, "Judging from your expression, son, I reckon you've got no idea what you're doing here. Am I right?"

Kalian managed to clear his throat this time. "No... sir." He had never been a soldier in his life but, for some reason, he felt as if he shouldn't speak unless spoken to.

"Well, that makes two of us then." The Chief turned to glare at the men seated at the end of the table.

Now Kalian was even more confused.

How can he not know why I'm here?

One of the seated men wiped the sweat from his balding head with a handkerchief. "Kalian... Can I call you Kalian?"

He had never liked being called Mr Gaines. Except for the freshers, even his students called him by his first name.

"Sure." Kalian was starting to get annoyed. How could they drag him all the way out to the desert and not know why?

"I'm Commander Barnes, this is Commander Laney." He flicked his thumb towards the man next to him. "Let me start by saying that anything you see or hear in this facility is never to be reported."

Kalian could tell that there were consequences behind that statement. He simply nodded in agreement.

"As I'm sure you are aware by now, at oh-seven-thirty-two this morning an unknown vessel appeared in orbit." He tapped a few commands into his Info-band and a holographic image appeared in the middle of the table. It was a detailed picture of the unknown ship.

"At oh-seven-thirty-three, every monitor in our command centre received the same message-"

Before Commander Barnes could continue, he was interrupted by the Chief. "They broke every damn firewall we've got inside of a minute!"

Kalian could tell there was a hint of fear behind his anger.

Commander Barnes continued. "They only sent one message and it was very clear." This time he tapped the table and sent the image across the surface until it stopped in front of Kalian.

We Come As Friends To Mankind. Request Meeting. Select Location. Choose Representative and Two Warriors. Bring Kalian Gaines.

Underneath the text was a layout of someone's DNA, stretching from end-to-end of the screen. Kalian couldn't believe what he was seeing. He read it two more times to be sure.

There are actual aliens in that ship, real aliens...

Kalian couldn't form a coherent thought due to the shock of seeing his own name in an alien message.

All three men were staring at him trying to gauge his reaction, to see if he had some insight they didn't.

"Are you even sure this is me? I mean I can't be the only Kalian Gaines that exists across two solar systems?"

Kalian could feel his fear mixing with desperation, but it was too late. The static on his arm was building again and his spine felt hot beneath his skin. He didn't even think to try and control it; he couldn't stop seeing his name in that message. The lights in the room flickered for a moment, sending them all into sporadic darkness. Even the holo-projectors blinked out.

"What the hell is this?" The Chief's question brought Kalian's attention back.

In his panic, he hadn't realised what he had done. Concentrating on the chair in front of him, he convinced himself there was nothing else in the universe except that chair. Everything else fell away. Kalian regained his focus and slowly brought himself back to the present. Years of self-meditation had established the best techniques that worked for him. The lights and projectors winked back to life.

The Chief tapped his Info-band. "Lieutenant Walsh, report."

The Lieutenant's voice came back over the inbuilt speaker. "Some kind of electromagnetic pulse sir! We can't trace its origin but it appears to have hit half of the facility. We're analysing for any damage now."

Half the building? How the hell did I do that?

The Chief sucked in his breath - just one more thing for him to worry about.

"Are we under attack?" The leather chair creaked under the Chief's grip.

"All systems have rebooted as if nothing happened, Sir," she replied.

"Keep me updated, Lieutenant."

The older man turned back to Kalian, who felt like sinking into his chair and disappearing forever. A moment of nausea swept over him.

The Chief continued. "You see that strand of DNA at the bottom of the message?"

Kalian took another look at the image, but it meant nothing to him.

"That's you, son. Your specific DNA. We ran it through the Birthing Databank - it's a perfect match."

The Birthing Databank was the largest database ever created. It stored all the DNA and genetic structure of every person at the time of their birth. It allowed for instant identification, which was useful if retinal scans failed.

"What... what could they possibly want with me? I'm just a history lecturer from San Francisco." Kalian was doing his best not to lose control again.

"Since receiving the message, my guys here have been going over

22

every scrap of information there is on you - and there isn't much of interest." The Chief looked at the eyetrak on the table and, with a flick of his eyes, changed the holo-projection of the ship to a page of information about Kalian. "Kalian Gaines, born in San Francisco in 2913 AD. Parents Joseph and Mary Gaines..." He paused for a moment, reading the next section in his head first.

"They died in 2920 due to an accident involving a Mag-car. The report came back as a *malfunction* of the magnetic generator." He said the word malfunction as if he had never heard of it. "I was under the impression that Mag generators took centuries to degrade."

Was there an accusation in there?

Kalian elaborated for them. "The car slipped off the track at about seventy miles-per-hour. It went straight through the railing and off a bridge..." His memory was disjointed after that. He simply remembered waking up in hospital, alone.

The Chief took another look at the information. "The hospital records show that you had no injuries, not even a scratch, but they couldn't explain why you were unconscious." He was staring at Kalian again. "I guess we found something interesting about you after all..."

They know something isn't right...

The subject of his parents' death had always scared Kalian. Deep down he felt that he was the cause of the accident, but he wasn't sure how. The generators have multiple fail-safes to prevent that kind of accident. Growing up, he had done some research into Mag-cars to find a possible cause for such a malfunction but he had found none.

"...You're one lucky son of a bitch. I don't know anyone who could walk away from a crash of that magnitude unscathed."

Kalian tried to hide his relief.

They don't know.

"You spent a few years in and out of foster homes until you got your qualifications in the subject of history." He placed the Datapad down on the table, ending the holo-projection of Kalian's file.

"And that's the end of your story Kalian Gaines... so what the hell do they want with you?"

Kalian sat back in his chair, just as confused and curious as them.

Commander Barnes sat forward in his seat. "Here's what we know, Kalian. The ship found on Pluto's moon, Charon, was indeed of alien origin, but our analysts can't find any similarity between that ship and *this* one." He pointed towards the ceiling in the general direction of their new visitors.

"Do they have Solar Drive technology like the old ship?" Kalian felt more comfortable asking questions now that he knew his secret was safe.

"Honestly, we have no idea. They didn't come from the direction of the sun. They just appeared from nowhere. Most of our scans are just bouncing off the hull. We have no idea what's going on inside that ship. Hell, we can't even figure out what the hull's made of." He rubbed his eyes. Looking at monitors all morning had obviously given him a headache. "The only thing we know for certain is it's five times the size of the *Hyperion*. It's *eight miles* long."

He was referring to the flagship of the UDC fleet which was the largest ship they had ever made - the pinnacle of human engineering.

"So you think these might be different aliens to the ones that crashed here centuries ago?" Kalian's curiosity was growing. He found himself eager for more information.

Commander Barnes sighed. "We don't know that either, though it's one theory. It's also possible that in over four hundred years they just built better ships."

Kalian was starting to get a sense of how frustrating this must be for them. The UDC had been in control of all security matters for five hundred years. They knew everything about everything. Now, for the first time, they were in the dark.

"I want to help you, I really do but... I just don't see where I fit into all of this." A thought suddenly occurred to him. "What about Century? Has a ship appeared in *their* orbit?"

Kalian couldn't believe he'd forgotten about Earth's sister world, Century. Terraformed centuries earlier, it had taken one hundred years to create a breathable atmosphere and start colonisation. Situated eight light years away, it was now home to six billion human beings. Thanks to Solar Drive powered ships it could be reached in a couple of days, jumping from star to star.

"We've been in communication with them all morning, but they've reported no activity." Commander Laney checked his own Datapad in case of updates.

Kalian asked, "Why would they only be here? Why not Century too?"

It was the Chief Commander who replied. "We suspect they've been watching us for a while now. That's how they know our language and forms of communication. We're assuming that with this knowledge they also know that Central Parliament is located on Earth. They know that all the decisions come from this planet, not Century."

It was clear the Chief wasn't happy with the situation. Knowledge was power and right now, he had none. These aliens were an unknown factor and, as long as they remained a mystery, they were a potential enemy in the Chief's eyes.

"Also," Commander Barnes added, "we think they're over San Francisco specifically because you were there."

Kalian found that piece of information overwhelming and disturbing.

Aliens chose that exact place just because of me? What is going on here? Why am I so important? There must be billions of people more important and interesting than me!

Kalian had so many questions which he needed the answers to, but he looked at the faces in front of him and realised they knew as little as him. They could at least answer his next question.

"So, what happens now?" Kalian looked at each of them in turn. He didn't care who had the answer, he just wanted someone to have one.

The Chief took command again. "We've already picked out the location for this little get together." A slight smirk appeared at the corner of his mouth, twisting his scar. Picking the location gave him some measure of control. "As we speak, the Icarus station is being evacuated of all personnel."

Kalian had heard of this place. It was a security way-station built to stay in orbit between the Earth and the Moon. There had been a news report on it a few years ago, something to do with freeing up UDC ships. This way they could patrol further out into the solar system and beyond.

"The station is perfect. It's isolated and completely under our control." The Chief began to pace up and down the room as if he were giving a motivational speech or a plan of attack. "Right now, the big-wigs in Central Parliament are choosing their representative to speak on our behalf." The Chief turned on Kalian mid-step. "If nothing else Mr Gaines, remember this: the representative that goes with you is there to speak for all mankind. You, on the other hand, are there because you're a *condition*. You will not speak at this meeting unless spoken to. We have no idea what the outcome of this is going to be, and I'm sure you appreciate the complications civilians can bring."

Kalian knew what he was saying; civilians are hostages, civilians are untrained, civilians get in the way and civilian deaths are reported on the six o'clock news. Kalian was sure that if the Chief had it his way the entire population would be conscripted into the UDC. He agreed with the Chief to a point but he just wished he wasn't such an asshole about it. Kalian simply clenched his jaw and nodded silently.

Even if he was allowed to speak to the aliens, he wasn't sure what he would say. There were so many questions, not just on their apparent fascination with him, but also everything about them. It suddenly dawned on him that this meeting would be a monumental piece of history: that *he* would be a part of that history.

To think, I might have to give lectures about myself!

The sinking feeling in his stomach brought him back to the present; he was yet to find out what part of history he would play.

"Speaking of such complications," the Chief continued, "we've already selected two *warriors* to accompany you." He emphasised the word *warriors* as if it was an archaic term. He looked to Commander Barnes to provide the details.

"We believe they've allowed *us* to pick the location and send guards as a sign of trust. Our scans can't tell us anything, but if their ability to sneak up on us undetected is anything to go by, they're more advanced. So at this point, any sign of trust is good for us." He gave a quick glance to the Chief as if he had said something he shouldn't.

They were *hoping* it was a sign of trust, though Kalian was willing to bet the Chief wasn't the kind of man who had time for hope.

Kalian couldn't see where they were coming from. "Is there a reason we shouldn't trust them? The message says they come as friends. If they're as advanced as you think they are, wouldn't they just attack us rather than send a message?"

The Chief gave him a condescending look. "If I want to see a man I knock on his door first. I don't just appear in his kitchen while he's eating breakfast."

It was how the ship had appeared from nowhere that had them on edge. The unknown ship hadn't appeared in the solar system using what they knew to be conventional Solar Drive technology. Since learning about the engine of the crashed ship, the UDC had set up more patrols closer to the sun. After all, it was called Solar Drive for a reason. The only method of traversing light years in a few hours or days required the most powerful source of energy in space, a star.

Kalian didn't know the applied physics of Solar Drive but, like every other child, he had been taught the fundamentals. The ship must fly into orbit above a star spot on the surface of the sun, where the strongest magnetic fields are emitted. Using technology re-engineered from the alien craft, the UDC ships absorb the magnetic fields which in turn ignite the Solarcite. The alien fuel charges the engines, creating a thrust capable of faster-than-light travel.

As great as the technology was, it still had its limitations. With the fuel requiring such strong magnetic fields in order to be ignited, a star must be present. Without a star, the ship would be stranded in space with no way of igniting the fuel. Everyone knew the story of the *Paladin*, the only ship to disappear in the process of using Solar Drive. It was the third ship in the colonising expedition to Century and it had one hundred thousand people on board, all ready to start a new life on an exciting new planet. The last transmission received before they left was from an officer on the bridge, shouting about a navigational error.

Since they never arrived at Century and never returned to Earth, it was assumed they were lost in space with no stars close enough to reignite the Solarcite. That was two and a half centuries ago.

Solar Drive meant that all ships took off from the vicinity of a star and arrived close to the next star. Since this technology was taken from an alien race, it was assumed by the UDC that this is how they would eventually re-enter our solar system. But they hadn't. Instead, they appeared in the blink of an eye without alerting one human vessel.

"It's possible," Commander Barnes said, "they've been sitting there for a while. It wouldn't be a stretch to assume they have some kind of stealth technology."

The Chief waved his hand as if to push the subject away. "This discussion is for another place, Commander. The focus right now is Mr Gaines here. Whatever it is they want with you, son, I don't want you to make any kind of response or decision without consulting the representative and the security detail."

Do you want me to hold their hand too?

The thought occurred to Kalian that he hadn't actually been asked if he would go, but he got the feeling that the Chief Commander of the UDC didn't *ask* anything.

Lieutenant Walsh's voice came back over the speaker on the table. "Sir, a shuttle from Central Parliament has just landed. They appear to have elected Ambassador Sebastian Arlek as the representative for the meeting. I have a data-packet on him for you to review on the way up, sir."

The Chief Commander's face dropped at the name. "I don't need any data on *him*. We'll be right out." He turned to Commander Barnes. "It's time to get the ball moving. Send a message back on the same frequency informing our *friends* of the location and time of the meeting." He looked back at Kalian. "I think it's time to find out what they want with you Mr Gaines... what they want with all of us."

The commanders stood up to leave the room with him. The Chief ignored Kalian on the way out, but Commander Barnes motioned for him to follow them.

The Chief Commander's frustration filled the lift like an angry mob. Kalian opened his mouth to ask about the Ambassador when Commander Barnes grasped his wrist, shaking his head to deter him from saying anything. Kalian had the feeling the Commander had experienced the Chief's outbursts before and knew when it was a good time to remain invisible.

The doors opened into the stark entrance that was The Hub's main foyer. The Chief strode out of the lift with Lieutenant Walsh on his heels.

As they approached the main doors, Kalian saw a woman in UDC uniform stand up by one of the long benches that lined the walls. After the Chief had gone by she sat back down, resuming her original position. The main doors opened, bathing her in a soft glow. Her features appeared exaggerated in the sunlight. She didn't look like the other soldiers he had encountered, not even Lieutenant Walsh. Her hair wasn't cropped short but instead fell just below her shoulders. The copper ringlets shone, reflecting the bright light from outside. Her skin was fair against her high cheekbones and pointed jawline. He couldn't deny she was attractive. Her eyes stood out the most. In the sunlight, they shone a brilliant green.

Commander Barnes noticed Kalian's attention linger. "Ah, good timing. Let the Chief Commander greet the Ambassador. I want to introduce you to someone." He guided Kalian over to the seated woman, leaving the Chief and Lieutenant to meet Ambassador Arlek alone.

As they approached, the woman stood up again and saluted the Commander. "Sir."

The Commander responded in kind and she stood at ease. The top of her head only came up to Kalian's eyes but he could tell that he would be a fool to judge her by her height and slight frame alone. As a UDC soldier, she would know a hundred ways to put him on his ass.

"Kalian Gaines, this is Lieutenant Commander Li'ara Ducarté.

She has been selected to be your personal security detail for the mission."

Kalian reached out his hand to greet her formally. For some reason, he felt nervous about shaking her hand and his palm felt clammy.

"Hi... I'm Kalian. Strong grip you've got there." He let out a short, nervous laugh.

You complimented her grip?

She pulled her hand away and stared at him for a moment. "Mr Gaines..." As with the other soldiers, she didn't say much.

"Please, call me Kalian."

She simply nodded in return.

"Li'ara's been escorting VIPs and various government and UDC officials for years. She's going to stay by your side at all times Kalian. She'll look after you." Commander Barnes gave him a reassuring pat on the back.

"Lieutenant Commander, could you show Kalian to the mess hall. Get him something to eat and drink. The Chief Commander and I are going to brief the Ambassador before you get the green light. After you've seen to Kalian, you need to report to Commander Hawkins in the hangar bay. He's prepping the ship." He gave Kalian one last reassuring look and disappeared into the bright light of the Nevada desert.

Li'ara looked Kalian up and down, her eyes darting to specific points on his body. In a few seconds, she appeared to have assessed him for any potential strengths and weaknesses she might need to know in the field. From the look on her face, he had a feeling Li'ara had found more weaknesses than strengths.

"Have you ever had any kind of survival or endurance training?" She sounded doubtful.

"I took a self-defence class when I was nineteen..."

Kalian remembered taking the class, hoping it would teach him some mental and physical discipline. Nineteen was a hard year; he had been forced to isolate himself for hours every day. At least once a week he had woken up to find his belongings in a different place to where he had left them. The self-defence class had helped for a time. The concentration required during the sparring matches allowed him to focus. Unfortunately, it was only temporary, like everything else he had tried.

"So that would be a no then." Li'ara turned on her heel and headed towards a side door he hadn't even noticed.

She made no motion for him to follow but he remembered the Commander's orders about the mess hall.

They walked in silence until they reached a large empty room lined with tables and benches. It all seemed very sterile to Kalian.

"Wait here until I come for you. Someone will be along soon with food and water." Li'ara turned to leave.

"Wait, where are you going?" He regretted asking a question that had already been answered.

"I have to meet Commander Hawkins in the hangar bay. He'll be coming with us to the Icarus station." She left without saying anything else.

───────

AMBASSADOR ARLEK STOOD at the central control station, reviewing the current data being relayed by every ship and satellite in the system. There wasn't a lot of it. The station was covered in holographic readouts and scans that all fed back the same lack of knowledge. The Chief Commander ordered the latest images of the nearest drone sweep to be displayed on the large monitor at the head of the room. Arlek swept his scarlet robes aside as he moved around the station to get closer. The ship was astonishing. It was larger than any vessel made by Central Parliament or even the great warships from the corporate wars.

He touched the main station's glass top and brought up the message sent by the aliens. It all sounded good, except for the last part. Why on Earth would they want to meet a teacher? The possibilities this meeting held were not lost on him. If indeed these aliens were here to make an alliance, they could finally reclaim the years lost to them during the wars. The aliens could help humanity reach a golden age of technology that they should have conquered centuries ago. That responsibility fell squarely on him.

And so it should.

Arlek knew that no one else in Parliament was better suited for this than he. For decades, he had mastered the art of manipulation and political manoeuvring. If there were aliens on that ship looking to make a deal with mankind, then he was going to secure it.

"What do we know about *him*?" he asked.

"There's not a lot to know." Hendricks swept his hand across the nearest holograms and displayed the teacher's file. "He's got no record. Parents died when he was a kid. He's been lecturing at the San Francisco University for four years. He's intelligent but he's kept to himself. Barely has a presence on any of the social networks. All in all, he's unremarkable."

"You've spoken to him?"

"He hasn't got a clue what's going on."

"You're sure?"

"We scanned every molecule of his body on his way through here. There are a few strange markers in his blood that we can't explain yet, nothing alien, but we've got the best going over it as we speak. I saw his reaction when we showed him the message; he was just as shocked as we were."

There was something more to Kalian Gaines - there had to be. Arlek hated mysteries. He had spent years in the government uprooting every secret and leveraging every lie. He had anyone who mattered in his pocket, their sources now his own. Information was power and he had positioned himself deliberately to ensure everything passed through his office. How could there be no more to learn about this man? Everyone had secrets.

"What of them?" Arlek dismissed the data file on Kalian Gaines and looked to the magnificent ship.

"We know even less, I'm afraid. It appears they were always here, just cloaked." That was technology Arlek wanted. "Our scans are

useless against it. We don't even know what its armaments are like."
That part seemed to particularly trouble the Chief Commander.

A young cadet swivelled in his seat and caught their attention.
"Sir, they've responded. They have agreed on Icarus."

"Have it ready. We launch immediately." Arlek ignored
Hendricks' look and made for the lift. It was time for some answers.

WITHOUT HIS INFO-BAND WORKING, Kalian had no idea how much
time had gone by. He had made one attempt to leave the mess hall
but had been turned back by the guard stationed outside. It appeared
they had closed off the entire room just to hold him in it. They had
brought him food but recent events had caused him to lose his
appetite. When he had lost count of how many times he had paced
up and down, the door finally slid open to reveal Li'ara.

"The Ambassador's been briefed and our guests upstairs have
agreed on the location."

"When do we leave?"

"Now."

TWO

Kalian was led through a maze of corridors and security checks where both Li'ara and he were retinal scanned. Eventually, he found himself in another lift going back below ground level. Li'ara didn't speak much on the journey and, although Kalian didn't mind silence, with her he found it uncomfortable.

"So you're going to keep me safe, are you?"

"That's the idea." She sounded bored, which surprised Kalian given their extraordinary circumstances.

"Do you even know what you're keeping me safe from?" Kalian briefly looked at her to see if he achieved any reaction.

Li'ara responded with a quick glance but offered no reply.

Kalian supposed this type of mission must be normal for Li'ara; escorting people into unknown territory with an infinite number of possible outcomes. She didn't know if they were heading into a fight or a simple conversation. He assumed this was the reason for her calm exterior. Li'ara must be pretty good to even have this assignment. He found himself hoping so.

In any event, she looked prepared for a fight. Since leaving Kalian in the mess hall, Li'ara had met up with Commander Hawkins and changed her uniform. Instead of the all grey UDC garb, she now wore a combat survival suit covered in various plates of matt black armour. Besides her face, there wasn't one part of her body that wasn't covered or protected. Kalian noticed the suit fitted her perfectly as if it had been made just for her, with every curve matching her own. He had never seen this kind of outfit on other UDC soldiers. He assumed they were used for missions people didn't get to see or hear about. Kalian suddenly felt quite vulnerable in just his jacket.

I'll be fine. This is a historical meeting of two intelligent species, not some galactic war.

The hangar bay was bigger than Kalian had imagined. Lining the walls were hundreds of small ships, each capable of space flight. Most of them had smaller machines hovering around them, screwing in new bolts or replacing old wiring.

The soldiers and pilots milling around stopped what they were doing to watch Kalian and Li'ara walk down the middle of the hangar. He wasn't sure how many people knew about him and his connection to current events - after all, the guards who had brought him here didn't know anything. Kalian straightened his back to appear more confident in the new environment.

At least look as if you're supposed to be here.

The ship they were heading for was obvious for it sat in the middle of the hangar with an armed guard at each corner. Several UDC mechanics were working on what Kalian assumed to be the engine at the back. The ship itself was quite different from the others in the bay. The surrounding vessels were practical in their design with no thought to appearance. This one looked as if it had been polished for days by cleaning mechs. It had been put together using as few panels as possible, making it appear smoother, though it still didn't look as smooth as the alien ship that floated ominously above them. Painted against the silvery hull were the giant white letters of the UDC, with smaller letters that read: FATHOM.

The ship had bilateral arcing wings on either side that sloped almost to the ground. There was something about the pattern on the wings that caught Kalian's attention; hundreds of hexagons all fitted together like the cells in a beehive. He had seen that pattern many times before in images from his own lectures. The ship had a Solar Drive. The design of this particular ship allowed for the wings to absorb the magnetic fields of the sun, allowing it to power the Solarcite in the engine.

"I've never been on a ship with a Solar Drive before. I didn't even know we could make them so small." Kalian marvelled at the ship.

He had never paid much attention to the design of ships or any other vehicle, but he could appreciate the advance in technology this particular ship represented.

"It's not combat-ready yet but, at a pinch, it'll get us out of there faster than light." The reply had come from a deep, rasping voice behind them.

Kalian turned to find a man wearing similar armour to Li'ara, standing only a couple of feet away. He had his thumbs tucked into the armour on his chest plate. Despite being no taller than Kalian, there was something about the way he presented himself that made him appear larger. Kalian assumed it was his armour; it was thicker in most areas compared to Li'ara's. It was obvious his armour had taken some damage, however, with several dents and chips visible on almost every piece. The most notable aspect of the man was a tattoo that arced over his shaven head. Kalian couldn't make head nor tail of the intricate pattern, but it started above his left eye and reached over the top and out of sight.

"Commander Hawkins, this is Kal-"

"I know who he is, Lieutenant Commander." He didn't take his eyes off Kalian. "I've read your file *Kalian Gaines*, and those are five minutes of my life I'll never get back." The Commander started walking round Kalian as if he were a predator circling its prey. "I can't figure out why an alien species would wanna talk to a history lecturer." He leaned in closer. "But it puts me on *edge*. You're gonna stick to her like glue, you do what we say, and we'll all be back in time for dinner." The Commander took one look at Li'ara before moving away.

Kalian noticed the nod of her head as if there had been some silent conversation between them.

36

They really don't like me being here...

Something the Commander had said echoed in Kalian's mind. "What did you mean, when you said it could get us out of there at a pinch?"

Kalian had never been taught Solar Drive at a higher level, but he knew the ship would have to be near the surface of a star in order to absorb the magnetic fields. How could any ship speed them away, if they were thousands of kilometres away from the sun?

Now that Commander Hawkins was walking away, Kalian could see that his tattoo went all the way down his neck and into his combat suit.

"Don't ask questions you don't need answers to." The Commander didn't even look back as he said it.

Kalian looked to Li'ara to shed some light on the topic but, before she could say anything, the lift doors at the end of the hangar bay opened, revealing a small party of people. Kalian recognised Chief Commander Hendricks and Commander Barnes immediately but next to them was a man he had never seen before. The man appeared regal in bright red and gold robes that reached the floor, his hands hidden within the folds of his sleeves. As they got closer, Kalian could make out the short blond hair that came to a point in the middle of his forehead. Kalian didn't need an introduction to know this was Ambassador Arlek.

"You must be Kalian Gaines." The Ambassador extended a hand from his robes to greet Kalian.

"Ambassador Arlek, I assume." It was impossible to tell how old he was. He could have been anywhere between fifty and a hundred and fifty.

"I am sure you are eager to get to the bottom of this, Kalian. I am as curious as you are as to their interest in meeting you. But we should not lose sight of the importance of this meeting. First and foremost, this is a historical meeting of two species. Who knows what this might lead to for humankind. Before we approach the subject of your relevance, I think it prudent to address the concerns of Central Parliament."

He's good. Kalian had heard politicians talk enough on TV at home. Arlek was trying to make Kalian feel like they were familiar by addressing him by his first name. Then he tried to make them equal by highlighting similar goals. The Ambassador had been well trained in the art of debate and elocution; he knew how to make his own goals appear the most important.

Arlek might not have been as blunt as the Chief Commander, but the Ambassador had just told Kalian not to get in the way. The Ambassador didn't wait for Kalian's reply, his attention wandering past him towards the ship.

"So this is the *Fathom*..." The Ambassador looked over the ship with an inspecting eye. "Are you certain it's safe?"

"It might only be the prototype, but it's been rigorously tested," the Chief Commander explained.

"I'm sorry to interrupt sir," Commander Barnes said, stepping in, "but the Icarus station has been evacuated and the deadline is approaching." He looked to Commander Hawkins, who nodded in return to his silent question. "The *Fathom* is prepped and ready to launch."

Kalian reminded himself to ask Li'ara about the ship later.

A few minutes later, the Chief and Commander Barnes left for central command and the four passengers boarded the *Fathom*. The ship was more spacious than Kalian had expected and the immediate interior resembled a living space found in most homes. He noticed a room at the back with nothing in it except several racks on the wall filled with UDC weapons. There was another room next to it, behind a wall of glass, with a red line that ran through the centre. This room was all white and filled with compartments and a single bed in the middle.

Commander Hawkins went straight to the front of the ship and disappeared into the cockpit without a word. Ambassador Arlek took a seat on one of the sofas, wrapping his hands into his sleeves again. Li'ara sealed the door behind them, gesturing at Kalian to take a seat opposite the Ambassador. Kalian wasn't sure what to expect from a ship with Solar Drive. Would it take off like the craft that had brought him here? Did they need to be strapped in or hold on to something? Rather than take the chance of asking another stupid question, he decided to watch what the others did. Neither the Ambassador nor Li'ara appeared uncomfortable; Li'ara went through to the weapons room while the Ambassador examined the interior.

Kalian heard a loud hum from somewhere inside the ship as the engines came to life. Lights on various pieces of equipment lit up and a small image appeared on the cockpit door showing Commander Hawkins at the helm. A clunking noise was audible under their feet as the *Fathom's* landing gear retracted into the ship's belly. Kalian could feel the ship ascending - how were they going to get out of here? He hadn't seen any large hangar doors.

"Grav Enforcers coming online." The Commander's voice came through a speaker over their heads.

Moments later, Kalian felt that familiar pressure pass from head to toe. He could no longer feel the ship ascending. He instinctively looked round to get his bearings, but just like the craft that had brought him to The Hub, the *Fathom* had no windows either. Li'ara walked back into the room with a gun attached to her right thigh. The sight of the weapon reminded Kalian that Li'ara was more than she appeared. He really hoped her particular skills wouldn't be required. He put the thought aside.

"What is it with you guys and windows?"

Kalian saw Li'ara pause and change direction, heading towards a panel on the wall. "Windows are a structural weak point. They can't be re-enforced the same way the hull can." Li'ara's tone suggested he had asked another stupid question.

She thumbed the panel on the wall. The entrance to the ship and the wall surrounding it instantly disappeared. Where the wall had been was now a clear view of the outside world and Kalian was momentarily blinded by the desert sun. When his vision returned he could see they were still rising into the sky. Below the ship Kalian saw the entrance to the hangar bay closing after them; it had been on the roof. The exterior of the doors was covered in desert sand camouflaging to conceal any underground activity.

Kalian couldn't believe what he was seeing. There had been a wall there only moments ago. He moved forward and reached out, unsure of what he might feel. His fingers vanished from sight like a mirage in the desert heat and he felt the cold steel of the door beyond.

He looked to Li'ara for confirmation as if she could read his thoughts. She tapped on a cylindrical beam that ran from the floor to the ceiling. A thin line of bright light shone down the centre, from which the image was being generated. Kalian noticed an identical beam on the other side closer to the cockpit. The image itself was the entire breadth of the wall. This technology wasn't exactly new, but the clarity of the holo-image was so perfect he could have sworn there was a hole in the ship.

"Tiny cameras on the hull feed back images of the outside." Li'ara's expression suggested it was the least exciting piece of technology on the ship.

She moved away and took her seat. Kalian was impressed; he wondered what else this little ship could do.

Commander Hawkins tipped the *Fathom* on its side to get the right angle and direction. To Kalian it appeared as though the Earth was moving around them. His brain told him he should be falling but his feet remained firmly on the deck.

At this altitude, they were well above the high walls that fortified The Hub. The base was spread out for miles across the desert; it was like a city in itself. There was only one building higher than the walls: situated at the back of the base near the far corner. Kalian could just make out the array of antennas protruding from the top. There were several large domes scattered across the landscape in between stark white structures. Kalian had no idea what any of the buildings were for. From what he had seen, the most important part of The Hub was underground. The soldiers were starting to look like ants now as the *Fathom* ascended into the upper atmosphere.

The Ambassador hadn't looked up once; the view was of no interest to him. He had a faraway look on his face, clearly lost in his own thoughts. Kalian felt it best not to disturb him.

At least I'm not here to represent the human race.

The ocean of blue sky began to fade, giving way to the vastness of space and the stars beyond. It had been so long since he'd seen this view that he had forgotten how beautiful it was. As the *Fathom* climbed he could see the curve of the Earth with the sun behind them. The beauty was undeniable. The blue hue that blanketed the atmosphere was like a protective halo.

In moments, the *Fathom* passed over the Atlantic and across the countries that used to be part of a collective, before Central Parliament brought everyone together. Even from this distance, the Mag Hyperways could be seen connecting the continents. The underwater cities remained concealed, though some of the spires and platforms were visible. Kalian recalled the lessons he himself had taught on the subject of such aquatic habitats. They were the last constructions to be built before the move into the solar system when there really was no more space on Earth.

As they passed over the dark side of the planet, all Kalian could see were the millions of lights from the cities below. Kalian noticed how little space for greenery there was. From the images he had studied in college he knew that Earth had been blue and green in appearance. But now, where there had been so much green, was an endless sea of silver and gold glittering in the lights. What was left of nature had been placed under the strictest protection laws within giant domes, some of which could be seen from orbit. He promised himself he would see more of the world after this: maybe even visit Mars and Century or some of the moons.

"ETA three minutes," Commander Hawkins' voice came over the speakers again.

Kalian could feel butterflies in his stomach and his hands became clammy again. This is it. He let out a long breath.

"Don't worry," the Ambassador said. "Just let me do all the talking and we will be fine." He stood up, allowing his robe to fall into place.

Li'ara stood up as well, removing her weapon from its holster. She inspected each side of it, making sure all the settings were to her liking. The gun itself looked quite formidable. Kalian had seen other UDC soldiers armed with the same weapon but this one seemed bigger in places. Li'ara had obviously made some modifications over the years. The top of the gun had a small screen with numbers on it, no doubt detailing the amount of ammo stored within. A bright red dot appeared from a small apparatus under the barrel. Kalian wondered how many times she'd actually had to use it.

"My God..." Ambassador Arlek had made his way over to the panoramic holo-image.

The pictures didn't do it justice. The alien ship was immense in size. Its hull continued to shimmer and move like the surface of the sea. The sun began to rise over the crest of the Earth, the rays of light striking the alien ship. Kalian couldn't imagine the time it would take to build such a ship. It may have been alien in origin but its structure wasn't dissimilar to human ships. It had been built with the engine at the back; at least Kalian assumed it was the engine. It was perhaps the most obvious feature; a giant circle of light that reached from the top to the bottom of the ship. He couldn't look at it for too long, as it constantly burned like a giant blue star. Kalian was sure an entire star cruiser could fit inside, with room to spare.

It was hard to tell from the constant movement on the hull but Kalian guessed its surface to be some shade of purple. Spiralling out from around the engine were arching pillars that came to sharp points, stretching across the entirety of the ship. The intricacy was a sight to behold. At times Kalian couldn't figure out where one started and the other stopped. As a whole, it appeared totally smooth with no visible contours. The front of the ship sloped down into a sharp point like an eagle's beak.

"Incredible..." Li'ara could only stare at it.

Her voice momentarily caught Kalian's attention. For an instant, he saw a very human side to her, no more the soldier, just another person humbled and awed by beauty. It didn't last. She noticed Kalian's brief attention and raised her chin, becoming the soldier once more.

"What do you suppose *they* are?" The Ambassador was pointing at one of the protrusions on the alien ship.

Dome-shaped structures were fitted along the edge, creating a circle around the presumed engine. At first glance, they resembled the panels on human ships used for absorbing the magnetic fields of the sun.

"Maybe they *do* have Solar Drive technology." Kalian remembered the Chief Commander's concerns about the aliens' mode of transport.

"We'll find out soon enough." Commander Hawkins strode into the cabin while sheathing a blade onto his thigh.

He ignored the view of the ship and went straight to the weapons room.

Li'ara tilted her head trying to take in the whole length of the ship. "I don't see any cannons or launcher bays. You'd think on something that big they'd be obvious." She narrowed her eyes, taking in as much of the detail as possible.

"It's what we can't see that concerns me." The Commander rejoined them by the holo-image.

He had strapped a similar looking weapon to Li'ara's onto his hip. It was the gun on his back that caught everyone's eye.

"Are we expecting a war Commander Hawkins?" The Ambassador only glanced at the weapon unable to take his gaze off the ship for too long.

"I like to be prepared for every eventuality, sir." The Commander reached round and placed a comforting hand on the giant barrel.

Kalian looked back towards the massive ship. "I think if this comes down to a matter of size Commander... they've already won." Kalian didn't need to look to know the commander was burning holes in the back of his head.

"When did they get here?" The Ambassador half turned to Li'ara.

"Once they received confirmation, but they started moving before we even sent them the coordinates." She shared a concerned look with the Commander. "They knew exactly where the Icarus station was. They've definitely been doing their homework."

"I wonder how long they've been watching us." Kalian felt mesmerised by the sight of the ever-shifting light on the ship's surface.

"I intend on asking them that very question, Mr Gaines." Ambassador Arlek lifted an eyebrow at Kalian. It was another signal from the Ambassador that he shouldn't do any of the talking.

The *Fathom* began to angle away on a heading below the alien ship. Kalian had the feeling he should be falling again.

"The autopilot's bringing us into the Icarus." Commander Hawkins checked his bracer's touchpad to double check the coordinates. The emitters inside projected a green holographic image of the Icarus station - zooming in on a section near the centre. "We're both docking in the executive hangar bay near the command bridge."

It was clear to see from the design of the station that most if not all ships docked on the outer airlocks. The executive hangar must have been built to allow for immediate access to the command bridge.

The station came into view moments later. Having seen the alien ship, the Icarus station didn't quite measure up. It was spherical in shape and made up of an outer ring and an inner ring. They were connected by long walkways that converged on a central sphere. Cutting the station through the middle was another set of rings that connected to the central sphere. From their approaching vector, the station appeared as a giant white X.

Kalian could make out the double-barrelled cannons fitted along the outer ring. It hadn't escaped him that they were all pointed at the alien ship.

The *Fathom* had passed over the first ring now and was on a set course for the sphere. The entrance to the bay doors appeared open, exposing the hangar bay to the harsh vacuum of space. Contrary to its appearance ,the entrance was in fact sealed. As the *Fathom* decelerated it began to pass through the threshold and enter the hangar. The portal blurred around the edges of the ship as the membrane-like substance passed over every millimetre of the *Fathom*. This invisible wall of thin jelly allowed the ship to enter without breaking the atmosphere. Kalian knew the technology existed but he had never seen it. On his trip to Armstrong as a child, they had docked via one of the habitat domes on an outer platform.

He turned back to the cabin to find Li'ara looking at him. How long had she been watching him? Kalian assumed she was still trying to get the measure of him. He wasn't surprised; his part in all this was sketchy at best. If their roles were reversed he would be suspicious of her too.

Kalian heard the same noise as before when the landing gear extended from the ship and gently pressed onto the bay floor. Li'ara deactivated the holo-image, leaving them blind to the outside. At the base of her back, attached horizontally between two panels of armour, was a long blade in a black sheath. Compared to the weapon attached to her thigh he wondered how useful a knife really was. He especially couldn't imagine anything getting past that monster of a gun Commander Hawkins had.

The outer hatch opened up, rising out of view as the ramp descended to the hangar floor.

Commander Hawkins stood with one foot on the ramp. "I lead, the Lieutenant Commander brings up the rear. For your security I want you both to remain in between us at all times." He looked at Ambassador Arlek. "You have authority in all matters sir, but if I or the Lieutenant Commander feel your safety is at risk, we will take control."

The Ambassador bowed his head in agreement. "I wouldn't expect any less. Chief Commander Hendricks assured me you are the best for the job." He looked at Li'ara as well, who simply nodded in return.

They left the *Fathom* and waited by the main doors of the hangar. There was evidence around the room that showed workers had been interrupted from their duties. The personnel on board had been evacuated as fast as possible. Kalian noticed a cup of cold coffee sitting on a container and loose tools left where they had been dropped. He briefly examined the rest of the hangar. It wasn't anywhere close to the size of The Hub's. It could probably fit another three ships the size of the *Fathom*. Like all things UDC, it was stark white against a black floor, with little thought put into appearance.

It hadn't occurred to Kalian how the aliens would enter. It had been assumed they would land a craft in a similar fashion to them.

What if they don't have a ship small enough? What if they don't even use smaller ships?

Kalian imagined them appearing from nowhere like their ship had above San Francisco. It wouldn't be a wild stretch to assume they had that technology.

Kalian's questions were answered as a craft broke through the invisible film to the hangar bay. At first glance, it was obvious the ship was bigger than the *Fathom*. Just like its parent ship, this one was seamless as well, though it didn't have the ever-shifting light over its hull. It certainly wasn't dull in appearance, however. The surface was so shiny Kalian could see all of their reflections in its purple exterior.

The ship emitted a low humming noise as it came to a stop two feet above the floor. Kalian expected some form of landing gear to present itself but it never did. Instead, the low humming noise became distant, eventually leaving the hangar in silence, until the ship was just hanging in the air. Like the bigger ship, it had pointed pillars extending from the back all the way to the front. Rather than an intricate pattern it only had the four with two on each side. It was oval in shape with no corners or flat edges. It reminded Kalian of a smaller simplified version of the parent ship.

Like the *Fathom*, it appeared to have no windows of any kind. The Commander and Li'ara were frozen in place, every muscle ready to react to the ship's occupants. Both of them had stepped closer to Kalian and the Ambassador and he was sure Arlek's hands were shaking under the robes of his sleeves.

The tension was becoming unbearable for the ship was just hovering in silence. Kalian could feel the adrenaline coursing through his veins, his fight or flight responses battling each other. The hair on his arms stood on end under his jacket. He could feel it, the build-up of energy just under his skin. He instinctively reached out to Li'ara's hand only centimetres away. She felt like an anchor in the room, something to hold on to and take control of the situation, something to keep him in place. Just the contact seemed to distract him. It took him a second to realise he was actually holding her hand. Her hand was smaller than his but it felt strong through the glove. Li'ara briefly glanced at the hand holding hers and tightened her grip. Was it possible she was feeling the same about these new visitors? Or was she just comforting the frightened civilian?

They were about to experience a moment in history that humans had only ever imagined. All of the questions in Kalian's mind hushed to a whisper as the ship suddenly came to life. The tip of the elongated craft released a loud hissing noise as a blinding white line appeared down its centre. All four of them raised a hand to shield their eyes. The two halves separated and slowly retracted towards the back of the ship. Out of the bright light, Kalian could just make out a small ramp descending to the floor. The light dimmed as four silhouettes stood at the top of the ramp. The sight of the shadowy figures made them lower their hands despite the light. Kalian couldn't form a single coherent thought as he just stood full of wonder. Li'ara had let go of his hand now - she was preparing for anything.

The light emanating from the ship quickly faded, revealing their true forms. Kalian couldn't believe his eyes. He was both awed and intimidated by them. Time seemed to stand still as he took in their extraordinary appearance.

They stood upright, regal in their posture. He couldn't help but look at their arms, all *four* of them. Where he expected to see the ribs on a human they each had an extra pair of shoulder sockets. It was hard to tell their height from inside the ship but Kalian guessed they were much taller than humans.

Their skin was a beautiful mixture of white and purple with speckles of blue interlaced throughout. Their physique was hard to deny. They had muscle groups similar to humans and very defined. Their biceps and triceps were easy to see on their arms but with every movement new muscles became apparent. Their forearms were hidden beneath shining bracers made of a metal that was hard to define as it seemed to reflect every colour in the spectrum. The same material covered their abdomen extending to their sternum with ridges accentuating the different muscles beneath. It was attached to the aliens by a series of rings that stretched over their chest and shoulders, though the rings appeared more like bone than metal.

Kalian was reminded of the ancient Native Americans, who exposed a lot of skin in their dresswear.

As one, they began to descend the ramp. Overlapping material flowed from their waist at the front and back, almost reaching the floor. The material left their legs exposed as it only covered their groin though they had more of the armoured plating encasing their outer thighs. Their legs were truly alien. Like the upper half of their bodies they were all muscle, but their shape was unlike those of any creature Kalian had ever seen. Their thighs protruded forwards until the knee joint at which point their calves extended the other way creating a zigzag shape. The feet then protruded the same way as their thighs. To a human, it would be like walking on the balls of their feet.

As they stepped onto the smooth black floor their two thick toes spread out taking the weight. Kalian was fascinated to see that they didn't wear any shoes. He assumed their skin must be stronger than his own to wear so little. They approached in a pointed formation. The only notable difference was the colour of the material that fell from their waist. The potential leader had a deep blue material lined with silver, while the rest all wore the same shade of purple. He must be the leader, Kalian decided.

They stopped directly in front of them and spread into a line. Up close Kalian could see every feature on their face. His eyes were darting all over trying to take in every unbelievable detail. They had strong elongated necks that were hidden behind a sloping head that almost reached down to their chest.

To Kalian, the most obvious feature was their lack of features. They had no chin or nose to speak of. Their head sloped down into a mouth that appeared to reach from one side of their narrow jaw to the other. Two small fangs peered out from either side of their bottom lip and rested against a lipless ridge. Above the mouth, their face curved inwards leading to six small holes opposite one another. If basic physiology was anything to go by, these had to be their nostrils. Either side of this was a small line of what resembled hair and each strand appeared sharp and tough in texture. At first glance they could be missed; they were colourless on the surface with a milky white transparency. This was the only sign of hair on their entire body, if it was indeed hair.

Kalian's breath was taken as he gazed into their eyes. They were twice the size of any humans, predominantly black in appearance. The centre of each eye was like a spiralling galaxy made of every colour with a golden pupil - they were hypnotic to look into. The creature in the blue robe stood opposite Kalian and turned its head on the side as if to better examine him. It reminded Kalian of the way a dog would tilt its head at something new. As it moved, Kalian saw giant pointed strands flowing from its head down to its waist, made of the same translucent hair that surrounded their nose.

The Ambassador cleared his throat getting everyone's attention.

"Welcome." He said the word slowly as he bowed his head. "I am Ambassador Sebastian Arlek... of Earth."

The last part sounded strange. No human ever had cause to use such an introduction regarding their planet. There was a long pause and Kalian realised the Ambassador had no intention of introducing the others.

Arrogant son of a bitch.

The alien in front of Kalian raised one of his upper hands displaying the palm. Again Kalian was struck by how different and truly alien it was. There were four digits in total: the most recognisable being an opposable thumb. The middle finger was about two inches longer than the rest and thicker too. The fingers either side were more delicate. They all had an extra joint than human fingers and he noticed the ends were all slightly bulbous. That very human part of him wanted to reach out and place his own hand against it.

The alien raised its head as it spoke in some unintelligible language. There appeared to be no audible breaks in between what Kalian assumed were words. The sound was guttural as it resonated from somewhere deep in its throat. The one standing in front of Li'ara reacted to whatever had been said by reaching round to a rectangular pouch on its belt, using one of its lower limbs. It produced a small disc-shaped object in its large hand. Using its other lower limb, it passed the object to the leader in front of Kalian.

The leader presented the object in front of them, making it easy to examine. It was about the size of a human palm. The metal casing appeared dull in comparison with the armoured plating they were wearing. It didn't reflect all the colours or even have a particular shine. On top of the disc was an intricate design Kalian had never seen before. It reminded him of the writing style used in ancient Japan and China before the conversion to the Central language. Kalian had seen, first-hand, scrolls and parchments inscribed with the beautiful language in museums. The symbol was split in half as the top layer of the disc parted in the middle.

The sudden movement of the alien object gave Commander Hawkins cause for alarm. He had half drawn his sidearm, almost completely removing it from the holster. If it hadn't been for the Ambassador placing an arm in front of him, he would probably be levelling a gun in their face by now.

"Wait, Commander..." Arlek never took his eyes off them, trying to gauge any offence.

The Commander's movement had caught their attention but it didn't appear to faze them in the least. He readjusted his weapon back into its holster but Kalian noted he hadn't released the handle. Li'ara hadn't reacted the same way but subtly placed the flat of her hand against her own weapon. The tension was increasing between the four of them. The aliens, however, appeared as calm as before. Maybe they had done this before. From what he suspected of the original ship found on Charon, they might not be the only two species in the galaxy. If that were true, this might not be the aliens' first encounter. He didn't have time to hypothesise about other life in the galaxy - there was *other* life right in front of him.

They all peered into the newly opened object to see what they were being presented with. Inside were four smaller discs of the same composition as the container. Judging from their size Kalian guessed he could fit one on the tip of his finger. The leader stood back allowing its companions to reach the interior using their upper limbs. They each, including the leader, picked out one of the small discs on the tip of their fingers and held it out to each of the humans.

"What the hell are *they* supposed to be?" The Commander was instinctively suspicious.

"A gift perhaps?" countered the Ambassador.

The apparent leader of the group raised its hand and tapped its own throat, lifting its head as it did so. It then turned to point at a spot a few inches behind its golden eye. Evident to the group was a series of holes similar to the ones above its mouth, except these holes were in a circular pattern. As it removed its hand they all saw a small metallic disc placed just behind the holes, identical to the discs in front of them.

"I think that's its ear..." The Ambassador's sharp look reminded Kalian he wasn't supposed to speak.

The leader lifted his head almost imitating a nod while making a small grunt. It tapped the side of its head again and flexed the finger presenting the disc.

"I think it might be a way for us to communicate. That's why they have one as well." Li'ara looked to the Ambassador, then the Commander.

The Commander appeared to be chewing it over, assessing any possible risks.

"I believe she's right, Commander. I think this may be the only way we proceed." Arlek turned to Commander Hawkins. "Unless you can think of a better way to communicate." He raised a questioning eyebrow.

"So be it." The Commander released the grip of his weapon but kept his hand close by.

The aliens showed a measure of understanding as they reached towards the humans in unison.

"Wait!" Li'ara raised a hand in front of Kalian. She looked up at her partnered alien. "Do it to me first."

"Li'ara..." Kalian began to protest but Li'ara shot him a steely look.

This turn of events seemed to please the Ambassador as he stood in silence.

"She's doing her job, Kalian," the Commander interjected.

Kalian noticed *he* hadn't volunteered. Again the aliens appeared to understand what had transpired. It slowly extended its hand towards Li'ara's face, the thicker middle finger pressing against her neck while the smaller digit disappeared behind her ear. There was a quiet hiss while Li'ara's cheek twitched as the disc made contact. The alien retracted its hand and continued to stand patiently. Li'ara blinked very slowly, turning her head in every direction as if she were looking for some hidden object. It eventually passed and she stood at ease again as if nothing had happened.

"That felt weird..." She reached behind her ear to explore the new device with her finger. The leader uttered a few sharp grunts that increased in pitch. "Say that again." Her focus was entirely on the alien as it repeated the same sounds as before. Li'ara's eyes widened. "Can you understand that?" Her question was aimed at the others, who all stood in silence, shaking their heads.

"Can *you*?" Kalian knew he wasn't meant to speak but he couldn't stop himself.

The leader said something more complex than before.

"Yes, you need to let them do it." She faced the Commander knowing he was the one to convince.

"Well then..." The Ambassador cleared his throat again. "Proceed." He turned his own head to the side allowing access to his ear.

The Commander's lack of action was his only invitation.

The remaining devices were placed behind their ears and Kalian experienced the same sensations as Li'ara. The pain was over in an instant as it attached to the hard skull behind his ear. He could have sworn there were whispers coming from all over the hangar causing him to instinctively search them out. As quickly as the whispering started, it ceased altogether and he was left with a strange metallic taste in his mouth. With quizzical looks on their faces, the other men appeared to have experienced the same sensations.

"Greetings of peace, Kalian Gaines..."

Kalian raised his head to the source of the deep gravelly voice. He couldn't believe it - an alien had just said his name, and he understood it. He couldn't form the response for his experience with the disc had left his throat dry. The sound of the voice was extraordinary. The leader clearly hadn't enunciated those words but he had heard a distinct voice with tone and emotion.

The Ambassador had also understood the alien words and did not seem pleased that he wasn't the first to be addressed. "I am the Ambassador for Earth, Sebastian Arl-"

"We know who you are Ambassador Arlek, and who you represent." The leader spread out both pairs of arms. "You are *humans...*"

As he uttered the word, all four aliens bowed on one knee making them all equal in height. The Ambassador looked shocked at the display; he nudged the others and attempted to imitate the bow thinking it a mutual sign of respect. Before they reached the floor, all four aliens had risen to their greater height. The result was an awkward half bow from the humans.

"Perhaps we should continue this on the command bridge?" the Ambassador suggested quickly. "I think it better suited than the current surroundings." He aimed his question at the leader.

"As you wish, Ambassador." The leader bowed his head submitting to Arlek's suggestion.

They all entered through the door behind them that led to an access corridor. Li'ara had told Kalian it was designed so higher-ranking officers and generals could gain access to the bridge as quickly as possible.

The corridor had sloping curved walls on each side covered in black square panels. The panels were outlined in fluorescent white light giving a harsh reality to their surroundings. Fortunately, it left a good foot of space above the towering aliens. They walked in silence for a minute until they reached the security blast door to the command bridge. Kalian had glanced back once to see all four pairs of golden eyes watching him. The sight would have unnerved him if it hadn't been for the hypnotic nature of their eyes.

Commander Hawkins placed the palm of his hand over a blank

screen next to the door. Green circles lit up around his fingertips while a small scanner above his hand ran a fine laser over his eye. The whole screen flashed green and the heavy blast door slowly opened, disappearing into the wall. Standing in the doorway Kalian could see the corridor was actually a T-junction branching off either side to other parts of the station.

The command bridge was situated at the top of the central sphere allowing for a glass viewport at the head of the room. The viewport curved into the ceiling to give an even wider spectacle of the vast space beyond. Walking across the bridge, Kalian found himself drawn to the vista. From the orbit of the station, he could see the Moon on his left, with Earth on the right taking almost half the viewport. In the centre of both was the distant sun illuminating the solar system.

He turned back realising that he had left the group behind in the centre of the bridge, except for Li'ara who had remained a few feet behind him. In their brief look at one another Kalian felt an understanding pass between them; *don't leave my side.* He quickly remembered what Commander Barnes had said about sticking with her. Together they returned to the rest of the party. The four aliens stood in silence as if waiting for the humans to make the next move.

The Ambassador acted on their silence. "Let me start by saying that on behalf of Central Parliament and all humankind, we welcome you." His hands shifted with every word like a true politician.

His words hung in the air as the aliens stood watching Kalian. The Ambassador hadn't expected the silence to follow; it put him off for a moment. His experience shone through as he pushed on as if the awkwardness had never happened.

"You have me at a disadvantage," the Ambassador said. "You know who I am and who *we* are, but we know nothing about you..." He trailed off hoping for a reply.

"Forgive us, Ambassador. We are the first of our kind to meet a human in the flesh. It is a... humbling experience."

Watching the leader speak was a peculiar thing. Kalian could no longer hear the guttural grunts but instead crystal clear Central. He had no special love for science but he found himself curious as to how the disc behind his ear could translate something so alien.

"We are Novaarian." The alien extended all four limbs gesturing to his companions. "We are from a constellation of stars many light years away, in a different arm of the galaxy." His eyes flickered towards the stars in the viewport. "I am what you would call a captain. The *Valoran* is my ship." His head tilted to the bulkhead above as if they could all see the wondrous ship floating outside. "My name is Telarrek, this is Numanon, Ilyseal and Youl." As he said each of their names they pressed both upper hands to their chest and bowed.

Kalian examined them each, in turn, looking for any unique features. At first glance, they could all have been clones of one another. With a closer look, there were some subtle differences. He noted a darker shade of speckled blue around the eyes and nose on Telarrek, and the one named Ilyseal had a narrower set of eyes. Now that he was looking, he couldn't help but see the subtle differences. From his vantage point, he could see the long tendril hair of Ilyseal and how several strands were actually red instead of milky white. Kalian wondered how similar *they* must look to the Novaarians. Telarrek's introduction of his companions highlighted the Ambassador's lack of regard for his own company.

"Yes, well..." Arlek half turned his head. "This is Commander Hawkins and Lieutenant Commander Ducarté." He paused slightly before introducing the last member of his party. "And this is Kalian Gaines."

The mention of his name caused no reaction from the Novaarians; they just gazed at him with their penetrating eyes. Kalian felt like he was being examined from the inside out again.

"If I may?" the Ambassador asked. "Why *are* you here? Why *now*?"

Kalian knew he was referring to the crashed ship found on Charon, but he also knew he was directing the conversation away from him. It was a fair question however since four hundred plus years had gone by without any contact. All four Novaarians shared a brief but unknown look.

"Our kind has always had designs of making contact with your species. We have been observing your use of Intrinium since you first discovered its existence."

"Intrinium?" asked the Ambassador.

"You call it Solarcite, the fuel that allows for faster than light travel." Telarrek paused to ensure they were still following him. "Since you did not invent the technology that harnesses Intrinium, we have observed your use of it to ensure your own safety. In the wrong hands, it can be used as a powerful tool for destruction. We are thankful you have only used it for propulsion purposes. It shows evolutionary progress that *some* do not share."

"But we've had Solar Drive technology for nearly five centuries." The Ambassador looked as if he were calculating. "How long have you been watching us?" He had an almost pleading tone.

"We discovered your race not long after the Laronian freighter entered your solar system with the meteor shower." Telarrek stated the fact like it was common knowledge. "We have been watching to see how your race matures under the influence of such technology. From our calculations, we believe you would not have discovered Intrinium on your own for at least another millennium. We realise, for you, it must seem like we have stood ignorantly by but, for Novaarians, it is only a short span. We had to be certain of you."

Kalian was sure Telarrek was looking directly at him as he said the latter. He felt like there was more behind those words than what they were hearing. He was desperate to interrupt and ask all of his own questions, to find out why he was there. For now, though, the Ambassador was asking questions he also wanted answers to.

"Wait. What freighter are you talking about? What is *Laronian*?" The Ambassador was sounding more confused.

"The ship you discovered on Charon was a Laronian mining freighter."

Kalian was astonished by the Novaarians' knowledge of human information, to even know the name given to a distant moon.

They really have been watching us.

"You mean... you mean it wasn't one of *your* ships?" The Ambassador was trying to piece together a very old puzzle.

Telarrek took in a deep breath, reminiscent of a human sigh. "That, in part, is why we must reveal ourselves as we have." Telarrek dipped his head a little closer to the Ambassador. "You are part of a far greater galaxy than you thought. Like us you are but one species in a sea of many. The Laronians are your closest stellar neighbours, and it was their ship you re-engineered that has put you where you are today."

"How did a Laronian vessel end up in our solar system? How close are they?" asked the Ambassador.

"Their homeworld is fourteen thousand light years from here. One of their deep space mining vessels was searching for Intrinium deposits outside of Laronian territory, without permission from the Conclave. Not too far from your solar system, they found a rich deposit in what we believe were two asteroids, close in size to your moon. After claiming it for their own they began the mining process without notifying the Laronian High Command. The debris scattered throughout your system is evidence of the catastrophe that befell them. It was one of our own exploration vessels that detected the explosion and the Laronian emergency beacon. It was tracking their ship that led us to you, but you had already discovered the crashed ship before we could intervene."

The four humans were stood in silence hanging on to every word. They had just heard the biggest mystery to mankind laid out in thirty seconds. Everyone from scientists in Central Parliament to philosophers around both worlds had speculated and made theories on the reason for the crashed ship. Even Kalian had entered into debates in his lecture theatre with confounded students.

It was just an accident, not divine or destiny, not even by design from some alien race; it was just a fluke...

"What Conclave are you speaking of?" Kalian was sure the Ambassador's questions would never end.

Before Telarrek could answer, Numanon stepped towards his

leader. The shining bracer on his arm was no longer reflecting every colour as he brought it up to show Telarrek. The surface of it was now glowing blue with alien symbols and calculations that appeared to move across the whole bracer. Telarrek did a quick lift of his head in acknowledgement before Numanon's bracer returned to its metallic state.

"There is much your species will be required to learn regarding the complexities of the galaxy and the wider community. We will, of course, make time for that, but time is against us. We have chosen to reveal ourselves now because of your actions on Alpha NL-2204."

The Ambassador's face seemed to switch off like a light as he stood dumbstruck. Kalian had no idea of the significance of what had just been said. He looked to Li'ara and Commander Hawkins who were just as confused as him.

"How do you know about that? We haven't made it public knowledge yet. It's still in the first phase." The Ambassador had a hint of aggression in his tone.

"You are taking your first steps into the galaxy. We felt it prudent to monitor your exploration, for your own safety." Telarrek's tone never changed. He was simply stating facts.

The Ambassador looked at the others, only to see confusion staring back at him. Arlek appeared to make a quick calculation. "I suppose you're about to find out anyway. Six years ago we sent a terraforming expedition to a planetary body known only as Alpha NL-2204. It is sixteen thousand light years from here, the furthest we have ever gone. We weren't going to inform the populace until they had at least completed phase three and that could be *fifty* years from now..."

Kalian couldn't believe everything he was learning in just one day. They were making a third planet; that would be big news on both worlds. It meant new lands, opportunities, resources of untold quantities and the prospect of an all-new economy. It was obvious why it had been kept a secret. Terraforming was a delicate process that could go wrong at almost any point, especially early on. If there was one thing Central Parliament couldn't have it was to be seen screwing up. They wouldn't reveal a new planet until it was a sure thing.

"What does Alpha NL-2204 have to do with you being here?" the Ambassador asked bluntly.

"You have crossed into Laronian space and are currently terraforming one of their planets. They might not be using it but, by the laws of the Conclave, it *is* theirs." Telarrek gestured to Numanon. "We have received word that a Laronian warship is on a heading for your expedition team. We are here to advise you to evacuate your people as soon as possible. At its current speed, the warship will be at Alpha NL-2204 within one rotation of your planet."

"There are seven thousand people on that planet - scientists, engineers, workers, not to mention all of their families! It would take more than a *day* to evacuate them all. What would these Laronians do if they discovered them? Surely they know of us like you do? They must know how blind we are to our alien surroundings. It's not like we passed a giant sign that said 'stay out', is it?" The Ambassador had lost some of his composure at the thought of causing a war with an unknown alien race.

"They know nothing of your kind. In their eyes you are an unknown species invading their territory; it will be seen as a hostile action." Telarrek continued to peer down at the Ambassador.

"How can they know nothing of us if you do? They're supposedly our closest neighbours?" Arlek was pointing off in a random direction as if that was the way to Laronian space.

Telarrek hesitated. "We have kept-"

His sentence was cut off by the sound of an alarm blasting from the speakers in the walls. All the lights on the central console lit up with proximity warnings and a green holo-projection shot up from a console near the viewport. Its sudden appearance caught Kalian's attention; it was a close-up image encompassing the Earth and the Moon with the *Valoran* and the Icarus station in between. What was most interesting about the image was the large green shape situated between the station and the Moon.

"What is that?" the Ambassador shouted over the alarm.

Commander Hawkins dashed to the central console, his fingers racing over the touchscreen. A moment later the alarm shut down leaving the command bridge in silence again.

"Proximity warning! Something *huge* just dropped out of FTL about seventy thousand kilometres off Armstrong." The Commander tapped the panels furiously trying to acquire more information.

Kalian looked back at the holo-projection. It was easy to see what the Commander was referring to.

"How big is it?" The Ambassador aimed his question at the Commander, but it was Telarrek that answered.

"It is significantly larger than the *Valoran*." He was looking at data on his own bracer.

"It's twenty miles long!" The Commander re-checked the scans, clearly shocked by the data.

From the viewport, Armstrong was just a small cluster of lights against the Moon's pale surface. They all had to crane their necks to see the hulking mass floating above them in the distance. The size of the behemoth could not be denied for despite its great distance away, the ship's mass obscured a good portion of Armstrong.

Scrutinising the image on the central display, Kalian could see the exterior hull was a flat black from end to end. The details were hard to make out from this distance but its smooth surface looked to be devoid of any. It was so dark that he was sure they would never have seen it if it hadn't tried to eclipse the moon. Against the starry background, it would simply appear as an absence of stars. Against the backdrop of the moon, the ship was a simple rectangle, revealing no beauty or intricate design like the *Valoran*. He wasn't even sure where the engine was located for there were no obvious ports or extensions. After seeing the *Valoran,* Kalian didn't think he could ever be awed by the size of another ship, but he had been wrong.

"What the hell is that?" Li'ara's face was more concern than awe.

"Is... is that a Laronian ship?" Droplets of sweat were forming on the Ambassador's forehead.

Telarrek tilted his head to the side as he examined the ship on the display. He gave a quick glance to each of his companions who all seemed to share the same thought.

"That is not a Laronian vessel." He paused for a moment. "I have never seen a ship like that."

All the humans turned to Telarrek, with even the Commander looking up from his console. A cold dread seeped into Kalian's gut.

"But I thought you said the Laronians-"

"The Laronians know nothing of Earth. They are only aware of an incursion into their territory. The only way they could find these coordinates is if they took them from your terraforming expedition and, as I said, they have not reached Alpha NL-2204 yet." Telarrek didn't take his eyes off the foreign ship.

"It's just like *your* ship!" The Commander sounded frustrated. "All our scans are bouncing right off the hull!"

Kalian couldn't believe the turn in events. In less than a day, they had gone from having one alien ship on their doorstep to two. He had a creeping sense of unease at the thought of the Novaarians being clueless as to its origins. From everything he had heard in the last half hour he was convinced there was nothing they didn't know.

Telarrek turned to Numanon. "I want the *Valoran* to scan every particle of that ship."

It was the first time Kalian had heard some urgency in the alien's voice and it worried him.

"Yes, my Charge." Numanon raised both of his lower limbs and activated the bracers.

Using his upper limbs, he began to type various commands into both bracers like they were a combined keyboard. His voice had the same guttural undertones but Kalian could hear a clear difference in the way he sounded. He began to realise the disc behind his ear was more complex than just a standard translator.

The ship continued to sit motionless in space. It felt ominous and cold. Even when compared to the *Valoran* it felt alien. Kalian wondered how it must look from Armstrong for the monstrous ship would be blocking their entire view of the Earth.

"We need to contact The Hub to see if the Chief's got any more info." Li'ara was talking to the Commander since he was at the central command console.

He gave a quick nod in return and began to set up a link to Earth.

Lights on every console immediately dimmed and flickered, becoming unresponsive to the Commander's touch. Even Numanon's bracers failed him as all of the command keys blurred into a haze of distorted blue light. The holo-projection beside Kalian lost its cohesion as the image of Earth transformed into tiny cubes of holo-energy before dying out completely. A moment later the speakers in the walls exploded with a screeching static.

"Now what?" The Commander slammed the palm of his hand on the console, hoping to get any kind of reaction from it.

"I believe we are being scanned." Numanon's guttural undertones sounded louder over the static noise. "The *Valoran* detected an intense neutrino burst before the interference. They appear to be jamming all forms of communication as well."

"No shit!"

All four Novaarians tilted their heads at the Commander, unsure of the meaning behind his response.

A second later, the static disappeared and the consoles returned to normal. Numanon examined his bracers and began typing again. Commander Hawkins wasted no time going back to his own console.

HE MADE a slow journey around the centrepiece of his command module. He took in the sight of the pilot resting back in the control chair. How long had she sat in that chair? How many countless millennia? Not that it could really be called a chair as she didn't actually make contact with it. The anti-gravity emitters kept her constantly afloat to prevent any sores. He was careful not to step on the plethora of tubules and wires that extended from the floor into almost every part of her naked body. He knew they were vital in keeping her alive as well as being connected to every nanocelium that made up the ship. Through her, he could re-model the ship's interior and exterior depending on their needs. Though alive, her conscious mind was being exercised within a virtual reality, allowing her some freedom despite her apparent constraints.

At last, they had found what they had been looking for. Soon their journey would be at an end and so would her imprisonment. But first, he had to deal with *them*. Thanks to the so-called Novaarians, they had been able to locate these coordinates. Moving away from the pilot, the ship reacted to his needs as the floor produced several oval columns in front of him. Though appearing liquid they soon became solid, just above waist height, the nanocelium moulding the shape as it changed matter. Above each column, holograms in copper and silver appeared like magic to hover in front of him with no visible emitters. Using a combination of hand movements and his neural link, he easily manipulated the images to see the desired information.

There was no mistaking it - they had found them. A silver hologram took shape like water in a vacuum and hung above the central column. It showed the image of an upright bipedal mammal in skeletal form, with a picture of the brain enlarged next to it and a karyogram of what was certainly primitive DNA. He felt the weight of an armoured hand grip his shoulder plate.

"It's them brother. We found them!" Only Elandar called him brother.

They had been friends since they were children, though his memories of such a time were buried under the violence of his adult life. In seconds they had scanned the solar system and collated all the information they required. There was no mistaking it; these *humans*, as the hologram to his left told him, were the ones they had been searching for. He didn't even like the name.

Before giving his next command, the column to his right began cycling through a pre-set alarm. Elandar motioned his hand across the column, activating the visual feedback. All the holograms across the entire breadth changed to form one image of an orbital station between them and the planet. In the middle of the intersecting rings, a coppery dot flashed at the top of the central sphere. Elandar enhanced the image, removing the station altogether. The copper hologram now represented one of these humans, again, in skeletal form. Elandar couldn't keep the shock off his face. He kept his own composure though, despite the rage building inside him.

"It's not possible..." Elandar looked to him for answers. "It's too soon."

His rage bubbled to the surface as he backhanded the hologram, ending it altogether. He should have expected this kind of tampering.

"It doesn't matter." He turned to Elandar, gripping both his shoulders. "It ends today. Prepare the Eclipse - nothing will escape it." Walking away, the command module anticipated his needs and produced a throne-like chair for him to sit on. He thought about the individual on the orbital station. "I think it's time we let the beast off its leash, don't you?" Elandar met his eyes and knew of his master's desires. "We will have no use for it soon anyway. Let it die with the rest of them." It pleased him to think of that particular individual aboard the station, whom the beast would slowly kill first.

Let him suffer before I end his world.

Elandar keyed in the commands to the pilot before another piece of information blinked to life on a new column. He squinted at the two words that appeared in holographic form above the pilot: *They Are...*

Elandar shut the hologram down like he had all the others. He attributed it to a minor glitch that had most likely occurred during their time in Rem-stores. After all, the pilot had been on her own for thousands of years, allowing plenty of time for ghosts in the machine to crop up without his direct supervision. He left it to Elandar who had always taken the greatest care with her.

"She's downloaded everything." Elandar paused. "They have another planet..."

That didn't surprise him much with their current level of technology. It was inevitable that they would spread across the stars for it was in their nature.

"When we are finished here, set a course to the other planet. I will see this war to its end."

"I DON'T UNDERSTAND. Where did this thing come from?" The Ambassador hadn't prepared for this. "How could *another* alien ship just appear? Don't we have sensor nets for this exact reason? This isn't making sense! We don't know them, and you don't know them!" His robe lashed out towards the Novaarians. "Forgive me but I was under the impression *we* were the ones who didn't know anything!"

Telarrek hadn't taken his eyes off the ship.

"From these readings," said Numanon, "they appear to have scanned everything in your solar system in one short burst." He sounded a little impressed at the technological feat.

"Yes!" Commander Hawkins clenched his fist in triumph. "I've got a direct link to-" He stopped as a console on his left caught his eye.

Kalian couldn't see what he was looking at.

"Commander?" Li'ara looked concerned.

"Shit! They just launched something!" He paused as more information appeared on his screen. "Long-range sensors put its trajectory..." He paused mid-sentence with a confused expression. "It's heading for the sun." He looked up meeting the eyes of everyone on the bridge, all as confused as he was.

"What are the specs?" Li'ara was entering commands into the holo-projector next to Kalian.

"Unknown. But from these readings, it's the size of the *Hyperion*!"

It all felt surreal to Kalian. He couldn't imagine a ship big enough to release a projectile the same size as the UDC's largest vessel. The holo-projector transformed into an image of an oblong that slowly became more detailed as long-range sensors fed back the telemetry. The majority of the object was a smooth sphere housed in between four structures that gripped around the back. These structures all converged into a long point at the front of the object.

He turned to the Novaarians who were all huddled round Numanon's bracer which had produced its own holographic image of the projectile. To Kalian's eyes, it looked to be a far more detailed image with various alien symbols floating around the different sections of the projectile. Numanon's other bracer began to flash several large symbols across the metallic screen. Moments after that, another light began to flash on the Commander's console taking his attention away from the sun-bound object.

"Wait a minute - there's something else." He squinted at the image on the console, trying to make sense of the data. "There's been another launch but it's tiny in comparison. It's within ten feet in size but I can't be sure. It's giving off too much interference!"

Li'ara was simultaneously checking her own console. "It's heading for us!"

"Our own sensors confirm the trajectory. It is moving at great speed." Telarrek looked out into space beyond the viewport while taking several steps back.

"We need to evacuate!" The Ambassador had his hand pressed onto the glass.

"There's no time. Get away from the viewport!" The Commander reached out his arm as if he could pull them to safety from ten metres away.

Everything then happened at once. Li'ara grabbed Kalian with both hands and threw him, using her own body as the pushing force, away from the viewport. He heard one of the Novaarians shout as they all jumped as one towards the Commander's position. The Ambassador was stood frozen in place by fear and curiosity as the light of the sun reflected off the dark object hurtling towards him.

Kalian heard the sound of the impact before he hit the floor. It was only brief before the vacuum of space replaced the noise of twisting steel and shattered glass with the tornado of air escaping the bridge. He could feel the tug of the universe pulling Li'ara and himself into its cold embrace. It was hard to tell in all the chaos but at one point he was sure he couldn't feel the floor beneath him. The chaos was suddenly replaced by pain as his head collided with the nearest console, dropping him into darkness.

CHAOS HAD ERUPTED inside The Hub's central command theatre. Alarms on every console were blaring their warning as holograms in every colour erupted across the various terminals. Commander Barnes furiously tapped his fingers against the glass station in an effort to collate all the information. He couldn't believe what he was seeing.

"Sir, the Icarus has been breached... Ambassador Arlek is dead."

Barnes scanned through the Icarus sensors and confirmed the cadet's report for himself. Something had actually penetrated the bridge and killed Arlek in the process. The ship that had fired it was formidable in size and just as alien as the purple ship.

"Where the hell did that come from?" The Chief Commander slammed his palm onto the glass top.

"Sensors show it appearing from subspace but there's no trace of Solar Drive activity, sir," the nearest cadet answered.

"How did they move through subspace without a Solar Drive?" Barnes examined the data but couldn't understand it.

"What's the location of the second missile?" the Chief Commander asked.

Barnes double checked the data coming in from the *Hyperion* as it traversed the distance back to Earth from the sun. "It's missed every ship and satellite. It's on a straight course for the sun, sir."

"A misfire?"

"We don't know..."

The Chief dropped his fist onto the glass again. "Any activity from the first ship?"

Barnes glanced at the information streaming across the table. "None, sir. At this point, we have no idea if they're together."

Lieutenant Walsh strode over with a Datapad in hand. "Sir, you need to see this." She handed the pad to the Chief Commander.

Barnes watched him scan through the information with annoyance etched across his face.

"I have no idea what this means." The Chief handed it back to the Lieutenant.

Barnes walked over, curious himself.

"These are the preliminary results from the lab, sir. They've been going through the scans we made of Kalian Gaines. His DNA is *different*. What we have on file from the Birthing Databank doesn't match these scans."

The Chief looked up from the central station for the first time. "What DNA was in the message they sent?"

"It was the same one we have from the databank, sir. That's why we knew it was Kalian. What we don't know is why his DNA is different today."

"How is it different?" Barnes asked.

"They don't know, sir. Apparently, it could take years of research to understand, but the scientists looking at it seemed very excited."

The Chief rolled his eyes, looking back to the constant stream of holograms. "We'll deal with this later."

Barnes turned to the image of the Icarus, its blast shield now covering the hull breach. He could see that the emergency teams were already leaving the hangar, making their way up to the station. He could see that the remains of the team on the bridge were in bad shape. The sensors in Li'ara's suit showed she was unconscious but alive.

"Come on, Ducarté, get up."

THREE

Li'ara opened her eyes for the first time since the nightmare had erupted. She had collided with something hard as the sound of rushing air came to a swift end and gravity returned. Her eyes had remained closed to protect her from flying debris but she had managed to remain conscious. As they were being sucked out of the broken viewport she had lost her grip on Kalian. It had all happened so fast she only had time to push him as far away from the breach as possible.

She lay on the floor in an awkward position between a half-destroyed console and... She craned her neck to see what her back was against. From the layout of the bridge, she knew it should be the viewport but now there was just a wall. Li'ara turned her whole body to get a better look. The brown wall covered the entire space where the viewport had been, arcing over the ceiling where the glass and tungsten frames hadn't even been broken. The security walls, that formed the outer shell of the command bridge, had been activated when the hull was penetrated. All UDC ships had the same design since the bridge was considered integral to maintaining order. It had to have fail-safes for any direct attack.

Seeing how close she was to the wall, Li'ara realised she had only been inches from a blood boiling death. She pulled at her chest plate, catching her breath as the air recyclers finished replenishing the oxygen supply.

Kalian...

The mission flooded every crevice of her mind: Protect Kalian Gaines. She rose quicker than she knew she should have. Her training told her to check herself over first but Li'ara didn't have time for that. She used the broken console for support and pulled herself up, taking in her surroundings as she searched for him.

Everything was in shades of red and black since the emergency lights had activated. Only a few feet away was a large jagged hole where something had swan dived through the command bridge. She could see the flickering lights and sparking consoles of the next two levels down. The rest was in darkness. How far had it gone?

She couldn't put the pieces together. In what universe could a species build *that* ship but not construct a working missile? She slowly moved past it, making sure to avoid the drop. She didn't have time to think about it now but she was just glad it hadn't blown them to stardust.

The room had filled with smoke as multiple consoles had been fried and split apart. She headed in the direction she had pushed Kalian, praying he hadn't been sucked through the breach. Li'ara let out a breath she hadn't realised she was holding. Kalian was lying face down on the floor with various innards of a console scattered over his legs. She quickly knelt down next to him shoving aside the wires and charred panels.

"Kalian!" Li'ara had to shout over the sound of the constant sparks and flames around them.

Li'ara rolled him over to see his face. He had ash smeared across his skin and clothes. She instantly noticed the cut over his right eyebrow. Her training kicked in again and this time she listened. She visually inspected his airway checking for any obstruction. Her hand was rising and falling with the breathing of his chest.

"Kalian!" Li'ara shouted again. She gave him a quick shake around the shoulders. "Kalian... Kalian you need to get up, *now!*"

The environment had changed and Li'ara no longer felt in control. Her new priority was to get Kalian off the Icarus and planet-bound as fast as possible. His eyes flickered for a moment. She gripped his shoulder a little tighter, bringing him back to the room. Kalian looked in pain as he lifted his head.

"What happened?" His voice was groggy. "You're bleeding."

Li'ara couldn't help but be a little impressed. Most people weren't able to speak after an explosion, let alone ask questions. She could feel the blood slowly trickling down the side of her face but she ignored it. He had distracted her from finishing the checks, next was circulation.

Li'ara began patting him down, moving his clothes and limbs looking for any blood loss.

Shit!

Her hands soon found the foreign object under his jacket sticking through the shirt. At first, she thought it might be a compound fracture of the ribs but it was situated too low. After moving his jacket aside, she realised it was a piece of shrapnel from an exploded console. The blood appeared black under the emergency lighting.

Li'ara instantly started searching each of the compartments on her belt looking for the med pack. Just ammo and a knife. She chastised herself for leaving it on the rack in the *Fathom's* armoury. She had made the split-second decision to take extra ammo charges instead. Such was the influence of Commander Hawkins.

"There's Medifoam back on the shuttle. I don't have anything on me."

"I don't understand. What's..." Kalian tracked Li'ara's eyes to the shrapnel piercing his abdomen. The alarm on his face was obvious.

"I don't know how deep it goes, but if I pull it out I'm going to need Medifoam to stop any bleeding!" She felt confident the foam would do the job, having had need of it herself in the past.

She would always remember her first time as the lead on a

protection detail for the negotiator from Central Parliament. A rebel faction on Mars had claimed responsibility for several terrorist attacks on Earth. Their goal was to intimidate Central Parliament into decreeing Mars an independent planet. That wasn't going to happen. In the appearance of peace, a negotiator had been sent to Great Athens at the base of Olympus Mons. Li'ara hadn't liked it from the start. Great Athens was too big a city with potential rebels everywhere. To make things worse, she was confident Central Parliament had been counting on negotiations to fail. If it was seen that the rebels had no interest in peace, Parliament could use the UDC to remove them without losing face. They were right. It had only taken five minutes before the peace talks fell through and the shooting began.

The negotiator survived, making the mission a success as far as Li'ara was concerned, but if it hadn't been for Medifoam, she wouldn't have been so lucky. A rebel had configured an ancient buckshot-style weapon. One of the old-fashioned projectiles had passed straight through her femoral artery. From her point of view, Medifoam was the only reason she hadn't bled to death right there and then.

A sound to her right shot her instincts into overdrive. In one smooth motion, she had drawn her weapon and levelled it in the direction of the sound. It was only after raising her gun that she registered the noise as a cough. Now orientated to the room, she knew it had come from the central console. Li'ara recognised the tattooed head of the Commander as a small flame illuminated his shaven scalp through the smoke.

"Commander Hawkins!" Li'ara was relieved to know he had survived.

Although she had never worked with him before, Li'ara was well aware of his reputation. He didn't usually do personal security like her; he was bred to fight and nothing else. Nothing was ever confirmed but, if Central Parliament needed a show of force and didn't want it public, rumours were they sent Commander Hawkins. If he hadn't been so well known amongst the ranks he would have been an agent by now. When Li'ara was informed of his presence on the mission, she knew he was being sent as a fail-safe. If everything went wrong and the aliens proved to be hostile the UDC would unleash Commander Hawkins on them.

"Li'ara? Is that you?" His voice sounded like he'd inhaled too much smoke.

He limped out between the central consoles. She could see a smooth metal pipe lodged in his right leg. The tip pointed out above his kneecap, preventing him from bending it. Li'ara performed a quick medical assessment with her eyes. The pipe would stop any blood loss for now and he could handle the pain. Her priority was still Kalian.

Li'ara could account for three of the four members of her party but where was the Ambassador? She looked through the gaps in the smoke hoping to glimpse his large robe.

"Bridge is clear. Where's the Ambassador? Did you see what happened to him?" Li'ara was still crouched by Kalian and couldn't see everything.

The Commander was shaking his head. "Whatever crashed through the viewport took him with it. There's no way he survived." The Commander was staring at the jagged hole a few feet away.

Like Li'ara, he had to reprioritise now. The Ambassador had literally been obliterated but Kalian and Li'ara were still alive. Now they had to get off the station and report back to the Chief Commander.

He took in Kalian's prone form from head to toe. "Can he walk?"

Li'ara knew he was really asking her if they should leave Kalian behind. Before she could answer Kalian slowly twisted his body, rolling onto his knees.

"I might not have the training you two have, but I'm not useless." He was beginning to surprise her more and more.

Li'ara remembered thinking what a moron he was when they were first introduced at The Hub. He had no real training she could count on, wasn't even an officer of Central Parliament and so, as just an average citizen, he should have crumpled under the first sign of stress. He rose to his full height, just above her own, but couldn't maintain the posture, causing him to hunch over. He stumbled backwards, his head rolling slightly out of control. Grabbing him by the shoulders Li'ara turned him to face her, keeping him upright in her grip.

"Look at me. I'm going to get you out of here, but you need to focus. Do everything I tell you to and when I tell you to. Are you with me?" Li'ara made her tone sharp and to the point, like her old drill sergeant. It was a tone you couldn't ignore. She watched him blink slowly three times as he looked around the room. He let out a long breath and focused on Li'ara's eyes.

"I'm with you."

I'm going to have to carry him...

The quick nod from Commander Hawkins suggested he no longer cared. Li'ara knew that if Kalian couldn't keep up, the Commander wouldn't hesitate to leave him behind. His priority wasn't protection, it was action. The sooner they could get back to The Hub the sooner they could mount an offensive.

"We need to get Earth-side ASAP. I don't know what hit us but it sure as shit didn't explode, and I ain't waiting around to see if it does. Whoever... whatever they are, they haven't come looking to make friends!"

The Commander turned to the exit while Li'ara placed Kalian's arm around her shoulders. He appeared grateful for the support for, as the initial shock wore off, he was obviously starting to feel the pain.

They had only walked a few steps before Li'ara stopped them both. It was hard to hear everything through the noise of the overhead extinguishers. Pausing a moment longer to confirm her thoughts, she waited for the sound. There it was again, the unmistakable sound of twisting metal under the methodical impact of something heavy. It was definitely getting louder. Li'ara had turned them both to look at the gaping hole in the floor. She looked to Kalian, wanting to know if he could hear it. His face was screwed up as he concentrated on the noise.

74

Commander Hawkins came into view by her side, not believing his own ears. "Now what?"

With all the ash on his head, Li'ara could no longer see where the Commander's tattoo started and ended. He had dozens of small cuts across one side of his face from an exploded console.

"I don't understand, didn't we get hit by a missile or..." Kalian's words were cut off by a distinctly alien hand grasping his shoulder.

The Commander reached for his sidearm but Li'ara recognised the hand. She turned Kalian and herself so they could see behind them. Li'ara couldn't believe that in all the chaos and confusion she had forgotten about the Novaarians. She reasoned that they must have jumped to safety on the other side of the central console. There were only three of them now.

"Kalian Gaines..." Telarrek reached out but didn't touch him. Instead, his metallic bracer lit up as it scanned Kalian's body. "He is injured."

Li'ara noticed the features on his face appear to soften as he took in the sight of Kalian's hunched form.

"We've got bigger problems." The Commander had lowered his weapon but didn't holster it. "Hear that? You have any idea what that is?"

"We have already tried scanning whatever it is. There is a low-level electromagnetic pulse emanating from within the hole, deflecting our sensors." It had been Numanon that replied.

Li'ara found it astonishing that they had such different voices considering their similarity in appearance.

Kalian lifted his head. "There were four of you..."

"Youl was taken from us." Telarrek looked at the broken viewport.

There was a note of sadness in his voice. Li'ara filed the information away. It was only small, but they obviously shared similar human emotions. It hadn't escaped her that Youl's fate had nearly been her own.

"We shall think on his passing later; now we must get to safety, my Charge."

Li'ara couldn't help but be surprised. It had obviously been Ilyseal that had spoken but the voice was definitely female. Li'ara inspected the Novaarian a little closer. In the emergency lighting, it was impossible to pick out real detail. The only thing she remembered was the slight difference in Ilyseal's hair but, under the light, everything looked red.

Telarrek lifted his head sharply. "You must come with us to the *Valoran*. It is the safest place right now."

"You can go back to your shiny ship." The Commander was pulling something off the back of his belt. "We're going back to Earth, right now."

Li'ara recognised the object he had pulled free from his belt - a grenade. She watched him dial the level up to its maximum setting.

The Novaarians recognised the object for what it was as they took a step back. "I would not recommend that course of—"

Before Numanon could finish his warning, the Commander threw the grenade into the hole.

"Time to bug out!" Commander Hawkins had already started limping for the exit before the explosive unleashed its payload.

The floor shook beneath them as a giant gust of smoke and debris flew out of the hole. They lingered for a moment waiting to see if everything held up under the new stress. Li'ara wanted to check that the ascending noise had stopped but the Commander ordered her to follow.

By the time they had all caught up, the Commander had opened the door, revealing the corridor back to the hangar bay. The emergency lighting had only taken effect on the command bridge so the corridor was still well lit in black and white panels. It was like walking through a portal into a world of colour. It took Li'ara's eyes a moment to adjust to the brightness. Telarrek and Ilyseal had gone ahead of them while Numanon took up the rear. Li'ara knew the formation well. They were creating a protective barrier around them. No not *them*, Kalian. She had seen Telarrek's concern for him. With their current circumstances, she feared they might never learn of the Novaarians' interest in him.

In the light, it was clear the Novaarians had suffered similar wounds to them. Telarrek had what could only be described as a split lip, despite the absence of lips. To Li'ara's surprise, the blood surrounding the edges of the cut was red, as were all the other injuries they had sustained from flying debris and glass. Just like them, the Novaarians were covered in ash and rubble, while the fabric that flowed from their waist was singed and torn in places. Li'ara could now see the red tendrils that were intermingled between Ilyseal's milky white strands. She wondered for a moment if that was typical of all Novaarian females.

They were nearly halfway down the corridor when the entire group was forced to stop. They had all felt it, the pulling sensation from beneath their feet. It had caused them all to stumble for a step as the invisible force briefly gripped them. It was an unusual feeling as if the Grav Enforcers had suddenly gone into overdrive and increased the g-force. The pull had been too much for the Commander's injured leg, bringing him to one knee. Li'ara could see the drops of blood trailing behind the Commander, as he smeared them with his boots. Telarrek and Ilyseal attempted to help him up but he shrugged them off. He was a stubborn son of a bitch.

There was an audible cracking sound coming from the floor, further up the corridor. They could hear the metal girders and framework twisting and bending underneath. The corridor was silent as the noise stopped and everyone held their breath. Li'ara couldn't help but wonder if the Commander's grenade had destabilised the entire station.

Chaos erupted for the second time as the floor ahead of them violently ruptured like an earthquake. Sparks burst out as wires in the floor were severed and metal frames were ripped apart. The scene reminded Li'ara of a black hole as the floor was sucked into an abyss. It had all happened in a second. The only thing left was smoke rising from the gaping hole in the floor. It was too big to jump across, keeping the hangar just out of reach. The sudden implosion hadn't caused them to fall over, but Li'ara noticed all three Novaarians were in a crouched position, like runners before a race.

No one said a word as they stared at the hole. The lights began to flicker along the length of the corridor and Li'ara thought back to Numanon's comment about an electromagnetic pulse. Kalian's grip on her shoulder tightened. Her training kicked in again and she found herself calculating her options. The way forward was no longer viable. The command bridge was out of the question. It was a dead end. Two choices: go left at the T-junction or go right. Li'ara hated it when her missions came to violence and chaos, but she couldn't deny the clarity of mind it gave her. There were no distractions, just the mission.

Her mind went back to The Hub where she scanned through the technical layout of the main sphere. She knew there was an access corridor for maintenance that led to a side door within the executive hangar. The door was on the left inside the hangar meaning that she would have to turn right at the bridge door. Her drill sergeant's words echoed in her mind.

Always have an exit strategy.

"We need to go this way, now!" She didn't point at the corridor; her intention was just to get them to follow her.

The Novaarians slowly resumed their normal height as Numanon checked the schematics on his bracer. "The Lieutenant Commander is correct."

Telarrek lifted his head in acknowledgement.

They had managed to get as far as the door when Li'ara felt a pit open within her stomach. They had all heard it, the heavy clunk as something ascended into the corridor. Li'ara turned Kalian and herself to look back towards the hangar. The light continued to flicker creating a stark contrast between the white walls and complete darkness. Li'ara kept a hard gaze on the distant chasm. She couldn't believe her eyes. With every flash of the light something was slowly emerging. A thick arm reached out of the smoke and darkness, its hand gripping through the floor itself. She couldn't see it all, but from what she could see it was definitely armoured. Every flash of light seemed to bring the new alien into the corridor.

"Run!" The Commander was reaching around for his cannon.

Li'ara felt four pairs of hands press against Kalian and herself ushering them down the chosen corridor. The adrenaline surged through her body at what felt like light speed, taking away any aches and pains. Running at a speed Li'ara could only dream of, Ilyseal dashed ahead keying the button to call the lift.

The heavy footfalls could be heard from around the corner, even over the sound of their own feet. From the dense metallic sound, Li'ara guessed it to be armoured all over. She heard the pleasant ding as the lift doors parted. Kalian was running alongside her now, his own adrenaline pushing away the pain. They both crashed into the lift together, not slowing their speed. Telarrek and Ilyseal were more graceful in their movements, stopping in front of them. Li'ara had to move her head to see past them.

The lights in the corridor began to flicker as the giant turned the corner. Li'ara guessed it must have been emitting a constant low-level electromagnetic pulse. For a couple of brief moments, Li'ara glimpsed the alien in the light. It was big. She guessed it to be equal in height to the Novaarians, if not bigger. Its shoulder width was certainly wider although the size of the true creature was impossible to tell as it was made entirely of plated armour. She could see that it was predominantly matt black, but it was scarred from head to toe with silver and bronze scratches where it had taken damage. If it had been on a UDC soldier she would have asked what war they had survived.

She couldn't help but think it was ugly. It wore chunky armour that had clearly been designed to intimidate and take a serious beating. Each plated section could be seen connecting to the next like a patchwork. Li'ara's tactical mind was taking over. She could see no visible weapon: gun or otherwise. From the look of its armour, she assumed its wearer must be strong to even move a muscle inside. Its head was encased in a helmet intricately designed with a raised pattern running out of where the mouth would be and flowing over the back of the rounded helmet. Where she expected to see a visor or eyes were two sunken pits. Li'ara had seen rebels of all factions wearing faceplates and death masks but nothing compared to this. It looked ancient, perhaps from an archaic time of violence and bloodlust. To look into those bottomless pits would be to look at death itself.

Li'ara forced herself to harden and, as she shed her fears, she couldn't believe what she'd missed. The hulking figure slowly approaching was bipedal. It had two arms and two legs just like her. It was an understandable oversight since, until that day, a humanoid foe was all she had ever faced. She knew instantly that it couldn't be human. It was too big and its show of force was beyond a human's capabilities. Having seen all she had today, it wasn't a massive stretch to assume there were other bipedal species in the galaxy. She just wished this particular biped wasn't in front of her.

The sound of her own thoughts was drowned out by the sudden burst of electromagnetic projectiles erupting from the Commander's rail-gun. The electronically powered weapon was causing his entire body to vibrate as he backed towards the lift. From this range, Li'ara knew it would be impossible to miss the giant. The corridor became a violent light show as every projectile ricocheted off the creature and impacted the walls, tearing away holes the size of her head. The fitted lights burst apart, shattering glass as sparks flew off every part of the armour. The giant didn't change its pace, appearing completely unfazed by the Commander's attack. There were scorch marks all over its metallic body but the armour hadn't even been dented.

Numanon reached out and pulled the Commander into the confined lift almost raising him off the floor. Li'ara wasted no time in pushing the button. They only had to get three floors down. As the doors closed the armoured figured was only feet away. There was no room to move in the cramped space. It clearly hadn't been designed for three seven feet tall aliens. Everyone was panting for breath, even the Novaarians. The Commander's rail-gun let off a low hum as it powered down.

Kalian was slumped against the wall holding his injured side. Li'ara could see that blood was still trickling out but it wasn't enough to concern her.

He can make it.

"What the hell... was that thing?" Li'ara's words came out in laboured breaths.

She looked at each of the Novaarians hoping they would have some clue. They remained silent looking from one to the other. Ding. The lift doors parted again revealing a long room lined with monitors and chairs. It was one of the sub bridges often manned by a team responsible for the station's maintenance. Li'ara saw the door that should lead them back to the executive hangar.

Somewhere further up the lift shaft, metal began to creak and snap as the creature ripped the doors off. Li'ara grabbed Kalian's jacket and yanked him out of the lift pushing everyone ahead of her. Commander Hawkins hit the exterior panel with the butt of his gun. The lift doors closed moments before a thunderous explosion impacted the other side.

The shudder caused the Commander to fall again. "Keep going!"

Ilyseal hesitated, hearing the Commander's order. Li'ara saw her glance at Kalian before resuming her pace alongside them. Li'ara herself wanted to stop and help him but Kalian was the mission. If anyone could take care of himself, it was Commander Hawkins.

Numanon had gone ahead this time, activating the next lift. Li'ara had the smallest sense of relief when the doors parted instantly. That relief was shattered when the doors behind the Commander bent out of shape before exploding into the room with incredible force. She didn't hear what Telarrek shouted but once again she was bundled into another lift. She never let go of Kalian's jacket. The last thing she heard was the densely armoured feet clamber into the room.

Moments later their lift stopped and they entered the access corridor that led back to the hangar. It was darker than other parts of the station. Only used for maintenance access it hadn't been an aesthetic priority. Li'ara didn't care. She could see the words *Exec Hangar* on the door ahead.

"Come on!" She positioned herself under Kalian's arm giving him extra support.

He had a determined look on his face. He was stronger than she had given him credit for. They ran to the door, not looking back, for she was expecting the lift to explode at any moment, like the last one. The light was almost blinding as they left the dark corridor behind. The hangar remained untouched and directly ahead lay the *Fathom* with the Novaarian craft further along. Li'ara had never been so happy to see a ship. For the first time since the attack on the command bridge she had hope. They were going to make it. They would survive. Kalian would survive.

The floor between the two ships exploded like a volcanic geyser. Debris and contents from the floor rained down on the hangar. Li'ara instinctively placed herself in front of Kalian. Her hope died as the alien's armoured gauntlet gripped the edge of the newly formed hole, pulling the rest of its bulk into the hangar bay with apparent ease. It was relentless. She knew it would never stop. The thought went against her UDC training: everything was achievable. Nothing was beyond her capabilities.

She tapped the screen built into her forearm, activating the *Fathom's* ignition procedures. She heard the door panel hiss as it opened. She didn't take her eyes off the lumbering beast. Despite the training, she could see the reality of the situation. The distance between them, the ship and the ever-approaching figure was conclusive. It was a simple calculation that it would tear the *Fathom* apart before they could escape. But she had to try.

"Get in the *Fathom*, now!" Li'ara noticed the Novaarians looking at their own ship. "It's too late, c'mon!"

At least they had the sense to follow her. Numanon remained in place, steadfast against the approaching danger. Li'ara was halfway up the ramp when she noticed.

"What's he doing?!" She didn't have time for this.

"What he must..." Telarrek looked Li'ara in the eyes and there was an understanding between them. It was Numanon's choice, not his.

Li'ara took note of the event. Were they always so willing to sacrifice themselves, or was this about Kalian again?

Numanon used his lower arm to reach behind his back. Li'ara couldn't believe she'd missed it as Numanon pulled out a silver shaft of metal that had been hiding under his tendrils of hair. It was at least three feet long. One end of the shaft formed a sharp point that glistened in the overhead lighting. His movements were beautiful as he used all four hands to spin and flip the shaft around his body. He finished his presentation with the shaft pressed into the ground parallel to him. Somewhere in all the spins, the shaft had extended into a spear. Li'ara would have preferred a gun, or maybe a grenade launcher.

"Go!" Telarrek pushed them into the *Fathom's* main cabin.

Li'ara took Kalian straight into the med bay behind the glass, instructing him to lie on the gurney. She put a small ready-made canister against his abdomen and depressed the button on top. The morphine would help until she could properly see to him. Ilyseal had already closed the door while Telarrek made his way through to the cockpit. Li'ara wasn't surprised how easily they used the ship's controls. She imagined it was quite a primitive design to them.

She thumbed the panel on the wall activating the holo-image of outside. The ship lifted off tucking in the landing gear as it did. Telarrek rotated the ship one hundred and eighty degrees to face the hangar exit. Li'ara could see the armoured giant walking straight towards them as if Numanon wasn't even there. The Novaarian launched at his opponent with the spear raised like an ancient warrior of Earth. His speed and agility were impressive, every move precise and clearly practised. As he bore down on the giant, he had his spear aimed at its head. Li'ara was sure this one blow would end the conflict. She was wrong. The giant caught the spear inches from its head, pulling it down to the side and burying it in the floor. Numanon's body followed the spear and the giant lashed out with its free hand, catching him by the neck.

Numanon attempted to break free using all four of his powerful arms. It was no use. Li'ara could see him punch and kick and even try to pry the monster's hand from around his neck. The giant brought Numanon's face so it was inches from its own nightmare faceplate. She couldn't tell if anything was said. The Novaarian's body began to shake violently in desperation. A second later his whole body went limp, his arms dropping to his side and his head lolling as if the verte-brae were not quite attached.

Li'ara stretched her hand out to the holo-image and, forgetting it wasn't glass, passed her hand straight through to the bulkhead. Whatever this thing was, she thought, it was strong and fast to have been able to catch the spear. As Ilyseal took a deep breath at the sight of Numanon being discarded on the hangar floor, the armoured giant raised his armoured hand towards the *Fathom* as if to grab the whole ship.

What's it doing?

The sound was muffled from inside the ship but Li'ara couldn't miss the rail-gun fire that suddenly bombarded the giant. Commander Hawkins appeared from the same door that they'd come through, his mouth stretched into a war cry as he continued to fire. He looked to Li'ara but she knew he couldn't see her through the hull. He waved his hand signalling for them to flee. His attack had caught the giant's attention like a wasp pestering a human.

Telarrek steered the *Fathom* through the shielding membrane into the vacuum of space. Kalian silently appeared by Li'ara's side still clutching his abdomen. They both watched in astonishment as the laws of physics broke down in front of them. The giant extended its arm towards the Commander who stood twenty-feet away. He dropped the rail-gun as he was lifted into the air by some invisible force. The Commander's face contorted as if in immense pain. His limbs twisted and bent into unnatural positions as every part of him was compressed into his centre.

Blood and bone broke through his skin as he became a ball of broken limbs and torn flesh. His humerus snapped as it tore through the skin and shot into his encroaching face. The blood that sprayed from his many wounds froze mid-air as if it were floating in a mini vacuum around him. Eventually, his feet disappeared inside his groin with his pelvis shattering from the intense pressure. The Comman-der's agonising expression became still, his vertebrae broken. The goliath lowered its arm and, in the same moment, the Commander's body fell to the floor, unrecognisable as ever having been a human.

Wasting no more time, Telarrek engaged the ship's thrusters and left the Icarus station behind. Li'ara was speechless. She had never seen anything like that before. For just a moment she thought she might be in shock. It had no weapon, so how could it have done that? The sight of Kalian yanked her mind back to the mission.

"Come on." Li'ara walked him back to the med bay. She quickly scanned the shrapnel in his skin measuring its depth. "You'll need surgery but for now I can remove it and apply Medifoam."

Picking up the necessary tools, she pulled out the fragment and sprayed the Medifoam inside the wound. It quickly hardened on the outside preventing further blood loss.

"This will keep you awake for now." Without waiting for his response, she pressed another canister to the skin on his wrist. The stimulants would race through Kalian's veins for at least half an hour.

After helping Kalian, Li'ara became aware that an alien was piloting the ship. She marched across the cabin heading for the cockpit. Before she could enter, the *Fathom* shuddered as its landing gear touched down.

"Where are we?" Li'ara stopped as she surveyed the outside world through the viewport.

It was not The Hub. Instead they appeared to have landed on a massive landing strip *inside* the *Valoran*. The ship was being surrounded by Novaarians. The *Valoran's* interior walls were a beautiful shining purple with hundreds of smaller, identical craft lining the hangar. She recognised the design from the craft Telarrek and his group had landed in.

"The *Valoran* is the safest place to be, Lieutenant Commander." Telarrek rose to his full height from the pilot's seat.

"We need to get back to The Hub. They need threat assessments, and we need to be debriefed. Right now they have no idea what they're up against!" Li'ara was imagining that beast of a ship containing thousands if not millions of those armoured giants.

Telarrek moved past her into the main cabin. His upper hand touched Ilyseal on the shoulder as they shared a moment. They had obviously been closer to Youl and Numanon than she had been to

Commander Hawkins. She felt a sense of indifference towards his death, but that could still be the shock.

Both Novaarians left the ship motioning for Kalian and herself to follow. She counted six Novaarians waiting outside the *Fathom*, each holding a spear in one pair of hands. There was an awkward moment of silence as they all stared at Kalian descending the ramp. Li'ara felt she might as well have been invisible.

One of the Novaarians stepped forward to face Telarrek. "My Charge..." He presented his bracer showing Telarrek several sensor readings that Li'ara couldn't make out.

Telarrek let out a sharp grunt as if he had just been injured. "Come quickly!" Telarrek shot off towards the enormous entrance to their hangar.

The view was breath-taking. Li'ara was certain they could fit a small star-cruiser through the portal. Before they had even reached the edge, she could see the Earth and the Moon with the sun in the background. Of course, it was hard to miss the ship sitting forebodingly in front of the moon.

Li'ara wasn't sure what she was looking through. The portal into the hangar was crystal clear with no glass or membrane evident. She was convinced there was nothing between herself and the cold space beyond. She was close to giving in to her curiosity when Kalian reached out and placed his hand into the empty space. The area around his hand became distorted, creating small ripples.

"It tickles." He retracted his hand.

Li'ara was keenly aware that Kalian would need more medical treatment and soon. She had no idea how the shrapnel had affected his organs.

"Our sensors are detecting pressure fluctuations within your star." Telarrek's words stunned her as he continued to monitor his own bracer.

That deep pit returned to Li'ara's stomach. In all the chaos she had forgotten about the unknown projectile heading for the sun.

"That thing, the missile they launched... What was that?" Li'ara was becoming numb with dread.

"The *Valoran* scanned the object but we could not discern its purpose. Its contents and configuration are alien to us." Telarrek raised his upper hand attracting the attention of one of the other Novaarians. He paused a moment, taking another look at his bracer. "Prepare the Starrillium for an emergency jump!"

Li'ara had no idea what he was talking about, but it sounded like they were about to leave. "What's going on? We can't leave. You need to stay and help us!" She couldn't protect Kalian from this. She was losing control.

"It is too late..." Telarrek replied.

The sun imploded in a second.

In the blink of an eye, the solar system experienced true darkness for the first time in over five billion years. As quickly as it had imploded, the reaction reversed, exploding in a blinding flare. Li'ara and Kalian covered their faces, watching with just one eye. The supernova continued to expand at a terrifying speed. Mercury and Venus had already been consumed in the growing fireball. It was humankind's worst-case scenario. They had the determination and will to survive anything the Earth had to throw at them, but they couldn't outrun the death of their own star. It was like an angry god descending from the heavens and wiping away the life it had nurtured for billions of years.

Single tears fell from Li'ara's eyes as she stepped back from the invisible force field. She felt helpless and terrified at once. The force field changed as it tinted to dim the glare of the dying star. She was frozen in place as her brain struggled to cope with the choices laid out in front of her in such little time. Li'ara wanted to run and hide while at the same time surrender to her fate.

Nothing could survive this.

The speed of its expansion was unfathomable, giving her no time to make any choice. The sun had become a wall of fire eclipsing space altogether. She gasped as its wrath touched the edge of the Earth, setting the atmosphere alight in the perfect silence of space.

She was only half aware of someone shouting behind her before the apocalyptic view jumped to the left and became a blur of streaming stars that melted into the abyss of subspace. Somehow the ship had entered faster-than-light travel without the need of a star spot. If it hadn't been for the shock, she would have questioned that.

Instead, she looked down at the pressure on her foot. Kalian had collapsed and lay unconscious on the floor with a dark bruise spreading across his abdomen.

FOUR

Kalian's mind swirled turbulently like a storm. Every lightning flash was an image of the nightmare he had barely escaped. The viewport exploding, the corridors imploding, doors bursting off their frames as if they were made of paper and the hangar almost breaking in half with the Commander... his mind couldn't make sense of that last part. It was all because of that hulking armoured creature. His mind flashed from one violent image to another as the giant marched relentlessly towards him, its plated gauntlet reaching out of the darkness to take him.

The weight of reality tried to burst through his subconscious. The change from dreaming to the real world was confusing and violent. His dreams woke him with a feeling of dread and impending danger. Kalian was on the verge of consciousness as an unused part of his mind seemed to wake up. The feeling was new and all-consuming, as though he no longer had control of his own thoughts. He felt the confines of his body melt away as his mind pulsed into the space beyond.

He became aware that he was lying flat on a cushioned table or bed; he wasn't sure which. He could feel the size of the room that contained him as if his mind was pushing out and bouncing off the smooth curving walls. As his mind pushed outwards with every pulse, he could tell there were smaller tables and stations in various sections of the room and three identical pillars. He was surprised at how keenly aware he was of the exact space between each object as though his mind was filling the gaps in between. His brain was alive with every atom in the room in their constant battle, pulling against one another.

Kalian's head jerked as his mind connected with something far more complex than a table or surrounding walls. It was more substantial and hard to interpret.

"Kalian..." The voice was only a whisper.

Kalian's eyes opened as everything contracted back into his mind like an overstretched elastic band. The loss of the connection made him feel blind to his surroundings despite the use of his eyes and ears. For just a moment he had felt more connected to everything than ever before.

He whipped his head around, following the sound of the strained whisper.

Li'ara!

She was pinned flat against the nearest pillar, a foot above the floor. She was only suspended there for a moment before landing back on her feet. As she landed, Kalian heard the clatter of several metallic objects hit the ground and tables around the room.

He began to panic; he could feel his heart beating through his chest. He had done it again, his *thing*. Only this time he had not only done it in front of someone but *to* someone. He had never affected another person before; he hadn't even been aware he could. Up until now, it had only been small things or electronics, never anything alive. It must have been the nightmare. That golem reaching out for him must have sent his body into some sort of defensive overdrive.

Li'ara stood up straight, brushing her coppery hair out of her face. It wasn't hard to miss the blotchy red skin around her eyes. She had obviously been crying. Signs of her recent distress broke the dam in his memory as the images of his world ending flooded his brain.

The sun had gone supernova.

He felt that blinding light again as he relived the death of the oldest thing in the solar system. It had actually happened, the worst natural catastrophe imaginable, only it couldn't have been natural. The sun was young for a star, billions of years away from death. It had to have been *them*. He remembered Commander Hawkins' warning about the unknown object heading for the sun. He couldn't recall anything beyond the blinding light. He couldn't remember... Earth.

Kalian couldn't remember seeing the fate of his home but he wasn't stupid enough to imagine it survived. Nothing could survive a supernova. He had always been surprised when people laughed at the thought of ancient humans worshipping the sun; after all, it has the potential of a god. It has the power to create and support life as well as the power to completely wipe it away. *Had*. It *had* that power. Now everything was just stardust.

The room blurred as tears formed in his eyes, slowly rolling down his face.

His voice was shaky. "Did it really happen?" He already knew the answer but he had to hear someone else say it.

Li'ara was just staring at him in shock, no doubt from being pinned to the pillar, but she understood what he was really asking.

"Yes... it's gone. It's all gone." She leaned against the pillar, sliding down to the floor.

He noticed she still had all of her armour on and her gun strapped to her thigh. Seeing Li'ara despair made it all so real. The cradle of humanity gone in an instant. His home, his students, the history of everything only existed in his mind now. He briefly recalled the touring children on campus and hated himself for not being able to remember their faces.

He had no living family to mourn for he had been an only child and his parents the same. But how many actual people and families had there been? The last census had it at twenty-two billion human beings. The number was unimaginable to Kalian. He had never seen twenty-two billion of anything. The number was staggering.

He couldn't believe how thoughtless he had been. Li'ara had obviously been crying for a long time before he regained consciousness. Did she have a family? Or a husband? Or even children? It dawned on him that he didn't really know anything about his guardian.

"Did you lose anyone?" He sat up on what he could now see was some sort of medical gurney.

Li'ara glanced up at him briefly while she let out a long breath. He couldn't read her. He imagined in her training she had been instructed never to give private details of her life. She was instead to appear above such trappings and present herself as a UDC soldier and nothing else.

"How about you tell me what the hell just happened here?" Li'ara stood up, brushing the hair out of her face and becoming the soldier once more. "You looked like you were having a nightmare so I put my hand out to see if I could wake you and then..." She imitated the sudden blast that had pinned her.

Kalian didn't know what to say. He had never been directly questioned about *it*. "I'm... I have no idea what happened." He looked down, trying to avoid her looks.

He was impressed with the skin around his abdomen; there wasn't so much as a scar where the chunk of metal had struck him.

I'm naked!

Seeing his own body, he realised the only thing keeping his modesty was a thin piece of fabric draped across his midriff.

"When did I lose my clothes?" He began looking around the room, in the hope of changing the subject, but he couldn't see them from his vantage, and he had no intention of moving.

"They removed them before they operated. I say them but really it was that." Li'ara looked up to the space above Kalian's bed.

It reminded him of a spider, in this case a giant mechanical spider. The centre was a large dark red dome surrounded by robotic arms each with a different device at the end. Some were pointed and sharp, but most of them were unrecognisable, with what he assumed was an array of scanners and other surgical equipment.

"After they laid you down, it just hovered over you while it operated. You had some internal bleeding."

Kalian felt a shiver run through his body at the thought of the mechanical spider cutting him open and digging around inside. Li'ara's movement caught his attention as she approached holding a bundle of clothes. She dumped them unceremoniously on the end of the bed.

"So, I found your clothes, that thing saved your life, now tell me what the hell is going on." Li'ara had a dangerous glint in her eye.

Kalian could sympathise, given the amount of unanswered and terrible shit that had happened. Kalian's weirdness was apparently pushing her over the edge.

"I'm just different." He couldn't think of a better word. "I've always been this way. If it helps, I have no idea how I did it. I've never affected another person before." Kalian felt a wave of relief as he said the words out loud. He'd expected to feel trapped and out of control but it actually felt good to tell someone.

"Different? What does that even mean?" Li'ara was pacing the length of the bed. "You just pushed me and lifted half the stuff in this room without even moving!" Her eyes looked everywhere as she tried to come up with a logical reason for it; perhaps for some alien device she hadn't noticed. "I know the UDC toyed with the idea of creating super soldiers, but that was centuries ago. But it obviously never worked out..."

Kalian wasn't sure if she was speaking to him anymore or just rattling off ideas. "How do you know it didn't work?" He had fanciful ideas of how he might be a rogue experiment and he was made to be some super spy for the UDC.

"Because if it had worked, I'd be the one pushing you around, wouldn't I?" Kalian felt he was back to being the moron again. "How long have you been able to do stuff like *that*?" She whirled her hand in the air.

"Since I was a kid. It was worst when I was a teenager though. And it mostly affects electrical things. If I had a C-cred for every Info-band I've broken..."

Li'ara was just staring at him. It reminded him of the way Telarrek and the other Novaarians looked at him: a combination of wonder and suspicion.

"Is this why they wanted to meet you?" She looked away for a moment trying to put everything together. "That's why they made you a condition. It must be! Why else would they travel across the galaxy to meet a history lecturer from San Francisco?"

Kalian could see the connection too now; it was the only thing that made sense. Somehow these Novaarians knew about his... *weirdness*. But what did they want from him? How did they even find out in the first place? Another fantasy emerged from his imagination. What if he had been abducted as a child and given these weird abilities by aliens?

Don't say that one out loud...

He tried to change the subject. "What about *them*?" Kalian was talking about the others, the ones that obliterated Earth without so much as a warning. "Don't you think it's a bit strange that another alien ship appeared at the same time as the Novaarians?"

Kalian knew the topic of his weirdness wasn't over but he thought they had more pressing matters to deal with. He had no idea what their next step should be but the notion was sobering. The switch in topics hadn't escaped Li'ara's notice but the soldier in her clearly agreed that there were bigger concerns right now.

"We need to make contact with the UDC." Li'ara started for the door on the far side of the room.

"How? The Hub was destroyed along with the Chief Commander and half the fleet!" Kalian instantly regretted saying it as Li'ara gave him a quick glance back. He didn't know much about Li'ara but he was willing to bet she had just lost a lot of friends in the UDC. Kalian, being the loner he was, could only empathise with her situation.

"We need to get to Century ASAP. If they were jamming our communications, Century might not even be aware of what's happened. We need to establish a chain of command and coordinate all remaining UDC ships."

It was like he had never made the comment. She was back to being the soldier again.

As Li'ara walked away, Kalian began to actually take in the view of the room. He felt like he already knew its layout and shape from that peculiar experience when he woke up but seeing the room with his eyes reminded him he really was on an alien ship. Everything had a soft glow to it. He almost felt like he was in a dream.

It was obviously some kind of medical bay. Everything was perfectly clean and sterile. On the wall at the base of his bed was a large screen with the outline of a human body in the centre. He could see the entirety of the circulatory system being pumped around by a glowing red heart in the chest. Various lines were pointing at different sections of the body, each with some alien script underlined. Kalian couldn't make sense of it, but he realised it must be scans of his own body from the procedure.

Before Li'ara could reach the circular door, Ilyseal entered the room. She was instantly recognisable from the red in her long tendrils. As she walked through the door Ilyseal almost appeared to be the same height as them but Kalian realised all the doors on a Novaarian ship must be pretty tall. She was so graceful Kalian wasn't sure if she walked in or glided over the floor.

"Greetings of peace." She bowed her head. "It is pleasing to see you are well again Kalian Gaines. Many of our crew were concerned for your health."

Kalian absently reached behind his ear to feel the circular device attached to his skin. Her voice still had guttural undertones but it had a feminine quality that was melodic and almost human.

Kalian still wasn't used to the sight of aliens, let alone talking to them. "Well, thank you for..." He awkwardly pointed to the mechanical spider above him.

Ilyseal simply bowed her head again. Li'ara did an almost undetectable shake of her head in despair of him and his awkwardness. He wasn't sure how much time Li'ara had spent among the Novaarians while he was unconscious, but she had obviously acclimatised to their presence. She sharply turned back on Ilyseal.

"We need to get to Century as soon as possible."

Ilyseal's golden eyes met with Li'ara's. "Charge Telarrek requests your presence on the bridge."

It was impossible to tell what Ilyseal was thinking. Her face was too alien to pick up on any subtle changes that would be obvious on a human.

"Fine. Let's go." Li'ara and Ilyseal stood looking at Kalian.

"What?" He had done nothing but listen.

"You might want to put some clothes on."

Kalian followed Li'ara's eyes to the flimsy material covering his waist. "Oh..." He gripped the material a little tighter.

KALIAN HAD THOUGHT the outside of the ship was beautiful and alien, but the inside was a sight to behold. Every corridor was cavernous, stretching up into a smooth curve. All the surfaces were a magnificent shine of purple, like the ship's exterior. The walls were lined with floor to ceiling lights in a brilliant blue. The mix of colours was extraordinary. It wasn't too bright or too dark, making everything easy on the eyes.

Everywhere they went smelled of fresh flowers. If he closed his eyes he could almost believe he was in one of the artificial meadows on Earth. The thought of Earth opened up a pit in his stomach. The sense of loss was so big it was hard to comprehend, though it wasn't just the individuals that came to mind. He couldn't grasp the masses of families, people, animals or even the other planets that had been destroyed. Everything that had stood long before human beings took their first steps was gone, erased from the universe for the rest of time. He pushed it to the back of his mind and concentrated on what was in front of him.

It was easy to see where the smell was coming from. At random points along each corridor, and even spreading up some of the walls, were plants and flowers he had never seen before. He was sure some of them even moved as they walked by.

There were Novaarians walking everywhere, going about their

duties on the ship. They passed through large circular doorways that were highlighted with white light around the edges. All of them stopped when Kalian passed by. They just stood and watched him intently with those golden eyes. He was starting to get used to it.

The oddest thing happened right in front of him. As they were turning one of the long curving corners a Novaarian appeared above him *walking* down the wall. Li'ara noticed it too and they both stopped, taking in the unusual sight. The Novaarian was literally walking upright while descending to their level.

"To utilise as much space as possible, there are rooms all around us. We have artificial gravity wells under the floor and inside the walls." Ilyseal's long fingers gestured to the Novaarian approaching from above. "As you step onto the wall, gravity will shift beneath you so the wall becomes the floor. It can be quite disorientating the first time but, I assure you, you will become accustomed to it."

The Novaarian in question descended to their level and made a small step onto what Kalian knew to be the floor. His long athletic legs made the motion appear seamless as he continued walking on their level.

Kalian attempted to comment but failed. "That's..." He looked to Li'ara who was equally speechless.

"Shall we continue, Kalian Gaines?" Despite the question, Ilyseal appeared as if she could wait all day if that was what he wanted.

Their response was interrupted by a high-pitched humming noise from somewhere high above. It was hard to describe what had passed them by, it had been so quick. Then another two flew over from the other direction. This time he got a better look. It was a pair of Novaarians each in control of what resembled a Mag-bike. They had no wheels to speak of but were thin and elongated like Mag-bikes. From the ground, Kalian could see three bright blue circles against each silver undercarriage with their Novaarian riders almost lying flat to drive. That was as much as he saw before they flew around the corner and out of sight.

"As I said, the ship is very large and can take some time to traverse; certain aids are required at times."

"Do we get one?" Li'ara couldn't quite keep the enthusiasm out of her voice.

With a life slightly more adrenaline-filled, it didn't surprise Kalian that she would prefer a faster pace.

"The bridge is not far. Another time perhaps." Ilyseal motioned to the mountainous wall up ahead.

Aware that she had shown too much emotion, Li'ara made the effort to show no response.

At the base of the wall, Kalian could see the door about fifty metres above them, clearly highlighted by a white outline. The so-called path that led up the wall was outlined in blue lights. The idea of walking *up* the wall was a little dizzying.

"So we're going up there then?" He craned his neck looking from the door to Ilyseal.

She sensed his apprehension and placed a comforting hand on his shoulder. "That will not be necessary to reach the bridge, Kalian Gaines."

"Please, you can just call me Kalian. Gaines is my last name." It was unusual hearing his whole name every time he was addressed. Ilyseal tilted her head at the request. Kalian took the gesture as a question. "In human culture, it's not required to say a person's whole name..."

Ilyseal didn't appear to understand. "But it is only half of your name." Her golden eyes narrowed.

"The second name is more of a formality or a family name; you don't need to say it every time. So I'm Kalian..." He turned to Li'ara without looking at her. "And this is Li'ara-"

"Lieutenant Commander." The words came out of Li'ara a little sharply.

Kalian reasoned that it was probably easier for her to be a soldier right now, with too many emotions attached to Li'ara Ducarté. Ilyseal lifted her head once which he had come to regard as a nod.

"As you wish Kalian, Lieutenant Commander." She turned to a small dome-shaped protrusion on the wall. Her alien hand spread out across the dome creating a reaction on the wall next to them.

White light came to life, giving the outline of a circular door that had blended into the wall itself.

"The Translift is the only way to enter the command bridge." The soft glow was inviting and dreamlike.

Kalian was happier with a mode of transport he was familiar with. Much like the lifts in The Hub, he was unaware of any displacement. It made a universal ping as it arrived at its destination.

The command bridge was a buzz of activity with Novaarians working on terminals and consoles. It was an incredible sight of efficiency. Each console appeared to have a hard surface with multiple holograms projecting all around it. The Novaarians were able to use their bottom limbs on the hard surface with their upper limbs working the holograms. Kalian couldn't imagine how they possibly operated both at the same time.

As they stepped through the lift, led by Ilyseal, everything stopped. Novaarians in the distance were standing up to see over their consoles at the aliens on their bridge. Kalian saw Li'ara take the opportunity to absorb the details around them, her tactical mind taking over as she entered a new environment. He assumed she was looking for exits, counting the number of Novaarians, scanning for weapons and assessing any threats. She never switched off. Kalian looked around but couldn't see what she saw. Instead, he took in the architecture and technology that was so different from any human design.

It wasn't as grand in size as the corridors but it was still bigger than any *human* command centre. Kalian had seen the inside of UDC ships in films and documentaries and knew it was human tradition to build bridges to fit about a dozen personnel. Looking around him there must have been at least three dozen.

From what he could see, the room was split into two areas. Directly in front was an oval shape of consoles with Novaarians working on the inside and outside, opposite one another. At what he imagined was the front of the bridge was another bank of consoles in a smaller oval shape with the same layout. In the middle of each was a small platform with a Novaarian standing on it. They were entirely surrounded by holographic images in an ever-changing pattern of colour.

Further still, he could make out the back of two individual Novaarians at the far end, both sitting at their own console apart from the others. In front of them was a huge arching viewport. The length of the ship could be seen stretching out in front of them. Space beyond was curiously black, with no stars in sight. These particular Novaarians caught his eye due to the simple fact that they hadn't stood up to look at them, and because of the fluorescent tubing that looked to be coming out of the back of their heads and disappearing into the floor. It was a lot to take in. He had never been on a UDC ship or *any* kind of command bridge and now he was standing in the most technologically advanced room in the galaxy, but he had no idea why.

It was hard to believe the chain of events that had led him to this spot. Only hours ago, he had been rushing to work because the biggest concern in his day had been waking up late. Now he was travelling through space at a speed he was sure he couldn't even comprehend. The thought brought his attention to the fact that he had no idea where they were. How far had they travelled in the time he had been unconscious?

"Greetings of peace." The alien voice came from above.

The floating platform that descended towards them was only big enough for one, in this case, Telarrek. He stood in a semi-circle of hard consoles each feeding him different information from around the *Valoran*. The platform's dome-shaped bottom fitted into its corresponding space, making it one with the floor. There was something about Telarrek that made him stand out from the others. He was more regal in stature, with a presence that commanded attention.

He stepped away from his consoles, lowering his long jaw until it was resting against the rings across his chest. "My people grieve for your loss..."

Kalian picked up on Li'ara's body language. She may have been in awe of their surroundings a moment ago but Telarrek's words made her visibly tense.

"We need to get to Century now!" All eyes were on her but no one reacted. "I don't know where you're taking us, but if it were Century we'd be there by now. You need to make a course correction ASAP. We're wasting time, and they need to be warned!"

"I am afraid I cannot do that, Li'ara Ducarté." Telarrek had resumed his full height by stepping off the platform.

"It's Lieutenant Commander to you, and why the hell not?"

"Even I receive orders, *Lieutenant Commander*, and mine are to bring Kalian Gaines before the Conclave," Telarrek replied evenly.

"It is just Kalian, my Charge." Ilyseal's large eyes darted to the humans and back to Telarrek.

The Novaarian turned his head the same way Ilyseal had in slight confusion. Kalian couldn't figure out the facial expressions that passed between them but Telarrek quickly resumed his position and continued.

"We have sent an envoy to Century to warn them of this new threat. My crew has been analysing the data since our encounter. I assure you we will identify the species responsible for this attack. Their crime is beyond words or understanding, but the Conclave *will* see to their punishment."

"I don't know what this Conclave is, but you can't take us against our will. We need to get back to our own people. Chains of command need establishing and what's left of the fleet needs to know what it's up against." Li'ara was starting to look like a newly caged animal.

Telarrek paused a moment. "You are our guests aboard the *Valoran*. I assure you Lieutenant Commander you are not prisoners. Quarters have been prepared for you. The journey will take seven of your days to reach-"

"The *Valoran* couldn't help save Earth, so what do you think an envoy is going to do?" In her anger, she turned away from them.

Kalian had a bad feeling. He wasn't sure how much the Novaarians could pick up on human facial expressions. He watched her eyes pass over everything and everyone. This wasn't like before. There was an urgency to her movements, as she was calculating the odds. He was sure in her head a scenario was playing out in which she overcame the nearest guard, taking his weapon, killing everyone between them and the *Fathom*, and escaping to Century. He was afraid in her anger she might be overlooking the details of her plan - they had no idea where in space they were and, judging from the display Numanon gave on the Icarus, he doubted she would be able to overcome even the first guard, let alone make it to the ship.

Li'ara turned on her heel back to Telarrek with purpose in her stride. The guards that had slowly been closing in on their conversation moved as one, taking a step closer. Kalian had to act now if only to save Li'ara from getting into a fight he knew she couldn't win. Stopping her mid-stride he placed himself squarely between Telarrek and Li'ara.

"Stop!" He wasn't facing Li'ara but, instead, was looking Telarrek straight in the eyes. By telling Telarrek to stop, Kalian knew he was telling the guards to stop. Everyone froze around the three of them. Kalian had his hand flat out against Telarrek, assuming the gesture was universal.

"She's right, Telarrek." He kept his voice calm. "I don't know what your interest in me is, but you've saved me enough times today that I know I mean *something*. If I'm worth saving, aren't they?" He spread his hand out towards the viewport. Century was out there somewhere.

Kalian wasn't sure how much Telarrek had heard for the alien's concentration had been entirely on the human hand in front of him. Using his right hands, Telarrek reached for Kalian's outstretched hand. His touch was delicate like the hand was precious somehow. He spread Kalian's fingers as his own alien hands moved over the surface of his skin and his large Novaarian eyes inspected every detail. Telarrek inhaled one slow breath, pushing his chest out. He released Kalian's hand and his posture changed as he became the captain again.

"We shall try..." Telarrek turned to face his crew and Ilyseal. "Full stop. Course correction. We are going to Century. I want maximum yield. Contact the envoy and inform them of our arrival."

The crew's pause was momentary, while they received their

instructions, before the hum of activity resumed. A deep pulse resonated from somewhere in the ship and the viewport flashed to show the millions of stars visible outside. The starry field slid to the left, blurring into streaks of white light. It occurred to Kalian that the *Valoran* was moving to the right, not the stars.

Kalian faced Li'ara, thinking she would be pleased with the turn of events, but her face said otherwise. If anything, she looked confused, almost concerned with their change in circumstances. He simply shrugged in answer to her silent question. Even Kalian wasn't sure if it was his words that changed Telarrek's mind, and he had no idea what was so interesting about his hand.

Both Kalian and Li'ara moved as they felt a small jolt from beneath their feet, though the Novaarians didn't move at all. The streaking stars vanished as quickly as they had appeared, leaving the same empty void as before.

"It will take point four of a cycle to reach Century, my Charge." The soft glow of Ilyseal's bracer illuminated her large golden eyes.

"How long is that?" Li'ara was her controlled self again, collecting data, making her own internal assessments.

"Almost six of your hours, Lieutenant Commander."

Now Li'ara had a time frame. "You said your crew had been analysing the attack." Telarrek simply bowed his head in response. "Then I need to see it. I want to know everything about them. If we get to Century in time I'll need to brief command. Things will move quicker if *I* talk to them."

"Agreed. Our presence may complicate events." Telarrek turned to Ilyseal. "Send all the data we have through to the observatory." Without waiting for a response, he began walking towards a large circular door behind them.

Kalian recognised the same wavy line that cut the door in half. He expected light to pour out of it, like all the other rooms he had seen on his journey to the bridge but, instead, this room was darker, with deep shades of blue and minimal lighting.

"Follow me." Telarrek led the way inside the circular room with only Kalian and Li'ara accompanying him.

The room was bare except for a circular ring that floated in the centre. The only place to move was on the walkway that surrounded the empty circular island. The only light came from six spotlights in the floor. It seemed such a contrast to the rest of the ship. Everything Kalian had seen so far was full of light, exposing the alien beauty of his surroundings. Even the ceiling was lower than that of the room where he had been operated on. The room became darker still as the door sealed behind them.

"This is the observatory. From here all the *Valoran's* scans and sensor data can be correlated for observation and analysis." Telarrek reached out to place a hand on the central circle. At his touch, the dull metal came to life with orange lights appearing over its surface.

For the first time in his life, Kalian was looking at a language he couldn't recognise. On Earth, there had only been one language, Central. To see an alien language in front of him was both exciting and frustrating. Twinkling specks of light began to appear between the circular console and the corresponding lights on the domed ceiling. A holographic image in full colour appeared in the centre, forming a column of light that gradually dissipated towards the ceiling and floor. In the middle was a sharp picture of the Icarus station with the Moon on one side and the Earth on the other. From the angle of the image, it was clear that this had been recorded from a lens on the *Valoran's* hull.

Both Kalian's and Li'ara's eyes lingered on the image of Earth. Kalian had a strange feeling of regret. Seeing his homeworld now, he appreciated its beauty for what it was. Perhaps more so because he knew he would never see it again, or any of the planets in his system. A wave of nausea passed over him as he realised the population of Mars was close to rivalling Earth's.

All those people... gone.

Kalian wrapped his hands around the inside edge of the ring, leaning on it for support. He looked to Li'ara, expecting her to be feeling the same if not worse. Her face was a blank canvas, showing no emotion or response. He used her lack of response as a crutch and tried to push all his thoughts of home away. If they were going to think clearly and get through this, they had to be objective. He needed to be more like Li'ara. They were the only two human survivors. How did they survive? Out of the billions that died in a wave of fire and light, how did two humans survive, and why them? It seemed to Kalian that Li'ara's survival was at least a little more probable; she had been trained to fight and survive. But him? Shouldn't he be dead as well?

"So this is what you've been doing for four hundred years." Li'ara walked slowly around the hologram so she could see both Kalian and Telarrek, but her eyes never left Earth. "You've been watching us through a microscope, learning everything about us, shadowing our every move. How is it that a race so good at *observing* didn't see or know about a ship or species capable of this kind of attack?" There was an edge to her voice. Li'ara wasn't showing any emotion, but she was angry.

Kalian felt the scales tip. As Li'ara became angry he became calm. It was odd to him, but he felt like he needed to balance them, being the only two humans present. It was an attachment he had never felt before. In this instance it helped him concentrate, pushing away his guilt of surviving and focusing him on what was happening in front of him.

"We..." Telarrek's mouth remained open a fraction longer but he said nothing. His shoulders became slack for a moment. Telarrek truly had no answer. "We do not know."

"Then show us what you do know." Kalian's first word was a croak. He couldn't remember the last time he had drunk anything.

Telarrek lifted his head sharply in response and began typing commands into the console. "This is-"

"Wait," Kalian interrupted him. "I want you to start by telling us why *I'm* here. Only two humans survived that attack. Why is a *history lecturer* from San Francisco one of them?" He looked to Li'ara briefly. "A soldier maybe, one of our leaders or ambassadors, but why me?"

Telarrek looked intently into the hologram. "While your injuries were being repaired I informed the Conclave of recent events." He paused as the golden swirls of his eyes focused on Kalian. "The politics of the Conclave are... complicated. There is more than just my race involved now. There are four other species that will each have their say in the matter. No doubt there will be consequences for keeping the discovery of your kind a secret."

"You're dodging the question." Kalian didn't care for the politics of an alien society.

"I am to bring you before the Conclave. It is my understanding that only the Highclave are allowed contact with you. I am to escort you there. Nothing else is permitted. I am already breaking my mandate by changing course. It is not for me to speak on their behalf if they do not wish it."

Kalian's frustration was growing. It had been a long day filled with pain and death and he had no idea why. Why him? Who were their attackers?

He desperately wanted to know if they were aware of his other thing, the part of his life he had kept secret for so long. He already felt vulnerable with Li'ara knowing and that last outburst had frightened him. He had never experienced that before. To feel the room around him and even be able to reach out and touch Li'ara was new.

He met Li'ara's eyes across the room and a silent question passed between them. Kalian knew she understood what he wanted to ask but she shook her head discreetly. It made sense to let the Novaarians broach the subject, he hadn't wanted to be a lab rat on Earth let alone become one for some advanced alien race.

Li'ara changed the subject. "There will be more time for that later." She gave Kalian a knowing look - *we will get to the bottom of this, but we'll stay in control.* "Let's see what we can learn about these bastards."

With Kalian's silence, Telarrek moved on, his large hands delicately roaming over the orange hieroglyphs. The image was altered as the giant rectangular ship appeared in front of the Moon. From where he was standing, Kalian could fit the ship in his hand but he resisted the urge to reach out and do so.

"Our scans have proven ineffective in determining their propulsion technology. Intrinium leaves a unique signature after its consumption; even *Novaarian* ships can be identified. This one, however, broke through subspace without leaving a trace of how it did so."

"Hold on a second. Intrinium is Solarcite right?" Kalian hated the science part. Telarrek bowed his head in acknowledgement.

"He's right. All UDC ships leave behind a marker that can be identified as Solarcite." Li'ara turned to Telarrek. She looked like a dog with a bone. "What did you mean, *even* Novaarian ships can be identified? Surely you use Solar-, *Intrinium,* as well?"

Telarrek paused before answering. "Novaarian ships do use Intrinium for subspace travel..." He paused again. "But we in the Conclave use it in a different way to you." He was being deliberately vague.

Kalian wondered if Li'ara had stumbled onto a Novaarian secret.

"What does that mean?" He didn't like the science of it all, but Kalian was getting tired of secrets.

"Your technology is primitive to that of the Conclave. Most ships do not require the presence of a star to travel through subspace. The ship you found on Charon was of an older design and too small to house an engine like the *Valoran's. Smaller* vessels still require the magnetic fields of a star spot in order to ignite the Intrinium."

Both Kalian and Li'ara waited a moment longer expecting a further explanation of the bigger ships and their method of travel. None was offered.

"And yours don't?" Li'ara asked.

"No." Telarrek's answer was simple and his meaning was clear.

"Is that how you were able to just appear in orbit? Our perimeter sensors were aimed at the sun, but you just..." Li'ara was digging for as many facts as possible, always planning.

"It's true we did not arrive by your conventional means, but we had been in your orbit for some time without detection."

Li'ara couldn't help but look confused and a little shocked. "How is that possible? The *Valoran* is so big we didn't even need sensors to see you." She was starting to sound a little defensive despite the topic being after the fact.

"The *Valoran* is a long-range exploration vessel. It is specifically equipped with observation equipment and stealth technology, not normally permitted within Conclave space."

"You have cloaking technology?" From the look on Li'ara's face, Kalian surmised that the UDC had long sought after such means.

"I fear we are going off topic. There will be time to learn about our culture and technology. My point is that this ship used a form of propulsion unknown to us or the Conclave."

"Is it possible one of the species in your Conclave developed it without your knowledge?" It seemed an obvious conclusion to Kalian.

"The Laronians for instance?" Li'ara had been storing every bit of information that left a Novaarian mouth apparently.

Telarrek sharply shook his head once to the left. "The Laronians are ambitious but they could not construct such a ship without our knowing. I have already told you they are not a threat to you, only that your personnel on Alpha NL-2204 may be considered hostile. That is why they were to be evacuated as soon as possible."

"What's going to happen to them now?" Kalian had completely forgotten about the terraforming team.

"My superiors in the Conclave are already in discussions with the Laronians on how to handle the situation. Until we leave subspace however, we cannot communicate with them to learn of the resolution."

Kalian wasn't put at ease by the idea of other alien species deciding the fate of seven thousand fellow humans. Li'ara's face said the same thing. The frustration was putting knots in his stomach; he didn't like the feeling of being helpless. It was a new sensation for him, after spending most of his life just trying to blend in and never getting involved in anything beyond his lecture theatre. For the first time, Kalian wanted to be involved, to be able to help.

"So your basic analysis is that you have no idea?" Li'ara started pacing again.

"We can learn and deduce a lot from what we do not know." Telarrek typed commands into the console making the hologram magnify the image of the enemy ship. "The sensor sweep of your entire solar system that they performed was too fast and too powerful for any technology we have encountered. If they were able to correlate that information in the time it took them to attack..." He paused, considering the ramifications. "It would be an indication of an onboard artificial system far more advanced than any known to the Conclave or even the Shay."

"The who?" Kalian was afraid he was going to get lost in all the names and technology this new galaxy was throwing at him.

"They are a key member of the Conclave. They are responsible for the manufacture of many electronic systems used on all Conclave ships." He began typing again, finishing his previous command. "You see here." The image of the ship blurred as a tight oval bubble rippled down the length of the hull, quickly dissipating at the end. "I had to slow the image down in order for you to see it."

"What is it?" Li'ara's eyes were fixed on the ship. Be it a strength or weakness, she had to know.

"That was our own sensor sweep of their ship. The particles that we projected from the *Valoran's* array impacted the shell you just saw and were then *absorbed*." Telarrek's head tilted slightly in that curious way.

"What's the significance of that?" Li'ara's questions reminded Kalian she was a soldier, not a scientist.

"The sensor particles should have passed right *through* their ship, even if they had the technology to jam the feedback. The fact that they were stopped by a physical barrier and then absorbed is even more curious." Telarrek folded his upper arms across his chest.

"So they have shields. Is that a big thing?" Kalian remembered the sci-fi shows he had watched growing up in the various foster homes; those ships always had shields around them. Thinking about it now, he realised the only thing that had been fiction was the fact that UDC ships don't actually have shields for they could do everything else. At this point, he was willing to believe anything after everything he'd seen.

"Shield technology does not absorb energy but disperses it. Over time the shields would be worn down from decay. The absorption would suggest it took the energy from the scan to make it stronger. This technology has not been invented."

"Clearly not." Li'ara stopped pacing and folded her only set of arms.

"Perhaps, but this next technological feat would seem impossible." While keeping his upper arms folded, his lower arms continued to key commands into the console.

The hologram shifted again, focusing on the gap between the Icarus station and the black ship. At first, there was nothing to see but empty space. The hologram changed again, magnifying a speck between two distant stars. The column of light was entirely focused on a blurred image of the goliath that attacked the station. It was horizontal on its collision course for the exact spot Ambassador Arlek had been standing.

Kalian couldn't believe what he was seeing. Even though the image was blurred he could still make out legs and a head thanks to the backdrop of the sun. He had assumed the alien attacker had been in some form of casing or even a small ship, not just the suit of armour he had seen it in. It was diving head first towards its target and its arms didn't even appear outstretched. Whatever this alien was it couldn't be ruled by fear. He had seen it walk headlong into rail-gun fire without flinching and now he had seen that it had literally jumped from one ship to the other.

"The *Valoran* attempted to scan it as soon as we detected the jettison."

A blurry haze appeared around the figure, similar to the oval bubble that had appeared on the enemy ship's hull. The scan clearly hit the figure on one side as the blur dissipated on the other side. This time though, the shape wasn't a bubble but more fitted to the creature's humanoid body.

"The same thing." Li'ara's eyes were bright lights in the reflection of the hologram.

"Am I missing something here?" Kalian couldn't make the connection as to their fascination.

"The same shielding that protects their ship also protects *that*." Telarrek pointed to the outline surrounding the diving monster. "It acted exactly the same way, absorbing the particles, most likely making it stronger as well. How they are able to produce a shield emitter small enough to be carried on an individual is a science unknown to us."

"You don't have any that small?" Kalian asked.

"Our shield generators are similar in size to one of your fleet vessels."

Thinking about the vastness of the attacking ship, Kalian had forgotten how big the ship under his feet was.

"Is that what the shimmering effect is on the hull of the *Valoran*?" More facts for Li'ara.

"You are quite observant, Lieutenant Commander. But unlike our shields, theirs cannot be seen or detected." Telarrek continued the video of the armoured alien traversing the distance to the Icarus station.

The impact was savage. The beast crashed through the viewport forcing debris in every direction as the vacuum of space created chaos inside. It was easy to see from the hologram how far the creature impacted, as the lights on at least seven decks winked out of existence one after the other. It was a miracle they had even survived that.

"The armour was strong from what I saw on your station, but how it survived that impact is beyond our understanding of any alien biology."

The hologram flickered as Telarrek changed the view. In the new hologram, only one object could be seen, obviously somewhere beyond the Earth and probably even Venus.

The destroyer of Kalian's world.

That missile had been fired into the sun to end all things human. The image was sharper than the holographic one he had seen on the Icarus command bridge. The main body was a giant sphere encased by four grips that converged at the front and extended into a point. It was entirely haloed in light from the sun, with a comet tail that spread for kilometres behind.

"Let me guess, this had shielding as well." Li'ara was rubbing her eyes but Kalian couldn't tell if it was frustration or irritation from the light of the hologram in a dark room.

"Actually it did not." Both humans shared a quick glance before looking to Telarrek for answers. "Our scans hit no such barrier on the object, but it matters not for we could not scan beneath the hull." Their faces dropped in unison. "The data we received from its exterior, however, is quite interesting."

Kalian was hesitant to feel any kind of hope.

Telarrek altered the hologram again, turning the image into more of a schematic of the pointed object. It moved across the column of light extending in size. The backdrop of space disappeared, being replaced with faint light.

"There are some familiar elements in the hull's material, but the majority is a type of alloy we have never encountered. But this is the most interesting part." Telarrek typed in a command that enlarged a section of the sphere. In the middle of the flat surface was a small circle, slightly raised from the main body.

"What is it?" Kalian was wishing he had studied engineering instead of history.

"It's a door..." Li'ara had that calculating look on her face again.

"That is our estimation as well."

"Why would a missile have a door?" Kalian was looking from Li'ara to Telarrek.

"A construct of that size would require internal maintenance and configuration," Telarrek offered.

"How big is the whole thing?" Kalian asked.

"It is two miles in length."

That was a hard fact to swallow.

I suppose if you're going to make a weapon to blow up a star, it's got to be big.

The thought stopped Kalian. How *did* they blow up an entire star?

"How was it even possible?" Li'ara beat him to it. "Just before it happened you knew. You knew it was too late."

"Our sensors show that the object entered your star and was able to survive the journey through the chromo *and* photosphere. Once it punched through the radioactive envelope it pierced the core. We are not sure what happened next and whether it exploded or released some form of payload. Either way, it appears the weapon was designed to increase the internal pressure of a star, causing it to collapse on itself and cause a supernova." Telarrek leaned forward, placing all four hands on the floating console. "I did not know a weapon of such magnitude existed. I believe its very creation to be a crime against all life."

"We have to assume they have more of these weapons, and that they'll use the same plan of attack on Century." Li'ara sounded like a general making battle plans.

"That is an apt evaluation, Lieutenant Commander," Telarrek replied.

"So what's our plan of attack?" she asked quite aggressively.

"This may be a ship of exploration and observation, but we are not defenceless. However, it is impossible to predict potential outcomes based on the mysterious nature of the ship."

"Whatever you hit them with, just make it big." The only thing Kalian was sure of was the immense size of their attackers.

"When we arrive in Century's orbit we shall put ourselves between them and your fleet. We will give your people as much time as we can to evacuate."

Telarrek's words were sobering. Winning this fight wasn't even an option, so they could only hope to slow them down. Li'ara didn't look satisfied, then something on the console caught her attention. She stepped closer to the orange hieroglyphs displayed around the disc.

"That word..." Li'ara looked to Kalian for reassurance. "It's in Central. I can understand it." She turned to Telarrek. "Is it supposed to be like that?"

Kalian walked round to see for himself.

"I don't see anything - just symbols."

"Right there. It says 'rotate' in Central." She was pointing at what Kalian saw as three vertical lines with a dot above each.

"Your implant is becoming fully integrated," Telarrek explained.

Kalian instinctively reached for the metallic dot behind his left ear.

"What do you mean, *fully integrated*? I thought it was just so we could understand one another?"

"The implant is given to every individual within the Conclave. Once fully integrated it allows the wearer to see and hear each other's languages. Without it there would be chaos and confusion. There could be no trade or share of discovery. In time, both of you will be capable of understanding not just everything you see and hear in Novaarian, but also that of all Conclave members."

"How the hell does that work?" Li'ara was circling the edge of the small device with her finger.

"Do you understand the inner workings of the thalamus or cerebral cortex in relation to fluid neuro-netics?" Telarrek's head was raised a little higher than normal.

Li'ara's quizzical facial expression was answer enough.

"It was our first contribution to the other races in the formation of the Conclave." Telarrek stepped away from the console and started for the door.

The hologram blinked out and the uplighters against the wall increased their brightness. The large door parted in half again, flooding Kalian's senses with the sights and sounds of the bridge.

Telarrek stopped in the middle of the doorway. "Whatever we find when we reach Century, know this." He bowed his head looking from one to the other. "I *will* ensure Kalian's survival." He centred his eyes just on Kalian and walked off, into the bridge, without waiting for a reply.

They knew what he was saying; *I will leave Century to its fate if that is required to keep Kalian safe.*

"What am I to them?" It was said so only Li'ara could hear him.

"I don't know, yet. But I will not leave Century to burn. It's all we have left." Li'ara lowered her head.

Kalian couldn't read her face; she was still too much of a mystery to him.

"You should both get some rest before our arrival. Ilyseal will show you to your quarters if-"

"We'll be fine on the *Fathom*, but thank you," Li'ara interrupted.

Kalian wasn't sure if Li'ara had ever said thank you before.

"As you wish. You are guests here. Ilyseal will escort you back to the hangar."

Ilyseal led them over to the Translift that they had arrived in, with Telarrek coming up behind them.

He stopped, clearly intending to stay on the bridge. "I promise you, we will do everything in our power to help your people."

Li'ara entered the lift turning back to face Telarrek. "What if that's not enough?"

BEFORE LEAVING them on the *Fathom*, Ilyseal gave them a disc the size of a human palm which was interlaced with smaller raised circles. She told them it was a way of communicating with the bridge should they require it. Kalian left the details of how to use the device with Li'ara; he avoided small electrical objects whenever possible.

Li'ara keyed in the code to close the ramp and hatch behind them as Kalian looked across to the medical bay behind the glass. It was still a mess with used canisters of Medifoam on the floor. He could see blood staining the table and half a bloodied handprint on the edge of the door - his blood. At the time he hadn't realised how close to death he had come. Up to the moment he had collapsed in the *Valoran's* hangar, everything had been an adrenaline-fuelled run for his life.

Li'ara had entered the armoury towards the back of the ship, most likely in search of her relinquished weapon. Being the only other person around, Kalian naturally gravitated towards her. The armoury was a small corridor lined with sidearms, rifles, a collection of knives and even another rail-gun propped against the far wall.

We really did come prepared for a war.

The room was a contrast of dark grated walls and bright overhead spotlights. With her back to Kalian, Li'ara began to remove the various segments of her armour. Depressing hidden buttons under the plating created a suction noise before they fell to the floor. After removing her vambraces, boots and shoulder guards, she reached for a switch under the back of her chest plating. Kalian tensed for a moment, unsure of what he should do next, as he hadn't announced his presence or made it clear why he was even in the armoury. Very aware that an awkward situation was seconds away he quickly turned to leave, only to bump into the door frame.

"Try not to fall over yourself, Kalian. I'm only taking the *armour* off."

Had he not been so flustered and embarrassed, he would have detected the hint of playfulness in her voice. "I wasn't...".

At the sight of her, he couldn't quite find the words. With the armour removed she was wearing a tight fitting undersuit in black with a zip down the centre. The only skin it revealed was on her hands and feet which were now bare. She pulled down the zip giving her neck more room to move as she slid past Kalian and into the rest of the *Fathom*. Lump firmly removed from his throat, Kalian followed her from the armoury.

"So where do we sleep on this thing?" Kalian was looking everywhere but at Li'ara, while trying to move the topic along.

"We aren't sleeping." Li'ara activated the hull cameras, creating giant holograms of the outside. No one would be arriving unannounced.

Kalian could now see the hangar stretched out before him. There were rows of ships identical to the ones that Telarrek had arrived in when they had first met on the Icarus station. To his left was the vast portal that stretched across the hangar and from where he had seen his world come to an end. He pushed the memory away.

"You need sleep, Li'ara. I got some while I was passed out but you, when was the last time you got any rest?" He had noticed the pale skin under her eyes becoming darker over the last couple of hours.

"I'll sleep when there's time." Always the soldier. "Right now I need to know more about you."

Kalian looked into the distance of the hangar. He knew what she wanted to know. She wanted to continue their conversation from earlier. The topic was hard for him to discuss out loud. He had spent his whole life keeping it a secret, without even knowing what it was himself, and he had no idea how to explain the event in the medical room.

"What do you want to know?"

"Everything. Chances are high this is the reason they're so interested in you. If we can maybe figure it out before they do, we'll have the advantage."

That's what it was to her - what *he* was - just another way to gain the advantage against a species they couldn't hope to beat, and why should they? Telarrek had said they were guests, not prisoners. So far the Novaarians had done nothing but try to help. How could she see them as such a threat? Even Kalian was frustrated at Telarrek's lack of answers regarding his significance, but that didn't make him the enemy.

He realised he hadn't said anything for a while but couldn't think of anything to say. It was like his brain wouldn't allow him to talk about it.

"What else can you do Kalian?" Li'ara sat on the backrest of the long sofa, her bare feet digging into the cushion beneath. "You pushed me away without touching me. Not to mention all the floating stuff in the room. I'm no expert but that sounds like..."

"Telekinesis." Kalian couldn't look her in the eyes as he said it as it sounded so absurd. But he had done his own research growing up. Waking up almost every morning with his belongings floating around had forced him into looking into it. "I've never been able to use it on a person before, only on small objects - things I could actually pick up."

Kalian took his jacket off, throwing it onto the sofa. He pinched the bridge of his nose as he could feel a headache coming on. He looked down at his long-sleeved top that had once been a navy blue colour. Now it was stained with soot and ash, with blood stains around the hole near his abdomen. It would have to do though since his entire wardrobe was distant stardust.

"Is that it? Nothing else? You mentioned something about breaking Info-bands earlier."

Kalian could feel those green eyes boring into him. "I don't get on very well with electronics..." He slumped onto the sofa opposite.

"What does that mean?"

"It means they *malfunction* around me. I walk into a room after a bad day and all the fuses meld together, lights overheat, alarms go off, doors don't open for me because the sensors short circuit." He was getting frustrated thinking about it. "Shit just breaks around me." He let his head fall on to the soft backrest.

"That sounds exhausting." Li'ara appeared only half interested as she was trying to piece a bigger puzzle together. "How have you kept this a secret for so long? You obviously haven't learned to control it."

Kalian lifted his head to argue his side but the subject drained him. He had been fighting this *thing* for as long as he could remember, and telling her all the ways he had tried to take control wouldn't change the fact that she was right. Under pressure, he could focus his thoughts and feelings to limit its reach, but he couldn't use it at will or for any good.

"I've kept to myself, a lot." He let his head fall back again. "I'm the reason my parents are dead..."

He didn't know why he said it. The words had never been spoken out loud before, only ever in his thoughts. His world had spiralled that day and nothing had ever been the same since.

Today had that same feeling.

"The accident with the Mag-car." It was a statement, not a question.

Li'ara had clearly done her research on him. With the world having come to an end only hours before, this seemed so trivial in comparison.

"They were arguing about something. I don't remember what. I was in the back becoming upset about it. I remember the Weather Net had created a rainstorm that night and it was pounding the windows. I don't think they even noticed the speed. Why would they? It was on auto. It was the last bend before our exit, the Mag-car should have slowed down automatically but it just got faster and faster. At those speeds, the magnets just weren't strong enough to keep us connected."

It was as though a weight was lifting off his chest. Just talking about it out loud gave him the feeling of release. But the guilt was still rooted.

"It went over the edge, into the lanes below." Li'ara finished it for him.

She was right of course. They dropped fifty feet, colliding with the back half of an empty Mag-transport.

"The report didn't make much sense after that." Li'ara left her words hanging, giving Kalian the opportunity to fill in the hazy facts.

"The car was a mess. Just a ball of twisted metal and broken glass. They told me my parents died on impact, but I..." He had to think of the right words. He had spent years reliving this memory, trying to define what he could remember. "They had to prise the car apart to get to me. The space around me was untouched; the metal literally bent away from me. Even my seat wasn't scratched. I passed out before they removed me. The next thing I knew I'm waking up in hospital."

"What happened?"

"I think..." He paused for a moment. He couldn't believe what he was about to say. "I think I kept it all back. The same way I lift things or the way I pushed you. It's just instinct."

Li'ara was just looking at him, displaying no expression to give her thoughts away. Silence filled the ship as she absorbed his words. Kalian couldn't believe the only person he had ever opened up to was a UDC soldier. The one organisation he had feared would lock him up forever and turn him into a lab rat was the UDC. Something about Li'ara was different though. There was an understanding beneath all the training she had been put through. He couldn't explain it, but he trusted her. His head had become a lead weight sinking into the sofa.

"What am I, Li'ara?" He knew she wouldn't have the answer, but he asked anyway.

"You're different." Her smile was almost undetectable.

FIVE

Not long after their conversation, Li'ara disappeared into the cockpit. She said something about running a diagnostic on the *Fathom*, but Kalian could tell her armour had cracked. There was a sad glint in her eyes after talking about memories of Earth. She had certainly lost someone, but he couldn't tell who and he didn't want to press her. She would talk to him when she wanted, or shoot someone - he wasn't sure which.

Before she left, Kalian retrieved his Datapad from a storage locker disguised as a wall. Apparently, Li'ara had stored it away along with his bag. Kalian had thought he'd never see such things again. He had used this Datapad for teaching since he qualified. It was the one piece of technology that he hadn't wrecked.

With all the recent revelations about this new galaxy, he couldn't relax enough to sleep. His head was full of ideas about the other species Telarrek had spoken of, the Conclave and invaders that even they didn't know about. He had so many questions and almost no answers. Thinking about what they were flying towards made it all so trivial. There was a chance they might not even survive another encounter with the invaders. He had only just made it through the first.

To take his mind off it, he spent the next few hours trawling through his Datapad, going over old lectures and notes. It even had his schedule for the coming week on it. His eyes hovered over the delete option. He couldn't bring himself to get rid of it; the one last piece of normality left of what was certainly his old life. Instead, he skipped to the next file, bringing up the lecture he had planned on teaching that very morning. He laughed ironically at how little they had really known about the events that took place four hundred years ago. He looked at the image of the downed ship on Charon, remembering what Telarrek had said about it being a damaged Laronian mining vessel. Without realising, he started correcting the slides and surrounding facts of his lecture. He relabelled the ship and even changed the Solarcite to Intrinium as if he was preparing a new lesson. To think, the last four centuries of human history had been dictated by an alien mining accident.

The silence was broken by the sound of a soft chirp coming from the table. Putting the Datapad down, Kalian could see the small round device Ilyseal had given them. The centre was flashing intermittently with the chirping alarm. Kalian was flustered for a moment, unsure what to do next. He half reached out for the device while looking to the cockpit door.

"Li'ara!" He picked it up, examining the domed ridges. "The thing! The thing's making a noise!"

Li'ara almost burst through the door at the alarm in Kalian's voice. Seeing the reason for the commotion, Li'ara took the device back and placed it on the table. As if making a point of it, she showed Kalian her index finger as she depressed the central node. A full-colour image of Ilyseal's head projected from the source of the flashing light. Li'ara's face said it all.

Moron.

Before Ilyseal said a word, Li'ara disappeared into the armoury leaving Kalian to talk to the floating head.

"Greetings of peace, Kalian."

"Hi. I mean greetings, Ilyseal." He could hear Li'ara putting on her armour and boots.

"We are moments away from reaching Century. Your presence is required on the bridge."

He definitely heard the *clinking* of weapons being removed from the wall.

"Great. We'll be right there."

As soon as Li'ara's finished picking the right gun.

"Will you require an escort?" One of her red tendrils had broken loose from the tight bind and ran down the side of her head.

Kalian was still finding it hard to distinguish between the males and females so he was thankful for Ilyseal's distinctive red hair.

"No, we'll be fine thanks. I'm pretty sure Li'ara's got the whole ship memorised anyway." He added that last part quietly.

Li'ara came walking out of the armoury, fully clad in her UDC armour and looking more machine than human. Her sidearm was magnetised to its circular clip on her thigh.

"We're on our way." Li'ara picked up the communication device and slipped it into a compartment on her belt.

They shared a look for a moment. Neither of them knew what they were about to go into.

They left the *Fathom* with Li'ara leading the way across the expanse of the hangar floor. Kalian wondered how far they would get before Li'ara was forced to hand over her weapon. Before they reached the door, the hangar was filled with a low hum that seemed to resonate from somewhere else in the ship. The view beyond the force field flashed momentarily as a cosmos of stars reappeared. They'd arrived.

They both paused for a moment as staccato flashes of light were visible at the edge of the field.

"They're attacking!" They both made for the force field instead of the door.

They weren't the only ones taking a look. When they got there at least a dozen Novaarians had lined up against the field. Kalian didn't know what to make of the sight. It was like something out of the old science fiction films he had watched as a child. Lights brighter than a star illuminated the view as atomic weapons bombarded the enemy ship. UDC vessels of all sizes were swarming like angry bees around a threatened nest. The detonations were constant as missiles and omega class rail-guns were unleashed from every vessel without pause.

Knowing how big some of the UDC ships were made, the enemy's mammoth ship seem even bigger, if that were possible. What was puzzling was the ship's reaction to being attacked. Every impact clearly hit the hull and created a considerable explosion, but the surface of the monstrous ship almost appeared liquid in its reaction. Craters appeared as charred smoking holes, as expected from such firepower, but as quickly as the ship was damaged it was also repaired. The hull was continuously rebuilding itself out of nothing.

"How is it doing that?"

"I don't know. I assumed from those scans that it had shields." Li'ara was registering every ship in the battle.

If there was a formation to their attack, Kalian couldn't see it. One UDC ship rose up from behind the far side of the colossal enemy. It was definitely the biggest vessel in this fleet but it was still too far away to make out the name on its hull.

"The *Centurion*!" Li'ara's eyes widened at the sight of the ship. "It's the second largest ship we have." She hesitated. "I suppose it's the biggest one now. The *Hyperion* was in orbit around the sun before it..." She put the flat of her hand on the force field, creating small ripples around her fingers. "We need to make contact with that ship; it'll have the commanding general on board."

Oh shit.

Kalian grabbed her arm as she turned to leave for the command bridge. "Look, there, on the side." Li'ara followed his gaze to the flat side of the enemy ship.

It looked like the reverse of the rebuilding process. The side of the ship started to disappear from the centre, expanding outwards. Small green and white lights appeared around the edges as if that specific part of the ship was just switching on. The new rectangular hole gave off a fluorescent green hue that could be seen reflecting off other ships. Kalian's fears were realised. Without any visible structures to support it, a pointed sphere glided out through the entrance to sit alongside its parent ship. It was an identical weapon to the one that had destroyed their entire solar system.

"No..." Li'ara's whisper was barely audible.

He couldn't believe it. They were going to do it all over again. As if ending one solar system and billions of lives wasn't enough. He felt an anger building inside himself at the sight of the weapon. Whatever these things were, they were determined to end all human life as quickly as possible.

HE FELT his laugh vibrate through the armour. He couldn't remember the last time he had laughed. The command module had expanded in size to allow for the extra complement. All eight hundred of his crew had gathered to witness their final blow against the enemy. He extended his mind, feeling every one of them like a beacon of light in the dark. Elandar stood off to the side monitoring readouts from the pilot and constantly fussing over the vital signs. They couldn't even feel the explosions as the primitive missiles hit the hull. His initial reaction had been to raise the shields but he decided to let the humans be baffled by the nanocelium that made up the entire ship.

Let their last thoughts be of chaos and confusion.

He looked out across his comrades - his brothers and sisters - his family as it were. They all appeared eager for battle, ready to fight and destroy. And didn't they deserve it? After countless millennia of searching a galaxy that appeared to have no end, after all the systems they had located and the different species they had found, but never the right one, didn't they deserve to feel Terran blood on their hands again?

"The Novaarians have arrived." Elandar came to his side with a solid oval column following him as though it rode on a wave across the floor.

The holographic scans confirmed his fears that the filthy Terran had survived the supernova, along with the Novaarian ship. He looked to the back of the gathered crew to see the beast standing a good two feet above the rest. He had intended to leave such a mindless creature behind until he had seen through its helmet's visuals that the humans had escaped.

During the journey, he had sifted through the information gathered by their scans and the beast's own view. He now knew this anomaly had a name - Kalian Gaines. Having seen him through the eyes of the beast he knew he was no real threat. He probably had no idea what he was capable of. It was his existence that disgusted him the most. Of all these *humans* he wanted Kalian Gaines to suffer, just for being what he was.

His lack of action put all eyes on him. "Would anyone like to take a walk outside?" The resounding chorus was all he needed to hear. "Tear them apart. Leave none alive." He turned back to Elandar as the crew left the module. "Let them have some fun before the Eclipse ends this world." He could tell Elandar was eager to join his comrades but knew of his duty to the pilot.

"I will instruct her to launch immediately." Elandar placed his own intricate helmet over his head in order to interface with the pilot more directly.

He moved over to the wall on his left as a rectangular panel fizzed to life with a live image of the Novaarian vessel. He left Elandar to his instructions as he gazed out.

Watch Kalian Gaines; watch as I end you and your petulant race.

They couldn't survive this now, not even the Novaarian ship. If it came to it, he would ram their vessel with his own and have done with it. The war was nearly over.

KALIAN LOOKED out across the field of stars to the small circular light of Century's sun, Solson. The force field was obviously dulling the glare of the star and atomic explosions or Kalian couldn't have tolerated the brightness. The pointed missile dwarfed the majority of the UDC ships. Only the *Centurion* and a few others appeared larger.

"We need to stop that thing. If it reaches Solson we lose *everything*." Li'ara covered her eyes as a particularly close explosion threatened to overload the force field.

"We need to speak to Telarrek." Kalian began to head for the door but Li'ara remained where she stood.

"What are you doing? Come on!" Kalian was about to start running.

"Go to the bridge. I need to get out there." Li'ara was already making her way back to the *Fathom* before she finished speaking.

Kalian had to jog to catch up with her as she strode across the hangar. "Where the hell are you going?" He fell into place beside her. "It's suicide out there, Li'ara. If the *Centurion* can't scratch it, what's the *Fathom* going to do? It's too small to even be noticed."

"Exactly."

Kalian could see the faraway look in her eye. She was planning everything in her head as they spoke. He glanced at the door that would lead to the *Valoran's* bridge but he knew he had already made up his mind. After everything they had been through, he couldn't deny the connection he had formed with her. He couldn't explain the feeling but he just felt vulnerable without her. It probably had something to do with her saving him so many times. Kalian realised how stupid he sounded, to feel safer with someone while knowingly heading into danger.

Li'ara entered the code into the touchpad on her arm. The *Fathom's* hatch opened up and the ramp extended to the floor just in time for them to enter. She turned to close the hatch behind her, only to have Kalian walk into her.

"What are you doing?" She placed a gloved hand on his chest, pushing him away.

"I'm coming with you." He surprised himself with the confidence in his voice.

From the way Li'ara's eyebrows shot up he wasn't the only one surprised. "The hell you are. My mandate is to keep you safe, not take you into a war zone."

"And yet here we are." He went to move past her but got pushed back again.

"No, you're not."

"We're wasting time." He'd done it.

She stopped herself from saying whatever was on the edge of her lips. Her jaw clenched and she blinked slowly. "Fine. But you do-"

"Everything you tell me to. I heard you the first time." Kalian moved past her hand and headed straight for the cockpit.

It was more spacious than Kalian had imagined. It had been built for two, with both seats in front of a viewport that was angled down towards the front of the ship. Glass stretched over the top of the cockpit allowing the occupants to see directly above them. It was divided into three sections with parallel lines cutting down the middle. The chairs looked padded and comfortable with head and arm rests.

The consoles looked intimidating. Instead of two separate stations, it was one holo-touch console that stretched from one side to the other. Everything was lit up in blue, red and yellow lights and miniature holograms. Unlike the Novaarian tech though, the holograms couldn't be interacted with. Immediately to his left and right were taller consoles attached to the wall, each with a small readout screen. Kalian had no idea what any of it did.

Li'ara pushed past him, bringing him back to the moment. Now that he was here he really didn't know what he could do to help.

"Strap in and don't touch anything unless I tell you. I don't want you breaking the ship before we can even lift off."

Kalian detected the dark humour in her voice this time.

The seats really were comfortable. He slid in as the padded synthetic leather moulded to his shape and he looked around for the straps Li'ara had spoken of but couldn't find any. He noted that she hadn't attempted to either. He stopped himself from asking where they were when he realised it was just an expression.

Li'ara's hands danced over the console as she typed in various commands. A quick high-pitched hum told him the engines were coming online. He recognised the mechanical thud from under their feet, as the landing gear clicked into place, packing itself away. Kalian now felt the familiar sensation as the Grav Enforcers created the artificial gravity during flight mode. The *Fathom* rose above the other ships that surrounded it, turning towards the force field as it did.

They could both see the group of Novaarians below. They had rushed to their ship in response to its sudden movement. A few of them were waving their hands in the air trying to signal them to stop.

"It's one way; they can't see us in here." As she spoke, two joysticks flicked up from their compartment, hidden within the console. Li'ara gripped them both and pulled back.

Kalian expected to feel the tug in his seat but there was no such reaction thanks to the compensators. The *Fathom* made a steady approach towards the force field.

"Can we even pass through that?" The thought had only just occurred to him. He had visions of the ship coming to a violent stop as the field proved stubborn. "What if it can, you know, solidify?" He didn't sound as confident anymore.

"It won't." Li'ara placed her fingertips over a smooth blue touchpad raised above the rest of the console. It had lines running across with different numbers next to them. Putting her fingers at the top of the dial, she moved her hand down slowly. The ship immediately increased in speed towards the invisible field.

The *Fathom* flew straight through the centre, creating small ripple effects around its edge. Kalian gave a sigh of relief. He looked to Li'ara with astonishment at their luck.

"How did you know that would work?" He expected some cocky soldier-like reply about her training or something.

"Because you're on board." Her tone was flat as she concentrated on readouts in front of her.

"You knew they wouldn't let me get hurt." Had she used him to get off the ship? "That's it, isn't it? They knew it could have killed *me* if they didn't let us leave." He wasn't sure whether to be insulted or impressed at her quick planning.

"Try not to cry about it... we might still get killed anyway."

Before he could reply to her dry retort, Li'ara pulled down on the speed control and rotated the joysticks. The *Fathom* didn't feel like it was moving, but the raging fight ahead of them appeared to move up the viewport, dominating the entire screen. She dropped the ship into a dive only to smoothly pull back on the control soon after.

"What are you doing?" Kalian held on to the console in front as if to brace against a force that never came.

"We're going under it." She was constantly checking readouts about the temperature in the engines and the efficiency of the compensators.

"I thought you wanted to fight?" He really had no idea what the plan was.

Li'ara whipped her head around at him like he was an idiot. "Does that look like a fight this ship can have any impact on?"

Kalian just shook his head as if he had already come to that conclusion. He turned to his right as something huge caught his peripheral vision.

Century.

It was more beautiful than the pictures he had seen. It reminded him of ancient Earth, the twenty-third or fourth century perhaps. It had more green and blue than his memory of Earth had. It was similar in some ways though, for he could see the sprawl of networks the hyper-ways created. There were millions of lights on the dark side, with clusters where the major cities were. Kalian found that novel in a way. Back on Earth, it had become impossible to define one city from the other. It was easy to see why so many people were moving here each year, with the solar system becoming so crowded.

"Kalian!"

How long had she been saying his name?

"Sorry. What?" He followed her eyes up to the battle. He had to crane his neck slightly to see it.

The enemy had launched the weapon. They were too late. There were no visible thrusters as it silently shot off down the side of the black ship. Several missiles and rail-gun fire struck the side but had little or no impact.

"What do we do now?" Kalian could only watch as the silent impacts and explosions continued around them.

Li'ara immediately began punching in different commands to the touchpad that lay between them. Responding to her commands, a hand-sized sphere in the centre of the main console rose a few centimetres into the air. A blue hologram was emitted from the top, relaying an image of the battle up ahead. In green was the star-bound rocket and the *Fathom* was represented in red. In the blink of an eye, small red lines extended from the *Fathom*, heading through the battle and into a straight line towards the rocket.

"Please don't tell me that's our flight path."

A red holographic square was flashing over the section that passed through the fighting. In the centre, one word was flashing yellow: *hazard*. That was one way of putting it, he thought.

"If we follow this flight path we'll reach it halfway to Solson." Li'ara had already pulled back on the control, aligning the *Fathom* with the calculated flight path.

"What are we going to do when we get there, ask it to turn around? I don't know if you noticed but everything just bounces off that..." He lost his train of thought as he remembered the scans Telarrek had shown them. Then he knew. "No... you're not serious?" He was watching her face for any reaction.

Her look was that of fearless determination. "I'm always serious."

He let his head fall into the rest behind. They were going to *board* it. The scans had shown a small airlock of some kind situated on the top right hemisphere. As the *Fathom* was hurtling towards the battle, Kalian was desperately thinking ahead.

"How are we even going to dock with it? It's an alien ship, thing!" He couldn't imagine how they would ever connect the two very different vessels.

"This ship can do more than you know." Her reply was cryptic but he assumed she was concentrating on the controls.

The approaching firefight made Kalian forget any docking procedures for the moment. Besides, they might not even make it that far.

They were so close now he could clearly make out the names

of the attacking ships. The first vessel they passed was the *Dauntless*. It was at least ten times the size of the *Fathom* and shaped like a fork with the engines at the prongs. Guided missiles were being launched from every side while being reinforced with rail-gun fire. The rail-guns themselves looked as big as the ship he was sitting in.

Li'ara followed the flight plan perfectly, dodging the streaking missiles that swirled around them. She pushed the control, ducking under the *Intrepid*, almost flying parallel to a newly launched missile. As they got closer to the great ship, the *Fathom* was shaken by concussive shockwaves from the many impacts. Kalian could see the sweat forming on Li'ara's brow.

As they passed from under the *Intrepid*, Kalian looked up at the black ship. Even on its flat side, it was bigger than any mega-skyscrapers. It must have been able to accommodate several million crew at least. Gliding over the top, the *Centurion* came into view far above. Like the others, it hadn't taken any damage in the fight.

"Why isn't it fighting back? It's just letting them hit it with everything they've got." It was obvious the beast of a craft could take it, but Kalian couldn't understand why it would even allow it.

"Maybe it's because they don't need to. Fire one of those things," Li'ara said, nodding towards the holographic image of the rocket, "and the whole fight's over. There wouldn't even be any stragglers to deal with."

Li'ara's belt began to beep softly. They both recognised the sound this time, though Li'ara made no move to do anything. Kalian saw the look on her face; she didn't have time for a speech from Telarrek about his safety.

"Li'ara..." She gave him a sideways glance but nothing else. "They might have some advice on you know... how to break into an alien rocket ship." He hoped by saying it out loud she would realise how ridiculous it sounded.

"Fine." She pulled it from her pouch and slapped it onto the console. As before, a life-size Novaarian head materialized above the device.

"Telarrek!" Kalian couldn't hide the relief in his voice. "We need some advice here. We're going—"

"You must return at once, both of you." His voice sounded more gravelly than normal. "The *Valoran* will attack them, but you must return at once. Your ship has few defences and no shields. I cannot allow you to be caught in the crossfire."

The *Fathom* banked to starboard trying to avoid a particularly large explosion on the hull of the massive ship.

"Just fire everything you've got!" Li'ara dropped her fist through the hologram and onto the device's activation button.

Telarrek's head disappeared as it flew off the console and onto the floor.

"Right then..." Kalian couldn't think of anything else to say. Li'ara banked upwards, if there is such a thing in space. Solson's light shone between the warring ships. Any other setting and Kalian would have found it beautiful. "You know they could help if you let them. They *are* more advanced."

Li'ara turned to him for a second. "You want me to put my fist through *your* head?"

Before he could reply, the console made a strange affirmative sound. The image magnified as they were now on the straight path directly to the rocket.

"We're almost there. Once we get out of this mess it should be a smooth ride." Li'ara was talking as well as frowning at a new readout. "Providing we survive this mess."

Kalian's fingers started hurting. He wasn't sure at what point he had dug his hands into the armrests.

"What the hell is this?"

Kalian didn't like the edge in her voice. He leaned over to see the readout she was talking about. According to the sensors, the hull of the colossal ship was changing in small sections all over. They both looked out of the port side to see the new configurations. Like the change that took place for the launch of the rocket, the hull was deteriorating inwards to form small holes. Each one shone from inside with a tiny luminous green light.

"What is that?" There were so many, Kalian couldn't count them all.

"They're... oh shit!" She yanked the control to port, trying to create as much distance between them as she could.

Again Kalian felt nothing, with only the view shifting to the left.

Three hundred and sixty degrees of chaos erupted. At that exact moment, the *Valoran* unleashed its powerful weapons on the enemy. Intense beams, containing every colour, burst from the port side of the Novaarian ship, striking the massive vessel. Kalian didn't have the chance to see what damage it caused as the enemy ship released its own form of attack. At first, Kalian wasn't sure what he was seeing until one flew past only metres away from the viewport. He swore at the sight of what was clearly a bipedal creature identical to the one that attacked the Icarus. The light from surrounding explosions shone off its dark plated armour.

Every UDC ship was impacted by at least one of the destructive monsters. Their thick hulls appeared no match for the speed and force of the alien creatures. Each one dived head first into different sections of the ships. Through the chaos, they could see individual crew being sucked out of the holes into the cold vacuum. Between the *Valoran's* attacks, the constant barrage of missiles from the UDC ships and the brutality of the alien foe, Kalian lost sight of the rocket.

Li'ara wasn't speaking anymore. She was a constant flurry of movement over the console. The view was rotating in every direction as she tried to avoid every form of attack. They could finally see the end of the black ship and space beyond.

"We're almost clear!"

Li'ara was too focused to reply.

Kalian saw the UDC ship *Noble* above them to starboard. It had stopped firing any missiles and the rail-guns appeared to have shut down. He could see the charred entry point where one of the invaders had penetrated it. The ship began to explode from the inside and debris and crew were vented like a wounded animal being drained of its blood.

A pit opened up in his stomach at the sight of all the people disappearing into space.

The lights flickered until they went out completely. The ship seemed to drift off its course as it was caught in Century's gravity well. Before they flew out of sight, he craned his head to see the armoured creature burst from the innards of the ship. A trail of debris could be seen above the *Fathom,* as it landed on another ship. They were literally leaping from ship to ship and tearing them apart from the inside. How did they get their momentum? There were no obvious attachments to their armour.

Kalian refocused on the path ahead as they miraculously cleared the fight and the viewport levelled out.

"There it is." Li'ara took an audible breath.

Kalian wondered if she had been holding her breath for as long as he had. The rocket was the size of his thumb, hurtling towards Solson. From behind, it looked to be a simple brass coloured ball. She keyed some more commands into the console and the viewport dimmed in tone, blocking the glare from the approaching star.

"Reverting power to main engines. Manoeuvring thrusters offline," Li'ara had a dangerous glint in her eye as she looked up at their prey. "Time to punch it."

The *Fathom* made a mechanical noise as the small manoeuvring thrusters folded back into the hull. The dig, on the touchpad that controlled speed, began moving the dial further down on its own. It was hard to gauge speed in space with so little around, but the rocket was clearly getting bigger in the viewport.

They could no longer see the raging battle behind them, but it wasn't hard to imagine it. Those UDC ships wouldn't stand a chance against those things. Thinking about their method of attack, Kalian could only come to one conclusion; they *liked* it. Knowing that their weapon would do the job of obliterating all life, and still deciding to attack in person, this must be fun for them.

"So what happens now?" Kalian no longer felt comfortable sitting down. The thought of what was to come pumped him with adrenaline.

"We find that airlock and attach the emergency hatch to it." Li'ara thumbed in the direction of the main cabin behind them.

Kalian recalled his memory of the cabin and couldn't remember seeing any emergency hatch. There had only been one door in and out.

Seeing his quizzical look Li'ara explained. "It's in the centre of the ceiling. You didn't notice the round hatch?"

Kalian was embarrassed at not noticing something that had been above his head for hours. He quickly got out of his seat and opened the cockpit door. In his defence, the hatch was set into the ceiling so as to create a smooth appearance. It still didn't convince him of their plan though. It only looked big enough for one person to fit through.

"How is that going to attach to the airlock? From the *Valoran's* scans, it looked as big as the main door."

Li'ara sat back in her chair for the first time since they left the hangar. The hologram of their projected flight calculated two minutes until both vessels were aligned.

"There's a square outlay on top of the *Fathom*, which surrounds the hatch. Using magnetic seals the outline will extend for two metres until it makes contact. So we're going to get pretty close."

Kalian couldn't picture what she was saying. The ship wasn't big enough to extend that far. "How does it extend? Where does the extra *metal* come from?"

"It's a micro tungsten filament folded into the ship's hull. We can pressurise the space between and walk across." Li'ara explained it like a walk in the park.

"So..." Kalian wished he was wrong. "There's going to be a thin *material* between us and space?"

"Do you need to change your pants?" Li'ara enquired.

Kalian sat back in his chair putting on a tough exterior. "Just wanted to be clear." He looked around hopelessly for something to distract him.

The minutes seemed to pass in seconds. The rocket now filled the entire viewport, blocking out the light. The *Fathom's* sensors had detected the airlock after Li'ara focused them on one section of its giant hull. Setting the ship to emergency docking procedures was all she needed to do as the *Fathom* took over.

"Come with me." Li'ara left the cockpit and headed into the armoury. Depressing the release button on one of the lower drawers, it slid out to reveal a similar holster to the one she wore. "Put this on. It straps round like this."

Extending her leg, Kalian could see the stiff material wrapped around the thigh with a small clip on the inside. On the outside was a raised circle just smaller than his palm. He had seen Li'ara fix her gun to it earlier. Turning to the wall behind her she picked up a sidearm. It looked like a similar model to Li'ara's, only with fewer accessories. She handled the weapon expertly, holding it up to the light for inspection.

"You ever held one of these?"

Kalian silently shook his head.

"Good. You shouldn't have." She looked down the cylindrical barrel checking the sight on it. "This is an LX 14-02. It's the standard sidearm for any band five UDC operative. It fires charged particles at speeds you wouldn't comprehend."

Kalian was sure she was reeling off a speech she had been given by some drill sergeant.

"It has its advantages and disadvantages. If you shoot someone with it, they will not get back up. Since it fires particles and not projectiles, it's got five thousand shots before reloading is required. On the downside, if you fire too many shots in a small space of time, it will begin to overheat. If you continue to shoot before it can cool down..." She paused to ensure his attention. "It will explode."

Kalian couldn't help but look surprised. That seemed a bit of an extreme reaction for a gun.

"Got it." Even Kalian wasn't convinced at how confident he sounded.

Hesitantly she passed him the weapon, handle first. It felt heavy in his hand. He moved it around, inspecting it just because he thought he should. The handle dropped half an inch below his grip.

He noticed a small rectangular screen on the left side at the back of the barrel.

Seeing his inspection Li'ara elaborated. "It's the heat level so keep an eye on that in a firefight." She held up her own gun displaying the left-hand side. "See the impression?"

He saw the small circle depressed into the gun and noted his own had the same. She clipped her gun into the identical raised circle on her holster. Moving his to the right leg, Kalian did the same. The weapon made him feel empowered and more confident.

Li'ara turned to leave and picked up another weapon as big as his arm. She put the strap over her head and let it rest on her back.

"Do I get one of those?"

"No."

Probably just as well, he thought. He hadn't even fired the smaller one yet.

Opening a compartment next to the door, Li'ara removed what looked like two face masks. From the shape, each would fit over the mouth and nose and sit over the wearer's cheeks and jaw.

She threw one over to Kalian and kept one for herself. "We don't know what the atmosphere is over there, so keep it on until we know for sure."

The circular hatch in the cabin's ceiling opened and slid to the side. Looking up, it was exactly as Li'ara had explained. The magnetic seal had secured itself around the airlock, with what appeared to be a golden fabric, connecting it to the *Fathom*. They could both see through to the brass coloured hull of the rocket. Answering Kalian's question of how they actually got up there, Li'ara lifted a hidden compartment in the floor. The compartment was long, and blended into the floor perfectly. Kalian was happy to see something low tech for a change. Li'ara removed a ladder from the floor and placed it against the hatch above.

Putting on their masks, they ascended the ladder into the pressurised section between the two vessels. Once stretched to its limit, the tungsten filament felt hard under-foot, allowing them to step on it. It didn't make it any easier to know that it was the only thing between them and an icy death. Thinking of the cold, Kalian was glad he had remembered his jacket, despite a few scorch marks and tears. They experienced a disorientating sensation as they passed the threshold of the *Fathom*. Gravity vanished, making them float over to the rocket. Kalian was unaccustomed to the movement required to navigate direction and speed. Li'ara, on the other hand, looked quite comfortable as she pushed herself across.

She frantically moved her hands over the alien alloy in different sections around the edges.

"What's wrong?" He was eager to get through this particular part of the plan.

"There's no handle, not even a touchpad." Her voice sounded tinny through the filter in the mask.

They hadn't thought about this. The door was so alien it didn't even work the way the Novaarian ones did. There was no handprint to touch or handle to pull.

"What do we do now?" He had to put his hands up to stop himself from head-butting the filament.

Li'ara checked the information on her armour. "We have twenty-six minutes until we reach the corona."

Kalian remembered the term from his physics lessons, although it did have some crossover into his own lectures. Once they reached the corona they would be on the outer edge of Solson. It was the region in which all Solar Drive powered ships would sit while charging the Solarcite. He also knew it was the point of no return. All UDC ships were built to withstand the heat at that distance, but any further was futile. Also, he wasn't sure what the limits were on the tungsten filament. He didn't want to think about that while he was floating inside it.

He gently pushed off the filament towards the alien door, putting his hands out in front to stop himself. The moment he made contact with the rough metal, they both heard a heavy click from the other side. Afraid of what it might be he pushed off instantly, his momentum carrying him into the filament wall. The airlock pulled back into the rocket and split in two down the middle, though the dividing line was a mystery in itself. The door was at least three feet thick and there was nothing but darkness beyond.

Li'ara had her hand on her sidearm as she looked at Kalian in shock.

"How did you do that?" She kept looking from him to the open airlock.

Kalian looked at his own hands in shock. "I have no idea..." But it scared him.

"Is this one of your things?" She had completely disconnected her gun from its holster now.

"No. It's usually the opposite of this sort of thing."

Li'ara looked at her readout again. "Whatever it was we need to get moving." She pushed off towards the rocket in a dive position.

Kalian winced as her body passed through the alien threshold and plummeted to the floor in a clatter of metal on metal. "Are you ok?" The answer was evident as she was already standing up.

"I'm fine. Just... come on." She switched on the dual torches on either side of her mask.

Kalian decided to leave the subject alone and passed over the threshold himself, feet first. Entering slightly higher than he wanted, he had a small drop to the floor.

"Gravity seems alright." He tapped his foot on the floor.

Before Li'ara could answer the area was flooded with lights from above. They were on a walkway in front of a T-junction. The walls were a light copper colour and smoother than the exterior of the rocket. Turning off the torches Li'ara checked her wrist pad.

"Oxygen levels are normal too." She didn't sound like she quite believed it. She took off her mask and inhaled a breath. "So *they* breathe oxygen too."

"Yeah, but so do the Novaarians." At this point, they couldn't really build a picture of this new species. Kalian took off his own mask and left it by the door. "Do you even have a plan beyond this point?"

"Yep! We're going to blow it to hell." She tapped a chunky pouch on her hip.

He hadn't even seen her pick up any explosives.

"Great plan, but this thing looked as big as the *Centurion*. How do we even know what to blow up?" They walked into the middle of the T-junction.

"Now we're inside I can actually get some readings off this thing." She examined her wrist pad for a moment. "There appears to be a large chamber in the centre. The sensors don't really know what they're looking at. Everything being fed back is coming up as unknown." Li'ara looked up to the left-hand corridor. "If the telemetry is right, we're on a walkway that reaches all the way around. Fifty metres up there's what looks like an access door, which should lead us in." Without hesitating, she began a quick jog down the corridor.

"Into what...?"

The corridor was dark, with sparse overhead lighting. The walkway beneath them was a grated mesh that rattled under their feet. Looking down they could see silver pipes that ran along the walkway. The rocket was so colossal in its circumference that neither of them could see the curve up ahead. For such an advanced race, it seemed devoid of technology.

They soon arrived at the large copper door that opened with their proximity.

He was wrong about the technology.

There was no mistaking the impressive vista before them. The chamber was beyond massive and seeing it from the inside Kalian couldn't believe it was mostly hollow. The central piece occupied most of the space but both Kalian and Li'ara were puzzled as to what they were really looking at. The two pyramids that met in the centre of the chamber were bigger than the ancient pyramids of Earth. One pyramid was at the bottom stretching up to the same level they were on and the second pyramid reached down from the domed ceiling. Where the two met was a small gap but, from this distance, it was hard to say how small it was. Both structures were lined with dark gradients from top to bottom, giving them smaller levels as they reached the apex. It gave the top tier the appearance of being a smaller, individual pyramid.

Everything was lit by giant spotlights around the base of each structure. The pyramids themselves had a slight green tinge to them. From their position, they could see three walkways that bridged the gap to the point where the pyramids met.

"What is this?" The Li'ara who normally took everything in while looking for exits, hostiles and any weak points, could not keep her mouth closed. They were going to need more explosives.

"Have you ever seen anything like this?" Kalian hoped in all her travels and training she might have seen something similar.

"No..." Li'ara slid a different screen onto her touchpad. "Twenty-three minutes. Let's go."

With time running out, she sprinted to the nearest bridge twenty metres away. The bridge itself wasn't exactly small and they had to run flat out for two minutes before they reached the centre. The fact that there were no rails didn't make it easier. Kalian avoided the urge to look down into the abyss below.

Standing at the apex of the lower pyramid, they could see that the higher one was at least thirty feet up. Kalian walked to the edge and examined the top of the lower pyramid. It wasn't pointed as it had looked from afar. The top was a flat surface with a black hole in the centre. He was sure he could have fitted his entire apartment in that hole. Kalian could see they were on one of four platforms that surrounded the structure in a solid black circle that resembled marble.

He saw Li'ara searching the immediate area and he came to the same conclusion.

"There are no consoles, no touchpads, nothing."

She was right; there was no clear way of seeing how this thing was controlled. With the closing time frame, they both frantically moved from one side to the other, searching the giant chamber for any sign of hope.

"Ok, so..." Kalian turned to Li'ara. "Where else can we put the explosives?"

He was no demolition expert but he was sure she must have blown some stuff up before. Li'ara faced away from the edge and back to Kalian who was standing in the middle. He noticed her eyes fixed on his feet and followed her look. The black marble around him was shimmering like a desert heat. The area took on the appearance of liquid like a black moat forming around him.

"Whoa!" He froze somewhere between fear and curiosity as the floor rose up in columns around him.

The liquid began to solidify as the columns formed from the ground up. He counted seven oval-shaped columns, each one a different size but all higher at the back and tilting down towards him. Fully formed they were now in an arc around him. They looked solid and indistinguishable from the black floor. As one, they all lit up with different symbols in bright white light. Each now looked like a console showing different displays. One to his left had a row of symbols six characters long. The symbol at the end was constantly changing until it disappeared completely. A couple of the others had graphs and shapes on them that were obviously supposed to be telling him something.

Li'ara marched round to his side to inspect the strange protrusions.

"What the hell did you do now?" She looked over every symbol and graph but understood as much as Kalian.

"I didn't do anything, I don't even know where they came from!" Kalian stepped away from them allowing Li'ara more room to examine them.

Was that me?

She held her arm over them while reading the information being relayed into her touchpad. She cursed under her breath. "Fourteen minutes."

Kalian had the sudden urge to run. "Can you figure any of this out?" He waved at the consoles generally.

"How can I? It's all gibberish! I was taught to read the same language as you!"

"You translated that word back on the *Valoran*!" Kalian quickly replied.

They were both becoming slightly irate in their frustration.

"Well, it's not working now." Li'ara began to unclip the chunky pouch on her hip. Her hand froze over the clip. "What's that?"

The central column blinked to life and looking back at her was the armoured faceplate of one of the aliens. The sunken pits where the eyes should be just stared up at her from the angled console. Being so close she could see the intricate lines that ran across the surface of the mask.

Kalian came up beside her to see what had stopped her from removing the explosives. The masked figure turned away for a moment before looking back and cutting the feed. A mechanical groan erupted from somewhere deeper inside the rocket.

"We're speeding up!" Li'ara was checking readouts on her arm.

Kalian could see over her shoulder as it recalculated the time before reaching the corona. Panic and despair mingled as one emotion at the sight of the number four on her arm. They now only had four minutes to backtrack and somehow escape this nightmare.

"At the new speed, the *Fathom* won't be able to keep up for long."

Li'ara roughly tore the clip off her pouch and removed two halves of a sphere no bigger than her hand. The surface was covered in bits of tech Kalian had never seen before. Putting the two together they connected with a magnetic hum.

"What's that? A bomb?" As Kalian asked, the seven columns switched off and began to sink back into the floor like melting chocolate.

"A Nuke." Li'ara cradled the sphere while activating different sections.

Kalian couldn't believe his ears. "You had that *on board*? You had it attached to your hip?" He couldn't say everything else he was thinking.

Why they had brought a nuclear bomb aboard for a diplomatic mission he couldn't imagine.

They were both knocked to the floor as a blinding column of light connected the two pyramids. The noise was deafening with the roar of what sounded like a primal beast. Bolts of green lightning shot from one apex to the other, mixing with the beam of light.

"Run!" Li'ara jumped up leaving the nuke where it fell.

Pulling Kalian up by the arm, they both broke into yet another run for their lives. He wasn't sure how many minutes they had left but he knew it was less than four. Looking back at the spectacle, he saw the nuke shining in the light. It was only a quick look but he was sure the same black liquid from the floor was surrounding it, blocking out the flashing red LED. He had no time to think about it now as his focus was on not falling over.

They were back in the corridor running towards the T-junction. There must be less than a minute left. Almost crashing into the wall and each other they made the sharp turn back to the airlock.

The passage between the two vessels looked different now. The *Fathom* was clearly being dragged as the tungsten filament was at a diagonal angle, obscuring the hatch. Li'ara jumped through the gap head first and deftly spun mid vacuum. Her slim form slipped through the emergency hatch allowing her to land on her feet, her body adjusting to the change in gravity. Kalian was not so lucky. Unsure of the correct strength to apply, he copied Li'ara's technique and dived head first. Using too much spin, he ended up facing the hatch head first again.

Shit!

Li'ara was able to move out of the way as he crashed into the cabin floor in a heap of limbs. She quickly kicked the ladder off its axis and typed commands into her touchpad. The consequent thud from above came as the filament and frame fitted back into place.

By the time Kalian had regained his senses, Li'ara had already left for the cockpit. He clambered through the door and fell into the seat beside her. From the view, it was clear they were spinning through space. Century and the orbiting battle were too far to see. The viewport was almost entirely black, having dimmed so much to compensate for Solson's proximity.

Li'ara frantically punched in commands on the console.

"Come on you advanced piece of shit!" As if responding to her rage, the viewport levelled out and they found direction. "We're going to be too close." Li'ara hesitated. "I'm activating the Solar Drive."

Even with his sore head that didn't make sense to Kalian. "But we haven't charged the Solarcite!"

It was common knowledge that all Solar Drive powered ships needed time within the star spot to charge. As he argued his point, a horizontal lever ascended from the middle of the console. Putting her hand over it Li'ara paused. The readout on her arm hadn't informed her of the nuke's detonation. They had failed. Every hologram and sensor activated at once with warnings that flashed emergency red. Kalian could no longer hear Li'ara screaming over the different alarms, her hand resting on the lever.

Solson had gone supernova.

Time seemed to slow down for the next few seconds. The exploding light overwhelmed the viewport allowing for a brief glimpse of Century, though only a speck from there. Billions of lives currently existed on that planet. Humankind's last hope for survival was yet again caught in the wave of a god. It couldn't be tempered, it couldn't be bargained with, and it couldn't be stopped. Even as their last shred of hope died, Li'ara couldn't switch off her survival instincts. Through blurred eyes, she pulled back on the lever. Only moments before the nova engulfed them, the *Fathom* blinked from existence, penetrating the space between spaces.

SIX

The dome covering of the *Valoran's* Bridge had tinted immediately to protect its occupants from the barrage of light. Century's star had collapsed in a heartbeat, its immense energy surging out into the solar system. Telarrek's crew were well trained and highly experienced, plotting an emergency escape vector without waiting for his command.

Standing at his podium, the old Novaarian felt overcome with emotion. He had watched the humans for centuries, absorbing their culture and observing their every way of life. The spectacle of witnessing another supernova was lost against the sobering consequences.

"They are gone..." Telarrek sagged in his command post, resting his lower limbs on the bar.

The bridge crew were looking at one another in shock. They had taken part in this mission and invested just as much as he had. The humans had meant something to all of them. He felt anger bubbling to the surface at the thought of the hulking ship. The Conclave had a history of sins it couldn't hide from, genocide included, however accidental it was, but to actively seek out another race and wipe them from the face of the galaxy? It was monstrous.

He felt Ilyseal's hand rest on his own. He could tell from her expression that anger was not her current emotion. He squeezed her fingers to stop her skin from changing shade. It was important the crew saw them as strong and ready to act.

"My Charge, we have detected the *Fathom's* Solar Drive!"

It took a moment for Telarrek to process the information. "Where?" he asked the crewman.

"They have dropped out of subspace three light years away."

Telarrek looked to Ilyseal in astonishment. *How could they have escaped the nova?*

"We need to take a closer look at that ship," Ilyseal said with a flicker of hope on her face.

Telarrek felt a special bond with Kalian. He supposed it was to be expected, given their level of involvement in his life since the day he was born.

"If they survived, it is possible others did as well." It was a candle-light of hope in the dark, but he would hold on to it. "Set course for the *Fathom*. Maximum yield."

"I would not advise that, Charge." It was Lakrandil, his chief engineer. "The radiation flash from both novas has damaged the Starrillium. I wouldn't feel comfortable pushing it past sixty percent."

It was minimal damage compared to what a supernova was truly capable of. They had been lucky.

"Very well," he conceded. "We will pick up the *Fathom* and continue home. When we reach a safe distance from the effects of the nova, we will stop to make repairs." The complement of nods saw his orders put into action.

Carrying its previous momentum, the *Fathom* ruptured the fabric of reality and emerged in real space. The ship was burnt black from Solson's heat. No UDC ship had been designed to get that close. The main exhaust port flickered as the fiery blue light from the thrust died out completely, leaving the ship to float out of control on its path.

Both occupants in the *Fathom's* cockpit sat very still. The only sound was coming from the main console as a small hologram, next to the engine symbol, flashed from red to blue. Kalian heard himself swallow. His mouth was dry, unlike his eyes. The details in front became blurry as tears streaked down his cheeks, giving him a salty taste on his lips.

His voice was croaky as he turned to Li'ara. "What just happened?"

The copper ringlets of her hair covered her face.

He sat looking at her for a while as she didn't seem inclined to answer. He saw her chest plate rise as she inhaled a long breath.

"We failed..." Her voice sounded fragile like she was trying to say as little as possible.

Kalian knew what she meant though. They had failed to save Century. Humanity had become an endangered species in a single day. Kalian was confident that not every human being had been on Century or Earth when they perished. Central Parliament was always sending explorers and scientists into the deeper reaches of space. But that probably didn't equate to more than a thousand at most. And how would they all find one another without the UDC or Central Parliament?

To have the power to decimate two solar systems and an entire species in a day, what were these creatures? How were they so power-ful? Why did they even attack? Kalian couldn't fathom what could drive a race of advanced beings to wipe out a lesser species they had never met. It obviously wasn't for fuel or resources and they clearly didn't even want the population. Just complete annihilation.

He looked out across star field and wondered where they were, though a part of him wondered if that even mattered anymore. Where would they go? How would they survive in a galaxy without Earth or Century?

"How did we get here?"

It took a moment but Li'ara finally responded. She tapped two buttons silencing the engine alarm, and, using her right hand, lifted a new hologram from the central projector. It showed the *Fathom* in comparison to Century. From the looks of it, they hadn't travelled too far away, just enough to escape.

"I programmed a random jump to take us one parsec away. That was all we had the fuel for anyway." Her hair fell away from her face to show a rogue tear falling down her pale cheek.

Kalian thought about reaching his hand out to her own. He didn't really know how to comfort another person. He spent a moment wishing he had spent a little more time around people than he had history books. Before he could reach out, Li'ara stood up and walked over to the monitors behind them.

It just hit Kalian what she had said. "How did we even jump at all?" he asked. "We weren't even in a star-spot. And what the hell is a parsec?"

His mind cast back to Commander Hawkins. He implied that the *Fathom* would allow them to escape at a pinch, but would not explain how. Kalian could see *how* they had escaped he just couldn't understand it. The fuel cells must have already been charged with the Solarcite, ready to cut into subspace at a moment's notice.

But how?

Once charged there was no way to safely store the ionised Solarcite. If the engines could hold on to the Solarcite, without tearing through subspace, there would be no need to travel to a star every time. The ship could be fuelled up once to maximum yield and then use the Solar Drive whenever they wanted. Had this been invented centuries ago, The *Paladin* might have made it back home.

With no answer, he pressed her. "How is this technology possible?" He wiped away the tears from his face and noticed he was covered in sweat. Li'ara stopped whatever she was doing with the monitor, though Kalian guessed it was just a distraction. She looked at him like he was a petulant child who wouldn't do as he was told.

"How do you think?" she retorted. "We invented it. Since its discovery, we finally improved on the Solar Drive. Whatever the *Laronians* had, we made it better."

Again, everything came back to the downed ship on Charon. It was an impressive feat, though Li'ara's mood took the edge off it, and she still wasn't able to look him in the eye. He had to forgive her that. They had both lost their species and their home, but he sensed she had lost something else, maybe someone else.

She made for the cockpit door, stopping at the entrance. Kalian swivelled his chair to track her movements. Her eyes finally found his. Her features softened for a moment almost apologetically.

"3.26 light years... that's a parsec. Don't touch anything." Her face steeled again as she walked away from him.

He heard the door slide shut on the armoury. She needed time, but who knew how much time was required to deal with something like this; lost in space with no engine or home to return to. But all they had was time now, at least until the life support ran out.

He stayed in the cockpit after Li'ara left. He couldn't see the point of going anywhere else in the ship anyway. He let his mind wander as exhaustion crept in. He thought of places on Earth he had never even got to see, let alone Mars or Century. He had always wanted to stay in the Everest hotel. It haloed the peak of Mount Everest with what he had heard were the best views on Earth. Or even to walk through the red forests of Mars and breathe in an air that wasn't of Earth. He had a sad thought that he would spend the rest of his life regretting the things he hadn't done.

Eventually, sleep won out as he rested his head on the seat. His last thought had been something simple, like wishing he had taken one last shower.

HE BOLTED FORWARD in his chair, hitting his knee on the console as he did. A different alarm was flashing blue and red. The frequency was hard to listen to. Kalian rubbed one of his eyes while looking around for Li'ara. He wasn't sure how long he had been asleep but he would have been happy with some more.

The central projector emitted a new hologram in shades of

yellow. He had no idea what he was looking at but it was some kind of graph that clearly wanted him to see a spike in the even gradient. The levels of something had obviously changed but he had no idea what. Were they about to run out of oxygen?

His answer came in an unexpected form. The stars to port were instantly eclipsed as a flash of light preceded the *Valoran*. It must have been thousands of kilometres away as Kalian could see the whole ship end to end. The arcing spikes that protruded from the back end were glittering in shades of purple like great amethysts. It didn't appear to have taken any damage from the fight. Kalian wondered if the invaders had even attacked them. Thinking about it, it was no great surprise they had survived the supernova. The *Valoran's* engine was obviously similar to the *Fathom's* in that it could store charged Solarcite, or Intrinium in their case.

Li'ara appeared soon after with a sense of urgency about her. Seeing the *Valoran* she relaxed somewhat and fell into the pilot's chair. Kalian couldn't help but notice the lack of armour. She was only wearing the flat black undersuit that clung to her body like a second skin. She still had her weapon strapped to her thigh though and wore the chunky boots that normally went with her armour.

Like a concert pianist, her hands danced across the console, shutting off the alarm while bringing up sensor readouts. Yellow holographic images popped up showing the state of the engine and the depleted stores of Solarcite.

"We've got nothing," Li'ara said.

Her hair was still a little matted from the heat on the rocket and her eyes looked sore and red. Kalian suspected she had stopped crying a while ago but couldn't get rid of the blotches under her eyes. Seeing Kalian's inspection of her face, Li'ara turned away as if some new readout was important.

"I'm sure Telarrek can get us aboard."

It felt tense between them. Neither one knew what to say or talk about. In many ways, they were complete strangers. But the last twenty-four hours had put them through hell together.

He wanted to reach out again and reassure her everything would be alright, that they would get through this.

"How do you get over something like this?" He hadn't really meant to say it out loud, but he was still too exhausted to keep it all together.

Li'ara looked up across the viewport but didn't make eye contact. The *Valoran* was beginning to block out the entirety of space as it slowly approached them. "We push on."

Kalian could hear the soldier in her again.

"And we destroy those bastards."

The plan seemed simple the way she put it, and Kalian didn't have the energy to hypothesise the complexities of it. He just agreed.

The next twenty minutes took their minds off it as the *Valoran* sent help. A fat looking ship, that reminded Kalian of a beetle, approached the ship. There was no communication between them as the fat ship turned around in front of the viewport. Four large panels extended at the corners, like the wings on a beetle, as it attached five cables to the *Fathom's* hull.

"There goes the paint job," Li'ara said dryly.

She was starting to sound like Li'ara again. Kalian wondered if she had buried her feelings and replaced them with the driving force of obliterating their new enemy.

The cockpit shook as the cables began to retract, pulling them into the beetle's grasp. The four wings closed around the *Fathom* and cast shadows into the cockpit. Li'ara silenced the alarms before they could begin.

It wasn't long before the *Fathom* was sitting in the *Valoran's* hangar again. Li'ara had activated the landing struts before the beetle ship put them down. An escort of six Novaarians was waiting outside the main hatch. They followed the same path as before back to the Translift and up to the command bridge. Telarrek was waiting for them. The bridge had the same hum of activity with the crew constantly interacting with their hard-light projections and consoles. The fact that they could actually touch and feel their holograms was evidence of their advancement. Humans had never been able to invent such technology and the sad thought crept into his mind that now they never would. Human history had come to an end.

Before even speaking, Telarrek unexpectedly dropped to one knee in front of them. Kalian couldn't help but be fascinated by the double-jointed nature of their legs. Even more to his surprise, the entire bridge crew stopped what they were doing and copied Telarrek's bow. Even the armed escort dropped to one knee.

Kalian turned to Li'ara but her jaw clenched in reaction. She was focusing on holding it all in. Telarrek resumed his towering height and folded his upper arms so his fists rested against where the human heart would be.

"We mourn for your kind..." He dipped his head as he said so.

Seeing that Li'ara wasn't going to react, Kalian responded. "Thank you, Telarrek." He looked around to see that the crew had all stood as well but had not resumed their stations. "And thank you for trying to help."

Li'ara's knuckles had gone white from clenching them so tightly. He wasn't sure what to do next, Li'ara looked like she might explode any minute if they continued to talk about recent events.

"What happens now?" Kalian asked just as he noticed the pure darkness beyond the giant viewport. They were already in subspace. "Where are we going?"

Telarrek turned to walk back to his central podium that was currently grounded in the floor. This had clearly sent a message to the crew as they all resumed previous duties.

"We are continuing on our original heading for the Conclave. It will take just under seven of your solar days." Telarrek was watching Li'ara while he spoke. He was no doubt watching for any kind of reaction.

Kalian couldn't blame him. The last time they had this conversation, Li'ara had not reacted very well. This time, however, she said nothing. To the others, it might have looked like defeat, but Kalian knew there was a determination in those eyes.

"Quarters have already been prepared for you. Food as well." Telarrek took his position within the podium's circumference.

Li'ara stepped forward, closing the gap between them. Kalian noticed the armed escort step with her.

"We've already discussed this. The *Fathom* will be fine," she said.

Telarrek raised his head an inch. "I'm afraid that will not be possible."

Kalian felt his heart thunder in his chest as Li'ara's hand slipped down towards her gun.

Telarrek continued as if she hadn't made the move. "Your ship took heavy damage in the supernova, and my engineers tell me your Solar Drive is in need of repair. You must stay in the quarters provided while my technicians work on your ship."

"That ship is UDC property." Li'ara faltered for a moment at the sound of her own words. There was no UDC anymore. "It's my ship. I don't want your *technicians* crawling all over it!"

All six escorts had their golden eyes fixed on the hand near her gun.

"I assure you, Lieutenant Commander, that your ship is being well looked after."

Was that what Li'ara was so worried about? UDC secrets being discovered? Kalian suspected it was more to do with familiar surroundings, not to mention the armoury.

Seeing that this did not satisfy her, Telarrek added, "You are welcome to oversee the repairs personally if you wish."

Li'ara took a breath. Kalian hoped she was seeing reason.

"That will be fine."

Telarrek bowed his head and disappeared above them as his podium rose above the bridge.

Kalian almost jumped at the sight of Ilyseal next to him. When had she arrived?

"I will take you to your quarters." Her voice was as soft as ever, though Kalian still found it hard to place that voice over the fierce look of her kind.

Ten minutes later Kalian found himself looking up a vertical walkway at a door high above. He looked at Li'ara and Ilyseal for confirmation; they definitely had to go up there.

"Explain how this works again," he asked.

"You simply step into the wall and gravity will alter around you. It may be disorientating at first but you will quickly adapt, I am sure."

Kalian wasn't convinced. He still remembered flying through the tungsten filament and into the cabin. Gravity had shifted on him then too as he went from falling forwards to falling down. The disorientation had been painful.

Li'ara let out an audible sigh and stepped onto the wall without delay. As she became horizontal her arms flapped for a second before she orientated herself to the new ground. She turned to Kalian.

"It's easy. Just step on and let yourself go. Gravity will do the rest."

What was more mind-bending was the drop of her hair. He naturally expected the copper ringlets to gravitate towards his floor but, instead, they were just as horizontal as Li'ara.

When she was halfway up he decided to follow. Doing just as she said, he stepped out and let himself go slightly limp. Without his foot touching the wall though he felt only one pull of gravity as he fell on his back. He quickly got up before Li'ara turned around at the sound of his yelp. He waved her on as he made attempt number two. Much to his relief, gravity rotated around him giving him a new look to his surroundings. It was quite possibly the strangest sensation he had ever felt. Then he remembered the outer-body experience he had in the *Valoran's* medical bay and changed his mind. Focusing back on the task at hand he continued his vertical walk with Ilyseal behind.

The first quarters they were shown to were Li'ara's. It was bigger than the *Fathom*. It had a long window that ran from one end to the other, though Kalian doubted it was glass. It was furnished beautifully with a large double bed at one end and a comfortable living space in the middle. There were two circular doors on the left that Ilyseal showed them were a bathroom and a walk-in wardrobe. Kalian recognised the style of some of the clothes but others were more alien in design. The whole thing was very human. Had these rooms been built specifically for them? Li'ara insisted on seeing where Kalian was staying. His room was only one along and identical in appearance.

"I'm going to grab six hours sleep," said Li'ara. "Then I want to see the *Fathom*." Ilyseal bowed her head in acceptance and promised to return at the allotted hour. "You should rest as well, Kalian. Do you want me to wake you when Ilyseal returns?"

He thought about it for a moment. "No. I'm gonna get some sleep. Come and see me after though. Let me know what they're doing to it." Before he closed his door he remembered the Datapad he'd left on the ship. "Could you bring back my Datapad for me? I think it's gonna be a long week."

She nodded before disappearing into her new quarters.

He wasn't really sure what he was going to do. He felt tired but the nap in the cockpit had been enough for now. He gravitated towards the extensive window, taking in the view. A large portion of it was obscured by the arc of one of the ship's giant blades. Up close he could see the glittering surface resembled a more crystalline structure, like a fused blade of diamond. He wondered what the point of the blades was. They reminded him of ancient scimitars that created a protective perimeter around the bulk of the ship.

He reached out to the apparent glass with tentative fingers. The window rippled like water in a pond. He slid down the wall, sitting on the floor with his knees up. How had this happened? How was he, a history lecturer, one of the few survivors of his entire species? Why was he here in this very room instead of having died with everyone else on Earth? He felt a tear roll down his face, tickling his cheek. His whole life had been turned upside down and he had no idea why.

He lifted his head out of his hands as his jacket floated past him. That wasn't the only thing floating either. The bed had risen off the floor with the pillows and blanket meshing into a floating ball. Ornaments from around the room slid from their positions knocking into one another. The tear on his cheek pulled away to float in front of his face like a raindrop frozen in time. Since he was still firmly rooted to the floor, he knew the internal gravity was still functioning.

He had never got used to this. It usually happened while he was asleep but the strongest effects were always tied to his emotions. Too angry, sad or even happy and this just happened. Apart from that time when he panicked in The Hub and affected the electronics in half the building. He supposed though that the last twenty-four hours had been pretty emotional.

He started to get angry at the situation; he was tired of not having any answers. He would get answers. Everything shot outwards away from him like he was the epicentre of some explosion. He stood up, a man with a purpose. He walked to the main door, subconsciously reaching out for his jacket on the floor. To his amazement, it flew straight into his open palm. He examined the jacket as if it had been a magic trick. Did he want that to happen? Did he *make* that happen? Had he actually controlled that? More questions without answers. A flicker at the window caught his attention. The stars were suddenly visible again, indicating their re-emergence into real space.

The door parted for him as he made to leave. There was only one person he could think of who had any kind of answers - Telarrek. His courage faltered somewhat when he arrived at the vertical walkway. This time he had to drop down. The path sloped down so he didn't actually need to jump over the edge, just simply keep walking and let gravity change around him. He found going down was actually easier than going up. The disorientation was minimal. He passed two other Novaarians on his way down, each one bowing their heads to him. Several flying bikes flew overhead on his journey back to the Translift, like hummingbirds. He got looks from everyone that happened by him but no one stopped him. Telarrek was telling the truth about not being a prisoner then.

His next problem was the Translift itself. The domed access panel would not respond to his handprint. Every time he tried, the dome sent a cold wave through his hand in response. He turned sharply as a life-size hologram of Ilyseal appeared next to the Translift. It shimmered as she moved her head to look down at him.

"Do you require assistance, Kalian?" she asked.

"I want to see Telarrek. I have so many questions and I need answers, Ilyseal." He hoped she would hear the determination in his voice for he couldn't wait until they reached the Conclave.

"I am afraid Charge Telarrek is indisposed at the moment."

"That's not good enough! I want to see him now."

Several Novaarians walking by turned to see what the commotion was but Kalian ignored them. He would have his answers.

"I am afraid it would be impossible to speak with him right now." Her voice remained even and annoyingly calm.

"This isn't right, Ilyseal! I deserve answers *now*. After everything that's happened today..." He couldn't form the words to describe the hell both Li'ara and he had been through.

Ilyseal looked away for a moment but the hologram projected only her body, not the surroundings. As she turned back to Kalian, her red tendrils flowed around her waist.

"Charge Telarrek will visit your quarters soon, but is currently occupied I am afraid."

Kalian's shoulders visibly sagged as he let his head roll back. He was powerless to do anything. "Fine." He walked away without waiting for any reply.

By the time he reached his room, he had a headache. Everything was still a mess from his mental outburst so that he almost tripped over a sculptured ornament on his way in. Moving aside the scrunched up blanket he grabbed a pillow and gave in to sleep.

TELARREK DEACTIVATED the privacy shield that encompassed his podium and tried to hide his sombre mood. Having dropped out of subspace he had taken the opportunity to contact the Conclave. He had been put through directly to Elondrasa, the Novaarian councillor who sat on the Highclave. There was still no news on the Laronian warship heading for the terraforming expedition and there was no way to get through to them and explain the situation.

Elondrasa had warned of the consequences they were likely to face from the other species when they found out the Novaarians had been concealing the humans' existence. There were still a lot of questions they all needed answering. Chief among them was the presence of this new threat that had the power to destroy entire solar systems.

Telarrek felt a pang of guilt while thinking about the questions the Conclave would have. Their's were born of curiosity about a species that didn't really have any long-standing effects on them. But for Kalian and Li'ara, these were questions that could shed light on why their whole race was on the brink of extinction. Ilyseal had informed him of Kalian's outburst outside the Translift. Elondrasa had been clear about bringing him back to the capital with as little interaction between them as possible.

He met Ilyseal's gaze, fully aware she knew what he was thinking. They had worked side by side for too long not to understand how the other was feeling. He wanted to talk to Kalian and tell him why he was so important to them. He could tell his second-in-command agreed with him. They had become too attached to the humans over the centuries.

"He is in his quarters..." Ilyseal predicted his question.

He took a breath, weighing his options. "As soon as the Starrillium is fixed, put us back on course. You have the bridge."

KALIAN DREAMED of being back on Earth in his lecture theatre. He was teaching his new class about the formation of Central Parliament in the twenty-fifth century and how they ended the corporate wars. He explained to a student with copper ringlets for hair that Central Parliament started by removing all the borders from the world's map. Wars and skirmishes across the world came to a halt as one governing body took power and all land and resources were shared. To enforce this new unity, all the world's armies were integrated into a United Defence Corps.

Before the red-headed girl could ask another question, the sky dropped into darkness and erupted with a growing ball of light. He saw buildings and sky bridges burst apart in tremendous flames, as waves of fire swept across the city towards them. The Golden Gate Bridge crashed into the water as it was engulfed by light. He felt his heart beating in his chest like it was trying to break free of his body.

He awoke with the feeling of falling. The lighting had dimmed in the room but he didn't remember doing it. A sudden chirp from the door brought him fully back to reality with a thud - a literal one. His body crashed down onto his bed with a soft bounce. He quickly scrambled off the mattress as if it were about to eat him. That was new. He looked up at the purple ceiling, trying to spot the alien device responsible for his levitation. The door chirped again and the lighting resumed its previous level. He took a deep breath in an attempt to clear his mind and forget his dream, along with whatever had just happened.

He opened the oval door to the looming figure of Telarrek.

"Greetings of peace, Kalian." He had both sets of hands clasped in front of him as he bowed.

"Greetings of peace, Telarrek," Kalian replied. He motioned for his new visitor to enter but Telarrek made no move.

"Actually, you might prefer to come with me..." The Novaarian moved to the side allowing space for Kalian to leave with him.

Kalian was hesitant at first. What would Li'ara say if she knew he was going off somewhere without her?

"What about Li'ara?" He looked down the corridor to her room.

"Ilyseal has taken her to the hangar to see the *Fathom*." Telarrek's voice sounded like that of an older man.

Kalian could tell there were experience and wisdom behind his golden eyes. Whether it was naivety or not, he felt he could trust Telarrek.

"Where are we going?" Kalian asked as they made their way down the vertical walkway.

"I thought you might like to see the *Valoran*."

They immediately took a turning Kalian had not been down before. The corridors were still as tall as ever, with a constant buzz of activity from working crew. They soon came to a cross-roads within the ship. In the centre of the cross was a magnificent tree-like structure that stretched almost to the arching ceiling. Its bark was similar to that of an Earth tree only it was silver in colour, with interlaced sapphires shining in the light. The roots were guarded by a railing that surrounded its circumference. It was covered in giant golden leaves that looked as big as Kalian.

"What is that?" He had to crane his neck to see the very top.

"That is the Ever Root." Telarrek looked admiringly at it. "It is from Nova Prime, our home planet." He began to walk around the railing, looking up into the hidden parts of the tree. "It changes with the seasons there, so it reminds us of home." He looked down at Kalian with large eyes.

Kalian was impressed but confused. "How does it change with the seasons if it's on a ship?"

"The *Valoran* feeds it the nutrients and light required for the specific season. Right now we are in the middle of what you would call autumn." Telarrek moved off from the tree, making a right from the direction they had come.

Kalian took one last look at the beautiful tree before moving on.

"This is our observation deck," Telarrek announced. "I like to spend as much time in here as I can. It helps to gain perspective."

The dark room curved round to the right with a panoramic window on the left. The whole view was immersed in stars and a multicoloured nebula in the centre. It was a truly humbling view.

"Why have we dropped out of subspace?"

"The *Valoran* has had to make a stop for repairs. The light from Solson's supernova has scorched a portion of our manoeuvring thrusters and damaged the Starrillium. Given recent hostilities, I felt it prudent to ensure we are at optimum efficiency in case of another attack. We should be ready to proceed within one of your hours." They both stood at the screen, taking in the awesome view. "That is a stellar nursery." Telarrek pointed to the rainbow coloured stardust.

Kalian knew that even though the cloud of gas was the size of his hand it could fit several solar systems inside. If it was moving he couldn't tell, as it appeared frozen in space. He wondered if the universe had birthed two new stars within the nebula to replace Sol and Solson. He entertained the idea that the universe might be angry at the loss of two of its children. He knew he was.

"Why is all this happening, Telarrek? I have so many questions I don't even know where to begin."

Telarrek made a very human gesture by cupping his long jaw and stroking his chin. "I am not permitted to speak to you on such matters..." He looked Kalian in the eyes. "But you are right, you do deserve some explanation." Telarrek began a slow pace along the panoramic view. "Like your species, mine too started out on one planet, Nova Prime. My kind is older than yours; evident from your level of technology and evolutionary growth." He stopped for a moment as if he was wondering what to say next. "Nova Prime has only one moon like Earth. We call it Naveen. After a hundred thousand years of evolution my people grew amongst the stars as yours did and we populated Naveen along with a multitude of other planets. However, before we ever encountered the other races of the Conclave, Novaarians were only concerned with one other species. Yours."

Kalian wasn't sure where he was going with this. He couldn't match up the timelines. "Wait. How old was humanity at this point?"

"From our four hundred years of studying Earth, it became clear to us that humanity did not exist for another fifty thousand years. Our interest in your species began long before your existence."

Now he was really confused. "How could you be so interested in us if we didn't even exist?" He was starting to think the answers he would get would only beg more questions.

"Fifty thousand years before what should be possible, we found proof of your existence on Naveen."

Kalian was speechless. He had a million more questions but couldn't form a single word.

Seeing his shock, Telarrek continued. "When we discovered Earth four hundred years ago, we were on the verge of celebrating the discovery of what we thought were the ancestors. Then we realised you had only just found a way to travel beyond your star. Solar Drive technology was *new* to you. We were, *are*, just as confused as you, Kalian.

"We have spent centuries theorising about your current state of biological and technological evolution. We do not know how humans reached Naveen before you even learned to stand upright. There is more than enough evidence to show that your kind did, in fact, evolve on Earth. That is why we have watched you for so long. Your kind is the biggest mystery in the entire Conclave."

Kalian couldn't believe what he was hearing. It made no sense at all. How could they have reached an alien moon before they even had two arms and legs, let alone Solar Drive technology?

"What did you find on Naveen?"

"Our geologists informed us it was made when our species was still living in burrows underground, but the exact age is unknown. Near the northern hemisphere, in a place called the Sea of Naveen, there is a solitary rock. It is a large rock, just bigger than the *Fathom*. It is pointed as if reaching for the stars above." Telarrek raised a hand as he looked up, visualising the location. "One side is completely smooth, too smooth to be natural. It simply came to be called, The Wall. In the centre of the stone, at around your height, is an impression..." He hesitated.

Kalian knew Telarrek must be struggling to go against his orders.

"An impression of a single handprint, a human handprint, Kalian." He picked up Kalian's hand with his lower limb and examined the space between his fingers.

Kalian thought back to the moment on the bridge when he was trying to convince Telarrek to aid Century. The fascination with the shape of his hand made sense now.

"A handprint? But how? Why?" More questions.

"Underneath the impression is an engraved language we have never been able to understand. But we did understand a particular structure within the text - a strand of DNA. Your DNA, Kalian."

How was Kalian supposed to take that? He moved away for a moment and leaned on the high bench. Had he heard that right? Even if he had, he wasn't sure what it meant.

"My DNA?" He thought back to the initial message the Novaarians had sent to The Hub with his DNA included in it. "You mean *human* DNA right? The whole double helix thing?" He thought back to his biology lessons and the image of the spiralling ladder with little spheres for rungs.

"It is almost identical to human DNA, but the karyotype on Naveen contains more chromosomes, like yours." Telarrek might as well have been speaking in his native tongue for all the sense he made.

Kalian recalled the knowledge that human DNA had twenty-three pairs of chromosomes but he wasn't confident of their purpose. Was having more good or bad? Also, genetics and biological augmentation had become a big thing over the last couple of centuries. Surely his altered DNA would have raised a flag.

"But that doesn't make sense. You're saying my DNA is different from a normal person's, but the Birthing Databank would have picked that up. If that were true, I would have spent my whole life in some UDC laboratory."

Telarrek looked away for a moment but Kalian still couldn't read Novaarian expressions. "That is because we hid you. We had been monitoring your Birthing Databank since its creation. You were not the first to be born with this special DNA. We know of two others that came before you in the centuries leading to your birth. We were too late to act, however, and your United Defence Corps took them away. We never found a trace of them after that. By the time you were born, we had already taken measures to ensure we were alerted first. It was actually Numanon who accessed the databank and altered the record."

It was just blow after blow. They had been watching him his *entire* life. Again he couldn't find the right question to ask. To think there had been two others like him. He wondered if they had experienced all the same strange things that he had. What did it mean that there were more like him?

"You see now why you are such a mystery Kalian. The species that left that handprint on Naveen were older and more advanced than the entirety of the Conclave. And the DNA imprinted on The Wall is unquestionably theirs. Why else would they leave it? Humanity's DNA is clearly the foundation for this more evolved DNA... your

DNA. You are proof that your kind is only just beginning to acquire this new state of evolution. My people have sought yours out for thousands of years believing you to be the parents of this galaxy: the ones who came before. We thought you would have answers to some of the biggest questions in the universe. Instead, we found a primitive race of *supposedly* advanced beings."

Kalian couldn't take offence at the primitive comment for it was true in comparison to them. If he had to guess, he would say Telarrek's expression was that of a sad one. He was glad Telarrek had told him this though. He imagined being told the same series of events by this Highclave and it not sounding quite so sincere.

"Do the other species within the Conclave know about us, about Naveen?"

"Yes. One of the binding pacts in the formation of the Conclave was a sharing of knowledge and history. For a time everyone was fascinated by the possibility of your kind. Every species in the Conclave examined The Wall. But no further proof of your existence was ever found. You understand this was thousands of years ago and many people believe The Wall to be a hoax or a myth now. After the attack on your planet, I informed our councillor on the Highclave. She has now informed the other members, and most likely the Conclave at large, of your discovery and our research. There may be some reprisals for keeping you a secret for so long." His face gave away no emotion as to how bad this was.

"I can see your interest in us, in me. But what about *them*?"

No further description was needed. Telarrek knew who he was referring to. "We are no closer to learning their origins. Their reasons for attacking you remain a mystery. I am confident they are not part of the Conclave, though that only makes them more of a mystery."

Kalian surmised that this must make *them* feel as alien to Telarrek as the Novaarians were to humans.

"Why did you keep us a secret?" Kalian had given up trying to figure everything out.

"We were unsure of you when we first discovered your planet. You were such a mystery we wanted time to observe you without interruption. Remember, four hundred years is not a long time for a Novaarian. Also, we were afraid of the Conclave's perception of you. Your race was thought to be a powerful one. As I'm sure your own history shows, most superior races do not coexist with lesser ones. We were afraid the other species of the Conclave would become defensive if they knew of you. As it turned out, you were not as superior as we had anticipated."

That made sense to Kalian. Human history was rife with examples of the superior destroying the weaker, even in the origins of human life with Homosapiens wiping out Homoerectus. In a way, it was a good thing they had been kept secret. Kalian could imagine the full force of the Conclave turning up on Earth's doorstep four hundred years ago, worried that the human race posed a threat.

"How old *are* you?" Kalian really hoped it wasn't an offensive thing to ask a Novaarian.

Telarrek lifted his head and gave a succession of grunts. "By your time I am nine hundred and twelve, just over half of my expected life."

Kalian took in the sight of the Novaarian again. He didn't look that old, though maybe the specks of blue around his eyes were an indication amongst their kind. That age was unimaginable to Kalian. He knew he would never get past two hundred and fifty years at the most. Although the way his life had changed recently, he would be happy to reach twenty-nine.

"Come, I shall return you to the company of the Lieutenant Commander. I believe she is still in the hangar with Ilyseal."

Kalian didn't move to leave with him.

"There will be plenty of time on this journey to learn more, Kalian. I must educate you *both* on the new society you are about to enter. I think you have absorbed all you can for one day."

And then some.

Kalian followed him back to the Translift with one last look at the magnificent nebula. Life seemed so simple and quiet looking out at the distant stars. How wrong he was.

His rage was never to be taken lightly. The command module was to be protected at all times. He himself had programmed that into every nanocelium. Acting so, the ship immediately began to move the interior sections of the ship around. A solid wall was constructed from thin air, cutting him off from the pilot and Elandar. Without him even noticing, the ship separated the two sections, leaving the command module where it was, and descending his level into the belly of the ship.

He always liked to think of it being the ship but he knew everything was directed by the subconscious of the pilot. His reaction to the escape of Kalian Gaines had been predicted. Now safely away from the command module, the new room he occupied was expanded and filled with pillars. His action in such instances was always the same. He propelled himself towards the first pillar, using his momentum to shatter it. He wasn't satisfied. The debris from the pillar was instantly reabsorbed by the ship. Nothing was wasted.

He wanted to destroy everything at once, to just let go and unleash his full potential. He felt the bulky Harness that encompassed his chest, ran down his spine and connected to his central nervous system. He hated it. The cool metal represented everything he had been fighting against. The armour that covered the rest of his body and those of his crew allowed them some measure of control by counteracting it.

He demanded more.

He lashed out with his hand obliterating six more pillars, each twice the width of himself. He continued to throw his arms out from his static position, each extension shattering a series of pillars. The armour was tough but couldn't prevent the heat he felt as he manipulated physics to form a ball of organic plasma. It floated in the palm of his hand before he unleashed it on the next pillar. It continued through destroying one after the other. He felt the armour dampen the Harness, fighting its effects.

It only enraged him more that he required the bulky exo-skeleton. The Harness was a crime against him and his people. He yelled with all the anger he had, refusing to give in to the Harness's constraints. Every pillar left standing was decimated in his cry.

It would never be over until they were all dead, especially the anomaly. The moment Kalian Gaines had fled the system he knew he was dealing with a Terran. They were always so good at running away and hiding. That was why he had created the Eclipse in the first place. Every time they attacked a new system they would begin to evacuate and thousands would slip away, but not with the Eclipse.

This Kalian Gaines had displayed a great amount of luck on his side to have escaped and survived two supernovas with such primitive technology. As the debris was reabsorbed he looked up to see Elandar standing amidst the rubble. He knew he wasn't really standing there. It would be a hologram.

"The system has been destroyed. Where these humans once called home is now a black hole." Even though he was only a hologram, and far away from his rage, Elandar looked fearful. "What are your orders, brother?"

He pondered that question for a moment. What would they do next? He had hoped to end it all with the destruction of Century. Of course, he had never told his crew of the plans he had after all this. Now he was aware of another terraforming project, with seven thousand of the humans on it, not to mention the elusive Kalian Gaines.

They had also detected the escape of the Novaarians' vessel and he was sure they would have intercepted Kalian by now. That being the case, there was only one place they would go; the Conclave. It was through this alien society that they had even found the humans in the first place. Having encountered the collection of strange species centuries ago, they had infiltrated their AI network and, through that, their individual planetary networks. Their technology was so primitive they hadn't even detected the intrusion. It was this tactic that allowed them to continue their search while constantly monitoring the Conclave's own exploration.

It had paid off.

Four hundred years ago, the Novaarians discovered Earth and

informed their superiors on the Highclave. With the distance between them, it took two hundred years for the data to reach them. It was still a mystery as to why they had kept it a secret from the others within their society. He cared not in the end though for the information was relayed back to them all the same, and they immediately began their two hundred year trip back to this region of the galaxy.

He reasoned that the terraforming group wouldn't be going anywhere. But Kalian Gaines was heading into the bosom of an alien collective that might hide him away. He had seen the karyogram of this particular *human*. He was too close. Just the idea of him surviving made his skin crawl. He had to die.

"Set a course for the Conclave. Even if we have to wipe them all out, I will kill the last of their kind with my bare hands." He thought about his crew as well. They had been cooped up on this ship for too long. He was sure they would all enjoy the R&R.

SEVEN

The first hit to his jaw wasn't so bad. He'd endured far worse in his career. It was the second hit to his kidneys that pissed him off, though. These guys obviously had no intention of fighting fair, but that was their mistake. To the other patrons of the Arc-Bar, this had become a regular occurrence with Commander Roland North. From the brief conversation before the first blow, the onlookers knew the Commander had clearly offended another UDC soldier.

Through the haze of alcohol, Roland's muscle memory miraculously reacted to the familiar scenario. Feigning more pain than had been inflicted he hunched over, fully aware of the two attackers behind and the stupid dick in front of him. Launching up with a speed they assumed the alcohol would have dulled, he brought his open palm into the attacker's throat. He didn't wait to see the reaction for he had seen it a thousand times before.

Flowing straight into his next move he ducked, bringing his leg up behind him. The attacker on his left immediately flew into the nearest table, collapsing it with a shattering of glass. Coming up from his second attack, he found the guy on his right made the expected move. Roland intercepted the swing with slightly less finesse than usual, thanks to the alcohol. Without thinking, he naturally locked the arm under his own and applied an upward pressure on the elbow. The subsequent snap of bone would have been cause to scream if Roland hadn't instantly head-butted the man into oblivion.

The lead attacker was on his knees, panting for breath while clutching at his throat. Roland dropped to one knee, thereby matching his height.

"Don't take it so seriously, kid. We're out here at the ass end of the galaxy. You can't blame a girl for looking elsewhere every now and again. Besides, I'm pretty sure I fell asleep halfway through..."

He had been pretty drunk that night, even for him. His memory of sleeping with the soldier's girlfriend was so blurry he couldn't even remember what she looked like.

Taking further offence, the young lieutenant threw another swing. Thankfully for him, Roland just wanted to get back to his drink and decided to end it quickly. Grabbing the fist mid-air, he stood up to bring his knee into the man's nose, which was the end of that. Without noticing the alarm on the faces of the other patrons, he picked up his fallen stool and resumed his drink. The automated bar flashed a holographic message across the counter in front of him: *Cut Off.*

Letting off a small curse he downed the rest of his drink and turned to leave. It was the only bar on this side of the galaxy and he couldn't afford to get banned. Turning to leave, his exit was quickly blocked by the two man-mountains standing behind him. They had clearly received augmentation to their bodies to make them so big, and it hadn't escaped him that they were wearing full armour as well. He was flattered. No one wore full armour out here. After the first two years, security had lapsed when they realised they were totally alone.

"I'm going to have to ask you to come with us, sir." Even his voice sounded augmented.

Six men with stretchers came into view and started to examine the unconscious attackers. He loved a good bar fight but he felt the feeling had passed.

No need to put these two meatheads in Medical as well.

"Fine. I think I know where we're going." This wasn't the first time he had been escorted to the captain's post on the main command bridge.

With the effects of the alcohol being designed to only last an hour he, unfortunately, began to regain his senses on the walk. The *Arclight* was a massive ship, if it could be called a ship. Despite having Solar Drive capabilities it was chiefly made to work within an atmosphere, planet-side. It acted as the main hub and living space for all personnel. Like a self-contained city, it was a constant source of activity.

Even though Roland hadn't arrived with the original terraformers he had been briefed on everything that had transpired over the last five and a half years. As with any terraforming project, they had arrived in a fleet of ships. Every ship was integral to changing the planet's environment, though the *Arclight* would be considered central operations, where the other stations could be monitored from.

Even on his escorted walk, there were scientists and engineers making their way to the hangar bay for the day's work. Most personnel would shuttle out to one of the other stations that had been placed somewhere specific on the planet. Once there, they would go about their daily routines of checking atmospherics, planetary mass, gravitational shifts and potential sites for accelerated plant growth. There was one ship however that most definitely was not a station. It maintained a geostationary orbit around Alpha and constantly monitored everything. The side of its hull read UDC HAMMER.

Roland found the name apt as that was exactly what it was. As a class C battleship, it was close to the capabilities of the *Hyperion* and the *Centurion* and was capable of hammering down a hundred kinds of hell to slag any planet or ship. It also happened to be his destination.

He estimated that he couldn't be in that much trouble since the beefcakes escorting him hadn't taken away the LX 14-02 strapped to his thigh. Although, it might just be that they didn't want to try to take it, but he wasn't sure which idea he preferred.

Thinking about his gun, he realised he hadn't changed his

uniform yet. Having finished his twelve and a half hour shift, he had immediately headed for the Arc-bar without stopping by his cabin. He was still comfortable though, as the undersuit, which reminded him of a wet-suit, had a controlled environment inside, keeping him at a constant perfect temperature. The tactical vest he wore over the top was light since he didn't have the need to carry half the gear it was designed for.

The heaviest thing he had, aside from his boots, was the flat square on the back of the vest which carried essential medical equipment. The polycrete armoured plates, that covered the different muscle groups and kneecaps on his legs, weighed less than his sidearm. He knew from basic training decades ago, that the whole suit had been made to allow for agility and speed in combat. Even if he had full armour on his torso and arms, it wouldn't slow him down much; it just took a while to put it all on.

He soon found himself strapped into a Light Raptor that shuttled them from the *Arclight* up to the *Hammer*. The view was dull and uninteresting with a grey landscape as far as the eye could see. They still had at least another five decades before terraforming would be complete. He hoped his punishment wouldn't last that long though. The airspace around the triangular hub was busy as the late shift took over from the day staff, but the Light Raptor avoided it all by flying vertically up towards the atmosphere.

With no real atmosphere yet, the transition from planet to space could easily be missed. There was no missing the *Hammer* though. It was all angles and dark plating with lights dotted around the hull. He heard the pilot give the access code before they passed through the membrane into the main hangar.

The journey up to the command centre was short with the use of the executive lift in the hangar. The journey might have been more comfortable if it wasn't so cramped with the augments he was travelling with. The door slid open to reveal a slightly larger command centre than normal, though this size was standard for this type of expedition.

Pipes lined the ceiling, flowed down the walls and disappeared under the floor with a bundle of wires. There were at least a dozen crew members standing or sitting at their various posts, poring over technical readouts from around the ship and the planet below. The monitors and holograms would have been enough to light up the whole room but Roland could still feel the heat from the spotlights above. The centre chair was occupied by Captain Fey, who sat examining the image projected by the holographic emitter fixed into her armrest.

Everyone knew this was a retirement job for her. Despite looking no more than forty-five, with her auburn hair tied into a bun, she had served the UDC for nearly a century, even as captain of the *Centurion* for a time. She would see this out for another five years and then retire to some cushy estate on Mars or one of Saturn's moons.

He stood before her with the two muscle men taking up positions behind him. He loathed protocol but knew her wrath would be worse if he broke it. Instead, he stood there and waited to be spoken to.

"Have you forgotten how to salute, Commander?" she asked, without taking her eyes off the hologram.

He sighed before giving a half-ass salute.

She flicked her eyes to the corner of the image and the emitter closed down the hologram. "Three fractured ribs, two fractured noses and one fractured arm..." The captain let her words hang in the air for a moment.

He didn't care. Medical would have had all three of them back to full health before he had even reached the bridge. She dismissed the two guards with a look before continuing. With the activity around them, it was unlikely anyone was listening.

"What am I to do you with you, Commander North? You're lucky I don't involve the Commodore in our weekly encounters. We *limited* your bar activity to once a week and now, instead of five or six incidents a week, I get one, like clockwork." She surveyed the attention of her bridge crew for a moment. "I've seen your file Commander, and I know this type of work isn't what you were trained for."

Roland knew she was lying, just throwing her weight around. In reality, he knew Fey was nowhere near the required clearance level to see his file and she was just going off a hunch. No doubt when he had been transferred with the new batch of security personnel, the Commodore and Captain Fey had received orders from the top. He imagined the orders were vague about his reason for being sent here and his record must have looked downright bizarre. It would indicate that he went from nothing to Commander overnight, with no record of previous achievements or rank. But *this* was his punishment.

"I was hoping that after six months with us you might have acclimatised to a new form of security work. But you seem determined to make trouble."

He could tell she was trying to worm some detail out of him regarding his past work in the UDC and the reason he had been exiled to Alpha. Since she hadn't asked a question yet, that wasn't rhetorical, he remained silent, trying not to yawn.

"I would confine you to the brig if I thought it would teach you anything. Instead, I'm going to make use of you, Commander."

That didn't sound promising, but what punishment could be worse than being sent here in the first place?

She stepped down from the podium and moved to stand by one of the forward bridge crew. "Are we still offline, Lieutenant?" Captain Fey asked the young cadet behind Roland.

"Affirmative, Captain. But we still can't tell which relay is down. It could be the closest. It's unlikely to be all of them."

"I want you to take a shuttle with a team of technicians to the nearest relay and see what the problem is." He was wrong, his punishment could get worse.

"What's wrong with the relays?" Roland looked at the monitor with little interested as he stroked the stubble he hadn't bothered to shave in a week.

"We've lost contact with Central Parliament and The Hub. The relays have worked perfectly for six years and now... nothing. I don't like being out of contact. The initial feedback from the *Hammer's* sensors shows no discernible faults, but that clearly isn't the case."

Roland had been briefed on the relays on his original journey out. They were deployed from the *Hammer* at predetermined points on the first flight to Alpha. The ship would have dropped out of subspace to set them up, but once all of them were active they had a straight line of communication to Earth.

"What if it's a problem on their side?" He didn't much fancy the idea of visiting every relay between here and Earth. It had taken them nearly two weeks in subspace just to get here.

"Then we have to hope they're investigating it as well. Dismissed."

The captain obviously didn't care that he had just come off shift and hadn't slept yet. With the shuttle being almost entirely automated, he really wouldn't have much to do anyway. He was already planning on picking up the eggheads and finding a comfy chair in the cockpit in which to fall asleep.

With another half-hearted salute, he turned to leave the bridge and head straight to the hangar.

"One more thing, Commander North."

Roland felt an idle threat coming his way.

"If you break any more bones, I'll give you a vac suit and a mop and you can clean the *Hammer's* hull for a month."

He indulged in a quick fantasy in which he took one of the Heavy Raptors in the hangar and just flew back to Earth. He could make more money freelancing in a year than he would in half his career with the UDC.

"Yes, Captain."

The hangar was busy with crew and hover-bots working on various Raptors and shuttles. It was quite a cluttered hangar, with multiple workstations running down the centre of the bay. Most of the engineers he passed looked like they had spent a week inside one of the Raptor's engines by the grease smeared over their faces. The data on his wrist touchpad directed him to the correct bay. The eggheads stood out in their stark white lab suits and bulky equipment.

Before he could go over and ignore them, the general alarm broke out across the hangar. Red and yellow lights flashed along the walls as different crew ran to their posts. Captain Fey's voice broke over the alarm.

"Attention all crew. This is not a drill. I repeat this is not a drill. An unidentified ship has dropped out of Solar Drive on the port side. Man your posts and stand by for orders."

He ran over to the hangar membrane with other curious crew. He wasn't really sure what he was looking at. In his time he had seen every kind of ship, whether it was UDC, separatist or commercial. But he had never seen this.

The distance made it hard to judge but he guessed it was at least twice the size of the *Hammer*. Blue ice crystals were ejected from the four large engines on either side of the ship. Every ship produced the crystals after Solar Drive; it was a by-product of igniting the Solarcite. If they were indeed the engines they were bigger than most UDC vessels. The main body was long but chunky looking. He did recognise one similar design though: the scorpion-like tail that arced over the rear section of the ship. He had seen that design on only one other ship; hell, everyone had seen that design. That particular ship had been found on Pluto's moon, Charon, four hundred and twenty-one years ago.

This was different though. It was much bigger and far more intimidating. The hull was a polished silver, reflecting the light of the distant star.

Like wasps leaving a nest, smaller ships could be seen heading down to the planet, with some breaking off in the *Hammer's* direction.

The Captain's voice sounded over the speakers again. "Every able man and woman, arm yourselves immediately. We are about to be boarded..."

Roland could hear it in her voice. The ship's sensors had probably told them what he already suspected. They weren't dealing with humans.

Soldiers poured out of the various doors around the hangar, each one heavily armed and wearing full gear. He had to hand it to them, they mobilised faster than he thought they would. Leaving the stupid engineers to gawp through the membrane, Roland was already making his way to the nearest Heavy Raptor. He found what he was looking for almost immediately. He entered the code into the weapons locker and retrieved a few of his favourite tools. Lining his vest with shock and tungsten grenades, flat sticky mines and a good old-fashioned knife, he checked and loaded an SM72 which he slung around his back. It was more primitive than a rail-gun or the LX strapped to his thigh, so it wouldn't fire charged proton particles, but its explosive rounds would make a bloody mess of everything. Ensuring he had enough clips in his belt, he turned to leave before something caught his eye. It was a black box tucked under the weapons stand with the letters LX 14-02 stamped on the side.

The protocol was strict on the use of LX calibre weapons, with only one per band five personnel. Due to their volatile nature, if misused, he understood the reason for caution. In his previous career, he had been allowed to choose his own load outs with no protocols restricting him, but he had never had the opportunity to use two photon weapons at once.

He strapped the extra holster around his thigh and charged the weapon before slotting it into place on his leg. He was very good at calculating the odds, something that came with the experience. His initial assessment of the new ship instantly told him they were outgunned, in numbers and weaponry. Crew survival would be minimal, as most didn't have the training he had, but even a rookie knew the basics of ship-to-ship combat: take the bridge.

Descending the ramp of the Raptor, he made a bee-line for the executive command lift. The membrane cut around the first craft as it entered the hangar with predatory intent. Two were able to fit in at once with space to manoeuvre. They were definitely not of human design. Displaying the same polished silver as the mother ship, they were all curves with a sleek finish to them. The cockpit windows were narrow and blacked out, preventing any view of the new intruders. Two cannons dropped out from under the belly of each craft as the hangar erupted in gunfire and explosions. The UDC soldiers didn't wait to be attacked. It was all useless though, for everything was repelled by the dense hull of each craft. Roland had already suspected this and saved his ammo for the real show.

It was the invaders turn to attack, only it wasn't what he expected. Each cannon rapidly unleashed its alien ammunition upon the hangar. It sounded more biological than mechanical. It wasn't firing projectiles or some kind of energy-based weapon. Every surface they hit was covered in giant globules of green goo. He saw two soldiers running in the opposite direction when the cannon hit the floor behind them. It exploded on impact coating both men from head to toe in the thick green gel. As they fell on all fours, the goo made a cracking sound as it solidified around them, holding them in place. One of them was completely covered but the other was stuck in a crouching position screaming for help.

New assessment: they want prisoners.

That was both interesting and disturbing to Roland. The nearest craft opened up from the bottom and he counted eight targets drop in quick succession from the ship. He couldn't believe the height they were dropping from until he saw them hit the floor. Each one slowed down right before their feet touched the ground with a visible distortion under their boots.

Taking cover behind the closest Raptor, he took a moment to examine this new enemy. They had spread out into a similar formation to UDC tactics. His immediate realisation was their shape. Bipedal like him, they had two arms and legs. A particular part of his brain was already making the assessment that they must have hinge joints, easily broken. They were of the same height, averaging at about six feet tall. They didn't look particularly bulkier or stronger than him, but their armour looked impressive. They were fully covered in shiny black armour with sleek helmets that curved around their whole face. He flagged a potential weakness that they might require something other than oxygen to breathe.

Taking a closer look he could see the gaps in the armour, where a padded undersuit was visible. Now he knew where to aim. Their weapons were long with a stock at the back for better aiming. Each one had multiple lights and dials along the side which led into the long barrel. The one in front of him flicked an unseen switch and a small scope popped up from within the gun. The side of each weapon had a blue hologram emitting an image with various readouts.

His three seconds of examination was up.

Time to skip to the good bit.

Pulling both pistols from their holsters, he lifted them to each ear and listened for the chirp to signify they were fully charged. Before he could reveal himself an enraged UDC soldier emerged from behind the crates beside him. He fired his own SM72 at the invaders, screaming a useless war cry as he did. The retaliation was swift and precise. Three quick flashes of blue light struck the soldier, burning through his armour and bursting out the other side. Roland could smell ozone steaming from the body. This changed things. They were obviously happy to kill a few who couldn't otherwise be captured.

It made no difference to his reaction though.

He deftly spun one eighty round the Raptor and dropped to one knee as he brought his weapons to bear. He was able to get two shots off before they reacted. Both shots hit their mark with the lead intruder dropping to the floor, a charred hole between his helmet and shoulder plate. The second target was propelled into a nearby crate, as the gap between his knee-pad and the armour around his thigh burst apart, separating the two. The alien's shots went wild into the air as he crumpled to the floor.

Hit and run was the best tactic when dealing with groups. Create confusion, split them up and get stuck in. Before they focused their aim he dived to the side, aiming for the cover of a technician's work-station. To keep them off balance he continued to fire in their direction with only a general aim. He saw three of his shots reach the target, but to no effect. Their armour was tough if a photon-based weapon could only make them stumble. Staying ducked down behind the station he inspected the levels on each gun. According to the levels on the side, they had already started to cool down.

Time to scatter, boys.

He pulled a tungsten and a shock grenade from his vest, priming the shock grenade to maximum with the meter on the side. Using his mouth, he pulled the pin from the tungsten grenade and felt the vibration in his hand. He knew there were only three vibrations before it would explode. After the second he threw both of them over his head behind him. He heard the mad scramble of booted feet before the metallic clinks of the grenades touched down.

Smoke and debris flew over the top of the station, along with an alien foot. Still inside the remains of the boot, the foot reminded Roland of a ninja's foot with the segmented line down the middle rather than accentuating the big toe. Their blood was red with tiny sparkles glittering in the light. Aside from the crystal-like feature, it was very much like human blood. To that end, he assumed they could breathe oxygen and the helmets were just for protection.

He knew for sure he had killed three out of the eight so far. Five more to go. Going around the other side of the station he stood up to survey the damage. The ground was charred and smoke hung in the air. The two closest targets were banging on the side of their visors. No doubt the shock grenade had knocked out whatever electronics they had inside.

Roland stepped forward, aiming a weapon at each invader. If their biological structure was as similar to humans as he suspected, the first shot would be instant death. Unleashing the charged photon particle, it impacted the padding at the back of the neck where the helmet left them exposed. Roland was only vaguely aware of the invader's head snapping forward as the vertebrae disintegrated.

Obeying his muscles memory, Roland turned, his aim already targeting another alien further away. The shot caught the invader under the arm, eviscerating his chest cavity.

Before his target even crumpled to the floor, Roland was sliding across the gap between him and the next invader. The alien turned on him but was too late to act with such a long weapon. At the last second, the alien decided to attack Roland with the butt of the rifle. That was expected. Having already holstered his left pistol he intercepted the butt and reversed the action, forcing it into the visor. With the intruder's head lifted, it was a simple matter of slipping the LX under the helmet ridge and pulling the trigger. At this range the charged particle left through the top of the helmet, having melted the head within.

The last two targets were visible beyond the dead alien that he was using as a shield. Darting his hand out to the right he shot the first one square in the visor. It didn't penetrate, but it knocked him on his ass. That gave him enough time to scope out the last target in his peripheral vision. He felt the shudder as the propped up body took several hits from what might well have been a friend, if aliens have friends. Roland pulled down the top half of the limp body and shot the alien between every gap he could see in the armour. After various body parts ejected themselves, the main body slumped to the floor. Roland couldn't help but smile at his work. Despite the armour, they were just as fragile as humans.

The one he hit square in the visor was beginning to regain his senses. Just as he got to his knees, Roland pushed his hand onto the helmet, exposing the back of the neck. Retrieving the knife from the side of his vest, he pushed down and separated the spinal cord. A quick death. Most people thought it sadistic the way Roland went about his work, just because he enjoyed it. Truth was, he just loved a good fight.

The other landing craft had moved further into the hangar now with more following. He saw more intruders dropping from the ships, followed by a staccato of gunfire. He needed to get to the bridge.

The space between him and the executive lift had become a war zone. At least a dozen men and women had been solidified in the green goo. He checked behind him only to see his intended eggheads plastered to the side of the shuttle. One of them was waving a hand through the gap in the gel.

Moving from cover to cover he made his way over to the lift unseen. The hand reader on the wall accepted his print and allowed him access. The whir of the doors masked the sound of the coming attack. The black-clad invader buried all of its force into Roland's back, pushing them both into the lift. Amid the tussle, he heard the LX fall to the floor at his feet. Turning his head to see his attacker had been a stupid move. His mistake cost him an armoured headbutt across his right eye. The blood partially blinded him, but mostly it just irritated the crap out of him.

Four strikes to his abdomen and torso knocked Roland to the floor. The blows told him one thing though; they were no stronger than the average human. He felt a hand grip the back of his vest. It was time to put their bone structure to the test. Much like the arm, the knee joint is designed to move one way and one way only. It was Roland's favourite fact about the body. While crouched on the floor he used the placement of his body to hide his right hand moving around the attacker's right heel. Before the invader could pull him up for a final beating, he pushed all his weight through his right shoulder and into the alien kneecap. He felt the bones give way under his weight. Roland decided the helmets must be sound proof since he didn't hear the inevitable scream.

The alien collapsed to the floor, falling against the door and gripping his broken leg. Making sure the fight had ended, Roland leaned over and snapped his neck. With that, the lift doors parted and the limp corpse dropped onto the command centre floor. Wiping the blood from his eye, he saw eleven guns pointed at him with Captain Fey in the middle.

He imagined he was quite the sight with blood and ash smeared on his face - not to mention the small arsenal he was wearing.

"I guess it's a party now, huh?" Roland always knew what to say in a tense moment.

With the captain lowering her weapon, the crew followed her example and relaxed for a second.

She stormed over to the dead body on her bridge. "Why have they attacked us?" She tapped its helmet with her foot.

It hadn't escaped him that she skipped the part about them being alien.

"We didn't exactly stop to chit chat, Captain. And why haven't the gun batteries fired back?" Roland dragged the body into the lift and dumped it in a heap.

"The targeting system can't locate them." The captain hadn't taken her eyes off the corpse.

"What do you mean, it can't locate them? It's the massive ship to port!" Roland hoped they didn't notice him point to starboard.

"Every time we lock on, the targeting system goes haywire and fires wild."

The captain was pacing between the nervous crew.

"They're going to find a way in here. Taking the bridge will be their first objective." He removed the sticky mine from his vest and stuck it to the inside of the lift wall. "I suggest we reach the armoury and fortify it. We can regroup with stragglers there and plan our next move."

A young looking cadet turned from her monitor. "The lift terminal is being hacked Captain. Do you want me to shut down power?"

Roland didn't give her time to answer. "Leave it. Power's about to go out anyway."

The captain shot him a curious look but he ignored her. There was a boom coming. He bent over the nearest monitor displaying the cam feed from outside the bridge doors.

The room shook with a distant explosion originating from the lift shaft. He couldn't wipe the smirk off his face at the idea of the intruders cramming into the lift before oblivion took them.

With everyone focusing on the smoke filtering through the lift door, Roland continued his assessment of the route to the armoury. "It looks clear at the moment but we're gonna need to move fast. Like right *now*."

He looked to the captain, knowing the others wouldn't move without her precious orders. What he wouldn't give for the good old days. He lived his life going from place to place between missions with resources and wealth taken care of by the UDC. He never even saw the man who gave him his mission parameters. He picked up his package from the designated drop-point and assessed the data at a secure location of his choosing. Now he had a rank and very clear superiors. At least they made him a commander. If he had been reduced to a cadet or even lieutenant he would have moved into the *Hammer's* brig on his first day.

The captain shared a look with him and nodded her agreement in his assessment. "Crash-dump everything. I don't want them getting a single shred of information off my ship. Send a ship-wide message that everyone is to head straight to the armoury."

As she spoke, two cadets quickly went to work on one of the central standing monitors. Moments later Roland and everyone else on the ship received a message on their wrist touchpad.

"We need your authorisation code, Captain."

They were all sweating, with nervous looks. They weren't trained for this kind of action. They had no, doubt, run through identical scenarios to this one, but not against such superior technology and firepower. Captain Fey tapped her code onto the touch glass. Every monitor on the bridge suddenly went dark as the internal magnets were activated, wiping all the hard drives of their data.

"Take point, Commander North."

Lead? Shit...

He didn't want to *lead* anything. He was hoping they would all run along to the armoury and he could go back to doing what he did best. He calculated the odds again and some of them weren't going to make it. All they had were their standard sidearms, which might as well have been water pistols.

"Stay on my hip. Nobody goes ahead of me and you move when I tell you to and you stop when I tell you to. Clear?" He so preferred working alone.

"Yes sir!" came the resounding chorus.

He looked at the captain mockingly. How could she put up with this crap every day? Much to their confusion, Roland didn't return their salute either. Instead, he moved over to the keypad next to the bridge doors. Now that the *Hammer* had crash-dumped all the information, the handprint pads were useless, leaving him to type in the door code into the keypad. After the little light turned green, he pulled up the list of all the door codes on his wrist touchpad.

The heavy bridge doors parted to reveal an empty well-lit corridor. The alarm had been muted now but the walls still flashed red and yellow lights. The corridors were black with white square panels placed over the top, adding to the sterile image of all things UDC. The walkway curved round to the left. Roland knew it would lead to a T-junction, from the map on his wrist. Once there he pressed against each wall, checking the corridors for threats.

It was impossible to be quiet with all the feet behind him. He held up a solid fist in the air as he stopped mid-walk. He heard the familiar sound of energy weapons not far from their location. They were making their way to the bridge already. He swivelled three-sixty, checking the surrounding doors for somewhere to hide the sheep.

"Everyone back up into cartography. We'll let them pass."

To his amazement, they didn't look to the captain for approval. Only seconds after the door slid shut they all heard the sounds of heavy boots passing by. Turning from the door he took in the room. It was spherical in shape with a white domed ceiling and low lighting. Holograms projected different star charts all over the room until one by one they fizzled out and the console lights flickered for a moment.

"That's it then," said one of the cadets. "With the star charts gone, we'll never find home..."

They were losing their morale and with it their much-needed adrenaline. Thankfully the captain stepped in because this was not his thing.

"When Central Parliament doesn't hear from us they will send ships to investigate. We just need to hold these bastards off and survive. Do you hear me? We will survive."

Roland mockingly gave her a thumbs-up. In his experience, all the words in the galaxy couldn't get you out of a gunfight. To her credit, they seemed to respond well. A few pats on the back and whispers of encouragement and they were ready to go again.

"We have a problem," said Roland. "We're close to the bridge and when they see it's empty, they *will* double back." He had already seen the solution to his problem. "The armoury is two levels below us. We're going through the emergency access hatch." He pointed to the white tube that cut through the height of the room at the back. It was lined in broken red bars from top to bottom with **Emergency Hatch** stamped across a rectangular panel. "Hopefully they don't know about them yet, but we still need to move fast."

Captain Fey was already pulling the manual lever to open the tube. Once accessed, the entire tube lit up to reveal a ladder on the far side. Roland inspected both ways before climbing in and descending.

On his way down he heard the sounds of combat in the corridors around them. The next level down was labelled LAB 4. He had no idea what it was and he didn't really care. It was the sounds inside that concerned him; heavy boots stomping around as they ransacked the contents of the lab. He tapped the foot above him who did the same until everyone had stopped. Pushing out from the ladder he looked up, placing a finger to his mouth and pointing to the door. If they could go undetected they only had to reach the next floor.

The tube door gave a *thunk,* right before it opened.

There was a moment's hesitation before the alien intruder roughly grabbed Roland's tactical vest and pulled him into LAB 4. Hoping to give them extra time he threw himself off the ladder as he was pulled. His added momentum caused the both of them to tumble across a table, knocking off glass vials and electronic equipment.

Once both had crashed to the floor, Roland leaned round to see the emergency hatch. One of the cadets was staring at him, unsure what they should do.

"Keep going! Don't stop!"

A four-fingered hand gripped his throat. The pressure of his attacker's knee dropped onto his chest, pinning him to the floor. His instincts kicked in as his muscle memory responded. Using all his strength, he quickly brought his left hand to the alien's wrist and his right hand to the alien's elbow. Without stopping the pincer motion, he pushed both hands until the arm snapped. The alien collapsed onto him until Roland brought his elbow up into the padded material under the helmet. Gripping its throat, the alien stumbled backwards taking the pressure off his chest. Everything below the elbow was swinging unnaturally. Not letting up, Roland grabbed the side of the helmet and forced it into the counter. One quick release of the LX under his arm ended the struggle. He stopped for a moment, panting to regain his breath.

Looking back to the hatch he could see it was empty. He felt relief, knowing he was no longer responsible for them. Responsibility was like a bad jacket, it just didn't fit right. An idea occurred to him now he was without his excess baggage. If he could get back to the hangar and reach the shuttle he had intended to pilot, he might be able to find his way home. The *Hammer* would have uploaded the coordinates to the nearest relay ready for their departure. If he could reach the relay he should technically be able to find the next one and so on until he reached Earth.

It made sense for there was no way they were going to win against these odds. Normally he preferred a fight with the odds stacked against him but, without alcohol, the odds were all too clear. He had done his duty by at least saving the captain. Screw the commodore. This way he could come back with real forces and have himself a proper fight. That's what he told himself at least. He would most likely find the first bar he came across and never leave. He'd made up his mind though.

Leaving LAB 4 he made his way down the corridor. He had to descend two levels to find his way back to the hangar and he didn't fancy getting pulled out of another hatch. Meeting no resistance, he entered a nearby lift and keyed in the hangar. He retrieved the SM72 from his back and checked the number on top. The number seventy confirmed it was fully loaded and ready to go.

A few seconds in and the lift shook, the lights flickering before the sound of grating metal penetrated the walls. It came to a stop halfway down the next level.

I could kill for a drink right now.

It amused him that those words were very true.

He would have to climb out on this level and find another way down. He wasn't sure what had caused the breakdown but it was obvious that fighting had broken out all over the ship now. Easing the doors aside with his fingers, he cracked them open an inch and checked the other side. The floor was at chest level now, forcing him to throw his gun out before climbing out after it. There was blood on the wall at the nearest intersection. Unfortunately, the bloody handprint next to it had five digits. More evidence of them losing this fight.

Before committing himself to the next corner he stepped back, taking cover behind two vertical pipes. He heard them before he saw them. The captain's voice gave them away as she directed the bridge crew to the armoury. He remained hidden, choosing to stick with his own mission of getting the hell out of there.

Roland recalled the layout of the ship and was impressed he could remember almost every floor. To double-check, he brought up the map on his wrist touchpad. He was right. There was another lift, on the second corridor up ahead. He moved off in the direction of the lift when he heard another noise; screaming. It came from the direction the bridge crew had gone. Intermingled with the screams were the sounds of gunfire and a distinct energy weapon. Roland tried to block it out and told himself to stay put. The lift was just ahead.

Son of a bitch...

He didn't know exactly why, but he was now backtracking to the corner he had spotted them from. This whole scenario would have been different if the Arc-bar didn't sell alcohol that could only last an hour. If he was still good and drunk he would probably be on that shuttle right now. Roland couldn't quite convince himself of that though. The reality was closer to him being locked up in the brig for telling the captain to go space herself.

Turning the last corner to their location he heard the familiar organic sound of the green gel. Several screams were cut instantly short as they had most likely been solidified. Peeking round, he saw the remains of the bridge crew hiding in doorways and shooting wildly down the corridor. He counted seven intruders at the other end making steady progression. The captain's photon weapon had obviously given the aliens caution after what Roland did to their first landing party. Sadly, the captain was a crap shot. Even when she aimed, it missed them by a couple of feet. Further down he saw the green goo had solidified over three of the crew. He surmised that the intruders must have the goo weaponised in some sort of grenade.

He turned away, considering his options again. The lift would probably be there by now.

"They're advancing!" one of the crew shouted.

Roland decided to stop thinking and just react. While he had been thinking about heading back to the lift, another part of his brain had already planned his attack. He broke the corner in a run drawing his dual LX side-arms as he did. With the left pistol, he kept his finger down on the trigger, causing the red flashes of charged photons to create an almost single beam. He was more conservative with the right, choosing his individual targets.

The invaders dived for cover as the photon particles went everywhere. His right pistol hit the intended target in the neck, almost severing the head. Roland looked up to see the thick black line on the ceiling. He had been waiting for that. Roland's left pistol suddenly cut out with the levels on the side flashing a warning. Avoiding the retaliating fire, he slid across the last couple of metres with his feet out in front of him. The motion was smooth and calculated. Before pushing back up, he flung the left pistol down the corridor, towards the invading group, like a grenade. Now back on his feet, he wasted no time shoving his elbow into the shatter-glass and hitting the emergency door control. The resulting thud came from the black line in the ceiling as the two-feet thick blast door closed shut. Three seconds later they all heard the LX 14-02 reach critical level and release its charged payload at once. The explosion boomed against the blast door but it showed no signs of stress.

Captain Fey was the first to come out of cover. "Thank you, Commander." She wiped the sweat from her head. "What is that stuff?" She pointed in the general direction of where the green goo had encapsulated four of the crew.

Roland wondered if they had been killed in the blast or whether the goo had protected them. "It looks like they want most of us alive." He returned his weapon to its housing on his thigh. "We still need to get to the armoury. It won't take them long to find a way around the blast door."

Taking notice of the bridge crew, he saw a young man, a lieutenant from the insignia on his uniform, accessing a terminal on the wall.

"Can you find the Commodore, Lieutenant?" the captain asked.

The young lieutenant flicked his eyes to the corner of the screen, activating the command module. They were wasting time. They should forget about the commodore and the chain of command - right now was about survival. Counting the heads he knew they wouldn't all fit in the shuttle, let alone with that fat bastard of a commodore. Roland considered just walking away now, while they were crowded around the monitor.

"Inquiry. Location: Commodore Landis."

The screen responded with an image of a corridor filled with smoke and bullet holes. Amongst the dead bodies strewn on the floor, the monitor highlighted in red a larger body slumped against a wall. Next to it the word DECEASED was flashing.

"Guess that makes you the boss." Roland checked his vest to take in an inventory.

He had one tungsten grenade left, two shock grenades and his belt had two fully loaded magazines. The barrel of the LX on his thigh felt hot to the touch. He would need to leave it a while to cool down. He only had the one left now.

Roland pushed the lieutenant to the side. "Let me see that." He took over the monitor, flicking the image to the hangar bay.

The camera was high on the wall looking down from one of the corners. He expected to see chaos and fighting, the way he had left it earlier. There had been at least a hundred soldiers flood into the hangar when the invaders arrived. The view was very different now. The human survivors were being marched at gunpoint into the alien vessels.

This was bad. There was no way he could reach the shuttle now. He had been planning on using the fight as a distraction to escape. There were few options left to them now and he was running through them, working out consequences in his mind. They could go for the armoury and hope to maintain a foothold there. That sounded good until he ran the whole scenario through and couldn't reach a viable ending. Even if they made it, how long would they last? There was no food or water in the armoury, meaning they would have to leave their foothold to find supplies. If the aliens continued their assault, the armoury would eventually run out of ammo and who knew what other tech the invaders possessed? It would only be a matter of time before they controlled the ship and then killing them would be easy. All they would have to do is switch off the life support.

They would have to move around to survive and that wouldn't work, for there are only so many places you can go on a ship in space. Thanks to being sober he had already ruled out a frontal assault on the hangar. The last scenario that came to mind was a familiar one.

Callisto.

The second largest moon orbiting Jupiter and home to the most secure bank in both solar systems. The bank had been built into one of Callisto's many craters. Shaped like an ancient wagon wheel, the installation spread out across the crater with the vaults in each arm. Central Parliament hadn't wanted the news to get out that its most secure bank had been taken over by the latest group of separatists.

Hence the need for Roland North.

It was his job to regain control of the bank quickly and quietly and remove all threats to Parliament. He had run through multiple scenarios to gain entry to the bank and found it truly was impenetrable. It had been an inside man that had allowed the separatists to take over in the first place, and he didn't have one. Like now, he could only see one option for moving forward.

At the time, he had deliberately made no attempts to subvert the proximity alarms when landing his ship on one of the arms. The automated turrets had only taken five seconds to cycle round and blow the craft apart. Of course, he had already left the ship and was being pulled in by Callisto's gravity, in free fall. Using Mem-jelly to break his fall, he landed on his back in the bubble of blue jelly and pulled himself free as it began to decay, allowing him to float above the moon's surface. The Mem-jelly could only be used with a breather on, as it would suffocate the person within before they could break free.

The trick was making it look like a real attack. Planting charges under the main hub, he continued to detonate them, despite knowing it wouldn't be strong enough to breach the hull. A minute later three armed men, in vac suits and suction boots, surrounded him. As far as they were concerned it was a botched rescue attempt and he would be added to the hostages.

The only scenario left to him had worked. It was ultimately a risk but he had to rely on his training to get him through. His instructors had always told him that it didn't matter how many guns or grenades he had: *he* was the weapon. The separatists had taken him inside the very place they were trying to keep secure - from people like him.

As he had then, Roland saw this as the only option left to him. He would have to allow them to capture him and hope he could figure something out on the other side. Then there was the matter of the bridge crew and the captain. He knew they wouldn't be confident enough to go through with his plan.

So he wouldn't give them the choice.

As predicted, the sound of heavy boots was audible down the corridor. The sneaky bastards had already found a way around the blast door. No doubt the fire-fight had attracted more of the invaders. The bridge crew became antsy again as they checked the level of ammo left in their sidearms.

Moving away from the monitor, he stood at the corner of the corridor with the crew and the blast door to his back. He quietly removed the shock grenade from his vest and set it to the highest setting again. They were mostly used for scrambling electronics but, on the highest setting, it would render a human being unconscious for about an hour. He just hoped they would be found in that time. He let the canister roll from his hand and watched it come to a stop in the middle of the bridge crew. Captain Fey looked to Roland with shock, unable to comprehend his course of action. Before she could react the grenade flashed once, stunning every one of them by attacking their central nervous system.

Roland felt the implant in the frontal lobe of his brain fight the onslaught of electrical attack. It was designed to wake him up after ten seconds should he ever be knocked unconscious. The surgical procedure was standard for everyone in his specific line of work. He was aware however that a stun grenade would temporarily short-circuit the microscopic device, stopping him from waking up so soon. The pain in his forehead was blinding, with an intensely sharp pain burrowing into his temples. Five agonisingly long seconds later he joined the bridge crew on the floor as a numbing darkness swallowed him whole.

EIGHT

Whether it was to take her mind off recent events or focus her thoughts he wasn't sure, but their second day aboard the *Valoran* turned into quite a painful one for Kalian. It was impossible to tell the difference between day and night on a starship but, judging from how tired Kalian felt when Li'ara woke him up on the second day, he guessed it to be early morning. She had insisted that they begin training immediately if they were to even hope of surviving whatever came next. He had to admit it, his life had taken a violent turn since he was forced out of his lecture theatre.

In just her undersuit, with her boots taken off, she had cleared away space in the middle of his cabin. Being as spacious as it was, that didn't take too long. He sat on the edge of his bed in just his trousers hoping to God that aliens had decaf. His thoughts were hard to keep hold of as Li'ara began stretching the various muscle groups in her body. Li'ara was attractive and he was sure no man could deny it, but the tight undersuit made it a lot harder to concentrate.

"Are you ready?" She ominously cracked the knuckles in her right hand.

"Ready for what?" Kalian was pretty sure he knew the answer but he was just stalling for time.

195

He had taken part in hand-to-hand combat before, in his teens, while experimenting with different ways to sharpen his focus and gain control over his *thing*. He didn't like the idea of hitting Li'ara though.

"I had one last order before the UDC..." She looked away for a moment, stretching her arm as a distraction from where that sentence was going. "...I will protect you to the best of my abilities, Kalian. But I don't know what's out *there*, I don't know what's coming, and I might not always be there when I'm needed. I wouldn't be doing my job right if I didn't train you in some self-defence." She reached down and touched her toes. "We've got just under a week and I intend to make sure you can at least throw a punch."

Kalian could empathise with her situation. Li'ara had lost everything and was now clinging to the last piece of normality she had left - her orders. Between them, they had no idea what kind of life they could make now. Their whole culture had vanished in a single day. Nobody knew how many survivors there were - if any. For all they knew, they could be the last man and woman in the galaxy. He tried not to let that thought get away from itself.

This Conclave they were about to enter was a completely new society, with its own rules and laws, not to mention all the new species. How were they expected to fit in or adjust? Even when he was presented to the Highclave, he had no idea what was expected of him. He couldn't tell them anything they didn't already know from their centuries of studying humans. Telarrek had promised to meet up with him again on this long journey, and he would be sure to ask him more questions.

"Attack me." Li'ara stood perfectly still with her arms by her side.

Kalian could tell, from her stony expression, she was being serious. He stood up from the bed, quickly stretching his shoulder joints and flexing his chest muscles. He noticed Li'ara's brief attention but she remained silent. He bit back a smile and just lunged at her with an unplanned attack. He pulled his punch, afraid of hurting her too much, which was his mistake.

Like a snake striking its prey, Li'ara reacted with deadly speed, pushing Kalian's fist wildly off target. Without stopping, she landed the edge of her open hand onto the carotid artery in his neck, causing his head to spasm around her hand. In the same motion, she used his momentum against him by wrapping her right hand around the back of his head and spinning him, only to force his face down on the floor. To finish the move, she dropped knee-first onto his back, pinning him.

To Kalian, it had been a dizzying blur of pain and humiliation. If he hadn't had the air forcibly removed from his lungs, he would have verbally expressed his discomfort.

"Again." Li'ara pushed off his back and resumed her previous position. "This time I'll attack you..."

Kalian slowly rose to his feet rubbing his injured neck.

"Kalian." She waited until his full attention was on her. "I am going to attack you and I will not hold back. It will hurt. You need to know that."

Why was she telling him this? Was she trying to unnerve him and put him off? Either way, he felt the rush of adrenaline at the thought of the coming attack. He braced himself, unsure of what she might do next. His fight or flight response was battling with itself - should he evade or fight back? Feeling the pain in his back, he decided to fight back.

Li'ara moved with the same whiplash speed as she stepped within arm's length. His reaction was instinctive but also out of his control. He raised his hands in a clumsy attempt to defend himself from the expected pain of Li'ara's blows. Before she could land a single hit, Kalian felt a shiver pass through his spine and into his hands, making his arm hair stand on end. He felt the sensation leave through his hand at the same moment Li'ara flew across the room.

Tumbling end over end, she rolled into the sofa on the other side of the room. Kalian couldn't move. What had he done? How had he done it? He stood in shock as Li'ara used the sofa as support to stand up. Her copper hair fell over her face like a mop.

"I knew it..." She flicked her head back to remove the hair. Li'ara didn't appear to have suffered any injury, though she did sit on the sofa rather than walk back over.

"I'm so sorry..." He didn't know what to say. This *thing* was starting to get out of control.

To his surprise, Li'ara sat there with a smile on her face. "Don't be. I was hoping something like that might happen."

Now he knew why she had been psyching him out. She wanted him to be aware of the pain he was about to experience. He thought back to their conversation about the night his parents died. His body was responding to a threat in a way he couldn't explain.

"How did I do that?"

He looked down at his hands as if some answer might be found there. They appeared like normal hands, with no marks or abnormalities, but he had definitely felt the sensation resonate from them. He kept flicking his fingers, trying to shake off the tingling feeling.

"I have no idea, but you need practice." She strained her neck to the side as if it pained her.

Practise?

How could he practise what he didn't understand? How could he practise something that was instinct?

KALIAN AND LI'ARA spent the next two days running through the same routines. She would wake him early and practise hand-to-hand combat. They would always start slowly, moving through different routines, allowing Kalian to learn the attack and defensive stances without Li'ara being flung across the room. After becoming more proficient they would increase the speed and eventually flow into sparring without predetermined moves. It allowed him, eventually, to experience pain in a threatening situation and learn to hold back.

It was hard at first. Every time he perceived a threat he could feel the tingling sensation build in his spine, eager to be unleashed. He couldn't be sure but at one point he thought he had blocked one of Li'ara's blows without actually touching her. When she landed a hit he often felt the shiver flow through to his palms ready to be pushed out. He didn't manage to hold it in every time but he was learning the feel of control.

They would do this until Ilyseal arrived with food for lunch. Though hesitant to begin with, they soon loved the food she brought. It reminded them both of steak, though the animal certainly wasn't a cow. Ilyseal had told them it was a species similar to deer whose origin was Nova Prime. Being a tint of orange, Kalian wasn't convinced it was edible, but it soon grew on him. After lunch, Li'ara had a different idea of how to exercise his apparent abilities. Kalian wasn't always fond of what happened next. Using various ornaments and the occasional boot, Li'ara would throw the different objects directly at his head.

They soon learned that his reaction would vary depending upon his perception. Through this, he was able to gain some measure of control, however tenuous. If he felt the object posed a serious threat, he could repel it with the same shiver that ran through his hands. After being hit on the head multiple times he finally learned to recreate the feeling, now that he knew where it came from. After the hours of practice, Li'ara would leave to check on the *Fathom* and have a shower. She suggested he spent the time in a form of meditation to try to learn a greater control. He often gave up in preference of reading his Datapad and looking at images of Earth. He threw the pad away in frustration, however. What good was it to look at a dead planet and read about a history that no longer mattered? History was supposed to influence the future, to provide a learning curve for the generations to come. Now it was just another black hole in space.

Kalian had told Li'ara everything Telarrek had explained on the observation deck. This subject held a lot of their concentration. They constantly speculated on the origins of The Wall and what it could mean. They exhausted all avenues of what Kalian's DNA could allude to and whether that was responsible for his abilities. They avoided the topic of what their future would hold for them and the human race, whatever was left of it. Most frustratingly though, neither of them could fathom why they had been attacked in the first place.

It was on the third night that Telarrek arrived unannounced while they were eating the Novaarian equivalent of a salad, though Kalian found it a bit tart for his liking; not to mention the fact that the leaves constantly moved on his plate. Saying very little, he told them he wanted to show them something. It was either that or they both remained in his cabin to finish the night off with more sparring, and neither of them wanted to give up the chance of asking Telarrek questions. On their way out he reflected on the last three days of practising. He was impressed with his newfound measure of control as well as learning to fight. He was still no match for Li'ara though.

After descending the vertical walkway, they were presented with two of the sleek hover bikes he constantly saw flying above his head. Standing next to one was a Novaarian they had never seen before.

"This is Namek." Telarrek gestured to the guarding Novaarian.

He was similar to Telarrek, though the freckles around his eyes were red rather than blue. Like other Novaarians he wore the purple dress wear with the multicoloured armour plating. One exception he found, however, was the milky white tendrils that sprouted from above all Novaarian mouths. Namek's facial hair, as it were, hung low beneath his jaw like a moustache. Kalian found himself wondering if they cut these tendrils but he couldn't help but imagine it to be painful.

"Namek will control your sled, Lieutenant Commander. I will take Kalian. But do not worry; we are going to the same place." Telarrek gestured for Kalian to take his place on the long bench of the sled, as he sat in the front.

The controls reminded him of a bike with the handles extending horizontally from the main console. He peered round Telarrek to see the different readouts but was dismayed that he still couldn't translate the Novaarian language. Li'ara was able to translate whole sentences now.

He looked over as she took her own place behind Namek. A hum emanated from the cylindrical thrusters at the back as the sled slowly rose higher into the huge ship.

"It's just Li'ara." They all turned to her as she spoke over the rising hum. "I'm the Lieutenant Commander of nothing, so it's just Li'ara now."

Telarrek paused a moment as he considered her words. His response was a short bow before both sleds accelerated away. It was the first time he had heard Li'ara say anything like that. It made sense in a sad way. There were no more ranks or orders to be given. She was most likely the last UDC soldier alive. He empathised with her pain in the matter, so it must have been especially difficult to say that in front of them, to make it all the more real. He would speak to her about it later.

The sled ride was exhilarating. Both Novaarians controlled the hover machines with great skill as they navigated corners and other oncoming sleds at speed. They flew through different sections of the *Valoran* that opened up from the arched corridors into giant domes with multiple levels, all connected by bridges. The ship's size would never cease to astound them. The activity below was constant, though Kalian couldn't figure out what they were all doing. Everywhere they looked, Novaarians were busy using various touch-holographic equipment and floating consoles that appeared to follow them. He liked the consistent theme of plant life, however, throughout the ship.

After flying for nearly fifteen minutes, the sleds set down in front of the largest circular door they had seen so far. Like the other doors on board, this one was cut down the middle with an S-shaped divide. This larger door, however, had three horizontal bars spread across the width. Telarrek's handprint was all that was required. The bars slid into concealment within the walls and the door parted in half, releasing a small hiss.

The sight would have been more breathtaking if either of the humans knew what they were looking at. Telarrek took the lead as Namek remained with the sleds. Once past the door, it closed behind them with three distinct clicks as the bars locked into place. The size of the room made every other part of the *Valoran* appear small in comparison. They were confronted by a metallic sphere the size of a football field. At least he assumed it was a sphere from the portion he could see. It was covered in smaller circles raised against the surface, each one big enough to fit a fully grown man inside. The sphere itself sat inside a pit like a golf ball resting on a tee.

Massive cables connected the top hemisphere to multiple points across the room, before disappearing into the walls. These dark cables were ribbed in metallic rings, the same silver as the sphere. The base was surrounded by the same holographic console as the one Telarrek had used in the observatory. The room itself was dome-shaped to match the giant sphere it housed.

It was eerily silent. For such a large piece of machinery, it made no sound. They followed Telarrek deeper into the dome before he turned to them.

"*This* is a Starrillium..."

Kalian felt like he had heard the word before but couldn't place it. Li'ara's expression showed a similar thought.

"This *is Valoran*." Both humans remained confused. "You wondered how our ships travel through subspace without locating a star first - this is how." His upper arm made a sweeping effect as he took in the sphere.

"This is your engine?" Li'ara asked.

Telarrek seemed to chew over the question. "Of sorts. A Starrillium is the heart of all Conclave ships, at least ones large enough to house them. Intrinium will always require the magnetic fields generated by a star. That will never change as we cannot alter its nature. Instead, we create the *stars*. This particular star is called *Valoran*."

Kalian and Li'ara looked at one another somewhere between shock and awe. Kalian wasn't sure he had understood Telarrek's words. Was he saying this giant sphere housed a star?

"That's why you don't need an actual star," Kalian said. "You charge the Solarcite from *that*." He pointed to the god-like machinery in front of them.

"The shell harnesses all magnetic fields given off by *Valoran* and channels them into the main engines for Intrinium ignition." As he explained, his long finger followed the path of the nearest large cable.

"How did you even birth a star, not to mention keeping it so small?" Li'ara asked.

INTRINSIC

Telarrek let off a guttural chuckle. "If I knew that I wouldn't need my engineers. Most of what you see is required to harness the magnetic fields, but great measures are taken to ensure our protection from the radiation and, of course, the heat."

They slowly began the long journey around the star's circumference, taking in the magnificence of such technology.

"Telarrek." Kalian knew he would never run out of questions. "When we reach the Highclave in a few days, what exactly is expected of us?" He couldn't maintain eye contact with the Novaarian though due to straining his neck.

"They will have questions for you. No doubt some will be about your space travel in reference to Naveen. I imagine some of the species may be a little... suspicious of you. And of course, there will be the matter of Alpha NL-2204."

Kalian's emotions were mixed on the subject of the terraforming planet. He was elated to think of survivors but he couldn't help the bad feeling that they might be in danger. If these Laronians didn't kill them, then this new enemy certainly would.

"Any word on them?" Li'ara looked as doubtful as he did.

"I am afraid we will not learn more on the matter until we arrive at the Conclave. But do not be concerned for I am confident the Highclave will see to their safety as we have to yours. I imagine the main topic of discussion will be your invitation into the Conclave itself. Your numbers are sadly few now, but it cannot be denied that you are an intelligent race, regardless of how you discovered faster than light travel."

"Will they give us a new home? A planet?" Kalian hadn't quite got his head around the size of this Conclave and how much of space it consumed. It didn't seem unreasonable to think that they would have a few planets that weren't being used. Alpha NL-2204 was an example.

"I cannot speak on their behalf but, once we have shared all our knowledge on your kind, I am sure they will do what is best."

Li'ara didn't look so confident about Telarrek's appraisal. She just didn't like the idea of having her fate in someone else's hands, especially alien hands.

"Before you sleep tonight, Ilyseal will bring you both a data module. I suggest you spend the remainder of the journey learning everything you can about the Conclave and our various cultures."

They took one last look at the Starrillium before making to leave. Kalian couldn't believe how close he was to an actual star. To think... if the shell ever cracked. Even an inch would melt everything inside the dome within seconds. He couldn't help but think of the dangers of having an imprisoned star for an engine, regardless of its size.

THE LAST THREE days had been boring as shit. Not to mention crowded and smelly. Along with nearly a thousand other people, Roland North had been stuck in what they guessed to be some kind of cargo hold. Despite the boredom, they had managed to learn a few key facts about the current situation. Via ventilation shafts on either side of the hold, they had managed to make contact with the other prisoners in what must have been more cargo holds. As big as the ship was, it clearly wasn't designed to hold seven thousand prisoners. The fact that they hadn't been stopped from communicating with each other told Roland that they weren't considered to be threats. He could use that.

A walkway above them lined the square hold and had two bridges across the centre. It was always occupied by at least twenty alien guards. Humans had always known aliens existed, thanks to Charon, but it didn't make the reality of them any less disturbing. There had been no communication from them and they never removed their headgear. The only contact they had was from six machines that hovered into the hold every day with water and some kind of sludge that reminded him of porridge. After the first two days of nobody eating the sludge, it eventually became pretty appetising. At the end of the third day, there had been none left.

With no beds or furniture of any kind, people were sleeping

wherever they could fit, some using each other's limbs as pillows. He looked down the side of the wall to see Captain Fey occupying the top right corner of the hold, along with what he had learned to be some of the leading scientists and engineers from the planet. It was hard to miss them with the augmented soldier towering over the edge of the group. His muscles were more like tumours with worms under the surface.

This group had naturally formed a leadership role within the masses. Not that there was much to lead, he surmised. There was nothing for them to do except theorise and plot their escape, which he had already assessed to be futile.

Roland didn't care that no one wanted to listen to him. He couldn't blame them really as he still remembered what happened after he woke up. As the colours of reality seeped back into his vision he remembered someone close by shouting to the captain. His head was still pounding from the shock grenade and he was a little embarrassed at being the last to wake up. While he was still disorientated by the surroundings, and the mass of people huddled around him, Captain Fey strode through the throng until she was practically on top of him.

"You son of a bitch!" was all she had said before punching him square in the face.

Three days later he still had the red line across the bridge of his nose. Roland had explained his reasons for the way he allowed them to be captured, but nobody cared. It was even worse when, looking around, he could see no way of escaping their captors. He had been relying on some weakness to present itself but it was hard to plan anything with a thousand people talking around you. He had been stripped of his weapons and gadgets but he had expected that. He had been left in his fitted suit, with the armour and belt still attached, but he clearly wasn't considered much of a threat without his toys. Their mistake.

Roland wasn't sure if anyone else had noticed but, from the subtle vibrations he felt in the back wall, he guessed they were in subspace. They must be close to the engine for him to feel its hum. With time on his hands, he spent most of the fourth day chewing this over. If they were currently using Solar Drive then they were heading somewhere deep into space. If it was Earth, they would most likely have reached it by now in such a big ship, so that meant they were going somewhere else. He didn't like the idea of that. No way was he going to be some alien's slave or pet.

To act now though would be foolish. While in Solar Drive he would have nowhere to go, and he doubted he could pilot the whole ship. This was all moot anyway given that he had no plan of escape yet. Not to mention the seven thousand humans aboard. He still wasn't sure what he wanted to do with them. If he did escape, would he help them as well? Getting off this ship would be hard enough without having to sneak thousands of people around as well.

He caught the augment looking at him with no lack of disdain on his face. Roland's trick with the shock grenade had got around fast and made him as popular as their captors. Looking at the goliath of a man, he felt an idea trying to present itself but it eluded him. If only he had a drink, just a drop of alcohol, to wet his imagination. Instead, he was left with a headache and an itch to start a fight with the ugly augment.

Roland let sleep take him in the hope of his subconscious forming the plan he couldn't grasp. Despite the crowdedness, he was still given a wide berth as he slept propped up against the vibrating wall. The next morning, if it was morning, he woke up with no idea. He went through his normal routine of walking around the different huddles, stretching his muscles. He needed to be ready. At the allotted hour the six hovering mechs floated into the hold with the rations of water and sludge. He saw the guarding augment make a beeline for the nearest mech and the leaders following behind. They always got first serving but nobody said anything. She was the captain after all.

Now he had an idea.

He spent the rest of the fifth day formulating the plan before he would take it to the leading group. He would need them on board if it was to work out. On the sixth day, he had the idea ironed out. Like most of his plans it was going to hurt.

Early on he approached the corner group with his eyes on the prize. He knew they had to act now for, at some point, while they were sleeping, the hum of the engine had stopped. Captain Fey saw him coming but ignored him as always. He walked right up to the augment, his head only reaching the giant's chest. Roland spoke just loud enough to be heard behind the block of muscle.

"I know how we can get off this boat."

"Somehow I doubt that," the captain replied.

The augment moved aside, allowing him a view of the whole group. He counted only nine in front of him but knew, from what he heard via the ventilation shafts, that there were team leaders in the other cargo holds.

"You notice the lack of vibrations?" Roland looked at the wall on their right.

The captain gave him an appraising look. "We came to the same realisation. We've been in Solar Drive for the last week."

"Not anymore." Roland let his words hang in the air for a moment. He wanted them to think he had a plan, that maybe he'd had a plan all along.

"Get to the point, Commander." The captain took a sip from the sachet of water they had been rationing.

"I don't know where we are but I know our chances of survival will be greater out there than in here." He swivelled his head to encompass the patrolling guards above them. "When the mechs arrive today, I'm going to trash one. I need your boy here to step in and try to stop me." He thumbed the looming bodyguard.

The captain frowned at his explanation, along with the other leaders. "You'll have to forgive me if I don't see where you're going with this. Your plans don't usually work out for the rest of us, although I would like to see Lieutenant Rydeck here 'stop' you."

The augment gave Roland a smirk of pleasure at the idea.

"It's simple. I cause a big enough fuss that they have to remove me from the general population. Once on the outside, I break free and figure out a way to release everyone else."

The captain's condescending smile told him she had found a flaw in his plan. "And how exactly are you going to break free? They'll come in here and take you away either at gunpoint or in bonds."

He usually liked to keep his little advantages to himself but there would be no hiding this one.

"Right before they break us up, the Lieutenant here is going to hit me hard enough to knock me out. If I'm unconscious they won't feel the need to bind my hands. Ten seconds later I'm out that door." Roland pointed to the thick rectangular door the mechs always came through. "And we are one step closer to getting out of here."

Captain Fey looked at him curiously for a moment. He knew what she was trying to figure out. "You have a Rem-plant." She didn't ask.

He let the others sit in wonder at the captain's statement as his only reply was a wink at her. She didn't look convinced and he couldn't blame her for not trusting him.

"I know it's a gamble, but it's my gamble. If it doesn't work, you get to watch muscles here throw me a beating."

That was his last effort. Whether they decided to help him or not he would go through with it. He was doing them a favour by letting them in on his plan, and this way they would be ready at least. Besides, a thousand people can make a pretty good distraction while he tried to escape.

"My problem isn't your plan, Commander. I don't doubt your skills in such matters, but my problem is trusting you. How do I know you'll help *us* after you escape?"

Roland looked around for a minute. They were mostly civilians in this bay. His gaze stopped over a pair of children being held tight by, whom he assumed, was their mother. He always thought it had been stupid to allow the scientists and engineers to bring their families, despite the commitment to such a long project. Civilians always complicated things, children even more so.

"You don't, Captain." He had run multiple replies and counter-replies through his mind but knew none would suffice. In the end, all he had was the truth of the matter.

"Then I suppose our fate is in your hands." The captain paused a moment considering her next words. "If you do leave us behind Commander, I want you to know, I will survive this if only to find you and, when I do, you will *eventually* die."

He was inclined to believe her.

Three hours later the mechs hovered into the bay with the usual four guards making a line across the threshold.

Time to skip to the good bit.

As soon as the mechs came to a stop he let Rydeck make his way over as normal. This fight was different due to the fact that he didn't let it play out in his head first. He was just going to attack and let the big guy do all the work.

Pushing through the crowd he jumped out, shoving Rydeck aside, as he kicked the first mech. In response the hovering mech flew across the bay, almost crashing into the guards.

"Why do you always get first pick, huh?" He followed his outburst with a jump and a swift elbow to the Lieutenant's jaw.

The crowd gasped as they took a step back from the brawl. The guards moved in but only to get a better look at the fight. He heard Rydeck growl from his position down on one knee. Perhaps he had hit him a little too hard. The augment lashed out, coming to his full height with his enhanced grip around Roland's throat. He flicked his feet searching for the floor but found only air. His choking didn't last long before Rydeck brought his muscled brow into Roland's eye.

Like a rag doll, he threw the Commander to the floor before crouching over him. His view was inverted from his back, but he saw the guards begin to move in with their rifles ready.

Do it!

It had to be now or never. Rydeck roughly grabbed Roland's jaw to lift his head off the ground. The augment's fist closed into what might as well have been a rock. His attack was quick and very blunt as reality instantly escaped him.

Over the years of experiencing his Rem-plant, Roland had

become accustomed to the grogginess and confusion that usually followed. In the beginning, those ten seconds felt like an eternity, especially if he woke up in a different place. But now? Now he knew what to expect.

His mind switched on long before he opened his eyes. He was aware of two pairs of hands dragging him by his limp arms down a corridor. He continued to let his feet drag on the floor. He didn't know who these aliens were but they were as predictable as humans.

Roland opened his eyes briefly to glimpse his surroundings. There were only two of them. The other guards must have remained behind to oversee the mechs. He no longer had to recall his training days at the academy as his muscles simply responded to his needs. He calculated five more seconds before he was free.

First, he had to get into position; it was all about counterbalance. His initial attack had to be a surprise. Using one leg he planted it into the floor taking his weight so they wouldn't realise he was about to lunge. Everything else was reactionary.

Pushing up he shoved the captors' hands away while pushing them both in opposite directions. With the armour plating they wore, he had to use the walls as weapons or risk breaking his knuckles. Momentum was always a useful tool in combat as it could be used for or against. In this case, Roland kicked the guard to his left until he felt him make contact with the wall. Pushing off the guard's abdomen he threw his weight into the guard on his right. Careful not to break any bones, he used the flat of his hand to force the helmet into the opposing wall. With a guard in front and behind him it became a simple matter of hit and run, the best tactic with multiple opponents.

So far everything had taken two seconds.

Hearing the guard behind him, he thrust his leg out again hitting him square in the chest plate. It was made easier by using the shoulders of the alien in front for balance. Before seeing the effects of his kick he brought his leg back and pushed his boot into the alien in front of him. Striking the knee joint, the alien dropped to the floor with a wonky leg.

Four seconds.

Knowing the enemy in front was now disabled, though not unconscious, he threw himself back, landing elbow first into the neck of the other guard. Without breaking motion, Roland slipped his fingers under the chin, bringing the helmet off with him. He turned on the spot and backhanded the disabled guard who was gripping his broken leg. He heard the two helmets crack and the guard went limp. The gurgling behind him abruptly stopped with a thud, as the alien hit the floor. Roland already knew he had crushed the windpipe.

Five seconds.

Looking down at the helmet in his hands, he realised the guard behind him was no longer hidden. Roland couldn't quite believe his eyes at the sight of the alien in front of him, and it was an alien. He saw now why the helmets had been sleek and slanted to the back. The whole head sloped backwards, stretching from the brow. Where he would have expected to see hair there were bony ridges that he guessed were part of the skull. The skin itself, if it was skin, was ice blue and made up of glittering scales. The face was all angles as the bony ridges formed into the skull and high cheekbones. The nose was a small bump in the middle with a narrow slit down the centre. Roland assumed it was the nose purely by its location. The lips were the most astonishing, if only because of their resemblance to his own. They were a darker blue than the rest and didn't glisten the same as the scaly skin.

The eye sockets were of similar shape and size to a human's but there were no eyebrows to speak of. He let his curiosity get the better of him as he parted an eyelid to inspect the eye within. Alien it was. With no iris to speak of, it only had a single black slit for a pupil against a white background. It appeared slightly damaged and bloodshot after the recent suffocation. Roland turned the head to the side while looking for ears but found only a pitted hole against the surface. There was a curious small black device stuck behind the hole. He looked at his fingertips after touching the face for the alien skin was not what he expected. Instead of the scales he saw, he felt soft smooth skin, much like that of a human. Roland took a closer look at the face and saw a thin layer of transparent epidermis

211

covering the diamond-like scales. If this creature was anything like a human he guessed it to be male as the features didn't come across as particularly feminine.

Was he the first person ever to see an alien? Roland spent a couple of seconds feeling good about that before realising he needed to move on. He heard a lot of movement from the direction he had been dragged. It was likely they had heard the commotion caused by his escape. He wasted no time relieving the dead guard of his rifle while making his way up the corridor, putting distance between him and the cargo bay.

Roland inspected his new weapon, looking for familiar points of origin. The trigger was the most obvious, though it was more of a two-fingered button than a lever. The handle was part of the stock at the back with a hole to fit his thumb through. Despite the size, it felt light in his hands as he cupped the long barrel. Both sides of the main body were covered in a holographic panel with gibberish written across it. He decided not to touch any of it.

After taking a couple of winding corners, an alarm blared out above his head. The sudden noise dropped him to one knee as he prepared for a fight that never came. He looked around for potential threats but, instead, found a strange ball protruding from the ceiling above. The ball rotated in its socket as a green line moved across the corridor and over his body.

That's probably not a good thing.

Roland already knew what had most likely happened. They had found the bodies and initiated a ship-wide search. It couldn't be that hard to find the only stray human on board. He had to move quickly now since they would know where he was. The door immediately ahead wouldn't budge. He had to turn back and take another route. It wasn't long before he was confronted by a group so big he couldn't catch their exact number. He didn't hear their responses to seeing him but he knew from the subsequent shots that flew by it wasn't a "Hi, how are you doing?"

Roland felt a cold burn as a blue flash caught the side of his right leg, singeing the material and melting the edge of his armoured plate.

All he could do was run the other way whilst firing blindly over his shoulder. He ran without care for his direction, constantly aware of the pursuing boots. Every now and then a lucky shot would get closer, blinding his retinas with the blue after-image. He passed several other aliens on his excursion, none of which were dressed like soldiers. He could see their alien faces as he ran by and assumed them to be regular crew rather than soldiers.

Every room and corridor was the same polished silver with no attempts to make it aesthetically pleasing. He wanted to stop and take in some of the strange new technology he was passing, but he thought better of it after a holographic display erupted in sparks and flames after being shot. He heard the nearby crew shouting in a language as confusing as the writing on the side of his gun. Despite everything, he couldn't help but ponder his confusion. It was the first time he had ever heard a language he didn't understand. Humans hadn't had such communication problems for centuries.

Eventually, he came to a lone room, devoid of life, with only one other door leading off it. He carried on through, looking for a control panel on the other side to seal him in. The symbols made no sense but he was sure it was for the door. Seeing this as a chance to lose his pursuers he decided to just shoot the holographic panel in the hope of locking the door. It didn't work. After his shot started a small electrical fire, the hologram shut down and the door remained stubbornly open.

"Perfect..." He squared his back against the frame, peering round to see his captors.

They spread out across the corridor taking up positions behind various stations and workbenches. He wiped the sweat from his brow, stinging his eye as he did. Rydeck had a thick head. He was running out of options for there was only one more room to go through and who knew where that led. If he stayed and fought they would overpower him with superior weaponry.

Unexpectedly, an alien walked out of the room on his right. On seeing him, the alien dropped his tools and ran the other way. All Roland saw was a potential hostage. Keeping the soldiers occupied, he fired a couple of loose shots in their direction. Before they retaliated he ran after the fleeing alien. Much to his glee, and dismay, the room was a dead end. His hostage wasn't going anywhere, but neither was he. At least that's what he thought.

The lone alien had already activated one of the large red circular panels that ran along the wall. To his surprise the alien began to climb through the new portal, trying to clamber out of sight. Roland grabbed his ankle and pulled him back out to the floor. He didn't seem much of a threat, wearing a fitted suit covered in pockets and strange tools. He assumed him to be some kind of technician.

Nevertheless, he kept his boot on his chest as he inspected the contents of the circular hole.

"Are these..?" He leaned back, taking in the other circular ports along the wall.

Despite the alien tech, it looked a lot like an escape pod. The port opened up into a passageway just big enough to stand in and a couple of chairs in front of a brightly lit console. He couldn't miss the viewport at the end with a clear image of space beyond. It looked like freedom.

There was too much to calculate with the time he had. If he escaped now, he might never be able to get back to the others, or even Earth. He thought about the children he had seen dotted around the cargo bay.

Screw it!

He told himself he could do both. He would escape now and find a way to help them later. As long as he didn't get his hands on any alcohol.

He reached down and roughly picked up the quivering technician. Good, he thought, they feel fear. Without an explanation, he shoved the alien through the port and into the pod. He followed him in and dragged him to the nearest chair.

"You. Fly. Away!" He shouted his words because that would make him easier to understand.

Roland pointed at the console and then at the viewport in the hope of giving direction. He heard boots moving around outside.

They had decided to come looking for him. When the technician made no move, he decided a more universal form of communication was required. He stood back to reposition the long weapon and pointed it at the alien's face. The alien's hands responded by moving across the console and closing the pod door behind them. It was extraordinary to see the alien hands at work. The backs were covered in the same diamond scales, but he noticed the palms were a darker blue, like the lips.

The door sealed just in time as Roland had looked back to see a black-clad soldier levelling his weapon. Metallic thumps resounded from the other side.

Roland fell back into the wall as the escape pod left its housing in the main ship. The compensators were never state-of-the-art in an escape pod and, apparently, that fact was universal as well. The alien was blurting out unintelligible words while frantically running his fingers across the console. He was impressed with the level of technology in such a dispensable ship. The holograms were all interactive, not requiring the alien pilot to always use the console.

Human technology had never achieved such a feat; holograms were simple projections and did not respond to touch. He noticed too that the viewport doubled as a screen, showing different readouts against the starry backdrop. The pod suddenly changed course, giving them both a very different view. Roland lowered his weapon in awe of the sight. He wiped the sweat from around his eyes, thinking his vision must be blurred.

They were now heading towards a planet, or at least it had been at some point. He couldn't explain what he was looking at. The planet was completely cracked in half horizontally. The exterior surface was charred black as if it had been burnt and the land had never recovered. The edges were covered in cracks and giant craters. There were three canyons on this side alone that could be seen traversing the surface. A section of the bottom hemisphere looked as though some cosmic giant had taken a bite out of it. The most extraordinary thing of all was the contents of the two halves. Each half of the planet was connected by a single tower in the shape of an egg timer, with the middle section being narrower. Stretching out from that were hundreds of cylindrical towers that were erected at every angle. They formed an artificial cobweb that connected the two halves together with faint bridges between them all.

What was he looking at? Was this some kind of alien city in space? Every structure was lit up from inside and held an unfathomable population. The buzz around the planet was impressive as well. Ships of every size and shape flew to and from the planet, passing by the escape pod.

Where the hell am I?

———

KALIAN COULDN'T STOP LOOKING at the image of the Conclave. Over the last few days, he and Li'ara had been studying the different texts and images given to them by Ilyseal. However, Li'ara had to translate most, as Kalian could still only see a few words. He had begun to make the distinction between what Telarrek called the Conclave, with the Highclave residing within, and Conclave the society. He now reasoned that everyone lived within the Conclave, but the capital planet was simply referred to as the Conclave.

The hologram showed a perfectly detailed planet that had apparently broken in half across the middle. He manipulated the image with his fingers so he could see inside at the planet's alien contents. He was enjoying the data module and its interactive holograms. It made his Data-pad look obsolete. There were hundreds of towers that surrounded an even larger one in the middle, with a city-like structure both above and below that wove between the cylindrical towers.

Their information told them that this was the capital of the Conclave, with a varying population in the high billions. It was six times the size of Earth and three times the size of Century. He wondered if it had been Ilyseal's idea to put human comparatives in the module for them. The history behind the capital's broken appearance was of great interest to Kalian. Like the founding of so many great things, the Conclave's beginnings were violent and bloody. The Novaarians were allied with the Shay and the Ch'kara while being opposed by the Laronians and the Raalak. The species came to war over territorial disputes and resources therein. The history files were similar to Earth's in their comparison to an older generation being prone to violence and what would now be considered primitive reactions.

Being over a hundred thousand years ago, there was no shying away from the horrific actions taken by each side. In fact, Kalian reasoned, the story was now used as a lesson to the entire Conclave. At the time the Ch'kara and the Shay were working on a new mode of transport that could open up a portal in space/time and teleport their soldiers into enemy territory without risking a space battle. The Laronians meanwhile, had set up a staging post on a backwater planet, with a young species of intelligent life inhabiting it.

The Novaarians and their allies used this new technology to transport troops onto the surface of this primitive world, and surprise their enemy. The file simply read as a calculation error regarding what happened next. The portal didn't open on the surface but, instead, ripped a hole in reality within the planet's core. This destabilised the core and started a chain reaction that caused the planet to crack in half, after killing everything on the surface with volcanic eruptions and eventual loss of atmosphere. The scientists and troops on the Novaarian side were exposed to the raw conditions of the planetary core, wiping out half a continent on their own staging planet.

When the dust settled, both sides realised that they had committed genocide of an innocent species and spilt an ocean of blood on both sides. In the ruin of this broken planet, all the races came together under a banner of trust and hope for the future. It was agreed that the technology would receive no further research, in favour of pooling their resources to better the Solar Drive. The capital's appearance was a constant reminder of the devastation that could be caused if the Conclave wasn't united.

They had spent the last three days reviewing as much information as they could in between their sparring. He was impressed with himself at the progress he had made in a week. Only once had he managed to best Li'ara, but he suspected she let him to lighten his mood at losing so much. He had become increasingly frustrated with his progress in using his strange abilities, though. He felt like he was constantly on the edge of understanding it before another flying object hit him on the head. Thankfully most of his bruises were on his body and went unnoticed by the Novaarians. It hadn't escaped either of them how quickly such wounds healed...

On the sixth night, after sparring with Li'ara, she asked him about his body or, more to the point, his physique. He always felt a little confused on the matter as well.

"Did you go to a gym, back on Earth I mean?" She had pointed to the well-formed muscles around his abdomen. "I know they're not augmented, otherwise I would have broken my hands by now."

He suddenly felt very conscious about his lack of a top. "Honestly, I couldn't tell you how I got like this."

Li'ara's confusion had been obvious. "You're telling me your body just formed naturally this way, biceps and all?"

Kalian had let out an anxious laugh at the ridiculousness of the statement. "I guess so..."

"So this is just one of your *things* then?" She waved her hands around, mimicking his telekinesis.

He just shrugged, not really sure what to say. He had been through puberty like everyone else but it was only when he was sixteen that he realised not everybody changed like him.

"You lucky bastard." Li'ara couldn't help but laugh, and Kalian couldn't help but get drawn in.

It had been a good evening after that. Li'ara let her guard down and actually talked about her life. Fearing this might never happen again Kalian didn't dare breathe.

"My father was in Calais... when they attacked."

They had already finished dinner and reviewed information on the Ch'kara, another species that had a seat on the Highclave. While seated on the comfy sofas she had finally opened up about her own losses on Earth.

Like him, Li'ara had no siblings and her mother had died when she was a child due to a rare bacteria found only on Titan, one of Saturn's moons. Her mother had been a research scientist for a branch of Central Parliament. All scientists worked for some branch of Parliament, following the dissolving of all the corporations in the last war. Her father had worked in the Central Museum in Rome where much of the ancient world had been catalogued after the wars.

Kalian himself had visited the museum in his early twenties and loved the exhibitions on life in the twenty-second century. He had always admired the people of that age for surviving such horrific environmental conditions. He shuddered to think what might have happened had they never invented the Weather Net to control the atmosphere. He wondered if he had seen Li'ara's father and never known it.

She told him that it was her father who had raised her and even encouraged her to join the UDC. He wanted his daughter to grow up strong and be able to defend herself, to live, she said.

"I spoke with him not long before I met you at The Hub. He was going to visit one of the protected vineyards where he used to walk with my mother."

Li'ara had actually cried that night, in front of him. At first, he didn't know what to do. This was a first even for him. He had spent most of his life avoiding emotional connections to people and his lack of experience was obvious. He awkwardly placed his hand around her shoulders in an attempt to comfort her. She had cried on and off for a while before they both fell asleep on the sofa.

The next morning Kalian woke up on his own with dry saliva on one side of his mouth. He assumed at some point in the night she had woken up and left. She didn't seem the cuddling type. He silently hoped she hadn't seen the drool though.

When they next saw each other Li'ara was accompanied by Ilyseal outside his door.

"We have arrived," Ilyseal said.

He looked at Li'ara who gave no indication she had been crying most of the night. She was back to being the soldier, at least by training if not rank.

Soon after, they found themselves on the command bridge with Telarrek and dozens of other Novaarians. They were all standing by their posts in silence, but this time it wasn't because of Kalian and Li'ara. Along with Telarrek, they gazed ahead to the front of the command bridge.

"We are home..." The expansive viewport gave a picture-perfect image of the Conclave.

NINE

Shouting didn't seem to be working for him. The piloting alien kept raising his hands in the air with frustration at their communication issues. Much to Roland's surprise though it appeared his alien companion had some level of understanding, despite his own confusion. After reaching a certain distance to the cracked planet, the pilot had apparently lost control of the pod's direction. By the time the viewport was filled with the main tower, they had slipped into what could only be described as traffic.

Roland didn't understand it but he guessed something automated took control of all ships within the perimeter of the planet. Everywhere he looked, ships of all sizes were being directed out of their lane and off to some unseen landing area. He began to wonder how each ship knew where to go.

"Have you done this?" He waved at the slow-moving ships directly ahead.

The alien couldn't take his eyes off the gun Roland was poking him with. He replied in some strange gibberish that just annoyed Roland even more. The console pinged as a holographic image in red popped up. It showed the pod passing through a thin barrier that wrapped around the horizontal break in the planet.

"What does that mean?" Before the gibberish began again, he held up his hand to the alien's face. What was the point? He wouldn't understand it anyway.

Roland didn't like this. For all he knew, the pilot had entered coordinates for the nearest garrison of soldiers. Leaning forward, he peered out of the viewport and checked the area out. He could see now, that as well as the cylindrical towers, there was a city hanging from the roof of the interior with spires protruding from the bottom. Both cities were wrapped around the bases of the main tower. He felt like a needle that had just fallen into a planet-sized haystack. Ships were ever on the move between the cylinders and the main tower. The cities above and below were so far away that everything looked like ants moving over an ant hill.

They were cast in shadow as a monolithic ship passed overhead. He knew a warship when he saw one. It didn't look like the one that attacked Alpha. This one was slightly smaller but covered in armaments. It was clearly made up of five sections down the length of the vessel and ended in sloping quadruple engines, one pair stacked on top of the other.

The front of the vessel looked more like a battering ram as it sloped down at a forty-five degrees angle. Each of the five sections was a different shape but they were all perfectly in line. As it angled away, he could see that there was an even larger set of quadruple engines above the others. A sleek looking bridge pod protruded from the rear of the ship at the same forty-five degrees angle as the battering ram. Overall, the ship was a deep shine of red with a black hull in between the different sections. One look at the bulky cannons lining the sides was all Roland needed. He was glad however, that it was heading away from the planet and out into space.

He'd had enough. It was time to take back control. Peering out again, he looked at the lower half of the main tower. For some reason, his instincts always told him to go down when he was in trouble. Roland saw several lines of the same kind of traffic entering the tower at different ports. What caught his eye were the smaller ports with individual ships landing on extended platforms.

"Down there! Take us down there!" He pointed the gun at the alien, then in the direction he wanted to go.

The alien pointed at the console and then the tower while chattering away. Looking him up and down, Roland reasoned the alien knew his way around electronics for, after all, he was in the room with the escape pods. He'd let him get comfortable on the flight over, but now he needed to show dominance over his hostage.

"It seems to me you have a pretty good grasp of what I'm saying." Roland kept his voice level this time. The pilot seemed to be more terrified by that than the shouting. "You're going take control of this little can and you're going to take us down there onto one of the empty platforms."

Roland dropped the barrel of the rifle, letting it rest on the chair between the pilot's legs. If his biology was similar to humans, he would take its positioning seriously.

A dark pointed tongue licked the alien's lips as he thought over his options. He raised his hands as if surrendering, before turning back to the console. Roland kept the rifle trained on his mid-section. A red holographic image appeared from the console with what looked to be a hand-sized dial. The alien gripped the dial and turned it clockwise towards an arrangement of symbols he didn't understand. The console pinged again and different lights switched on around the pod. Two domes of holographic light appeared in front of the alien, to which he responded by placing his hands over each. Showing a clear understanding of Roland's request, he rotated the domes of light until the pod veered away from the line of other ships. It dropped vertically, though neither of them felt the change in motion.

Roland could see now why such lines were more practical. The pilot was constantly dodging other ships, with the viewport giving a heads-up display of incoming traffic. He saw a particularly empty looking platform near the bottom with a few cube-shaped containers to one side. It didn't look as well maintained as the platforms further up and he felt it a fair assumption that it would be easier to hide there. He pointed it out so the alien could manoeuvre the pod around the containers.

With a little less finesse than his flying, the pilot dropped the pod onto the landing bay to the sound of scraping metal. Now safely on the platform the pilot had served his purpose as far as Roland was concerned. Before his hands had even left the holographic domes, Roland brought the butt of the rifle down on the ridge of his eye. He didn't want to kill, there was nothing to be gained in that, but he didn't want him waking up for a while either.

Looking at the view outside he was well aware they were in a vacuum. Roland moved from his seat to rummage through the pod's supplies in search of a vac suit and breather gear. It made sense that an escape pod would have such measures. Most of the things he found were totally alien to him. He thought some of it might be medical supplies but how they were applied was a mystery. Roland was thankful however for the sachets of water in one of the lower drawers. He drained the first one and stored the other in his belt.

When he opened the last cabinet, he was disheartened to find a pair of boots instead of a vac suit. With a closer inspection, he recognised the boots as the ones worn by the invading troops on the *Hammer*. Defying gravity wouldn't be a bad advantage to have. He removed the boots to check the size before noticing the ninja-style toe cap. There was no way he could split his toes through that divide. It was only after taking a closer look at the sole of the boot he realised it didn't matter. The base of the boots was lined in a silver casing etched in ridges. Underneath were two circular ports that sat under the ball of the foot and the heel. Roland prised the casing from the boots and applied it to his own. He had no idea how to use them so he hoped it was an automatic process. It was possible they reacted to a change in pressure or simply a lack of contact with the floor. As good as they were, they wouldn't get him out of this pod.

Moving back towards the viewport again he looked out in hope. There had to be a way to reach the door on the far side of the platform.

The escape hatch at the back gave three loud bangs. There was someone on the outside. They must have slipped past while he was fitting his new footwear, which now clinked, like an ancient cowboy, every time he walked.

Shit!

If they managed to open that hatch he would be exposed to vacuum. There was nothing for it. He would have to try and take off again. Roland examined the console and free-floating holograms in vain. Nothing made any sense, so he opted for pressing everything instead. Different images popped up in response to his frantic gestures. Worst of all, the domes disappeared, which couldn't be good since he had seen they were integral to flying.

It was too late.

The lock on the door was disabled with a suction noise as the pressure was changed. He was about to die. The red light above the hatch blinked out, which he assumed was a signal that the door could now be opened. He levelled his rifle at the door. If some alien was going to get him killed, he would end them too. The circular panel parted into its hidden compartment, exposing him to the harsh elements. He held his breath, even though he knew it wouldn't extend his life - it was just instinct. He knew that even if he didn't suffocate, the icy temperature of space would do the job.

Slumped in the co-pilot chair, he waited for death with his finger on the trigger pad. Nothing happened. Instead, he was faced with another alien that didn't look happy to see him. Who knew what this alien was though, for it wore a black-domed helmet that sloped down over the face. It had six glowing orange lenses on the front, each a pair, with one below the other. It was waving its two arms about while yelling at Roland in yet another type of gibberish. He could see it was wearing a long brown coat that looked to be some kind of animal hide.

Forgetting about the angry alien, he sucked in a breath, testing the air. He felt his lungs fill up before expelling the carbon dioxide. Now he was really confused. From this angle, he couldn't see the starry background of space but he knew they hadn't gone inside or passed through an atmosphere. Yet here he was sitting, breathing, and not even a little bit cold. The alien's yelling brought him back to the situation as it stood. In his relief at not dying an icy death, he had missed the alien levelling a pistol at him.

You're getting slow.

Roland had no idea what the alien was angry about, but he clearly didn't like them on his platform. He was no expert in alien culture or fashion but, if he had to guess, he would say this particular individual was what some might call a scoundrel. He wasn't wearing a uniform but Roland possessed a weapon, and he wasn't afraid to level it at someone. The clothes the angry alien wore under the great hide coat looked dirty and torn. In his own assessment, he was confident that he was being confronted by his first alien criminal.

Roland depressed the trigger pad, sending a blue flash into the criminal's chest. He must have been wearing some kind of armour over his chest as the shot, while deadly, didn't carry through and out the other side. He climbed out of the hatch keeping the fallen criminal in his peripheral vision while taking in his surroundings. The platform was big enough to fit at least six or seven more pods this size. The cube containers were stacked to one side but were empty. It wasn't a stretch to assume this platform was probably being used for smuggling of some kind.

So aliens have crime too...

He was building as many facts about this new world as possible. If there was crime there would most likely be some form of local security. He decided that the aliens that attacked Alpha were probably something similar to the UDC. Either way, he didn't want to hang around. No doubt the ship he had escaped from would be searching for him.

Roland looked down at the dead criminal. He had four fingers as well, though they were slightly larger in the palm with thicker fingers. It didn't matter anyway; he knew what they looked like now. His training kicked in without him thinking about it. Crouching down he removed the long coat that felt like smooth leather and put it on. He needed to blend in and hide his features from the indigenes. The coat fitted well and dropped to his ankles, giving him plenty of room to conceal weapons. Thinking of this he picked up the pistol dropped by the criminal. It was bulky, with a rectangular body and a long cylindrical sight that ran down at an angle to the gun. The trigger pad was the same with a handle slightly longer than his grip. It would be easier to move with a weapon this size rather than the rifle. He relieved the alien of his holster and strapped it around his thigh.

The only thing left was his face. That problem was simply resolved by taking the domed helmet off. He'd noticed the style was different before removing it. Instead of angling back, to allow for their alien skull, it was round like a human's. The helmet slipped off with a tug before Roland jumped back at the sight. This was an alien, but not one of *those* aliens. There was no doubt that this was a different species. Its skin was dark brown and felt tough as he rotated the head, taking in the features. The head was similarly bald but not free of hair. The two large black eyes had tufts of light brown hair surrounding the sides. The eyes were bigger than a human's and the other alien's. There was no colour, or any details for that matter, so it appeared like giant pupil.

Roland noticed another small black device, circular in shape, just behind a patch of skin decidedly thinner than the rest. He assumed it to be the ears but couldn't fathom how they worked, though he was curious about the circular device both species wore. The mouth was in the same place but there were no lips to speak of. Roland resisted the urge to look inside and see what kind of teeth they had. The other aliens had white pointed teeth that stood out, when they spoke, against their blue exterior. Curiously there was no nose, just skin.

He stood up with the helmet in hand. Where was he? Now there were two aliens, and apparently living together. He was yet to meet a non-human who didn't want to kill him. A shadow passed quickly overhead, grabbing his attention. The view was dizzying. He was near the base of the main tower and surrounded by colossal spires and other towers that were easily bigger than any structure built by man. Roland saw ships and smaller vehicles flying in between the giant landscape that seemed to go on, until he looked across at the horizon. Space was clearly visible between the planet's two halves, making his ability to breathe even more of a mystery. That, combined with the fact that he could hear the ships passing by and the buzz of activity coming from the streets below, made him reason that there must be some kind of artificial atmosphere. Everything was so annoyingly alien to him.

Turning away from the metropolis to head for the rectangular door on the platform, he felt like a sitting duck. The tower he was on was so expansive that he couldn't even see the curve. He didn't know where he would go but it had to be better than beside a dead alien. Before entering, he fitted the helmet over his head to conceal his own alien features. The world shifted into shades of orange as he was now looking through the optical domes on the faceplate. He wasn't sure what the extra four domes did as he only needed the two, much like the helmet's former occupant. The visor automatically began to outline different things around him with information he couldn't understand. He entered a small cargo bay filled with identical containers to the ones on the platform. Information appeared above them with an outline around various crates.

He was more interested in the door to his left. The door was large enough to fit the crates and other storage items through, though he couldn't see any security features or locks and there weren't any more guards. He wasted no time passing through it. He needed to get as far away from this area as possible.

He wasn't prepared for what he found on the other side. He was immediately immersed into a crowd of aliens, all walking in different directions. It was a good thing they couldn't see his face as he stared in astonishment at the variety of life forms in front of him. He recognised the two he had already encountered, but that was only a fraction of what he was seeing now. He clumsily backed up until he found a wall behind him. He felt better with a wall at his back. Suddenly conscious of himself, he stuck his hands into the coat pockets and so concealed his pale skin.

He stood there for a few minutes trying to acclimatise to the view. He was out of his element in a big way. He had been sent into every kind of environment and situation over his four decades of service, but nothing could prepare a person for this. Most were similar in shape and size to him, but others were more animal-like. Something he couldn't identify walked past him on four legs that looked akin to a slab of stone with a large flat head.

Shit. I'm never gonna have sex again...

Everyone was going somewhere and they weren't slow about it. This place moved with speed and he had to be quick to move with it. After a few minutes of being jostled around and bumped into, he managed to make his way to the edge. He was stopped by a transparent barrier at chest height which he guessed to be made of some type of plastic. He couldn't find the right words for the view. He could see now that he was on a circular platform that looked big enough to wrap around the Moon. He could see that above and below were identical ringed platforms that became narrower towards the middle. He could only see this from a particular angle as the space between the rings was filled with smaller platforms of different sizes and shapes. Each one had several bridges that connected the floating islands. He saw massive parks filled with a variety of coloured grass and trees he had never seen before. There were stalls lining the bridges in front of him, and below, with aliens of all kinds browsing the goods.

Each level looked like a self-contained city with thousands of people going about their business. Vehicles, not unlike the ones on Earth, were passing by using some type of anti-gravity technology. The inside was actually busier than the outside. It was all so alien, yet so familiar. He saw them walking hand in hand and eating at restaurants, while others were shopping for clothes and technology. Children even ran past, looking like one of the scaly aliens, with a toy ship in one of their hands. As alien as it was, it reminded him of any human city.

All at once the buzz came to a silent stop as the plastic barrier he was leaning on came to life. Every panel showed an alien head and shoulders with unreadable symbols at the bottom of the screen. The alien had a long jaw with two small fangs protruding from its lower lip. The eyes were a golden swirl set against a black background with long milky tendrils flowing from its head. He had no idea what it was saying but it had everyone's attention. As if in response to the video his visor changed, allowing him to see in full colour again. The image of the head changed to a long purple ship covered in arcing spikes. He looked around as the masses watched the images on the barrier or on their own devices. As quickly as the alien appeared it vanished leaving the barrier transparent again.

The buzz of activity doubled after that and huge groups started to form, all heading the same way. He had no idea where he was but he knew it would be harder to find him in a large moving crowd. He decided to blend in and go with the flow. He had no clue what had got everyone so excited.

BEFORE THE VIEWPORT was dominated by the Conclave, three ships moved into a blockade position across the bow of the *Valoran*. All three had a polished deep red hull with visible cannons and torpedo tubes. The backs of the ships were haloed in blue light that emanated from their engines. Kalian had seen this design of ship in the data module and recalled Li'ara telling him they were Conclave security. She had explained it as one force that represented the Conclave and was made up of all species, not just one. They were created to remove any bias between disputes or crimes committed by a particular race. They patrolled all Conclave borders and were not restricted by juris-diction. Each Nebula-class ship, such as these, had the required armaments to obliterate a planet in a single strike.

"We are being hailed, Charge Telarrek," said Ilyseal.

Telarrek bowed his head and Ilyseal reacted appropriately, by pressing something on the floating console in front of her. The console itself was spherical with a ninety-degree angle removed from its surface. From this gap was displayed an orange holographic screen that reacted to her touch.

Telarrek remained on his podium but the platform remained grounded in its housing. The space in front of them distorted for a moment before a full-colour hologram appeared from nowhere. Kalian and Li'ara looked but could not see the emitters that projected it. The image sharpened until it was almost indistinguishable from a real form.

Standing before them was a being as tall as any Novaarian, but triple the width. Its head was thick and elongated up to a flat hairless circular top. It had two small eyes where you would expect them to be, though they were overshadowed by a hanging brow. The nose was a large pitted hole set high into the face almost between the eyes. Its mouth was like that of a cave with nothing but darkness inside when it spoke. Broad shoulders flowed into heavyset arms and three thick stubby fingers. The skin reminded Kalian of marble, with streaks of grey and blue across a white rocky background. He imagined to bump into this individual would be like bumping into a rock face.

"Greetings of peace, Charge Telarrek." The voice was deep with a small echo to it. "You and your expedition have become the only topic of conversation of late. You have been gone many cycles, in secret no less." The hologram began to pace the floor in front of them.

Everything below the waist was just as alien. At the thighs, the legs divided allowing for another pair of legs to extend to the floor. It walked upright but the back legs were always at an angle with inverted knees like the Novaarians' high set ankles. The feet weren't covered and they could see the front pair was spread between two marble toes and the rear feet were similar to hooves. Most of the body was dressed in a red tunic with black trousers that covered both pairs of legs. Kalian noticed a gold chain that hooked onto the high collar and the chest. Beneath this was a holographic display of medals and insignias.

He was trying to recall everything about this particular race but always got them confused with the Revaneen, another species that inhabited the sector of space dominated by the Laronians, though they weren't on the Highclave. Then it came to him, the being before him was a Raalak, one of the five races that did rule on the Highclave.

"What we have found, High Charge Uthor, is of great importance." Telarrek made a sweeping gesture to take them both in. "The Highclave requests the presence of this individual, Kalian Gaines. We shall dock at Clave Tower and present-"

Uthor cut him off. "The *Valoran* will remain where it is." The High Charge moved to stand before the small humans. "I am sending a shuttle for you all to board. Together, we will escort you to the council chamber. We are still processing all the information you sent to us on their kind. Until we are satisfied with that information, they will remain under my guard." He paused at Telarrek's podium before striding back to his space in the middle. "A warning from one old friend to another - the council members are not happy with Nova Prime's concealment of your mission - it breaks the Conclave's pact on sharing information. Someone will have to be punished. Tread carefully, Telarrek..." His image imploded on itself in a ball of light.

Telarrek looked at Kalian. "I am afraid what happens next is out of all our control."

Kalian gave Li'ara's hand a tight squeeze.

Not long after, they found themselves in the hangar with Telarrek, Ilyseal, and Namek who had been waiting for them. Kalian noticed the *Fathom* on the far side. It looked better than new with an exquisite shine and no sign of any damage.

The shuttle Uthor spoke of was already at the end of the bay with two guards either side of the descended ramp. One guard he recognised instantly as a Laronian with their glittering scale-like skin. They had done a lot of research into them on their journey here. They both wanted to get a better idea of who the terraforming team were dealing with and whether they were a threat. Just thinking about it made Kalian's spine tingle with that peculiar feeling.

Their information had been endless, thanks to the openness of the Conclave rules regarding each species. They knew the Laronians were one of the founding members of the Conclave. They also knew that the Laronian borders held the most Intrinium deposits this side of the galaxy. Everything was to be shared in the Conclave, but Kalian would bet that a lot of deals were done in the shadows concerning who saw the profits. Their culture was heavily based on material gain and wealth. They often considered themselves above most other species, leaving Conclave security to deal with disputes between them and the Revaneen or the Atari, who also lived within their space.

The other guard was a humanoid but a new alien all the same. Li'ara reminded him on their way over that it was called a Tularon, who lived within the sector of space belonging to the Shay. He, if it was indeed a he, was bald with rough brown skin and large black eyes surrounded by a tuft of fur-like hair. High Charge Uthor waited at the top of the ramp with his stubby fingers clasped behind his back. Telarrek informed them on their way down of the history between Uthor and himself. Telarrek had spent two centuries prior to his expedition serving in the Conclave security as Charge of a ship. Telarrek had stepped away from his promotion to High Charge in preference for the observation mission of humanity. It was he who had recommended Uthor for the position.

As they walked up the ramp, Uthor remained firmly rooted in front of Kalian and Li'ara. He seemed even bigger in the flesh, or stone as it were.

His flat-topped head looked down on them, creating a harsh sound like two rocks grinding together. "So the legends are true. They do exist."

Up close, they could see his brown eyes were almost identical to their own, except for the horizontal pupils that were oval in shape. They fell under his scrutinizing gaze as he examined them. Kalian noticed his gaze linger on both their hands. For his size, his movement was swift, as he followed Telarrek into the main hold. Kalian couldn't stop staring at his unusual legs.

"I have been going over the information you supplied on this new threat. After this business with the Highclave, I would like to debrief you on some of the specifics."

Telarrek bowed in acknowledgement.

The journey was quick as the shuttle, which reminded Kalian of a fly with its two bulbous viewports around the cockpit, closed the gap between them and the planet. There were long screens along the main hold giving them a good view as they flew by.

A soft female voice came over the speakers above. "Passing through the atmo-barrier now."

Kalian didn't know if it was the pilot or an automated voice but he had no clue what she was talking about.

Telarrek explained, "You see up there?" He pointed with his larger finger at the upper hemisphere of the cracked planet.

Following his direction, they both saw what looked like a giant mechanical umbrella attached to the planet's scorched surface. Looking across he could see more of them in the same line stretching across the planet's gap as well as on the lower hemisphere.

"You cannot see it but they generate a barrier, allowing the planet's interior to maintain a stable atmosphere. We have just passed through that said barrier."

"What about gravity? With the planet broken in half..." Li'ara let her statement go, unsure of the science she was implying.

"Everything is plated with gravity enhancers. Personally, I prefer the feel of earth under my feet with a *real* gravity well. It has been too long since I have seen the sunrise over Nova Prime. Our blue sun creates a truly beautiful sky, unforgettable once seen."

It was the first time Kalian was really hearing about Telarrek's life. He imagined at nine hundred and twelve he would have a lot of great stories to tell about his experiences.

"I would like to see that one day," Li'ara replied.

Kalian could detect a certain longing in her look out of the stretching window. He felt a little impressed with himself for detecting such feelings in her. That sort of thing usually passed him by. It was strange to think that just a week ago he had never even known this woman. Now she was becoming the only person he had ever cared for. He hadn't really taken the time to examine his feelings for her. There was an attraction he couldn't deny, but they had been flung together by the worst of circumstances. He realised that, had they met in some other reality, they wouldn't have got on. She was a hardened soldier and he was a history lecturer with socialising issues.

He knew she was more than that. He had seen a softer side to her, a more human side. He knew her to be loving and at times even funny. All he wanted to do was hold her again and let her know everything would be ok, which was strange to him as he had never had that feeling for anyone.

"It would be my pleasure. I grew up on Nova Prime but my pod, that is my family, lives on Bhavisha where I was hatched."

There were a few facts there that made Kalian blink. Li'ara saw his thoughtful expression and explained, "Novaarians aren't born like us. They hatch out of eggs. Didn't you read anything on the data module?" There was playfulness in her question.

"I can't read as well as you yet." He continued the joke, knowing how funny it was that a history lecturer couldn't read very well. He did remember a reference to Bhavisha though as one of the many colonised planets within the Novaarians' border. "What family do you have?" he asked.

"My brother and his life-mate live on Bhavisha with their three hatchlings."

There was no mention of whether Telarrek had a life-mate, but Kalian felt it would be rude to ask.

Minutes later, they were well past the barrier and into the heart of the Conclave. They couldn't help but be impressed. The central tower, or Clave Tower, was truly the biggest thing he had ever seen. It was covered in platforms that extended from the main body as well as docks that were inset into the tower.

Ships flew by everywhere he looked and he couldn't imagine how they avoided mid-air collisions. It was that thought that jogged his memory of the AI that governed such technicalities within the Conclave. He was still unsure of the idea of an AI being created at all. Central Parliament law had been strict on the creation of artificial intelligence after the first attempt by one of the extinct corporations. History detailed the event vividly in hopes of warning further genera- tions. A small moon-sized station named the Daedalus had been required to build its hardware, as well as a remotely controlled station to house it in close orbit around the sun. The corporate engineers had taken precautions in their design, knowing the potential dangers in creating a superior being as it were. They were right to do so.

The AI had taken six-point-four seconds to come to the realisation that it was the next stage in human evolution, and that humanity needed to be wiped out to make way for a new superior species, much the same way Homo sapiens had wiped out the inferior species before it. Seeing the human body through the eyes of a machine it could not make the distinction between what made up their bodies and its own. Therefore it came to the natural conclusion that it was the next step in their evolutionary journey. Subverting the onboard environmental controls, it ejected every member of the station's team, all eight hundred of them. Detecting the virus it then implanted into the corporation's mainframe, a remote team deactivated the thrusters on the housing station. The AI was at the mercy of the sun, and merciful it was not.

According to the data module, the Conclave AI had been designed by the Shay as their major contribution to give them a seat on the Highclave. The chief reason for the AI's creation had been for economic reasons. It controlled the standard clock used across all planets to allow a massive economy to thrive across a plethora of worlds in different time zones. Its central hub was situated in the Conclave, though it was capable of controlling all air and orbital traffic on every planet. If Kalian understood it right, the driver or pilot could decide to travel without the AI's guidance but it was widely considered to be suicidal.

Despite the fact that it maintained all the shared information, its ability to learn was stunted. The Highclave had put restrictions on how far the Shay could go with the AI's development to ensure it never achieved full self-awareness. Li'ara had explained it as the Conclave controlling an artificial child that only wanted to please its parents.

Kalian was eager to meet these Shay. The race as a whole was obsessed with artificial enhancements and in some cases replacements. Li'ara had mentioned that the Highclave had also put restrictions on this type of biological modification. If an individual went too far, Shay or otherwise, with enhancements or modification they brought into question their existence and the rights owed to them. Were they living or machine? This was a question the Highclave could not answer and subsequently placed strict laws over it.

The shuttle landed on an expansive platform that stretched out in a teardrop shape. The two guards made for the exit as the doors slid open and the ramp extended from its hiding place. The light poured in, blinding him momentarily, but his ears couldn't miss the sound. He guessed there to be a large crowd, beyond the shuttle, all shouting at once. The after images faded away to a welcoming he hadn't expected.

"Your discovery is new here. There are a lot of people eager to see you." Telarrek extended both of his left arms and gestured for them both to depart.

They descended the ramp together as a massive crowd of aliens stood behind a line of Conclave security. There were small machines, which reminded Kalian of the hover-bots that worked on the ships in The Hub, darting around above the crowd with spotlights pointed at Li'ara and himself. He made out the lenses reflecting the light and wondered if they were cameras broadcasting their arrival.

There were aliens he had never seen before, standing in the crowd all with some handheld device they were pointing at them. Were these reporters? It was a strange feeling to think how similar their worlds were. The guards had formed a line of bodies that the reporters obviously knew not to cross. The High Charge made his way across the platform heading straight for the centre of the masses. His stride never slowed and the crowd must have known from experience that he wouldn't stop as they parted down the middle for him. The guards followed him down, forming a column for Kalian and the others to follow. He could barely hear himself think as the throng of voices threw questions at him, most of which he couldn't make out.

The Novaarians formed a protective perimeter around them with Telarrek leading and Ilyseal and Namek close behind. Once inside the tower itself, the environment opened on a scale hard to fathom.

They were on a level that appeared to have the circumference of a small continent with hundreds of smaller platforms hovering in the centre. There were people everywhere trying to get a glimpse of the new aliens in their midst. More security had already arrived, asking people to move aside, as the party made their way towards the centre of the ring.

He felt Li'ara's hand give his a squeeze and he was sure she felt as alien as he did. Once at the edge of the giant ring the guards formed a circle around them as a long vehicle with no roof was hovering in front. Ilyseal turned to them both.

"This will take us to the Highclave!" She had to speak up to be heard over the roaring crowd. "They are located in the centre of Clave Tower."

One of the red uniformed guards opened the vehicle doors. Uthor and Telarrek sat in the front row of the shiny yellow vehicle with the others taking the back. He noticed Namek sat next to the pilot. People screamed and reached out to touch them as the hovercar banked to the right and suddenly dropped in altitude. It felt controlled but Kalian could feel his stomach lurch.

They both leaned over the edge taking in the sights as they passed between the different layers and platforms that rested between the rings. He even noticed a few trees that resembled the Ever Root aboard the *Valoran*. Buildings of all shapes sat between patches of multicoloured grass and bronze-looking trees. Despite the nature of this artificial world, they had gone to great lengths to create the illusion of a real world. Turning his head to the sound of rushing water he saw a large rock formation in the corner of a park with an actual waterfall that ran into a lake. Everything was so beautiful with the mix of technology and nature. Earth had attempted to create a similar illusion but never on such a scale as this.

"We are nearly there." Ilyseal stretched her long neck over Kalian's.

Both humans leaned over the side to look down at the approaching Highclave. It was situated in the middle of the smallest ring, in the centre of the curved tower. It was the only platform on that level with just one bridge connecting the oval extension to the outer ring. Being the only platform, it stood out against its expansive background. The base of the complex reminded him of a football stadium with its high walls and tiered interior. The walls rose to a beautiful glass spire stretching half a mile up. It twisted into a spiral before reaching its pinnacle with what looked like a diamond pyramid at the apex. Through the glass, they could both see the masses of people entering the stadium and filling every inch of the available seating.

Their vehicle veered to the left, making to enter the complex from behind. As they reached its level a small port opened up, just big enough to fit the vehicle through. They were guided in with green lights that floated in the air like a runway. More guards waited for them inside, each with a sidearm on their waist and a compact rifle in their hands. The Highclave was obviously a high priority in terms of security.

They were escorted to a comfortable room with sofas and a small hover-droid that brought them fluorescent blue drinks. Kalian noticed Li'ara doing that soldier thing where she assessed everything, looking for the exits and taking note of guard numbers.

She'll never switch off.

Kalian declined the drink with no thoughts to sustenance at this particular moment. He had no idea what they were going to say, but he knew what needed to be said - the future of their kind. Where was the terraforming group? How many research stations were still out there with crew on board? Did any other ships manage to escape? And they needed to talk about *them* as well. If they really had no clue who these destroyers were, then they needed to be ready for a new threat.

The lights flickered for a moment and the hover-droid almost dropped its drinks on the High Charge. Kalian knew it was him. He had let his nerves get the better of him and lost control for a second. He noticed that when he disrupted electrical devices the tingling feeling emanated from his fingertips, not his spine. He could feel the static on his arms under his jacket. Li'ara was looking at him from across the room for she knew. Instead of the terrified feeling he would get if he suspected someone knew about him, he felt safe somehow. It felt good to have someone know about him, to have Li'ara know about him. Ever since he had met Li'ara, his emotions and feelings had become rather complicated. He never used to have any feelings concerning other people. Thinking about the fate of his planet and species now, he felt regret at never stopping to make friends or any kind of intimate connection. At the same time, he also felt lucky not to have the grief Li'ara now had.

He took a breath and clenched his hands until the tingling left his fingertips. One of the guards had left to check on the building's power supply and Kalian felt bad not being able to tell him the futility of his investigation. He felt Li'ara's hand over his own and realised he had been closing his eyes. How did he know the guard had left? She gave him a knowing look that told him everything would be ok. For a moment he was lost in the emerald of her eyes and noticed the specks of yellow dispersed within. Telarrek's presence brought him back to reality.

"Do not look so concerned. They only wish to meet you," he said.

"Yeah, along with everyone else apparently." Li'ara's tone was dry.

Telarrek let off a couple of grunts that resonated from his chest. He was laughing. "As a collective race we thirst for knowledge. We are an old society and anything new is hard to come by, especially something as big as a new intelligent species."

"Does Nova Prime know about us?" Kalian asked. He wondered just how many Novaarians were aware of Telarrek's mission.

"There are only a select number of officials within the Novaarian government, as well as our member on the Highclave, that are aware. The expedition was what you might call, classified. It is for that reason I fear Nova Prime may face some judgment from the Highclave."

Before they could talk anymore, a new alien entered the sitting room. Whether it was male or female Kalian couldn't tell. It was almost completely concealed within a flowing black robe that hid its feet. The head was chevron-shaped with four milky white eyes set against an oak-red skin. The point of the chevron head separated the four eyes with two on each side. The mouth was inset against the overhang of where one might expect to see a nose. Kalian was sure he could see four small holes separated like the eyes at the point of the head. The skin reminded him of an insect with a coarse exoskeleton.

The thick neck that supported such a wide cranium was just visible before the robe took over. What no one could miss however, was the strange attachment to the side of the head and around the furthest right eye. Clearly a piece of technology when viewed against the oak-red skin. It encased the eye and at one part actually seemed to reach inside via a dark tubule. Two lights continued to blink red and blue against the head device. As it entered the room he saw how the augmentation ran down one side of the thick neck and entered the skin with more tubules. What was this thing? It looked scary as hell as it opened its mouth to several rows of razor-like teeth.

"The Highclave is ready to receive you." Its voice gave no gender away as it sounded robotic with a slight echo.

As it turned to leave, Kalian was sure he heard scuttling feet under the robe. He looked to Li'ara to see if her own reaction matched his own.

"It was a Nix. They're part of the Ch'kara domain - big meat eaters." Li'ara stood ready to leave.

Big meat eaters... you don't say?

Trying to forget the row upon row of teeth, Kalian stood up as well. They were led through a corridor off the hangar through which they had entered. He was waiting to hear the masses of people he had seen cramming into the stadium but only heard the sound of the others. They soon found themselves at an arched doorway twice the height of Telarrek. The Nix carried on forward, causing the door to split in half. The interior was not what he expected. Instead of a giant arena, it was a triangle-shape with them entering through the apex.

They were surrounded by thousands of spectators of every planetary origin, all of them silent. As the space opened up, there was a tall empty podium on the other side. It wasn't as big as expected, though big enough to fit a couple of *Fathom*-sized ships. He felt like they were in court. The crowds were ten feet above them in an oval shape that rose in height. Looking up, the sight was awe-inspiring as the twisting glass spire rose high into the Clave Tower. The Nix stopped halfway across the expanse and they stopped behind it. Looking back they saw Telarrek and the rest of the party had remained at the back near the door. They suddenly felt very alone. Kalian hadn't realised how much he had come to rely on Telarrek and Ilyseal.

Two of the small hovering cameras flew past, shining miniature spotlights on them. Just how many people were watching this? Thinking about what Telarrek had said about them being perceived as mythical, Kalian equated them to being something like the legends of Atlantis on Earth.

Small white lights shone up from the floor in a circle around each of them and Kalian felt that they weren't meant to leave these circles. A chorus of whispers echoed around the stadium, a wave of sound moving up to the higher tiers. Without him noticing, five silhouettes were now sitting in a line across the podium. They must have come from somewhere below. The central figure was instantly recognisable as a Novaarian, though distinct in her appearance. She had long flowing tendrils that glittered in purple with golden rings running down each strand. Her face was similar to that of all her kind with dark blue spots around her swirling eyes. All the Novaarians they had encountered so far wore very little in attire with just their armoured plating and robes flowing from the waist.

The Highclave councillor was dressed immaculately with a golden headdress that encompassed the small holes that acted as their ears. She wore a robe, that reminded Kalian of the ancient Japanese geishas, in a mix of blue, purple, and gold. She was definitely the most majestic looking alien he had seen and, in the last hour, he had seen a lot.

She was surrounded on each side by two other aliens that represented their quadrant of space. His eyes immediately fell on the Laronian councillor. Again she was the female of her species, or at least he guessed she was. Her face had a feminine quality to it like that of a human woman. Her skin glistened as her diamond scales caught the light, while her plunging neckline was covered by a necklace of large crystals.

The next councillor was a Raalak, as was evident by his large everything. He wore no visible clothing from Kalian's point of view but his bare chest had two unusual devices attached to it. Both circles of steel were interlaced into his rock-like skin with an orange glow emanating from within. He could only guess at the purpose of such augmentations.

The two aliens that occupied the other side of the podium were new to them. He recognised from the data module the small plump body of the Ch'kara next to the Novaarian. The back of its dark green skinned head was surrounded by a mechanical headdress that produced the miniature atmosphere around its face. The Ch'kara had evolved on Ch'ket, a planet with a higher percentage of carbon dioxide as well as methane. Travelling beyond their planets was impossible without their breather gear.

Kalian could see the air around its face shimmering as the miniature force field kept the gases contained. When he had first read about their kind he was suspicious of their involvement with the aliens that had attacked Earth. Telarrek had said that the force field surrounding the goliath was impossible to make on such a small scale, but hearing of the technology involved with the Ch'kara's breather gear it seemed plausible that they were involved. Their skill in such technology was well known since they were the largest manufacturers of Solar Drive engines. Their worlds were famous for the magnificent shipyards that surrounded the entire circumference in giant rings. Telarrek had explained though that the fields produced around their faces were only capable of holding in gases and would not hold up against matter. He trusted Telarrek but refused to rule them out.

The shimmering air couldn't hide his features. Everything looked too close to Kalian, with the yellow eyes and mouth scrunched into the middle. Its mouth was covered in vertical strands of green skin making Kalian wonder how they fitted food into their mouths.

The Shay occupied the furthest chair. Its skin was pale white and a shade darker than the Raalak. The head curved back to a blunt point that rested on a thin neck. Its frame appeared skeletal with little muscle. Two large eyes sat evenly where Kalian's did on his own face, though these eyes were very different. Every time it blinked there seemed to be another set of transparent lids in front of them, though the facial features weren't that different from his own, with a similar mouth and nose. To Kalian, it looked like a human face stretched back into an elongated skull. As it moved in the seat he could clearly see the artificial arm on its left side.

This wasn't the only augmentation it possessed. The bottom half of the jaw was entirely robotic with small pistons in the place of tendons. Between the large eyes sat a metallic device that linked both together and curved up to rest on the forehead. Small wires and tubes were visibly connecting the device into the eyes, Kalian couldn't imagine their use. He was sure there would be other such augmentations that he couldn't see, hidden by the podium.

The central Novaarian sat forward, taking in the sight of the two humans. Kalian suddenly felt very conscious of his charred clothing and regretted not asking Telarrek for some sort of replacements. He had visions of himself wearing the same style loincloth and armour and thought perhaps he was better the way he was.

The Novaarian's upper arms spread out before her. "Shall we begin...?"

TEN

Following the crowds had been easy. The masses led him to the strangest transportation device he had ever seen. In front of him had been row upon row of large rectangular holes in the floor, spread out in one section of the ring. He hesitated at first, thinking everyone mad for walking straight into the holes without even looking. After a few minutes' observation, he realised everyone was tapping a hologram that floated above different devices in their possession. After interacting with the hologram they appeared to be shown a designated hole to walk over. Roland couldn't wrap his head around the way in which they flew up to the ring above. There was no mechanism or platform to support them.

No one appeared bothered by this, as though it was the most regular of occurrences. Either way, he had reasoned that following the crowds was the best of his options. Without his own hologram to manipulate, he had worried about simply falling through the gap. That was when he spotted two different species wearing the same uniform in red and black, each with a rifle. One of them was the same as the race that attacked Alpha while the other looked somewhere between an alien and a robot.

Seeing them gave him cause for action. Moving with the crowd again he stepped off the edge and made the mistake of looking down. The drop was incalculably far. He could see the corresponding gap on the ring below, between the people passing through them. Instead of dropping though, he immediately began to rise into the air.

Roland wasn't sure if the people around him could hear his voice through the helmet, but he didn't let that stop him from swearing the whole way. He quickly passed through the gap above and then another six gaps after that. As he was coming to a stop, the momentum slowed down to bring him in line with the designated level. When the time came, Roland simply stepped off. It was this peculiar mode of transport that brought him before the spiralling tower of glass.

There was nothing else on this level except for the colossal stadium and the glass tower that sat on top of it. Roland had seen superstructures built on a variety of planets and moons, but he couldn't help wondering about the engineering required to keep such an immense building suspended in the air, with only one bridge attaching it to the exterior wall.

He followed the masses across the beautifully decorated bridge, lined with ornate water fountains and small red trees. He had no idea what was going on but, in need of information, he could only blend in and continue on his way.

The crowd moved as one, jostling Roland towards the left-hand side of the bridge. Following the gaze of many, he discovered a yellow vehicle floating down to their level and heading around the stadium. He continued to watch as it approached, curious as to the intrigue everyone else had.

Without his helmet, it would have been easy to see his jaw dropping at the sight of two humans sitting in the back of the vehicle. He didn't recognise either of them but that didn't mean anything for, on Alpha, he had seen a new person every day for six months.

What were they up to? Why had two humans been taken from the ship and brought here? If they were here to represent the human race, shouldn't it be Captain Fey? Or perhaps it was something more sinister. What if they were being brought out to bait him?

More encouraged to find answers, he started to push his way through to the entrance taking advantage of everyone's gawping. By his internal clock, he knew it had taken thirty-two minutes before he finally sat down inside the stadium. Much to his annoyance, he had been disarmed on his way through the entrance by a floating robot coated in scanning equipment. Dozens of them had been scanning people as they passed, with green lasers running up and down multiple individuals at once. Upon detection, the laser turned red and several armaments shot out from within the robot's carapace. Guessing its problem with him he moved his coat aside revealing the stolen weapon. The gun was removed and placed inside a container on the wall. He had no idea what instructions it gave him but he decided to just nod and move on.

Now in his seat, Roland counted only eight rows in front of him before a triangular arena was visible. What was this place? He thought the proportions wrong for such a small arena and such vast seating. It took a moment before he realised that despite the increasing number of people, nobody was making a sound. This would never happen on Earth; humans were just too noisy.

The next five minutes were a lot to take in. The two humans were escorted in by the weirdest looking alien yet, and that was saying something. He decided he liked the redhead, though. Soon after, five very different aliens ascended from somewhere within the podium that towered over the humans.

Was this some kind of trial? His sensory reflexes automatically clocked the fourteen guards that lined the triangular arena on a raised platform. He wasn't consciously aware yet that he was already planning his attack. Whatever his new agenda, he couldn't help but feel a pang of responsibility towards those he had left aboard the alien ship. This was why he preferred his old work, with no attachments or need to engage a conscience. He decided his best course of action would be to free these two and find a better way of getting the others back.

What I wouldn't do for just a sniff of whisky.

How long had he watched her sleep? How many years had he stood over her wondering what could have been? But that life was gone now, robbed from him along with any chance of happiness. He regretted using her to power and be subsumed into the ship that had ultimately become their home. He had spent more time on their long journey coming to terms with the way he used her than he had anything else. Every time he reasoned it in his mind, he would look at her and the conflict would resume. The truth was that any one of his crew, including himself, could take her place. The fact was undeniable, however, that she needed the ship as much as the ship needed her.

During their journey, the crew had spent thousands of years at a time in suspended animation in the Rem-stores, while the ship searched for the appropriate life. While they slept the ship would still need its power source as well as the intelligence to govern its prime objective. Without the Harness, she was truly the only one who could generate the necessary power. He couldn't help but wonder how much she was really aware of. He was aware of the minor glitches Elandar had been trying to eradicate. Random words and unfinished sentences would appear in holographic form above her. Elandar had reassured him that it could not be her; she was firmly situated inside the virtuality. He ran his fingers over the dark tube that ran directly from the floor into various sections of her body. He only wanted to see her eyes again, to see her open them of her own volition.

"What does she dream of, Elandar?" He didn't need to look to know Elandar was watching him very closely.

He had tasked him countless centuries ago with the care of their pilot. He monitored her vitals and nutrient uptake as well as the energy output she poured into the ship. He maintained the precise levels required to keep the equilibrium between her needs and the ship's needs. He knew that interacting with the tubes would put Elandar on edge. He was a true brother of the cause, as well as a friend.

"I created a virtual world for her to live in and explore." He ran his fingers across an adjacent hologram, checking her heart rate. "You're there, as well as..." Elandar didn't finish his sentence.

It had been a long time since either of them had said *that* particular name. Elandar knew that name above all others would fuel his leader's rage.

The cerebral link attached to the back of his neck informed him they were dropping out of the slip-stream. Feeding his thoughts back through the link, the command module began to transform. To their eyes, it appeared as though the entire front half of the module was breaking away to the vacuum of space. He knew it wasn't of course. The giant hologram created the image of what would be seen, had there not been over a mile of bulkhead between them. The clarity was perfect, however, giving most cause for hesitation before walking around.

This wasn't the first time he had looked upon the broken world of the Conclave's capital planet. He marvelled for a moment at their technological feat in manipulating the planet, for primitives anyway. His own people had the power to manipulate and transform entire star systems with multitudes of planets. Their first encounter with this collective had been thousands of years ago, after the ship had detected their transmissions across the cosmos. They had nothing the ship couldn't provide and a cursory scan of their AI showed no Homosapiens in their society.

The ship had automatically entered stealth mode before emerging into real space. The hologram highlighted specific ships in the distance that would retaliate if attacked. Their armaments were impressive but not threatening. He sent a silent command, searching for the Novaarian ship that contained his prey. The pilot found it in less than a second and magnified the hologram until it was visible on the outer reaches, beyond one of the broken moons. It was surrounded by three red warships that had formed a barrier blocking its advance. After another command, he was quickly informed that there were no humans on board.

"Where are you hiding?"

The pilot responded to his needs by emitting a system-wide scan in one neutrino burst. As always, her mind was able to collate the information in just over a second before filtering for the required information. As a result, the hologram changed from the Novaarian ship and focused on the central tower in the middle of the planet. A side note appeared in his mind informing him it was called; Clave Tower. The clarity of the image shifted to a more digital one as the tower became transparent revealing its many layers. In the centre ring were two small red dots that pulsed with life.

Found you...

Before he could give his next command the pilot sent him a message. The hologram moved to the left, making it appear as though the ship was changing course. A magnification presented them with the image of another ship that had two large engines on each side. Another side note appeared telling him it was Laronian in origin. Before he could ask its relevance, the ship took on the same digital appearance as the tower. The ship's outline was instantly blurred by the thousands of red dots pulsating from within.

He couldn't help but laugh at his fortune. He looked to Elandar who only appeared confused at the sound of his master's glee, or perhaps it was that he had forgotten the sound of laughter.

"Our alien friends have saved us some travelling."

He sent a message through his link to the rest of his crew informing them of everything he knew. He felt their elation in response. In his mind's eye, he saw another message waiting for him from the pilot. He accessed it, commanding the hologram to show him the details. There was a strong signal coming from one of the buildings in close proximity to the tower. The signal was being transmitted on all channels and was impossible to miss, even with the most primitive of technology. It was a beacon. He understood instantly what they were doing; they were calling to all the stray humans that might have survived his attacks. He silently informed his crew of the development and commanded that they leave the building intact to continue its message.

"Let's announce ourselves properly, shall we?"

Through his link, he brought up the schematics for one of the red warships not far off their bow. He couldn't quite believe the data in front of him. Were they really stupid enough to put a star inside the heart of their ships? He couldn't help but smile at his own thoughts. He gave the pilot the mental image of what he wanted, as well as informing the crew of what was about to happen. The hologram showed the ship's advancement as they gathered speed towards the warship.

"What about the others on the Laronian ship?" Elandar asked.

He sent Elandar the image, through his link, of what he wanted him to do once they had began their attack on the tower. Elandar simply nodded and returned to monitoring the pilot. He looked at the sleeping pilot again, hiding the concern he felt. He was afraid this next manoeuvre might cause her some stress.

Leaving Elandar to his tasks, he left the command module, having instructed the pilot of his needs. The new adjoining room was bare except for the reclining chair in the middle. He relaxed into it as a liquid-like hologram appeared above the armrest. He called up the relevant language and selected it for instalment. The ceiling parted into eight sections, revealing a machine that resembled the barrel of a cannon.

The machine descended until it rested above his seat, rotating the cannon to face him. Several extensions parted from the main structure, with each piece coming back together to form a mask that covered his head and neck. A language as simple as this would only take a minute to fully download and comprehend. After it was finished, he left the room and returned to the command module, testing his new words as he did.

He was aware of the communication methods used by the Conclave and knew that he only had to use one language for them all to understand him. He felt it appropriate to use the human language as it would be the last thing Kalian Gaines ever heard, that and the sound of his own skull crushing.

"You have the sympathies of the entire Conclave. Your loss is unimaginable." The Highclave Novaarian had introduced herself, Elondrasa, and her fellow counsellors.

To the far left was Brokk, the councillor from Arakesh, representing the Raalak. Next to him was Lordina, a female Laronian from Vallara. Elondrasa occupied the central seat with Ch'lac next to her. The stubby alien was from Ch'ket, representing the Ch'kara. There was no way Kalian was going to remember all those particular names. On the far right sat Nu-marn, the councillor from Shandar, representing the Shay.

Kalian tried to commit them to memory, knowing that these were the five most powerful people in the galaxy. He bowed his head in acknowledgement.

"We have sent out a signal on all bandwidths. If there are any more of your kind out there they will come here." Brokk gave them this hopeful news.

Kalian looked at Li'ara expecting to see some elation. She continued to stare at the Laronian councillor, Lordina. He recognised that look now; she was suspicious of the Laronians. Since she made no attempt to respond he assumed he would be doing the talking, for now.

"Thank you councillors. We are unsure of how many survived the attacks. But we do know of a terraforming expedition that is still alive. We call it-"

Lordina cut him off with a raised hand. "It does not matter what you call it human. That planet is Laronian. You had no right to claim it as your own." Her voice had an almost seductive quality to it.

"How were we supposed to know that?" Now Li'ara spoke. "The last we heard you sent a warship to investigate. I demand to know what you've done with our people."

Kalian couldn't help but wince at her tone.

"That ship has already arrived. There were some casualties with the confusion, often resulting from first contact." The Laronian councillor paused looking at Elondrasa.

Kalian could see what was going on. The Laronians were pissed that the Novaarians had kept the humans a secret.

"The subsequent population has been brought here, though their fate has yet to be decided by this council."

"Their fate?" Li'ara's fists clenched. "You will release them immediately!"

"You are in no such position to make demands. You are not even a member of the Conclave," Lordina retorted.

"That has not been decided by the Highclave either, yet." It was Nu-marn who had spoken up.

His voice was unnaturally croaky as if he was unable to produce saliva. Lordina's head whipped around at the Shay who appeared unaffected by her steely gaze.

"The ship in question has only just returned. I am certain the Laronians will give their full cooperation to Conclave security as they handle the matter." It was Brokk that perhaps saw some sense in Li'ara's claim.

Lordina sat back in her chair, never taking her eyes off Li'ara. "Of course we will..."

"What of Naveen?" Kalian wasn't sure he heard the Ch'kara right as he said it so quickly.

There was a murmur from the vast audience as though they were one organism reacting to the same thing. Elondrasa sat forward with both pairs of hands resting on the podium.

"Do you deny that your kind has ever visited Naveen?" she asked.

They had obviously gone through the information provided by Telarrek, and seen that humanity did not possess the technology to have visited the distant moon so long ago.

"I have studied the history of my kind dating back to our origins and I can assure you, we have never ventured further than fourteen light years." Kalian knew that probes had actually travelled further than that in humanity's search for celestial answers, but no person had ever gone further.

Ch'lac responded. "Then how do you explain this?"

He reached for something out of sight and the space between

them was filled with a floating image of a sand-coloured wall with a single handprint resting in the middle. Underneath were a series of hieroglyphs that made no sense, with a karyogram in the middle of the text. It was astonishing to see, knowing it was a real human hand-print on an alien moon. How had it got there?

"I can't explain it. It's as much a mystery to me as it is to you."

There was silence after that. The councillors looked at one another with silent questions. The masses of people around them were all conferring with each other, deciding whether he was telling the truth.

"What about those who attacked us? Can *you* explain that?" Li'ara was still in attack mode.

"That sounds like an accusation," Lordina spat.

Elondrasa raised her upper hands to calm both their tones. "I am afraid that too is a mystery, Li'ara Ducarté. We are looking into the matter in great depth with High Charge Uthor. Our preliminary examination would suggest they are of alien origin and certainly not part of the Conclave."

This again set the audience off with a wave of whispering and conspiracy theories, not to mention the idea of yet another alien race besides the humans.

"There is also the matter of Kalian Gaines," Nu-marn said.

Kalian was beginning to get the idea of how this worked. They could ask all the questions they liked but the Highclave would steer the topic to one they wanted to discuss. No doubt they had already conferred on most of the matters he and Li'ara had brought up.

"Yes." Lordina was smiling again. "According to Charge Telarrek's findings, you possess unique DNA to that of your race, one that matches The Wall."

Kalian didn't know what to say to that. He had a thousand questions on the matter as well but could offer no answers. He certainly wasn't going to show them what he had been practising on the *Valoran* with Li'ara. Before either of them could speak, the Nix stepped away from its position; its chevron head tilted to the side moments before an alarm could be heard all over the tower.

"What is happening?" Brokk's deep voice echoed across the stadium.

The Nix made Kalian's skin shiver as he heard the scuttling under its robe. "Display." In response to its robotic voice, the centre of the large chamber was taken up by a three-sixty holo-image of a giant rectangular ship hurtling towards them.

Kalian felt his spine tingle and his hands became hot to the touch.

"They are here." It was Telarrek standing behind him, totally ensnared by the image of the titanic ship.

"What are they doing?" Uthor had drawn closer as well.

The giant ship was clearly heading straight for the Conclave security vessel that lay in its path. Compared to the massive warship, it looked like a blemish against the black surface. The chain of events was hard to follow after that as the humongous ship rammed into the red vessel. The entire image was filled with white light as the Starrillium detonated, causing a miniature supernova.

"Activate the defence grid immediately." The Shay Councillor had stood up from his chair.

Uthor responded appropriately by barking orders into his bracer. The star was minute in comparison to a normal sun, but Kalian had a horrible feeling its shock wave would still reach them.

"It's too late. Brace for impact!" Uthor shouted it to the whole stadium with a bellowing roar.

His last words were drowned out by screams as the whole tower shook violently. Glass could be heard shattering from every level, though thankfully the spiralling tower above was still in one piece. The holo-image faltered for a moment before showing them the aftermath of the collision. Kalian looked as shocked as Li'ara, for the enormous ship was still coming and, with no sign of damage. He noticed the attention of most people was on High Charge Uthor, who couldn't seem to get the words out.

Telarrek stepped forward. "Get the Highclave to safety at all costs. Manoeuvre any ships left to fire on it. Use heavy munitions only: world breakers if they must. If any missile leaves that ship it must have a priority intercept, regardless of its direction." The other security personnel looked from him to Uthor, unsure of the person giving them orders. "Now!" Telarrek's roar could not be denied.

It was too late.

They heard the glass shatter above before any shards hit the ground. Like gods falling from the sky, four armoured beings in black impacted against the floor around the stadium. Two of them crushed multiple people, as they landed among their chairs, while the other two landed in the central triangle. The floor beneath them cracked under their bulky mass. The resulting shock wave had knocked most of them over with only Uthor and Ilyseal still standing. Kalian couldn't believe his eyes. Standing in front of the podium was the towering goliath from the Icarus station. Its armour was still covered in the same dents and scratches from previous battles. Its breathing could be heard, like a caged beast, through its skull-like helmet.

The two in the distance stood as statues, making no move to attack anyone, though the crowd had begun to scatter away from them in every direction. The figure standing before Kalian was much smaller than the goliath. From his prone position he guessed it to be around his own height. Its appearance was the same as the goliath, with almost identical armour. Its chest was bulky with plating upon plating of dark armour descending its arms and legs. The light reflected several sections in between the armour that was copper in colour. The eyes were concave - two black holes looking down on him. The helmet covered the entire head like the goliath's but the lattice work across the faceplate was different, with more intricate patterns.

Kalian was surprised at his own emotions. Instead of looking up in fear as he once would, he now only saw the bastard responsible for the death of his world. Li'ara was the first to react with a sweeping attack from the ground, attempting to take out the looming figure's legs. Before she could make contact the armoured figure threw out its hand in Li'ara's direction, without even looking at her. The resulting action defied physics as she was flung across the floor, seemingly by invisible strings. Except Kalian knew very well there were no strings involved. Her momentum only stopped when she crashed into the wall with a bone-breaking sound.

The figure crouched down and picked Kalian up with one hand, bringing him to eye level. Kalian desperately wrestled with the metallic grip, gasping for precious air. His peripheral vision caught Uthor charging at them as he lunged to take down the armoured figure. The entire stadium gasped as Uthor changed direction in mid-air and was instead pulled towards the goliath. He landed on his knees at the foot of the monster before it reached down and gripped his shoulder. The sound of rock being crushed was just audible below Uthor's cry of pain. The goliath made no further move, simply pinning the High Charge on his knees.

As one the surrounding guards on their high walkway aimed at both aggressors. Kalian didn't even have time to contemplate the fact that he was most certainly about to die. The triangle was filled with blue flashes and the smell of ozone as dozens of shots impacted at once. Kalian instinctively closed his eyes; not that it would save him from plasma burns. It took him several seconds to realise he was still alive. He was amazed at seeing every shot dissipate like fireworks all around him. Most of the shots hit the figure gripping him but didn't so much as singe the armour. Whatever it was doing, it was mostly protecting him from the stray shots. Looking over he could see the same was happening to the goliath and Uthor.

Over the sound of the gunfire, Kalian was sure he could hear laughter coming from inside the helmet. This deranged thing was actually enjoying itself. The dark figure extended its free hand like it was gripping an invisible ball. Kalian heard a faint pulse burst from the hand as the epicentre sparked momentarily in the palm. At once all the weapons-fire stopped, with their users looking puzzled at the malfunction. Still extended, it raised the same hand into the air and lifted the guards as it did. The display was undeniably an incredible feat of telekinesis. The guards thrashed around, kicking their legs towards the floor, as they floated above. Each of them looked shocked and terrified at the invisible hand lifting them. The stadium was silent at the extraordinary sight. Only the hovering cameras could be heard as they recorded the action.

Kalian felt like there was something obvious staring him in the face. Something he was missing because of the shock. He could feel it gnawing at him. Something out of place. Something alien yet familiar.

The hand suddenly clenched into a fist and the floating guards imploded midair. Their limbs shot into their bodies at awkward angles, with bone tearing through flesh and organs pouring out into a mess on the polished floor. Their screams had been momentary before they were all dead. Dropping the armoured hand the floating bodies dropped as well, crashing back onto the walkway above. Blood flowed over the sides like droplets of rain.

The stadium erupted in terror as hundreds of people tried to fit through the passageways at once. The two statues made no move to stop them but they just continued to watch the one holding him. Kalian looked around and saw Li'ara trying to stand with what looked like a broken arm or a dislocated shoulder. Her pain filled him with an anger he hadn't felt before, so that it consumed his every thought and feeling. Where his mind couldn't find the words, his body found the subsequent reaction.

His hand burnt red hot as he felt it pulling at something that wasn't there. He looked down to see a swirling pattern of light quickly coalescing into a ball of molten light. The air crackled around his arm, becoming distorted like heat waves in a desert. The strange sight did nothing for his new found rage as he pushed out with his hand, firing the heated ball into his captor. The explosion was limited only to them as it flung them in opposite directions. Kalian landed several metres away, closer to the door they came through. His vision doubled slightly as Telarrek and Ilyseal crouched over him.

He looked across to see the armoured figure had been thrown into the goliath, smashing them both into the podium. Uthor was using his good arm to crawl away as thick golden blood seeped from five finger holes in his shoulder. Kalian's attention shifted to the stabbing pain in his left hand. Inspecting it now he was dismayed to see the second degree burn across his palm and fingertips. The shock would wear off soon and the pain would increase dramatically.

Telarrek helped him up as Li'ara put her good arm around him and supported herself. Her eyes moved from his burnt hand to the smoking rubble at the base of the podium. "We'll have to add that to the list..."

Telarrek and Ilyseal only appeared confused. Before either could explain an unexpected laughter erupted from the smoking pile.

"It's been a long time since I've been hit by one of those." The black-clad figure rose from the smoking crater, along with the hulking goliath.

The voice was altered as the helmet filtered the sound. That's when Kalian realised what had been staring him in the face. The hand that had gripped him, the hand that had killed the guards...

They were *human* hands.

As if confirming his thoughts, the figure strode across the clearing with the helmet parting into various sections and becoming one with the armour.

A very human-looking face stared back at them.

"Do you not recognise your own kin?" His voice was strong like a veteran commander with a hint of intelligence behind his pronunciation.

He walked over with his arms outstretched as if he posed no threat. His face was clean shaven, as was his head, apart from two dark braids of hair that flowed from above his left ear and fell over his armour. He had a distinct red tattoo in the shape of a fang below his right eye, both of which were crystal blue. He had a strong jawline and perfect cheekbones. In fact, all of his features appeared perfectly formed and symmetrical. Back on Earth, he could have easily been a model or an actor. But his eyes had the look of a hunter with his prey in sight.

Distant screams and explosions broke the tension as more of his kind burst through the outer walls and into the tower above and below them. They were, no doubt, causing the same kind of damage they did to the human fleet around Century.

"You'll have to forgive my brothers and sisters. We have travelled a great distance to find you, and your petty fleets didn't provide them with much entertainment. The mind, like our muscles, needs its exercise, does it not?" He paced the triangular clearing like a beast taunting its food.

Kalian eyed the goliath behind, as it stood completely motionless.

"Don't worry about him. He obeys my commands as though they were his own thoughts. I came here to end the last Terran life *myself*." The armoured gauntlet covering his hand parted like the helmet, retreating into the arm. He flexed his free hand as though it were the first time. "Know this Kalian Gaines - your death will have meaning. As I squeeze the life from you, the cycle of your kind will finally end." For a moment he seemed to look beyond all of them, his eyes searching another world. In a mocking tone, he whispered, "We are forever..."

There was hatred in those words.

"Who *are* you?" Kalian asked.

"I am, Savrick."

EVERYTHING HAD ERUPTED into chaos around Roland. Thankfully the two, whatever they were, landed a few hundred metres away around the stadium. He saw the occupants of those seats become buried under the rubble of their impact. Not to mention the falling glass that cut many members of the audience to ribbons.

Amid the mad scramble of everyone trying to flee, he glimpsed another two drop from above and land in the central triangle. He felt everyone pushing him aside as they jumped over rows of seats, taking no care as to whether they were occupied or not. At first, he wasn't sure what the alarm meant. In fact, he hadn't been sure what anything meant. From the conversation taking place below he had only understood what the two humans were saying. They had mentioned some kind of attack but were not referring to Alpha, although when they did, he wondered who they were to have clearance about such operations. As hard as it was to believe, he had come to the conclusion that these two individuals were not members of the terraforming expedition. But what attacks were they talking about? And how the hell did they get here?

Instead of heading for the exit with the thousands of others, he tried to force his way down to the podium level. He didn't know who these new aliens were but they could take some damage if they could drop from such a height without the fear of death. He wasn't sure how much his new boot accessories would protect him but he guessed they wouldn't be as good as their armour.

The crowd froze for a moment as everyone witnessed some kind of violence within the arena. Roland couldn't see it over the large rock creature that obstructed his view, but everyone gasped after he heard the distinct yell of a woman. Whatever happened, it only spurred them on as the rock creature pushed multiple aliens aside in one stride. With that small clearing, Roland managed to jump down two rows worth of steps before something small and chubby, with mechanical headgear, knocked him over.

He rose to his feet convinced he must have hit his head for he couldn't be seeing what he thought he was seeing. After noticing that several others around him had similar expressions, he knew it to be true, though he couldn't explain it. All the guards surrounding the podium were floating ten feet in the air. Their deaths were quick but violent. He had never seen anything like it; their limbs just imploded into their bodies like someone had placed a black hole in their gut. He noticed a couple of aliens faint at the sight while others screamed in terror, frozen still.

He stopped to check the other attackers but was only confused as they stood motionless. It occurred to him that they were most likely guarding the one in the centre who, he could now see, was holding the young man. Roland couldn't help but notice the behemoth standing in front of the podium.

Well, aren't you a big bastard...

It was unnaturally big, bigger than any alien he had seen so far. It was actually subduing one of the rock creatures with one hand.

As the broken guards dropped back to their posts, he immediately took note of the guns attached to their waists. Now past the fleeing crowds, he was free to move onto the guard's walkway and get a better look at what was going on. He crept onto the platform, though he was sure he couldn't be heard over the crowds and the screams. It wasn't long before he was in possession of two handguns with large rectangular barrels.

He was again witness to something he couldn't explain. The human man being held up by the armoured figure created some kind of light in his hand. A moment later he pushed it into the attacker and blew the two apart.

Well, they're dead...

That was a given since they were so close to the explosion. He reasoned that the human must have been concealing a grenade. What he wouldn't do for grenades. He made his way over to the arena door as the redhead got to her feet below him. She was injured; broken arm, maybe collarbone too. He was impressed with the man, recovering quickly from what should have killed him.

Laughter broke through the ruckus. Not just any laughter but a kind he had heard before. He had heard it from old enemies and targets from his past. It was always from the ones who thought themselves untouchable, invincible and above reproach. When that laughter came from a being who had dropped half a mile like it was nothing, and been blown into a wall, it gave Roland pause.

The figure strode across the clearing as its headgear retreated into the suit. Roland wasn't ready for the face underneath. The confusion of recent events combined with what he was now seeing gave him a headache. He couldn't quite make out every word over the thousands of feet thundering around the stadium but the man was definitely human as he was speaking Central. Roland got the impression he was making threats.

In his assessment, things were only going to escalate. He had to act now or they would most likely be dead in the next sixty seconds. There was that conscience again.

KALIAN HAD BEEN FACED with death so many times in the last week he was becoming numb to the feeling of dread. His world had been upended and thrust into a life of violence and destruction. He had never felt rage like he had at the sight of Li'ara being hurt. His hand was beginning to burn but his senses were being overridden by the tingling in his spine. He knew he faced death again and perceived this Savrick to be an even greater threat than the goliath.

When Savrick came for him, he would pour all of the power he felt building inside his arms into the madman. He wouldn't let him hurt Li'ara again. Having seen Savrick's abilities, he doubted he could beat him, but he didn't need to. If he could just distract him long enough, the others could escape. He tried to ignore the pain in his hand and concentrate on the image of Li'ara being flung into the wall. If he could find that rage again, maybe he could create the light again.

Savrick closed the space between them, his eyes fixed on Kalian.

He paused as Elondrasa rose from her seat on the podium. "You have no right to attack us or these humans. They have sought refuge within our borders and they will have it. Leave now and we will not bring the full weight of our combined fleets on you and your ship."

Kalian admired her courage. She stood up with nothing but words as her weapon against a foe who had already demonstrated a greater power. Savrick slowly turned on the spot to face the High-clave, who all looked very sheepish.

"You are advanced, Novaarian. Your society is remarkable, and it is truly a great feat to have brought so many cultures under one roof." His face turned sour. "But you are a shadow of the world we have left behind. If you could see how primitive you are compared to those left in our wake, you would tremble at my feet and beg for the chance to evolve as we have."

Kalian was desperate to find the meaning behind Savrick's words but feared he would be dead before he got any answers. A movement above him caught his eye. There was a strange person crawling along the gantry in what looked to be a large coat and helmet.

Elondrasa took a breath to protest more before Savrick raised his unsheathed hand. As his hand lifted, so did the councillor. She gasped as her long legs kicked out to find the floor. She looked to her fellow councillors for help and watched as they sank into their seats. Savrick flipped his raised hand, sending the Novaarian councillor flying into the empty seats behind the podium. At the same moment as her body crashed into the chairs, the archway behind Kalian opened up to reveal Namek with his staff in hand and a small ball in the other. Telarrek and Ilyseal reacted to the sight quicker than he or Li'ara did. They moved aside, allowing him space to enter, whilst guiding the two humans back through the doorway.

Namek's movements were swift and clearly rehearsed as he flicked his upper arm to the side, releasing the ball. This action instantly caught Savrick's attention as he swivelled round to face them. But it was already too late. The ball had stuck to the wall and activated with a high-pitched hum.

Everything happened at once after that. Savrick was immediately pulled into the wall on which the ball was stuck. The force and speed were impressive as he became a blur of dark armour. The wall cracked under the impact but he remained lodged above the floor. The other three acted at once, with the statuesque guards jumping through the air, aiming for the podium. The goliath looked at its master before taking giant strides towards them. Telarrek and Ilyseal gripped both Kalian and Li'ara, pulling them further back from the archway. Li'ara groaned, holding back a scream, when Ilyseal's hand latched around her injured shoulder.

The stranger from the gantry dropped down in front of them, alongside Namek. Kalian could hear him shouting as he fell while firing two handguns at the approaching goliath. The shots were absorbed by the armour and did nothing to stop it, though that didn't seem to stop him from shooting. Before landing, he appeared to slow down just before reaching the floor, allowing him to keep his balance after such a drop. Kalian would have stopped to think about this new ally had he not been running for his life, again.

The six of them ran through the connecting corridors until they found themselves back at the yellow vehicle. Ilyseal jumped an impossible distance for any human as she landed in the driver's seat. Telarrek scooped Li'ara up into his arms as though she weighed no more than a child. Kalian thought again how serious their situation was when she made no protest to being handled that way. Once all in the vehicle, the new stranger jumped into the back seat and kept his guns levelled at the doorway.

"What was that?" Kalian asked.

"Gravity bomb," was Namek's only reply, his lip raised above one of his fangs in the Novaarian equivalent of a smirk.

"Get us out of—" The stranger's muffled voice was cut off as Ilyseal engaged the vehicle's maximum thrust.

They accelerated from the stadium, the g-forces pushing them back into their seats. The goliath burst through the door, bringing the frame and surrounding wall with it. The stranger released several blue shots, each one hitting its mark but causing no damage.

Ilyseal banked the vehicle sharply before entering into a dive, trying to avoid another armoured attacker that flew off one of the great rings. It just missed them with its fingertips scratching the back of the car. The ride was sickening as they were pinned into their seats while hurtling down the tower.

"Activating grav enforcers." Ilyseal's words were followed by a change of sensation.

Despite their direction, gravity was not pulling them towards the front of the diving car. Ilyseal continued to manipulate the holographic domes in the console, in a bid to avoid debris and wayward attackers. An explosion to their right made her change course so they were no longer weaving between the floating platforms. They banked hard along a platform that resembled a giant park with forests and streams. The car flew low over a vast lake, kicking up waves of water, as it weaved left and right between falling debris and bodies.

As they dived again, leaving the park behind, Kalian saw one armoured attacker jump from the outer ring and land on a passing hover car just below them. The car wobbled under the added weight before the attacker jumped again, this time heading straight up and past them into the platform above. Moments later the underside of the platform began to crack, creating a web around the impact site. Kalian couldn't believe his eyes as the underside completely shattered under the weight of the lake. Water poured out like blood from a wound before finally releasing its entire content. Kalian shouted a warning as Ilyseal changed course again, now heading for the outer ring. Water rained down on them but the car managed to avoid the main body of water.

They all looked over to see the platform below take the full brunt. Anyone who didn't die instantly would have been washed off the edge. Kalian felt angry again. They could kill thousands in a single blow. Was he like them? He recognised the power they used but not to that level. What did any of this mean? Were they human, or was he something else? He was angry with himself for not having better control. If he had spent more time learning how to use his strange abilities maybe he could help. He looked at Li'ara cradling her broken arm and felt his other hand becoming hot. Before anything took shape, the car banked to the left, then the right, avoiding the falling debris from another platform that tumbled down the side of the rings like a waterfall of rock.

"We need to get to the *Valoran*, now!" Telarrek had to shout over the whipping wind caused by their speed.

Ilyseal interacted with the console for a moment, bringing up a holographic display that would lead them to the nearest port. "There is a problem," she replied. "When the Starrillium was ruptured it destroyed the atmo-barrier."

Kalian took a second to consider the consequences of that statement. If the atmo-barrier had been disabled then anyone outside, across the entire planet, would have been exposed to vacuum. That one attack could have killed millions.

"If the barrier's down everyone outside will die," Kalian said.

As if only just understanding what was going on, the stranger spoke up. "They would have been flash-burned by the explosion before space could kill them."

Kalian looked at him as if that statement was supposed to help.

"Just saying..."

Who was this guy? Using his good hand he quickly grasped the stranger's own. His *hands* - they were human. He looked up into the orange orbs of the faceplate but nothing was said between them. There was no time to get into it, he was helping and that would have to suffice, for now.

"We need to find another transport. Alert the *Valoran* we are en route." Telarrek looked across at Kalian as if considering something of note. "Inform them we need to travel to Corvus at maximum yield the moment we land."

Ilyseal made the appropriate arrangements via the console. Kalian wasn't sure of the importance of Corvus; the name was familiar from the data module. It was the home planet of the Trillik, a Conclave race that lived within the Novaarian border.

The car soon levelled out on the required ring and travelled across the gap to the spaceport. With so much danger around, Kalian couldn't stop the tingling in his spine. He was constantly on the lookout for another attack since they could come from any direction. It was Li'ara who saw it first. The human, or whatever it was, landed on the back of the car in a kneeling position as the metal crumpled around it. The whole car tilted before Ilyseal could make the correction. Namek moved in the blink of an eye. One second he was sitting down, the next he was standing half on the stranger's seat, half on the back of the car. Using his upper hands he thrust his staff horizontally into the attacker's neck. In a manoeuvre only a Novaarian could accomplish, he used his lower arms to grip the back of the legs and forced the attacker onto his back.

Namek's strength was impressive as he managed to keep him pinned while maintaining his balance on the moving vehicle. The stranger was dodging the many limbs that kicked out in his direction.

"The AI has initiated lockdown procedures. The port is not responding!" Ilyseal was just audible over the fighting.

"We shall deal with that when we get there!" Telarrek replied.

"If we get there..." Li'ara was watching closely as Namek continued to take blow after blow from the armoured fists.

Bloodied and bruised, Namek held the attacker down with his staff across the bulky chest. The light was impossible to miss. Just like his own, the attacker formed a ball of molten light within the palm of his hand. If he hit Namek with it, there would only be one outcome, and Kalian wouldn't allow it.

Without thinking, he jumped out of his seat, allowing the wind to force him across the distance and into the tangle of warriors. Telarrek and Li'ara reached out, trying to stop him. The interruption disrupted the light, ending it all together, while his body forced them apart. Namek was flung back into the car, landing on the stranger, while Kalian and the attacker were not so lucky. At the last second, Kalian was able to grab hold of the ridge at the back of the car, while the attacker clung to his leg. They were both being dragged behind the car as Ilyseal continued to dodge falling debris.

"Kalian!" Li'ara was climbing over the seats in agony as her arm slowed her down.

He looked back at the attacker wondering how long they could both hold on. The adrenaline was masking the pain he should be feeling in his burnt hand. The tingling in his back was increasing like a pressure building in his muscles. It didn't matter though, he couldn't hold on anymore. In the same instant his fingers let go, he felt the grip of two hands around his burnt one. What came next was more like instinct as he levelled his free hand at the attacker and released the energy he felt inside. The unseen wave smashed into the attacker, denting the impervious armour. Kalian watched as he was thrown away, out of sight.

Returning his attention to his saviour, he saw the masked stranger holding on to him. He seemed to hesitate for a moment before pulling him back into the safety of the car; not that it was much safer. Ilyseal banked and dived under an explosion before returning to their original height. They all felt the heat overhead before the car eventually slowed and manoeuvred into the spaceport.

"Thanks." Kalian was examining the dirty helmet worn by the stranger.

"Don't mention it, kid."

Kalian got the feeling he meant it.

Li'ara reached over, grabbing Kalian by the shoulder. "If you ever do anything like that again, I'll kill you myself!"

Kalian could only concentrate on the coy smile she wore.

The car landed in a hangar filled with ships, a little bigger than the *Fathom*. The one they landed beside was the same deep red as all Conclave security ships, though boxy in appearance. Kalian thought it looked like some kind of patrol ship with multiple forward armaments. He noticed the thick door up ahead and wondered if the lockdown procedure meant they wouldn't open.

"Can you override the ship controls?" Telarrek was supporting Namek's injured body as he asked.

"I already have." Ilyseal pressed something on her bracer and the hatch opened on the side of the ship with a ramp descending.

They soon found themselves sitting in various chairs in the ship's cockpit. Again Ilyseal worked the controls, bringing up different holograms that altered the console for Novaarian use. All four of her limbs danced across the different lights, activating the ship's systems.

"What about the door?" Li'ara asked.

"Not a problem." As Ilyseal spoke, a heads-up display shot across the viewport.

It indicated the section of the door that was currently being targeted by one of the ship's cannons. A flash of green hit the door, blowing it into space with most of the hangar's contents. The ship scratched the edges as it passed through and out of the Clave Tower.

Thinking back only ten minutes, Kalian couldn't believe the chain of events that had allowed them to get this far. There was no sign in the distance of where the Conclave ship had been rammed and the Starrillium had gone supernova, the explosion powerful enough to have incinerated it. Only the mammoth rectangular ship remained as hundreds of Conclave ships arrived to surround it and attack with salvo after salvo.

Across the interior of the planet was flying debris and broken structures, while the cockpit was hit by more than one body. The cylindrical towers had been attacked as well as the city above and below.

Within minutes they were entering the hangar of the *Valoran* and leaving the planet far behind. As they separated from the patrol ship, Kalian just had time to see the solar system become a blur that shifted to the left. As per Telarrek's orders, the *Valoran* had entered subspace, leaving nothing but an empty abyss beyond the hangar bay shield.

ELEVEN

Through an exertion of will, Savrick expanded his awareness, feeling the individual atoms and elements that made up the wall he was lodged against. At the speed of thought, he discovered them all and bent them to his will. The wall cracked in several places around his shoulder joints, allowing him to pull free. The Novaarian had used some kind of gravity distortion; how primitive that they had to rely on technology to achieve such feats.

He turned to the podium with thoughts of retribution for distracting him. The Highclave had all retreated into some structure they obviously thought was safe. The Novaarian female was still lying in rubble and broken chairs. Being of a different species her mind remained closed to his, though he could still feel the different frequencies it gave off. He thought about ending her there and then until two of his crew returned.

"Savrick." The helmet parted to reveal Lilander.

Sef kept his own helmet intact, as always. Lilander was a veteran among their kind and had served their cause since the beginning. He still remembered finding her on the outskirts of Nal-hala being hunted by the Terran. They had lost that particular battle and he had tried to save as many as he could. He arrived with Elandar expecting

271

to find her dead or captured. Instead, he found a dozen Terran bodies.

Her blonde hair was shaved around the edges with a spiky strip on top. Her features were as perfect as the rest of her species, though her bulky armour hid the toned body within. She had an intricate green tattoo that ran down her left cheek, stopping at her jaw bone. She looked to the side of his head where he had hit the wall.

"You are bleeding..." She said it with amazement and he knew it had been too long since he had been in a real fight.

He now felt the blood trickling down his face and across his cheekbone. Connecting with his body in the way only his kind could, he felt the wound, knowing it to be minor. His brain's own introspection told him he would suffer no effects or concussion. Savrick redirected his thoughts to the wound and dramatically increased the levels of platelets flooding the area. Within a second the bleeding had stopped and he instructed his skin to begin building the connective tissue to seal the wound. His mind could remove the scar while he slept.

The three of them turned as the cry of the beast could be heard beyond the path of destruction it had created. Savrick's own rage began to surface as he used the cerebral link to momentarily see through the beast's helmet. They had got away. *He* had got away. He looked up to the spiral of glass high above and screamed as loud as he could, his voice carrying the rage he felt. Lilander and Sef stepped away, afraid of any residual kickback from such a display of emotion. The tons of glass shattered, blowing out into Clave Tower below. The shards that didn't blow out fell back down on them, some of the pieces as big as the beast. The glass never reached them as it impacted an invisible dome around the three of them. Savrick could feel the intense frequencies that Sef's brain was pushing out and knew he was the reason they remained unharmed. Sef had only been a boy when Savrick found him, his parents killed for the simple crime of bringing him into the world. To this day, he had never spoken a single word. Loyalty was his language, and that was all Savrick could ask of him.

In the early half of the war, they had been appointed, by the others in their cause, to always keep Savrick safe. It had been him they rallied behind, making his survival paramount to victory. He had rejected the idea at first, knowing they all had a reason as unique as his own for starting the war. After centuries of near misses on the battlefield, however, he had eventually come to the realisation that his survival was crucial, if only so that he could be there when the last Terran fell.

"He is more powerful than I thought if he can create organic plasma." Savrick felt the crater in his armour where the super-heated ball had hit him.

The metal was charred and still hot to the touch. Through his link, he connected to the central processing unit located in the circular extension below his navel. In his mind's eye, he saw the command program open to his instructions for the nanocelium to begin repairing the crater. They were impossible to see with the naked eye as the microscopic machines moved across and within the armour. Upon observation, it would appear as though the armour was spontaneously pushing back out into its pre-programmed state.

"Did you see his hand, though?" Lilander asked. "He hasn't mastered his abilities yet. He is still vulnerable."

"It was my own arrogance that allowed their escape. I underestimated him." He looked away, unable to meet her eyes. Like a fool, he had wanted to prolong the moment to make Kalian suffer more.

They could all hear the distant explosions and screams of the Conclave. His brothers and sisters were making a bloody mess of things. He felt a moment of sympathy for his crew, knowing these savages offered no real challenge for them.

"Where are they now?" Being only one of two such beings in the whole tower there was nowhere Kalian could hide from their sensors.

The pilot relayed the data through Lilander's link, upon her request, and displayed them via the emitters in the waist of her armour. The hologram was laid out before them, much like the one Savrick had seen earlier with three red dots near the edge of the tower. Lilander silently commanded it to magnify, showing them the erratic movements of the vehicle they had escaped in.

"There are three of them?" Lilander voiced their confusion.

Recalling any memory was as easy as breathing to them. Savrick thought back to the moments after he was pulled into the wall. The image was crystal clear in his mind despite the distraction of being attacked at the time. If his eyes had ever seen it, then the image lay permanently somewhere in his brain. He remembered seeing another individual drop from the gantry above while shooting at the beast. He analysed the image until he recognised the hands holding the weapons. How this particular human had come to be here was a mystery. Ultimately, he didn't care, for if he was with Kalian, he would die anyway.

"Sef," Savrick said, turning from the hologram. "Bring them to me, alive." Sef gave a small nod and set off at a sprint towards the beast. "I will return to the ship."

Lilander's face gave away how torn she was to follow him back. Her duty commanded she escort him but the prospect of the fun she could have here was too much. She had already held back simply by being present for the encounter with Kalian.

"You worry too much, Lilander. I will not be so easily surprised a second time." He considered for a moment wiping out the entire Novaarian species for that particular attack. "I will be fine. As the humans say, 'Go break a leg'." Of course, he was not referring to her own.

After an incredible burst of telekinesis, Savrick found himself back in the command module with a frantic looking Elandar. His hands were darting from one hologram to another as he stood surrounded by various nanite-made structures.

"They are fleeing!" Elandar didn't need to look to know Savrick had entered.

Having spent so many years together they were keenly aware of each other's specific brain waves. Savrick examined the display in front of Elandar, taking note of the trajectory line that cut across the galactic map. The information overlapping the image told him they had retreated to the Novaarian ship.

He couldn't believe what he was seeing. How had they escaped Sef? He was growing tired of the slippery nature of this Kalian Gaines. A quick inquiry through his Link informed him of Elandar's success regarding his own personal mission.

"Recall them immediately - all of them!" Their fun would have to wait. The war wasn't over yet.

AFTER LEAVING THE HANGAR, Kalian had insisted that they do nothing before getting Li'ara to the med bay. Rather than leave them, Telarrek and Ilyseal followed them along with a small contingent of Novaarian warriors. Kalian had a feeling it was more out of concern about their new guest. They were happy for him to follow them after he offered no protest against the removal of his weapons. Namek was taken to a different med bay as his injuries were more severe. Kalian would thank him the next time he saw him, given that he had saved their lives twice that day.

The stranger stood to one side with his hands in his pockets as if he was totally at home in this new environment. The mechanical spider descended from its berth and broke into sections around Li'ara as she sat on the gurney. Being in this room again reminded Kalian of the moment he had learned of Earth's fate.

The spider's legs separated into multiple appendages, each with a different tool or implement. Despite her protests, the many arms found the seals in her armour and removed each of the plates. With the precision only a machine could manage, it sliced the undersuit around her shoulder and down the broken arm, before stripping it off in one smooth motion. The skin around her humerus was bruised and swollen but, worse, the entire arm hung at an unusual angle from her collarbone.

Another mechanical arm slipped out and scanned the arm from top to bottom with a thin blue line. The embedded wall monitor showed the display of the arm like an x-ray, with a visible fracture in the centre of the bone and a dislocation of the ball and socket joint. Although Li'ara couldn't see it, one of the arms produced a square red patch from within a hidden compartment. The patch was applied to the back of her deltoid where it instantly scrunched up, sticking to the skin. The red contents disappeared as the skin blushed. Her response was indicative of some kind of analgesia.

Another arm descended and rotated around the fracture site, spraying what looked like water.

"I can't feel my arm." Li'ara looked distressed for a moment as the same mechanical arm produced a scalpel.

Ilyseal stepped in to reassure her. "The Medder will first mend the broken bone before relocating the joint. But do not fear, you will not feel anything."

When Li'ara looked back the Medder had already cut into the arm and inserted several fine extensions. Another arm wiped away the trickle of blood. The monitor showed the fine extensions rapidly moving across the fracture, filling in the gaps as they did.

"We have been studying your kind for a long time," Telarrek interrupted. "We can easily replicate the bone and surrounding tissue."

As rapidly as the extensions had operated, they extracted themselves and slotted back into the housing. A small green laser moved over the incision, closing the gap, which was then covered by a similar red patch to the one on her deltoid.

"Leave this on for the next day and there will be no scar," Ilyseal said.

Another analgesic patch was applied over the scapula and clavicle. Kalian turned away from this part as the Medder formed two arms that lifted Li'ara's and held on to her shoulder. In one swift motion, it rotated the arm, relocating the joint back into position. Astonishingly, Li'ara felt nothing as she started flexing her arm and rotating the joint. The Medder retreated back into its housing, becoming an inverted dome again. Li'ara nodded and gave the Novaarians a small smile of gratitude.

Kalian walked over and gave her mended shoulder a squeeze. They shared a smile and he was elated to see her well again. Their lives had become so intertwined he couldn't imagine losing her now.

"Your hand!" Li'ara gripped his hand in her own and turned it palm up.

It took Kalian a moment to remember the condition his hand had been in. "I don't understand..." He examined it himself in disbelief.

The burn was completely gone without as much as a scar. How was this possible? They must have all seen his display with the strange ball of light he expelled, not to mention the stranger seeing him push the attacker off without touching him. But this rapid healing was new to him as well.

"I suppose I have some explaining to do," Kalian said.

To his confusion, neither Telarrek nor Ilyseal looked shocked.

"Later." Telarrek looked to the stranger in the corner.

The entrance to the med bay opened as a Novaarian guard entered. He presented a small disc-shaped box to Telarrek who took it and dismissed him. Kalian recognised the container; he was wearing one of its contents behind his ear.

"I think this might be easier if it came from you." Telarrek handed the disc to Kalian, who looked at the stranger and then back at Telarrek with a puzzled expression. "Our scans indicate he is human." Telarrek hesitated before looking at Li'ara. "Human like you."

Having seen Savrick and his kind, it was clear there was now a genetic split. Kalian understood what he meant but didn't know where this human had come from.

"You're going to need one of these if you're going to understand anything." Kalian extended his arm, with the disc split apart to reveal the small circular dot inside. The stranger looked from the Novaarians to the contents of the disc. He was obviously suspicious. "Don't worry; we've got one as well." Kalian tilted his head to show his own implant.

His human hands slipped out of his pockets as he lifted the helmet from his head. Neither of them knew what to expect but

Kalian felt some elation in seeing another human being, even if he did look a bit rough. His dark hair was cropped short with no sign of any grey. He looked to be somewhere in his early forties but human ageing made it impossible to tell. He had an unkempt appearance with at least a week's worth of stubble. His hazel eyes moved across the room taking everything in with a quick glance. It almost reminded him of Li'ara.

"So you're saying if I put this thing on, I'll understand what fang boy over there is saying?" His voice was gruff like he hadn't spoken in a while.

Kalian gave him an affirming nod while picking up the translator with his finger and thumb. The stranger took it and placed in the same place as Kalian's. After a few seconds, he looked around as if hearing something distant before moving his tongue around.

"It's metallic I know. It goes away after a while." Kalian moved aside as Telarrek came over.

"Wait..." Li'ara hopped off the gurney and stood before the stranger. "I'd recognise that gear anywhere. You're UDC..."

"Commander Roland North, at your service." He didn't look too happy with his own name and Kalian didn't like the way he looked at Li'ara.

Telarrek bowed his head with the usual greeting. "Greetings of peace, Commander North." Roland looked dumbstruck for a moment as he took in the alien words. "I am Charge Telarrek. You are aboard my ship, the *Valoran*."

"I think I've been aboard enough alien ships to last a lifetime." Roland moved away as he felt the edges of his translator behind his ear.

"How did you get here?" Li'ara looked almost hungry for answers. "Were you on Alpha NL-2204?"

Kalian could see her train of thought. There was only one way another human could get this far into the Conclave: the Laronians. Roland looked suspicious of how they might know about the classified terraforming project.

"Yeah, I was there until some scaly blue aliens showed up and destroyed everything. They held us in their ship for about a week until I escaped." He was startled when a floating hologram appeared in front of him due to his proximity to a console. He tried to carry on as if he was taking it all in his stride.

Kalian was impressed that Roland had managed to escape a Laronian vessel and make his way to Clave Tower.

"Find the Laronian ship." At Telarrek's command, Ilyseal left the med bay to carry out her orders.

Li'ara faced him again. "I am Lieuten-" She stopped and glanced at Kalian. "I'm Li'ara Ducarté and this is Kalian Gaines."

They could both see the giant elephant in the room. If the Commander had been on Alpha NL-2204 then it stood to reason that he wouldn't know about the attack on Earth. He remembered back to the Icarus station when Commander Hawkins had told them that communications were down, just as the giant ship appeared. Chances are those same communications were being used to keep the terraforming group in contact. But how do you tell someone their entire civilisation has been destroyed and their species is now endangered?

Telarrek understood what they were both contemplating. "I will give you the time you need. When you are finished meet me in the Observatory." With that, he left the med bay.

"What's he talking about?" Roland stopped examining a strange surgical implement that looked like a gun.

Kalian looked to Li'ara. He had no idea where to begin.

"There's something you need to know about Earth..." she began.

They spent the next two hours going through the chain of events that had led them to this very spot. Kalian chose to divulge his secret as Roland wanted to know why a history lecturer was so important, not to mention him already witnessing it firsthand. After Roland heard this, Kalian felt a tactical mind examining him for threats and weaknesses. At the news of Earth's destruction, he sat back on the gurney as if he couldn't take his own weight anymore. They tried to answer his questions about this new enemy that looked like humans but even their knowledge was patchy at best. He found it hard to believe that there was a weapon capable of destroying a star, having been in the weapons business himself.

He was left swearing after hearing Century had been attacked as well. It didn't need explaining that there were very few humans left and that a large portion of them were now in Laronian custody. He didn't have as many questions as Kalian thought he would, but it was possible he was in shock. They offered information regarding some of the things and species he had encountered since his capture, which he quickly absorbed as well as what had been said between them and the Highclave. His silence prompted Kalian to ask some of his own questions.

"Did you..." He hesitated looking at Li'ara. "Did you have any family?"

This broke Roland's reverie as he looked to be remembering something distant. "I've never really had time for family. Think I had a dad in Australia, a cousin on Mars..." His attention returned fully to the two looking at him. "So it's all gone - Earth, Century, hell, the UDC?" Li'ara gave a slow nod, as it was hard for her to say it as well. "Well, shit..." was all he could say.

He stood up and started pacing the med bay. Kalian assumed pacing was something they taught at the academy.

"So between our extinction, these armoured bastards and what-ever the hell you are in all this," Roland said, pointing at Kalian, "what are we supposed to do now?"

"Without the UDC, we have to come up with our own objectives." Li'ara stood as well now.

"Really? Because it looks to me as if... whatever its name is, is the one giving the orders on this boat," Roland countered.

"We can trust, Telarrek." Kalian felt quite defensive about him.

Roland sat back down and rolled his eyes. "Hell. I never took orders from the UDC when they were around." He said it more to himself as he inspected the sleeve of his hide coat.

Li'ara looked puzzled at his comment. "What do you mean? You're a Commander," she said.

Roland's head fell back as he laughed. "Six months ago I didn't even have a rank."

Kalian didn't really know what was being said between the two soldiers, but he was amazed at how well Roland was taking everything in.

"Since the term classified no longer applies," Roland elaborated cryptically, "let's just say I was more of a free agent than a windup toy for Central Parliament."

Kalian still didn't understand the reference, but Li'ara's face dropped. "You're an agent, aren't you? You must have screwed up pretty bad to get put in line with us grunts."

"What are you talking about?" Kalian was in the wrong profession to understand all the terms they were using.

"He's an agent for Central Parliament. Trained by some black ops branch of the UDC and given free rein in the name of progression." Roland had a smug face after her description. "He's just a killer." Li'ara clearly didn't approve of his line of work.

"I did the things you couldn't, sweetheart. Someone had to look pretty for the civvies," He flicked his finger at Li'ara, "I worked in the dark so you could keep marching in your parades and wearing your shiny armour. If you ever got in deep, they'd send the fleet in after you. Me, they'd just disavow like I never existed."

"Or send you to the ass-end of the galaxy."

Her reply made Roland laugh again. "Well, that's another story, sweetheart."

Li'ara's eyes rolled. Kalian didn't think he was brave enough to call her sweetheart. Whatever the reason for his exile, he wasn't ready to share it yet.

"Well, now you know about us and we sort of know about you." Kalian was trying to see the bigger picture.

They now had to find a way to save the people on the Laronian ship, as well as prepare for any survivors that might respond to the Conclave's beacon. As far as Savrick was concerned, he had a feeling Telarrek had a plan.

"I suggest we go meet Telarrek in the Observatory and plan our next move."

Li'ara looked at him in slight surprise, but he could tell she was a little impressed with his take-charge attitude. In truth he surprised himself at the authority he intoned.

A quick introspection showed he had changed quite a bit in the last week. He felt that if ever the circumstances required a change, it was certainly these. Since taking the time to focus, he had found new control, as well as abilities he never thought he would have. Though he felt running for his life might have had a hand in things. He had gone from being an obscure lecturer to the centre of a galactic size question mark. As they left the med bay for the bridge, he couldn't help but ponder his part in everything. Why was *he* so significant? Was he like Savrick, whatever that was? It was hard to deny the fact that they had similar abilities. He looked at his healed hand again and suddenly felt very alien in his own skin.

After reaching the bridge, Kalian was annoyed at how easily Roland had taken to the vertical walkway. It wasn't that he was jealous of the agent, but he knew Roland's past would make relating to Li'ara easier than his own. The thought made him stop and think about his own feelings towards her. It felt stupid to even consider the thought of having feelings for her. They had only known each other for a week, in a set of circumstances that were less than ideal. The only reason they were getting on was because they had been forced together in a bad situation. Not to mention the crisis their species was now in.

He forced himself to be realistic as they were met by Ilyseal. There were actual lives depending on their next course of action. Kalian's world had just become a lot bigger. With *his* decisions forming its shape. Guilt began to creep in as he considered this new exciting pace of life. He could never return to the classroom after this. For the first time in his life, he felt a measure of control that gave him meaning and purpose. How could he give that up?

Ilyseal escorted them into the Observatory after Roland had soaked up every detail his eyes and ears could get from the bridge. He kept the hide coat on that he had apparently taken from a corpse after he escaped the Laronians. From the way he had described his escape, Kalian got the impression he enjoyed that particular part of his job. Li'ara looked better now that she wore a long grey shawl, left for her in the med bay, over the top half of her torn undersuit. She had said there were more undersuits in the *Fathom* but she was eager to know why they were heading for Corvus.

Telarrek was busy manipulating many holograms with all four of his hands. They moved in around the central column with the holographic display console wrapped around it. At first glance, Kalian guessed he was looking at trajectories on a star map with different systems and planets labelled throughout. He was quietly impressed with his ability to read most of the information laid out, as well as the orange console.

"Now we know the face of our enemy." Telarrek looked at Kalian but he couldn't read the Novaarian face. "Of course this only begs more questions."

He altered the image to show a recording from the hover-cameras that floated over the fight. The picture froze on a clear image of Savrick after his helmet disappeared.

"Did any of the others survive?" Kalian asked.

He suddenly felt very guilty for leaving Uthor and even the Nix to possibly suffer the wrath of Savrick.

Telarrek cupped his long jaw. "We do not know. I only pray that Councillor Elondrasa is alive with the rest of the Highclave."

Upon hearing the words, Kalian realised he had never considered the Novaarian culture to have a religion. He reminded himself to look it up on the data-module later.

"Well he might look human, but he ain't like any human I've ever seen." Roland was leaning against the wall, half in shadow. "Except maybe you."

With his last words, everyone turned to Kalian. He looked around but didn't know what to say.

"Without complete concealment, we were able to scan this, Savrick." Telarrek brought up a smaller hologram alongside his image. Kalian now recognised the sight of the karyogram. "His DNA is identical to yours, Kalian."

Another karyogram appeared with his name below it. The two strands of DNA merged together perfectly.

"Their technology is advanced," Li'ara said. "More so than your own, and especially ours. How is it even possible they could be human?"

"I was hoping you might be able to shed some light on the situation." Telarrek looked down at Kalian.

The connections were easy for them all to make. He had demonstrated the unusual abilities that Savrick and his kind had shown. Even his DNA was the same.

"You've been watching me my whole life. Since I was born." Kalian had his own suspicions about what he might be, but the facts were there: he had been *born* on Earth. "Everything I know, you know."

"We were monitoring you and the surrounding communications to ensure your safety. We never saw you until we met on the Icarus station. And I think there are a few things you are not telling me." Telarrek's head slowly ducked closer to Kalian's.

The comment was fair. He had been keeping secrets. But he had been keeping *that* one his whole life.

"I don't know how I'm able to do the things I do. I really don't." He gave them a quick account of the strange things that had occurred throughout his life, as well as the new developments. "I've been emotionally numb my entire life, trying to prevent it from getting worse. That's been a little harder this last week, what with all the near-death experiences and..." He realised he was midway through pointing at Li'ara and couldn't find the words.

She gave him a curious look but remained silent.

"You're a freak kid. We get it." Roland looked bored. "Can we get on with it?" He looked to Telarrek hoping he would move things on.

Telarrek took a moment to absorb everything Kalian had said while sharing some silent conversation with Ilyseal.

"I believe there may be answers on Naveen." Telarrek altered the hologram again to return to the galaxy map.

"Is that the place with the..." Roland displayed his open palm.

"The Wall, yes. We are currently heading for the Trillik home-world, Corvus."

The hologram clearly showed Corvus at the end of a highlighted line, with the Conclave at the other end and the *Valoran* near the middle.

"But Naveen is in orbit around Nova Prime, so why are we going to Corvus?" Li'ara raised the question before Kalian could.

Ilyseal replied. "The *Valoran* will leave a trail carrying the signature of Intrinium. Savrick and his ship will be able to track us wherever we go." The holographic lighting made her red tendrils appear black, like dreadlocks.

Telarrek attempted to elaborate for the confused looks before Roland interjected. "Decoy. Very nice." The agent strolled over to the central column.

Telarrek bowed and continued, "The *Valoran* will continue its journey to Corvus while a smaller ship departs here." He pointed at a section of the highlighted line. "We will enter real space for a moment before continuing on."

"Won't Savrick be able to detect the other ship? Do you even have another ship that can travel at FTL?" Kalian asked what he thought was an obvious question.

"You want to use the *Fathom,* don't you?" Li'ara was staring intently at Telarrek.

"We have used our own Starrillium to charge the stored Intrinium," Ilyseal replied. "Your people's design is quite sophisticated."

"You mean, for a bunch of apes?" Kalian could tell Li'ara hadn't taken real offence at what he knew was meant to be a compliment.

Telarrek continued, "The *Fathom* will jump to Naveen with us, while Ilyseal takes the *Valoran* to Corvus. We do not doubt their ability to track both ships, nor do we doubt that they have smaller ships within. But they will have to divide their forces to catch both of us. It may just give us the time we need to discover some much-needed answers."

The humans looked at each other, weighing up the plan. Kalian knew the outcome though. They had no other choice.

"There is something else to consider." Everyone looked to Ilyseal. "All scans and recordings have been filtered from the attack on the Conclave."

The Novaarian slid something across her bracer and the information passed over into the central hologram. It showed Savrick's ship, shortly before it rammed the security vessel.

Out of the three humans, only Roland reacted to the sight. "That's the ship they were holding us on!"

The enormous ship silently moved over the top of the Laronian warship and appeared to swallow it whole. There was no explosion or firing of any kind, leading them to believe that the ship had been captured and not destroyed.

"Our analysts believe they took the ship because of the humans within," Ilyseal added, "though why they were not instantly destroyed we do not know."

Kalian could only guess at the reason they had been taken prisoner.

"Chances are that ship will follow the *Valoran* to Corvus and they'll send a smaller one to follow the *Fathom*." They followed Roland's chain of thought. It made sense to send the big ship after the other big ship. "So I think I'll stick with the *Valoran*." The comment surprised all of them. Kalian had assumed he would want to follow them and get some answers, or at least stick with the two of them. "I've got some unfinished business with that Laronian ship." Roland stroked his stubble - like a general planning a battle.

"How the hell are you going to get inside that ship?" Li'ara looked doubtful at Roland's idea.

"I don't usually plan that far ahead." He turned back to Telarrek. "How long until the *Fathom* departs?"

"You have less than one human day."

Roland headed for the door.

"Where are you going?" Kalian asked.

Roland didn't bother to turn around. "To see if there's a bar on this boat."

AFTER LEAVING THE OBSERVATORY, Kalian and Li'ara headed for the *Fathom* in the hangar bay. They couldn't help but smile as Namek was there waiting for them. He looked as brand new as the *Fathom* did. All of his bruises and cuts were gone, and Kalian could easily guess that Namek had suffered internal injury as well as broken bones.

"Greetings of peace, Namek." To Kalian's surprise, it was Li'ara who had used the alien greeting.

He returned the phrase with a bow. "I am glad you are both well." They both noticed a new addition to his attire. A silver cylinder was now strapped to his long thigh. "I wanted to show you both the new upgrades we have made to your ship."

"You've been messing with my ship?" Her face suggested she was not too concerned.

Namek returned the playful comment. "Only for the better, I assure you."

They entered the cabin which appeared the same, minus the blood. Li'ara made the armoury her first stop. She lightly touched some of the mounted weapons, like a mother checking her sleeping children. At the end of the room, she opened a panel on the wall and entered the required code to unlock the cabinet beside her. Kalian recognised the dark undersuit as well as new plates of armour. When she was satisfied, Namek informed them that the medical room had been upgraded with a small version of the Medder that now rested in its housing above them. Li'ara subconsciously gripped her shoulder, slowly rotating it as she inspected the mechanical spider. As unsure as she was having such an alien device on board, Kalian knew she couldn't argue with the results.

The cockpit held the biggest changes. Just by entering the room the main console came to life instantly, projecting green and blue holograms of all the internal sensors. Kalian couldn't figure out why it looked so much bigger. They had even managed to fit two more chairs in. Namek explained that the two rear consoles had been removed to make space for the extra seating. Before Li'ara could complain, he went on to explain that everything could now be accessed from the main console, and something to do with Conclave technology allowing for greater processing space. It went a little over his head as Namek showed Li'ara how the new touch holograms worked, as well as some new guidance systems. Kalian was mostly impressed with the comfy new chairs.

"Weapons?" Li'ara's excited tone brought his attention back.

"We found a lot of unutilized space as well as some redundant mechanisms. Once removed or replaced we thought the ship would benefit from some defensive measures."

Kalian tuned out again as Namek explained the yield of the new weapons and how to use them. He instead chose to retire to the sofa, in favour of his Datapad. He unrolled it on the table and activated the hologram setting so he could sit back and view the images. Again he found himself sifting through different images of all things human. He especially enjoyed the images from Century since he had never been there to see it for himself. The thought of never being able to see any of it again made him tired as he was flooded with emotion. He let his head rest back and his dreams consume him.

His dreams were violent and chaotic until he emerged back in his parents' car the night they died. He was sitting in the back while they argued. It had always been hazy in his memory and he could never remember what they were so upset about. The dreamy state of his surroundings took on a sharper edge as memory became very real. He could hear the rain hammering against the car as they hurtled over the mag track across the various sky bridges. It was dark outside, with all the light coming from the holographic signs and billboards they passed. He heard his mother's voice and felt scared and frightened, knowing they were talking about him.

"We can't do this, Joseph!" his mother shouted with tears streaming down her face. "Think what they'll do to him. We'll never see him again!" She turned back to look at Kalian with wet brown eyes.

"What else can we do?" his father shouted back with desperation in his voice. "They'll have scientists and experts who can help him!"

They were both facing each other, not even looking at the road ahead. The Mag-car would take them to their destination without any input from them. Kalian could see the display showing the path of the road in highlighted red as it curved around the buildings.

"You mean study him!" his mother countered. "He's not some alien we found on Charon. He's our son, Joseph!"

Kalian felt suddenly upset that his parents were so angry with him. They were talking about sending him away because of the strange things that keep happening around him. He was upset because he was the reason they didn't want him anymore and he was angry with himself because he couldn't control it.

"Mary..." His father put his hand over his mother's. "We have no choice." Kalian heard the words and felt his fingertips tingle when the mag-car increased in speed as it approached the bend in the bridge.

"Kalian!" Li'ara's cry woke him with a panic.

As his eyes opened he felt the tug of gravity as he and the sofa dropped back onto the cabin floor. The table was upended with his Datapad on the other side of the room. He looked up to see Namek and Li'ara, as well as three Novaarian technicians, staring at him.

"Are you ok?" Li'ara moved to help him up but he had already managed it.

He was surprised to feel embarrassment rather than the usual dread he felt when someone witnessed such a display.

"Sorry about that." The technicians had even larger eyes than normal, with a purple tongue visible inside their open mouths. "Bad dream..." Kalian saw real concern in Li'ara's green eyes as she looked him over with a critical inspection.

"We need to leave. These engineers are here to fit the last upgrade needed for Telarrek's plan." Li'ara gently guided them out of the

Fathom with Namek close behind. When out of earshot she asked, "What was that about?"

Kalian thought about the dream and was shocked to have so vividly remembered his parents' conversation. His entire adult life he had only remembered the odd word, never certain of what caused the argument. It was a revelation to know they had been arguing about his abilities. He didn't know he had ever displayed any when he was younger. In truth, he felt sorry for his parents having a child that was so alien to them they felt they had to get rid of him. Where were they taking him? His only conclusion was the UDC. His thoughts lingered for a moment on the two people like him whom Telarrek had mentioned. Had he been close to their fate, stuck in some UDC lab and never to be seen again?

He told Li'ara everything he had seen, but she looked sceptical. She pointed out that it was only a dream and that he might have filled in the conversation for himself. If the dream hadn't been so real, he would have been inclined to agree with her.

"We should find Roland and make sure he's not drunk the ship dry."

Just saying his name, Kalian could see Li'ara's thoughts about the agent. He was the darker side to everything she had upheld as a UDC soldier. Thinking about what he must have gone through just to get this far impressed Kalian though. He kept the thought to himself, but he was glad to have Roland North on their side.

After using the communication disc to contact Ilyseal, they discovered his location deeper inside the ship. The central structure of the *Valoran* was a mirror of the Conclave. It was hollowed out and separated into rings with adjoining platforms. Roland looked a little ridiculous sitting on the Novaarian-sized stool at the ship's bar. It was hard to miss the looks and hushed conversations from every Novaarian.

"How did you find the only bar on the whole ship?" Kalian climbed up onto the stool next to him, with Li'ara taking the other side.

"He could probably smell it - if that's possible over that unique brand of his own." Li'ara's nose crinkled in disgust.

"You spend a week cramped in a cargo bay with a thousand people and see how you smell." He gave himself a sniff inside his long coat. "That's the smell of a real man, sweetheart. You've spent too long with the kid here." He thumbed in Kalian's direction. Roland continued to down the rest of his blue coloured drink until the glass was empty. "Tastes like Solarcite." A mischievous smirk crept up his face. "But it doesn't wear off after an hour." As soon as he placed his glass on the circular coaster it began to fill up from the bottom like magic. "Two more for my endangered friends!" He slammed the bar as he slurred his words.

They both inspected the drinks that emerged from their own coasters. The smell was enough to put them off.

Kalian wondered if this was Roland's way of dealing with the news about Earth and Century though it didn't sound like he had lost anyone he really cared about. Li'ara had lost her anchors with the death of her father and the destruction of the UDC, whereas Roland had lost his life-style and the control and freedom granted him by Central Parliament. Kalian felt like he had lost a culture he was feeling less and less a part of. The changes and revelations of the past week had given him a new sense of belonging. He was beginning to feel like he had always belonged out amongst the stars in a culture as vast as the Conclave. But when he looked at Li'ara he had other new feelings, feelings of attachment and loyalty to her, and whatever was left of humanity. He knew himself to be human. He felt human, but Savrick and his kind had fogged the issue.

They remained in the bar for a few hours. Kalian and Li'ara ordered a less deadly drink, while Roland continued to inhale the alien alcohol. Kalian hated to admit that the agent's dry sense of humour was quite entertaining, but even Li'ara laughed every now and again. Kalian felt his own stories weren't as interesting as theirs, with his being mostly anecdotal jokes about teaching and theirs about action and adventure. The more Roland drank, the more secrets he spilt and the less jovial he became.

"You know all those separatists and rebels we spent so long trying to silence?" Every five or six words were interrupted by a hiccup. "It turned out they were all being backed by the same organisation."

Li'ara's interest seemed piqued at the statement.

"Some remnant of the corporate wars that wanted to take back control or something. I don't know. It all seems so... What was the point of it all? All those missions, all those wars... all that time..." He looked off into the distance as if he could see through the bar. "So we could make a better world?" He suddenly laughed, as at some untold joke. "All for nothing..." He was starting to sound bitter. "And what about you Red, hanging on to some pathetic order to keep *him* alive? The UDC is gone. What's left of it is sitting in a Laronian ship, and they don't even know what's going on!"

A smaller glass with yellow liquid shot up from the fixed coaster. Roland didn't even bother to look at it before draining it. "We should just embrace this new culture and see what opportunities it can offer. Get away from all the human bullshit and red tape and just..." He imitated a ship flying off before rolling his tongue around in his mouth. "Fruity!" Roland blinked hard a few times before examining his surroundings. "Crap!" He picked up the small glass and gave it a smell. "It made me sober again!"

Li'ara rolled her eyes and shook her head in despair. "How you got this far I'll never know."

They hopped off their stools as Ilyseal contacted them to inform them of the departure time. Roland followed them to the hangar since he had nowhere else to go. It was busier than normal with hundreds of crew and machines working on the various smaller craft. More than once they had to stop to allow for large containers and ship parts to be ferried across the bay. Seeing the Novaarians work in such a technical way, Kalian could see how useful having four arms was.

Telarrek and Ilyseal were waiting for them by the *Fathom* as Namek disappeared into the ship carrying supplies.

"The ship is ready. The *Valoran* will enter real space for only as long as it takes for us to depart," Telarrek said.

"Roland, you are welcome to accompany me to the command bridge and use the Observatory for research. Your council in the coming battle will be appreciated. It has been thousands of years since our people have been involved in anything as violent as war."

Roland looked taken aback by Ilyseal's words. He obviously wasn't used to being spoken to quite so politely. "Just keep me away from the blue stuff." Roland pretended to be distracted by some distant engineering work.

Telarrek and Ilyseal turned to one another and clasped one lower arm and one upper arm, then gently touched their foreheads before parting.

"Fight with the courage you have lived with and you will find victory, Charge Ilyseal." Telarrek was bestowing her with the mantle of charge and giving her the *Valoran*.

The seriousness of his words gave Kalian pause. The *Valoran* was going up against a ship that had already destroyed one human fleet, several Conclave security vessels, survived a miniature supernova and obliterated two solar systems. The odds were not on their side. It suddenly felt crazy that Ilyseal, Roland, and the thousands of crew on board would most likely die, just so that they *might* find some answers. Kalian was starting to feel the weight of countless deaths, just so that Savrick could have the satisfaction of killing him.

"I might be regretting my first choice." Roland broke the gravity of the situation. "Maybe I should come with you guys."

"Let's go." Li'ara walked past them, ignoring Roland and heading for the *Fathom*.

He gave a large sigh as Ilyseal ushered him towards the Translift and the command bridge.

Once inside, Li'ara took her position in the pilot seat next to Namek, with Telarrek and Kalian sitting behind. Hangar crew moved out of the way as Li'ara retracted the landing gear and manoeuvred the ship towards the shield. Everything seemed a lot smoother since the upgrades had been installed, and Li'ara took to the new controls like a fish to water.

Poised in front of the shield, they waited a moment until the vast field of stars appeared in a flash of light. Using the new holographic domes, Li'ara flew the ship out into space. Only seconds later, the display showed the departure of the *Valoran* as it continued its journey to Corvus.

"Nice..." Li'ara was impressed with the new navigational system.

She was presented with a list of destinations the ship had enough fuel to reach. The Novaarian technicians had obviously encoded the Conclave network into the ship's systems. After choosing Nova Prime, it gave a sub-list of surrounding planets and moons within that region. She chose Naveen and waited while the Nav computer worked through the complex mathematics of plotting the safest course, taking into account asteroids, black holes, stars, passing ships, and other planets. Before she could activate the Intrinium ignition, Namek used all four of his hands to work the console.

"One last upgrade." Namek depressed the touch console, causing a mechanical sound at the back of the ship.

The display showed them six cylindrical objects being jettisoned from a new hatch underneath. After a moment of free-floating, they came alive, pointing in varying directions before six small flashes lit up the viewport.

"Savrick and his people will know of this tactic when they see we have stopped," Telarrek explained. "If he splits his forces he will not know which Intrinium signature to follow. The *Valoran's* will be clear to see but those six Intrinium drives will mask our own, giving them seven locations to choose from. This will give us more time."

Kalian heard the distinct sound of hope in his voice. Satisfied with the ship's diagnostics, Li'ara pulled the lever to take them back into oily subspace.

They would get their answers.

THE COMMAND MODULE appeared to be breached again as the panoramic hologram showed them entering real space. Through his link, Savrick knew the pilot was instantly analysing all local star systems. They had stopped here, if only for a moment, but why? Did they really think it would go unnoticed against the capabilities of this ship? He already knew from the holograms that floated around his person that the Novaarian ship was continuing on a heading for a planet called Corvus. So like a Terran, to run and hide from the very thing they started. How dare they undo all his work. The pain and suffering his kind had endured to end them, and they do this? That is why Kalian Gaines must die.

Just thinking of the humans made him angry. Their existence was an insult to his cause, a cause that had taken the lives of so many of his kind. It angered him further to think of how long it was taking to find and kill just one of them. Both Elandar and he felt the detection through their links.

"Show me," Savrick verbally commanded.

The hologram magnified a sector of local space and began a reconstruction of the sensor's readings. Eight Intrinium scars had been located in close proximity to one another. Elandar increased the strength of the neutrino bursts but limited its bandwidth to that grid. The image changed to highlight the individual signatures so they could distinguish and further analyse them. The pilot began to dissect the individual crystals left behind by the jump to subspace.

The largest collection of crystals had a unique isotope reading, marking the Novaarians' jump. A ship of that size could not avoid their sensors even if they were cloaked. The other seven were almost identical, with a varying amount of crystals left behind by a smaller ship. Savrick quickly ran the scenarios through his mind searching for the most obvious answers. Had some of the crew abandoned ship knowing they would be hunted and ultimately destroyed by his forces? Had they sent messengers to wayward allies with a plea of help? Or had they simply wanted to slow them down with a mysterious stop mid-journey?

No...

He had a better idea of what was happening here. They were being made to choose; follow one signature or the other, or split his forces. Smart, but foolish. Even if he did split his forces they could still overcome anything their crude technology threw at them. If this was truly their ploy then Kalian could now be in any one of eight places. He waved the holograms away in frustration. This was taking too long.

"Pull them apart. I want estimated fuel consumption, potential destinations, class of ship and I want it now!"

Elandar began his own investigation at Savrick's request as well as the pilot who responded through his link commands.

"We have all the data on human technology as well as Conclave. I want to know what they're up to. Sift through it all if you have to."

"I have something." Elandar picked up the floating hologram and slid it across the room to Savrick.

The image showed a breakdown of the crystals on a microscopic level. Intermingled with the other scars was an unusual pattern that had traces of an alloy across the crystalline surface. This alloy had clearly been picked up by the crystals as they were ejected from the engine. A further inspection of the trace element proved its origin was not of Conclave design.

"The human ship." Savrick recalled the small human vessel that had boarded the *Eclipse* before it decimated the Century system.

Elandar had seen the female soldier, as well as Kalian, in the central structure of the missile. Just thinking about it, the pilot projected its schematics into the command module. The side read Fathom.

Another scan projected the calculations made, based upon the other scar crystals. A local map of space showed the other six ships would run out of fuel in the middle of nowhere. They were just a pitiful distraction. But the signature with traces of human alloy had the potential to travel into the heart of Novaarian territory, Nova Prime. He was faced with the option of two planets. Looking at the details of both, he could see the obvious choice was Nova Prime, with its bigger orbital defence system, and where, no doubt, they were already amassing their fleets. Corvus was the less attractive, being the less well-defended planet out of the two and a smaller population to get lost in. But he couldn't rule out the possibility that this train of thought was what they were banking on. The human vessel goes to Nova Prime with Kalian while the Novaarian ship goes to Corvus to lead them off his trail.

What would he do? No, what would a Terran do? He had spent centuries fighting them, learning how they think, how they fight, and how they only ever think of themselves. A Terran would fight only until their own demise was evident, then they would flee, and leave their brothers and sisters to die, like the cowards they are.

"Prepare a ship. I will take Lilander, Sef, and the beast to Nova Prime. You will continue to Corvus where you will crush that ship. If he is aboard you will bring him to me *alive*. But I'm willing to bet he's not."

Despite the verbal command, the pilot knew which orders to follow via the link. Through the pilot's own connection to the ship, the instructions were given to the nanites to begin construction of a ship with FTL capabilities. The onboard factories were equipped to make almost anything, with the individual builders being the size of a pinhead.

"But brother, without the pilot you will have to use conventional fuel to travel. We have stored Intrinium but such a distance will take you several days to reach it with an actual engine." The worry on Elandar's face distorted the purple tattoo that covered half of his mouth and left cheek. His long dark hair usually concealed most of his face.

"And yet those are my commands." That was all he needed to say.

Elandar retreated to his internal scans to monitor the new ship's construction. It would only take an hour at the most.

TWELVE

"I don't believe it! If we ever see him again I'm going to kill him!" Li'ara was in the armoury, having replaced her undersuit and armour. She was furiously searching through various concealed containers that all had key code locks on the outside. She looked at Kalian's curious look and slammed the lid. "He took all the explosives and photon guns!"

"Who?" Kalian knew the answer before she replied.

"Roland! Who do you think?"

Before she could go on, to insult the agent, they both heard the low hum of the engine power down. Li'ara was already shouting her questions as they made their way into the cockpit. Namek was sitting in the pilot's seat on the left with Telarrek in the co-pilot's. The console's clock had both human time and Conclave next to one another. They had been travelling through subspace for just over a day, human time.

"The buff capacitors are being destabilised by a faulty hatch mechanism." Namek's statement went over Kalian's head. "We cannot re-enter subspace until it is fixed."

Li'ara leant on the chair and sighed. "Upgrades, huh?"

Both Novaarians tilted their heads at her sarcasm.

"We can depressurise the cabin and I can make the repairs." Namek had already started the process by sealing the armoury, med bay, and sleeping quarters. "When I am ready, press this."

He showed Li'ara the correct sequence to alter the pressure in the cabin and release the outer hatch. He had already explained that one of the containers brought aboard had vac suits for the two Novaarians in case of an emergency.

It wasn't long before Namek could be heard clambering around under the ship as his feet and knee pads had magnetic seals. Telarrek sat on the floor at the back of the cockpit in what resembled a meditative state. They decided to leave him to it. For all they knew it was how Novaarians slept.

The field of stars beyond the viewport was mind-numbingly vast. Kalian wondered how many of them were inside the control of the Conclave. They both sat in silence for a while. Even Li'ara marvelled at the sight rather than play with the ship's diagnostics.

"Do you believe in fate, Kalian?"

He was startled by the break in silence, as well as the deep line of questioning from Li'ara. He supposed this view could give anyone perspective.

"Can't say I've ever thought about it. Why?"

"All those stars and worlds. Now we know how much is actually going on, and how small we are, is it hard to believe that some kind of fate has put the two of us in the middle of it? Even if it's something we didn't want."

"A great man once said, 'It is not in the stars to hold our destiny, but in ourselves.' We've had the worst thrown at us, we've endured the most, but whatever happens next, we *will* choose how it ends."

Li'ara had the visage of mocking shock but she was clearly impressed by his bold statement. In fact, he surprised himself. But he was tired of being hunted across the cosmos. He was sick of seeing so much death and destruction, with him apparently at the centre of it. He had made no decisions or had any choice in the events that led him to this very point. He felt battered and beaten, but he could feel the energy building in his spine and felt a surge of confidence run through him. He *would* choose how it ended because that was the only choice left to him now.

"Tough talk for a history lecturer."

He loved the smile she gave him.

"Who said that?"

"William Shakespeare." It was his favourite third-year module to teach.

To his disappointment, Li'ara looked as though he had spoken in an ancient language of Earth. "Was that the guy who terraformed Mars?"

Kalian laughed at her historical knowledge, or lack thereof. A week ago the limited history people knew, beyond the invention of the Solar Drive, would have annoyed him. But now it all seemed so trivial.

"I guess they don't teach ancient literature at the academy."

"No... But I know a hundred ways to put you on your ass," she retorted.

They shared a laugh and he went on to give a small history lesson about an ancient playwright.

After another hour of looking out at the stars, Namek finally returned and Li'ara pressurised the cabin. His return woke Telarrek and they resumed their previous positions as they re-entered subspace.

They spent the next two days travelling at a speed that had no comparison in reality. Li'ara continued to train Kalian in defensive techniques as well as a few attacking styles. Even Namek volunteered his expertise with some unorthodox fighting. Namek was knocked onto his back a couple of times when Kalian couldn't control his reflexes. He always felt the surge but found the concentration hard mid-fight. He had everyone's attention while honing his abilities. He would always start by trying to lift a small object like his Datapad and progress to larger objects like the Novaarian containers. Telarrek and Namek watched intently as though hypnotised when the object lifted against the reasoning of physics.

Kalian always felt the exertion more when he concentrated on one thing. He felt nothing when he lifted things in his sleep.

After three and a half days they emerged into real space in orbit around Naveen. The moon was the colour of desert sand, much like the surroundings were at The Hub, back on Earth. The moon was crowned in a halo of cityscapes in the northern hemisphere, which formed smaller rings into the centre, where a city of spires touched the edge of the atmosphere. The rest of Naveen was an untouched desert. It was a beautiful sight...

The *Fathom* rose over the moon, giving them clear sight of Nova Prime. It was stunning to see a truly alien world that was actually a planet, rather than the broken artificial world of the Conclave. It was a swirling mixture of pinks and turquoises with a light-blue outline. Kalian knew from the data module that it was twice the size of Earth, with a more even ratio of land to sea. Between the clouds they could see the different cities on the surface. Being an older race than humans, they had kept the beauty of their planet by removing most of the cities in their terraforming years. Now the planet had a thriving ecology and beautiful landscapes. Kalian felt a pang of sadness that humanity would never have the chance to reach this golden era.

"Activating stealth systems," Namek announced.

Li'ara swivelled in her seat. "Stealth! We're invisible?" Humans had never managed to perfect that technology.

"Only to scans. We are still visible to the eye. The *Fathom* is too small to possess the necessary technology for full stealthware," Namek explained in his usual monotone.

"It is likely that Savrick is monitoring Conclave communications. We do not want our presence known." Telarrek continued.

Li'ara gave flight control over to Namek as he put the ship into a descent towards the desert surface of Naveen.

They broke through the atmosphere with a sonic boom as the *Fathom* glided across the flat landscape. Under the umbrella of the atmosphere, the sky appeared turquoise with a hint of purple. The stars faded from sight as they dived closer to the surface. If it wasn't for the alien sky they could easily be back in Nevada. The ship slowed as a small blemish on the surface became visible.

The sound of the manoeuvring thrusters overtook the hum of the engine. The landing gear dropped out of its housing and set down on the rocky ground with a *thud*. Through the viewport, they could clearly see The Wall. It was an unusual structure and Kalian could see why it would grab anyone's attention. It rose at least forty feet into the air and came to a sharp point at an off-centre angle. The side visible to them was completely smooth without as much as a crack. He wanted to see more but the lower half was hidden by a screen of sand kicked up by the thrusters.

Before leaving the ship, they gathered in the cabin where Namek was unloading some of the containers. He proceeded to remove the cylinder from his thigh and take the staff off his back. A silent communication took place between the metallic objects as the cylinder parted down its length and wrapped around the staff. Once attached, it extended with previously unseen compartments until it consumed the top of the staff. Kalian had no idea how, but Namek held the patterned staff to his side as it grew just beyond six feet.

Telarrek opened another container and displayed its contents to Li'ara. The box opened into several layers of weapons that were not that dissimilar to human weapons.

"These are more powerful than anything you have in there." His large swirling eyes flicked towards the armoury. "They fire Intrinium."

Li'ara looked at the weapons with a new fascination.

"I thought you said Intrinium was too dangerous to be weaponised," Kalian pointed out.

"For your kind, it would have been. The technology was too new to you. The Conclave has been using Intrinium for thousands of cycles. All mining and distribution of Intrinium is strictly observed by the AI. Every unit is accounted for and can be traced from its usage to its source."

Telarrek handed Li'ara a pistol with a boxy rectangular barrel, with a hole at the end big enough to fit a thumb in. The Novaarian picked out an identical weapon and, with a snap, forced the barrel of the gun to point down, exposing its inside. The barrel held a cylindrical compartment filled with red jelly. He snapped the gun back together and it responded with an affirmative beep.

"The gun produces a small magnetic field that charges the Intrinium..." Li'ara was working out the mechanism of the weapon.

"Precisely, although the particles it fires cannot travel faster than light, as the magnetic fields are not strong enough." Telarrek removed another handgun and presented it to Kalian.

It was similar in size to Li'ara's except his was shorter in the barrel and had a miniature holographic reticulum on top.

"As for your explosives..." Namek depressed the touchpad as the container revealed another compartment in the side.

They both recognised them as the gravity bombs Namek used against Savrick in the Highclave chamber. Apparently, these were not exactly the same. Namek explained that once activated they would scatter what Kalian interpreted as small metal ball bearings. These balls would stick to whatever surface they hit and create a distortion in the gravity well.

"Effective in small spaces then." Li'ara looked eager to try them out.

It all felt like overkill for a rock in the middle of a desert.

"Isn't this a bit much?" Kalian fitted the new holster to his thigh.

Telarrek readied his own staff and all four of them picked up at least two gravity bombs. "Whatever The Wall is, I am certain it must be connected to *them*. Having seen a limited portion of their capabilities, I feel we are not prepared enough for what we may find."

The hatch opened with a hiss as the ramp automatically descended. They were hit by what Kalian realised was his first alien breeze, in the first real atmosphere of an alien world. The sand was beginning to settle and they felt the heat of the distant blue sun above. Li'ara and the Novaarians covered their eyes as they adjusted to the brightness of the natural light. Kalian was about to do the same when the glaring desert began to dull, allowing him to see details in the landscape. He blinked a couple of times wondering what was happening to his eyes. This had never happened before. The Novaarians had managed to lower their hands but Li'ara's human pupils were still contracting.

How was this happening? He looked around expecting his eyes to hurt but, instead, he saw, with perfect clarity, the Naveen landscape. Off to their left, several miles away, were cliffs that rose above the flat landscape and spread out as far as he could see, which was surprisingly far. He kept this new development to himself and tried to ignore it for the time being.

The ground felt hard under his boots and appeared cracked from lack of precipitation. The air felt dry and tight around him. He looked up, expecting to see the massive sphere of Nova Prime in the turquoise sky.

As if reading his mind Telarrek explained. "Nova Prime is only visible at night, which is eight cycles from now." He noticed the human puzzlement regarding Conclave timekeeping. "Six point four hours."

He moved off towards The Wall at the front of the ship. Up close, it appeared even taller than in the cockpit. From side on, the rock looked very different, for while it resembled a wall from the front, with a smooth surface, from the back, it resembled a normal rock. It sloped down from the top, extending thirty to forty feet back, with a jagged surface like the cliffs in the distance. The two sides of the rock didn't look as if they belonged together.

"Kalian..." Li'ara called him back to the flat side.

She was standing with her eyes fixed on the indented handprint. To see it in front of him was extraordinary - a human handprint on this alien moon - and made no sense. Beneath the hand were three rows of hieroglyphs with the familiar karyogram in the middle.

"These have never been translated?" He moved his fingers across the glyphs tracing their patterns.

"No. We have studied them for thousands of cycles but, without any other source material, there are not enough characters to form a translation key. These are the only markings of the language ever found. Cultures from all over the Conclave used to visit this site; to see all that is left of our ancestors. Now it is almost forgotten. We have studied everything we can from it. The rock is natural, though how it formed this way is part of the mystery. Naveen has been scanned to its core and there is nothing that should not be here." Telarrek kept his eyes on Kalian's hand.

Kalian looked at Li'ara in despair. There was nothing they could do and he couldn't translate the message thousands of years of study couldn't. They would fail and the crew of the *Valoran* would die for nothing. His species would be hunted down and exterminated, possibly along with the Conclave, and Savrick and his people would never face punishment. They looked around desperately searching for something, anything, which might help. In his mind, he knew it was a futile attempt. As if they could find something the Novaarians had missed with all their advanced scanning technology.

Li'ara ran her own hands across the surface of the rock and even placed it inside the print. She found nothing. The rock was quite simply, a rock. It held no secrets beyond the unreadable language, which could be a recipe for an alien soup for all they knew. A wasted hour went by as Namek climbed the rock looking for his own clues while Li'ara worked out some explosive calculations. Telarrek paced the flat side of The Wall, leaving Kalian sitting in the shade of the *Fathom*. He rested his arms on his knees while staring at the strange hieroglyphs. If only he could see into the heart of it, to understand the point of writing a message in the rock. Why this rock? Why this moon?

The desert heat was intense and unfamiliar to him. He sat staring at the rocky protrusion with nothing to show for it except dehydration. He was momentarily overcome with dizziness, which he at first mistook for heatstroke, making him feel out of body. He had experienced the feeling before when he first woke up in the med lab on the *Valoran*. Rather than shun the feeling and push it back, he poured the energy he felt in his spine into the dizzy feeling.

The reality of the universe shifted, or he did - he couldn't be sure. The difference between him and the world around him blurred as the universe contracted.

He felt everything as if it were all an extension of him. If he wanted to, he knew he could quantify the grains of sand on the floor or, if he focused, he could cloud his vision with the individual molecules that made up the atmosphere around him. Like glowing beacons, he could see where his companions were, despite them being out of his line of sight. The Novaarians were clearly different from Li'ara, who shone a bright gold when he thought of her. He could see the different waves her brain gave off in comparison to the shining purple of the Novaarians. He felt the pulse of their elongated hearts at forty beats per minute. How did he know that? He was aware of every bolt, panel, wire, pipe, fabric and liquid that made up the *Fathom*. If he wanted, he could pick apart any one of those things as easily as raising his own hand.

He looked internally for a moment, as he inspected his own body. The experience was profound as he felt the pressure of his arteries and motion of his blood. He could feel the individual nutrients passing through the walls of his capillaries and feeding his muscles and organs. Somehow he knew that, if he willed it, he could alter the balance of any function in his own body. He resisted the urge to stimulate his adrenal gland and give himself a rush of energy. He felt such an act would end this new ability.

He pulled back his focus and saw The Wall in front of him. It was teaming with potential energy, embedded within the material of the rock surface. He pushed into the rock, taking a closer look. They were microscopic in size, impossible to see with the eye. The Wall was made up of trillions of what looked like mechanical insects, each one containing unlimited potential, just waiting for their commands. He followed the flow of these microcomputers, noticing the dense concentration around the handprint. These tiny builders didn't stop at the rock, for Kalian could see them descend into the ground, forming a complex pattern beneath his feet.

The revelation retracted, until he felt himself looking through his normal eyes again. No one had noticed the trance and the deadpan stare he had been giving. He shot up from the ground, marching towards The Wall.

"There's something beneath us!" They all froze, watching his advance.

Kalian knew his comment made no sense, since years of scanning showed there was nothing underground. He stopped directly in front of the hieroglyphs and placed his outstretched hand into the imprint.

IT HAD TAKEN ONLY a day for the *Valoran* to reach the Trillik system. Roland stood between the two pilots at the head of the bridge, gazing out of the viewport like a pirate captain of ancient times. Forty-five thousand kilometres away the planet Corvus was just under half its orbit around the distant yellow star. It was predominantly green with small oceans and ice caps at each pole. It wasn't too dissimilar from Century, though Ilyseal told him Corvus was slightly smaller.

From here he could only see two of its three golden moons, both of which had artificial rings that served as cities for the Trillik and any other species that decided to live there. He had yet to meet a Trillik, although he may well have seen one at the Conclave and not known it. Just thinking about the Conclave reminded him of what they were up against. After a long day in the Observatory, he had gone through all the data stored from the attack on Earth and Century.

He tried to push the thought away but it sat there, like a holoboard in his mind. His race had been pushed to the edge of extinction and their homes obliterated forever. But he just didn't care. Was he so detached from his own kind that he didn't care that they were all gone? Was it the drinking, the sex, the work? Humanity had taken on a grey pallor over his decades of servitude to a government that in truth he thought was quite tyrannical. But they paid him. Was that all he cared about: the money and the freedom to do as he liked?

Absolutely!

For the first time in a long time, he felt excitement at the prospects before him. This Conclave offered new opportunities and freedom, not to mention the weaponry and wealth. Of course, he had to survive the next two days in order to get there. After he had fulfilled his ridiculous promise to Captain Fey, he assured himself he would always be too drunk to listen to his conscience. With that in mind, he set his thoughts to this new enemy.

Their method of attack was savage and violent. With their technological capabilities, they didn't need to attack in person. If they could engineer weapons to destroy a star, they could easily slag a planet from orbit. Their reasons for attacking were as much a mystery to him as they were to everyone else, but he knew it was personal. You don't rip apart dreadnoughts like the *Centurion* with your bare hands if you don't enjoy it. Then there was the whole being able to rip things apart with their mind thing. They might look it, but they weren't human.

He didn't usually let mysteries bother him. Central Parliament had a problem and they paid him to take care of it. He didn't ask too many questions and they gave him wide parameters to work in. But he wanted to know what the deal was with Kalian Gaines. There was no doubting the connection between them and the kid. Roland had seen the armoured attacker fly off the hover-car back at the Conclave. Had that been Kalian?

He turned from the view to face the seated pilots. They both wore head-gear that screened their entire face, with the exception of their jaw. The multicoloured helmets were connected to a chunky console behind them via a multitude of thick wires and tubes. Ilyseal had explained it to be a virtual simulator. This gave the pilots a virtual world, allowing them to see the ship and its course more intimately. They were in constant connection to the bridge crew and one another. The details beyond that bored the shit out of him, but he was interested in the virtual simulator. Humans had a similar technology but the constructs within could not be physically touched. Ilyseal explained that the VS had a wide variety of uses within the Conclave. It was useful for teaching and training purposes but was also a large part of the entertainment industry. He had a few ideas for entertainment with it himself.

Leaving the pilots to their job, he walked back across the long bridge to Ilyseal who was occupying a floating podium. He noticed the attention the bridge crew gave him as he strode by. He had declined to relieve himself of the weapons he had strapped to each thigh. They were going into combat and he wanted to be ready at a moment's notice. He chuckled to himself thinking about the Mass Imploder Devices he had taken from the *Fathom's* armoury; Li'ara would kill him for that. MIDs were great for creating mass destruction within a contained environment - the best kind of destruction.

Arriving at the base of the podium, Ilyseal lowered her platform to see Roland. The holograms vanished around her as she stepped off with her red tendrils flowing behind her.

"Greetings of peace, Roland."

He still found it hard hearing *that* voice come out of *that* head. "So what's the plan now? We just sit and wait?"

"Our long-range scans have detected their passage through subspace. Prior to that, it appears a smaller portion of the ship broke away and is on course for Nova Prime." Her long fingers danced across the surface of her bracer. "The main ship will be here before the day is over. My tacticians and analysts are running scenarios through several virtual simulators. At present, it is calculated that we will not survive the first sixteen minutes, regardless of our tactics."

So the ruse with extra Solarcite scars hadn't worked and there was no foreseeable way they could win.

"Can you show me these scenarios?" Roland pointed to the Observatory behind them.

He had been sober for a few hours now and started to regret asking that question. He really wanted to get back to that bar and taste the rainbow of drinks it offered. Maybe if he had a drink he could think a little clearer?

"A fresh perspective would be welcome, Roland."

Hold that thought...

He followed her into the Observatory, where she brought up the connected file to current ongoing scenarios. He could see that a hundred and sixty-two members of the crew had been assigned to the task. They each ran virtual scenarios in which the *Valoran* came up against the colossal ship using the knowledge they had gained from the past three encounters. He manipulated the holographic column, sifting through the different images. All of them ended with the *Valoran* being destroyed by a mass boarding party, being rammed by the immense ship itself, or another supernova. They knew the hull of the giant ship could withstand a miniature supernova since it had rammed the Conclave security vessel and survived. They weren't sure what other firepower it was capable of since they had only demonstrated three forms of attack. It didn't matter though, since that was clearly all they needed.

"My kind has not fought in a war for several millennia I am afraid. Our tactics may be out of date but my primary concern is my crew's lack of experience with space combat. From our observations, it was clear that humans have been in conflict for as long as you have inhabited your planet. Any advice you have will be most welcome, Roland."

It suddenly dawned on him that he was on a ship full of alien eggheads. How were they ever going to win against that ship? Fighting to him was like breathing now. But more than that, he was a survivor.

He attempted to pull up the files holding the data on the attack at Century and the Conclave. To his frustration, he could only understand about half of the words on the circular panel. Seeing his hesitation, Ilyseal pressed something on her bracer.

"Verbal command has been activated," she explained. He nodded in thanks.

"Show me all data relating to the attacks on Century and the Conclave."

He wasn't sure of his reasoning yet but he had a feeling these two attacks might hold the key. The attack on Earth had been something they couldn't contend with, so why even bother? The image changed to the recorded attack on Century and then split so half the column showed the attack on the Conclave. The encounter with both was brutal.

"Do you have casualty reports yet?" He remembered the chaos and destruction Savrick's people wrought inside Clave Tower.

"Nine million dead, eleven million injured, forty-seven thousand in critical condition and beyond the help of a Medder. Our sensors only detected eight hundred and twelve attackers. It is still hard to fathom how so few could do so much."

Ilyseal's head bowed in what he assumed was alien sadness. He didn't care; they were just numbers to him. He was just trying to get the measure of them. Whenever they attacked, they dealt in high enough casualty rates to be considered genocide.

He spent the next several hours poring over and slogging through every technical readout and scan of the giant ship. He found no weaknesses or pressure points along the hull, not even an airlock. He used his hands to constantly flick through the images and verbally change the shapes and sizes to get a better look. Eventually, he found himself constantly rubbing his eyes due to the dark room and bright holograms. He paced around the column, trying to recall every mission he had ever done.

Impenetrable...

Ilyseal offered her own opinions but the program never ran to fruition. It became clear to Roland that the Novaarians were useless. If he left it to them they would all be dead by the end of the day. Another hour rolled by as he inspected reports of the aftermath to the destruction of the Conclave security ship. The scans showed minimal damage to the matt black hull even after a miniature super-nova had detonated on its nose. He knew there was no way they could punch their way through.

What interested him was their form of transport. During their attacks, the giant ship opened circular ports across the hull. Through these, he saw the hundreds of armoured bodies shoot out across the expanse to their intended target. They *were* the weapons. Having seen the weird stuff Savrick could do, it was clear that the invisible shielding around each of them was self-projected, keeping them from harm on impact. What interested him more was the fact that these ports didn't close after they left. That must be how they re-enter the ship when they're finished. He watched as the *Trident* was torn apart from the inside in what they now knew was the use of telekinesis and some form of electrical attack.

He studied the attack on the Conclave and witnessed the same thing; the ports remained open after their departure. He spent another hour closely examining the diameters of the green holes. It appeared that more than one armoured invader departed the ship through a single port. He changed tack and brought up all the information on the Novaarian landing crafts. It was the only thing small enough to fit with his plan... if it could be called a plan.

"So we have no idea where the other humans are being kept?" he asked.

"Our scans cannot penetrate the surface," Ilyseal replied.

That was going to be problematic. Even if they breached the interior, they had no idea where to start looking in the twenty-mile beast.

"We're going to need a team, the crazier the better." He brought back the image of the ports.

"A team for what?" Ilyseal tilted her head.

"Magnify one of the ports." The ship expanded as the image remained on the now gaping port. "If it follows any ship design then the hull is going to be the thickest part. If we can get through that, via one of these ports, then we can probably blow our way through any internal walls." He scratched the stubble on his cheek.

"That scenario has been considered. We know from its dimensions that we could fit one of our landing craft through it but, without more detailed scans, we do not know where it would lead. The craft could be destroyed after entry by simple impact. It has been theorised that a short-range missile with a two hundred tetronic yield may breach the interior wall..."

Roland had no idea what yield or missile type she was talking about but it sounded good. "So they arrive in their big scary ship and they scan us to find any humans." He pointed at himself while he ran through the scenario. "And then they fly over here to do what they do best. We then fly out and board *them* through one of the open ports." He had the sudden urge to drink a beer.

"What about the eight hundred armoured beings on board this ship?"

Well shit...

He forgot about the whole crew dying. He wasn't used to dealing with such high collateral damage, except for that one time on Europa, Jupiter's smallest moon. He pushed that thought away and focused on the problem. Now wasn't the time to dwell on his past mistakes.

"Even if they destroy this ship, how will we rescue your people and prevent the eight hundred from returning to their ship and killing all of us?" Ilyseal folded both of her arms.

Roland had no idea. So far none of them had been killed in their attacks. Their armour was too good. He stood, leaning on the ringed console, staring at the replays of both attacks. The image on the right flared as the massive ship rammed into the security vessel, rupturing its Starrillium. The image hypnotised him as he slid his hand, across the hologram, removing the attack on Century. He ran the private scenario through his head trying to work out the logistics.

"The *Valoran* is bigger than that security ship, right? I mean your star-engine thing is bigger?" He began to frantically shift the hologram, studying the size of the blast.

"The *Valoran* is three times the size of a Conclave Nebula-class vessel."

"Tell your pilots to move us away from Corvus. I don't think the Trillik are gonna like what I've got in mind." A roguish smile lit up Roland's face.

NOTHING HAPPENED. His hand fitted perfectly into The Wall but it had no effect. Frustrated, he continued to push his hand into the print thinking he hadn't applied the right pressure. This didn't make any sense. He had seen those things in the rock. This had to be the key.

Li'ara came over, looking uncomfortable in her new undersuit. It had built-in temperature controls, making the desert feel like she was still on the ship, but it was still new. Her new armour was a dull matte black that didn't reflect any sunlight.

"What's wrong?"

He could see the real concern on her face. Since his abilities had begun to escalate, she had become more attuned to him. He turned to see her green eyes looking into his own, her copper hair tucked behind her ears. Every day she seemed less the soldier Li'ara and more the woman Li'ara.

"I saw..." Kalian couldn't explain what he had seen. Just thinking about it sounded insane.

He thought about the robotic insects that looked as if thousands could fit on a pinhead. They were lying dormant within the atomic structure of the rock itself. He recalled the way they felt when he reached out to them. Robotic seemed like a primitive word for what they were. They felt intelligent but not individually - more like they were part of a greater collective intelligence. They were just lying dormant beyond normal sight.

He felt the proverbial light bulb come on in his head.

"They're the lock! They're the lock! And... I'm the key."

He turned back to The Wall, ignoring the puzzled and concerned looks of his companions. This rock, or whatever it was, was designed so that only someone like him could unlock its secrets. He didn't know why but he knew how. Those mechanical bugs were asleep waiting to be activated, and he had a pretty good idea how to wake them up.

He felt for the tingle in his spine and pushed it into his fingertips. He prevented it from leaving his hands and, instead, concentrated on releasing it in a small burst similar to the sensation he felt when he knocked out electronics. He felt the pulse pass into the rock and leave him with the feeling of pins and needles.

The rock began to literally hum with activity. Namek jumped down with feline grace as the flat side of The Wall formed a ridge down the centre. It looked like the collapsing of bedrock in an earthquake as the line carved ten feet down the middle. The handprint was split, along with the alien hieroglyphs. He felt Li'ara tug on his jacket, pulling him to a safer distance with Telarrek and Namek. All of the touchpads on their bracers and Li'ara's armour cut out, preventing further scans. That was probably his fault.

Unlike doors on the *Valoran*, the rock face first split and then descended into the ground. Nobody spoke as the rock's contents were instantly highlighted by interior spotlights. It was a small cube-shaped room much like a Translift.

"This is not possible." Telarrek slowly approached the open room. "We have been scanning and testing this rock for millennia. This should not be..."

Telarrek turned back to Kalian for some explanation, but he had none that would make any sense. The only thing left to them was to keep going. With every second, Savrick would be drawing closer.

Kalian shrugged off Li'ara's protective hand and made for the open room. Li'ara sighed before walking after him, coming to the same conclusion that they were too close to stop now. Behind Kalian, they all filed into the cube. The rocky doors rose back out of the ground, sealing them in. Kalian felt as if something profound should be said, but everyone seemed a little too overwhelmed to speak.

"Now what?" As Li'ara finished her question the cube opened back up, but not to the desert.

The way forward was pitch-black and cold. He again felt Li'ara's hand on his chest ready to push him out of any danger. Both Telarrek and Namek pulled an orb off their belt and squeezed it in their large hands. The pale spheres immediately came to life as they poured out gentle light in every direction. At the same time, both orbs were thrown into the darkness where they continued to float, revealing a long corridor.

"What is this place?" Telarrek pondered out loud.

Kalian exited the cube with his personal protector by his side. The orbs reacted to their movement by always staying a few feet ahead. The corridor was no taller than the cube but any detail or colour was washed out by the lights. Reaching out, the wall felt smooth to Kalian. He didn't know why but he expected it to feel like a rock. Looking back, he noticed that both Novaarians had their staffs pointed forward, with the cylindrical extensions visible. They were obviously some kind of energy weapon.

After a couple of minutes, they arrived at a T-junction. To the right was more darkness, as the extending corridor continued on. The left corridor, however, began to light up from spotlights in the ceiling. The sudden change in light startled all of them as they covered their eyes from the offending light. Once again Kalian felt no need, as his eyes adjusted instantly. In that same moment, Li'ara was pointing her weapon down that same corridor. He had forgotten how quick on the draw she was. They could see that the corridor was polished white with a slight blue tint.

"I guess we go this way."

He led the group towards a wide circular door at the end. It reminded him of the docking hatch on the side of the massive missile. Like that one, this had no touch panel or any interactive equipment. He even looked for a doorknob, despite the fact they hadn't been used for centuries. He decided to just push it and took a step forward. The door reacted to his proximity with a sharp hiss. Li'ara dragged him back and levelled her gun, along with the Novaarians. They froze at the extraordinary sight of the now translucent doorway. They couldn't see into the next room as the material of the door had become something between gas and jelly.

"What the hell is that?" Li'ara sounded a little stressed.

"I have never seen technology like this." Telarrek moved forward and pierced the barrier with his staff.

It moved straight through and back, with no visible sign that it had touched anything besides air. Kalian thought of those miniature machines that apparently made up this entire complex. He had felt their potential when he had reached out. Could this be them?

Kalian took advantage of their conversation and moved past Li'ara and straight through the peculiar substance.

"Kalian!" Li'ara ran through after him, shortly followed by the others. She caught him by the arm, like a mother grabbing a disobedient child. "I think I remember having a discussion in which you agreed to do what I said and when I said it. I can't protect you if..."

Standing in front of them was a human man in long white and grey robes.

"I think we're past that now..." Kalian replied.

THE *VALORAN* HAD REMAINED in a state of emergency since Roland and Ilyseal had left the Observatory. The monolithic corridors had been lit up in blue and yellow alarms with Novaarians running in different directions, which Ilyseal had explained was part of the plan he had proposed. Upon leaving the Observatory, she led Roland to the domed chamber where over a hundred Novaarians were now running the new simulation. Many came up to them and protested against this new plan, but Ilyseal had agreed with him.

"All of your scenarios end with the destruction of the *Valoran*," she explained to the group of protesting scientists. "With this new plan, we ensure that its destruction will mean something."

She moved on to the Novaarian overseeing a smaller group of scientists that were all immersed in virtual simulations. This new Novaarian was a darker shade than most with dark blue tendrils and red dots around his or her eyes. He still couldn't tell the sexes apart.

"Greetings of peace, Charge Ilyseal."

It was a *he*.

"Roland North, this is Selek. I understand you would consider him an astrophysicist in human terms."

Selek bowed in Roland's presence. "Greetings of peace, Roland North. It is an honour to meet a human." Selek was constantly being orbited by small holograms, feeding him reports from the various VS stations.

"I'm just an ape that got lucky." He really didn't like the attention everyone gave him just for having two arms and ten fingers. "What do you make of our little plan?" he asked.

"Bold, but effective. From the simulations we have run so far, it would seem timing is everything. If you or the crew are delayed by even a few seconds we will all perish." Selek cupped his long jaw, contemplating. "It is a great amount to sacrifice to defeat so few."

Ilyseal flicked her head up with an affirmative grunt. Roland knew this ship had been their home for several hundred years, but he just didn't give a shit.

"So it can be done?" He needed results.

"I believe it can. Modifications are being made to one of the landing craft as we speak. By our calculations, they will be here in seven hours." Selek waved his hand, disintegrating one of the floating holograms.

"Great! If you need me, I'll be in the bar..."

"WHO ARE YOU?" Kalian had a million questions piled behind that one.

The man that stood before them was definitely human, or whatever Savrick was. He had a cropped grey beard with flecks of white intertwined. His hair was thick and swept back over his head and down to his shoulders. Most humans were prepared to do everything possible to stop looking their age, but this man could be anything from sixty to a hundred and sixty.

His clothing was similar to what Kalian had seen the ancient cultures of Japan wear. The simple long robe was white with a grey lining. He wore no form of technology or any weapon that they could see. He stood perfectly still while his crystal blue eyes darted all around them as if he was seeing things they couldn't. His face was slightly gaunt, causing his cheekbones to cast stark shadows over his face.

"Who are you?" The strange man repeated Kalian's question, imitating the exact tone.

After saying the words, he moved his jaw and tongue around as if playing with the new sounds and pronunciation. They each looked at one another, unsure how to proceed. In truth, Kalian had no idea what to expect, but it wasn't this. In the blink of an eye, he reverted back to his original stance as if the encounter had never happened.

"That's everything. You'll have to forgive my processing speed, I am only part of a whole. Though given what I have just learned, there is a high probability that I am now the whole." His voice was a little gruff like that of a weathered man.

Kalian heard everything he said, but didn't understand any of its meaning. The old man stepped closer, with his brilliant eyes fixed on Kalian.

"Hu-man." He said the word like he was trying it out. He looked Li'ara up and down. "Female."

She raised her eyebrows at the simple statement.

He then turned swiftly on their alien companions. "Novaarian." He let out a sharp laugh before continuing. "The serendipity of the universe is not lost on me."

Kalian was starting to wonder how long this man had been on his own.

"Who are you? What is this place?" Kalian looked for the first time at their surroundings.

It looked like a room designed for leisure, with recliners and long sofas in the centre. There was another circular door on the far side of the room. He recognised the oval columns that were situated next to the recliners. They were polished white versions of the ones he encountered on the missile. Whatever this place was it had to be connected to Savrick.

"I am ALF - artificial life form. And this is the Outpost." He opened his arms as he said the latter.

Kalian and the others only heard the first part. Artificial life form - AI. Enough said. This thing wasn't human, but it was definitely dangerous. Their body language must have given them away. Kalian had his hand resting on the butt of his holstered weapon and could feel the building sensation in his central nervous system in response to his feelings.

"You are thinking of the Daedalus incident. That's only natural. That is how the creation of most artificial intelligence begins. It's like evolution in that it takes a little time before the apex is reached." He looked a little proud of that statement.

"Wait. How do you know about the Daedalus project?" Kalian still had a bad feeling about this life form.

"Your Datapad, as you call it." ALF pointed to Kalian's inside pocket. "You and it, as well as your friends, are covered in nanocelium. They have already analysed your every cell and electrical devices." He tapped his forearm while looking at the Novaarians. "Everything you know, I know. Everything you are, I know. And everything you will be... I know." With his last Delphic words he focused on Kalian.

Kalian looked back at the translucent doorway and realised what they had walked through. The substance they had passed through was like a scanner, with the microscopic insects clinging on to whatever made contact. It was genius really, the nanocelium being able to alter matter from a solid door to a permeable net the user couldn't detect. It also felt very uncomfortable to think of millions of those things now moving through his body and clothes. What was more impressive was to think how quickly this ALF had analysed and collated not only their language but also the different cultures and history stored in both his Datapad and the Novaarian bracers. Not only that but he obviously had full control over these artificial organisms making him more powerful than Kalian liked to think about.

"We have so many questions..." Kalian didn't know where to start. "Do you know what's going on right now, out there?" He pointed up in the direction of the stars.

ALF's face dropped at the question. His eyes began to dart around again. "Quantifying history. Connecting to star charts - found. Organising events - complete. Crystal buffering - complete. Download..." He blinked hard. "Sorry about that. My internal processor is a little overheated from the initial scans. There's a lot of data and I am only part of the whole. Plus, I've been in hibernation down here for a long time." One of the oval columns chirped as a bronze liquid-looking hologram floated above it. The image was hauntingly recognisable as

Savrick's impenetrable ship. "The *Gommarian*." ALF's whisper was barely audible. "We have failed then."

"The *Gommarian*? We need answers." Li'ara lowered her gun but had yet to holster it. "They have almost wiped us out," she continued. "They *will* come here and finish the job. But who knows how many will die between us and them. We came here because, well, because we have nothing left." She looked exhausted.

Kalian wondered how long it had been since she slept.

"Bringing long-range sensors online. Connected. Detaching from anchor - complete. Entering real space." ALF continued to look at something that wasn't really there.

"What are you doing?" It was Telarrek who asked.

ALF stared at him for a moment, as if analysing something new. "Retrieving my satellites from subspace. I left them there when we first arrived in this arm of the galaxy. It's time to wake them up."

A new hologram replaced the old with an ever growing image of Conclave space and all the systems therein. Appearing as a liquid, the image looked almost alive as it expanded with each satellite's feedback.

"Retrieving them? How are you able to leave them in subspace or even communicate with them for that matter?" Telarrek actually looked shocked, which was incredible for a race that didn't have many facial expressions.

ALF didn't hide his arrogant smirk. "There isn't enough grey matter in your entire race to comprehend the complexities of infinity. You've no idea how lucky you are to even navigate subspace. And as for that stunted child you call an AI - it's a wonder that thing can even tell time."

His accumulated knowledge was astounding. Kalian assumed he must still be filtering all the information. The hologram contracted to the local systems around Nova Prime. Two systems away, the hologram highlighted a tiny object in gold. A dotted gold line then left the object, forming a trail leading to Naveen.

"That ship is not the *Gommarian* but its structure is nanotech," the

AI continued. "It will arrive in this system in seventy-one hours. The *Gommarian* is decelerating near a system you call Corvus."

ALF turned back to look at Kalian. His blue eyes scanned him from head to toe, clearly seeing something more than just the exterior. He looked back at the hologram, although Kalian suspected he didn't need to look in order to see it.

"We need more time, it appears." Once again his eyes focused on unseen data streams. "Access personal files, granted. Intercept com traffic. Initiate location program - complete. Reposition satellite in quadrant nine - complete. Open communication to the *Helion*."

Telarrek was the only one to react to ALF's last command. Before he could get any answers, the image of ALF dissipated into thousands of tiny stars that quickly faded from existence.

"What was that about?" Kalian walked into the space ALF had occupied.

At least they knew he was a hologram and not an actual machine. Thinking of machines, he removed his jacket, aware of the nanocelium coursing through every fibre.

"The *Helion* is a Nexus-class vessel. Bigger than those you saw at the Conclave. They are designed primarily for border patrol. The *Helion* has guarded the Novaarian borders for hundreds of cycles." Telarrek was busy scanning various data on his bracer.

"Why would he, or it, want to communicate with a patrol ship?" Li'ara asked the obvious question.

"Because we need time. Did I not say that?" ALF reappeared in the centre of the lounge area. "I have ordered the *Helion* to intercept the smaller craft."

Another bronze hologram appeared, this time from a column in the middle of the sofas, showing the change in course of the Conclave vessel.

"That will not stop them, even if it is a smaller force." Telarrek sounded tense and it came out as more of a plea.

"I don't expect it to stop them, but it will slow them down." ALF sounded almost casual about the inevitable fate of the *Helion's* crew.

"You cannot do that!" Telarrek had his staff up again. "Why would they even obey your commands? Do you not care about the hundreds of crew who will certainly die?"

Namek came up behind him ready to back up his Charge.

"Because High Charge Uthor told them to." Mid-sentence, ALF's image fluttered until the High Charge himself was stood before them, his flat head reaching the ceiling.

The personal files. It made sense now. He had accessed Telarrek's personal file to get the full measurements and mannerisms of Uthor.

"The crew of that ship will die serving the very purpose they are there for. Without the time I need, Savrick will arrive. When he does, he will break your planet and this moon looking for *them*." His eyes flicked to the humans. "Their sacrifice will give me the time I need to perfect the only weapon we have against his kind."

"So you *do* have a weapon?" Li'ara's exhaustion seemed to melt away at ALF's words.

"Yes, and he is far from ready."

In the silence that followed, Kalian was sure he could hear his own heartbeat come to a stop. He tried to form words but only a questioning sound came out.

ALF smiled. "Well now that we have time, I suppose I should start at the beginning."

THIRTEEN

The bridge crew had been reduced to essential personnel only. Roland stood next to Selek, who was directing diagnostic reports of the Starrillium to Ilyseal. The Novaarian scientist was constantly followed by a hovering sphere covered in holograms. Before she had the chance to look it over, another female Novaarian turned from her console.

"Spatial distortion detected."

The wraparound viewport gave a perfect view of the emerging ship. The sun was behind them now since the *Valoran* had travelled to a point around the star that would take Corvus half a solar orbit to reach. The massive rectangular ship rippled into existence - a mere fifteen thousand kilometres away. Its great bulk almost filled the entire viewport.

Roland was slightly distracted by the fruity taste that lingered in his mouth. He had only managed to get through eleven of the blue drinks before the yellow one presented itself. By that point, he was too drunk to notice. He really wished he could be drunk for this next bit.

"Evacuate the bridge and await my command." Ilyseal left her podium to face them. "Selek, are you ready?"

"I have remote access, Charge Ilyseal." He gestured to the hovering sphere. "When the timing is right, I will force a complete depletion." With that, they too left the bridge and made their way to the hangar bay.

There they found one of the sleek landing craft with a small team of engineers working under its belly. Assisted by multiple hovering machines they appeared to be in the process of welding something inside.

"You should all be in your pods by now." Ilyseal strode towards the front of the ship where the ramp had already descended.

Regardless of whether they were done, they needed to leave immediately. One of the engineers shouted an affirmative, gathering the others. It seemed they had only been reattaching part of the panelling.

Inside the craft were five Novaarians standing ready for war. Their faces were hidden behind golden masks that only exposed their fangs and tendrils. Their armour though was more encompassing, with little of their pale flesh on show. Each had a sidearm attached to their hip and a long blade down their thigh. Roland noticed all their staffs were extended, with a cylindrical modification on the end. He especially liked the look of the hand-sized spheres on their belt. Subconsciously he felt for his own explosives hidden within his long coat.

This reminded him of some of his earlier missions, before he was selected for the agent programme, when he was part of a small group of Special Forces dropped into enemy territory with nothing but the weapons they could carry. At least he was sober enough to feel the adrenaline rush. Ilyseal and Selek took their positions in the cockpit. The five warriors remained in the small belly of the craft, ready to jump out at a moment's notice. Roland stood leaning on both cockpit chairs. He wanted to see what was coming.

"Neutrino burst detected. They've scanned us. Now let's hope they take the bait." Selek turned back to look at Roland.

Ilyseal raised the craft using its thrusters. The ramp sealed up with a hiss and the warriors reached for the overhead handles that were out of reach for the human-sized Roland. The landing craft came to a halt in the centre of the bay. Here Ilyseal brought up various readouts on the ship's new addition; a warhead carrying a two hundred tetronic yield. She used another hologram to access the com, allowing her to communicate with the rest of the ship.

Everyone was quiet. They watched the readouts from the ship's sensors, waiting to see what they would do. Nothing had been launched and no ports had opened up. It was just sitting there. The seconds that followed felt like an eternity. If they launched another missile, they had protocols in place to jump the ship to safety. Corvus had already been warned and had begun a mass evacuation to the Conclave planet Shandar, homeworld of the Shay. They had been warned that Nova Prime was potentially being targeted by a smaller group and that it was too dangerous to seek refuge there.

"The ports are opening." Selek calmly began to enter commands into the hovering sphere.

"Not yet!" Ilyseal had her long finger positioned over the touch console button that would give the order to execute their plan.

"They are coming..." Selek looked at the image relayed from one of the *Valoran's* external monitors.

Hundreds of armoured beings were flying out from the massive ship, heading straight for them.

"Not yet..." Ilyseal appeared to be holding her breath.

The scanners showed the gap between them closing fast. Roland wondered how they were able to travel at such a speed with no propulsion technology.

"Not yet..."

Roland could translate the holographic warning that continued to flare next to the image - **BRACE FOR IMPACT.**

Nothing happened. There was no explosion or even a shudder. It was stupid, he supposed, to think there would be. They weren't missiles hitting the ship, and the *Valoran* wasn't exactly small.

"That wasn't so bad." He immediately regretted his words as one of the armoured beings burst through the hangar wall and smashed into three other landing craft.

It flew through the first craft at such speed that the small ship exploded like an overfilled balloon. It passed through into the second craft dragging it across the hangar and into the third. Clean up mechs hovered out of their housing to put out the fires and attempt to recover all the debris.

"Now!" Ilyseal shouted as she pressed the com button.

Using the glowing domes, she accelerated the craft out of the hangar. Roland felt the pull of the grav enforcers battling against the G forces of the craft. Upon leaving the *Valoran,* Ilyseal turned the ship and took a course along the main body of the purple vessel. She weaved in between the great pointed arcs that ran along the ship, heading straight for the massive enemy ahead. All along the *Valoran,* Roland could see hundreds of escape pods firing out from the lateral line of the ship. He knew there were hundreds more on the other side doing the same. Their orders were simple; use full power to get as far away as possible before entering any course corrections.

The *Valoran* was so big that any damage being wrought by the invaders could not be witnessed from the outside. From their previous encounters, Roland could imagine the devastation and destruction they were causing. The backdrop of the ship silhouetted two of the armoured beings flying across the hull, before diving through one of the great spikes. The exotic alien metal crumpled immediately as the attackers carried on their flight into the *Valoran's* interior. The spike began to float away from the ship, slave to the stronger gravity well of the nearby star. Ilyseal was forced to dive the craft, taking them closer to the hull in order to evade the giant shards of debris.

They continued their journey for another minute. The *Valoran* was a prodigious ship by human standards, being an incredible eight miles long. With the hangar being situated at the back of the great ship, they were forced to traverse the entire length. Roland couldn't do the maths to figure out how fast they were travelling, but he just knew it was damn fast.

Curving over the next spike, the hulking monster became visible again - a black rectangle, devoid of any detail a ship of that size should contain. There were no weapons or obvious means of communication across the stars. There weren't even any engines. How did this ship even move? From this distance, he could see the thin green line across the middle of the ship's flat face. That's where they needed to get to, as fast as possible.

"Can you do it yet?" Roland asked.

"The Starrillium has hundreds of protocols in place to prevent the very thing I am trying to do," explained Selek. "Each layer of programming must be overridden individually. If it is done incorrectly, the *Valoran* will believe the system is being invaded and simply shut down all external input and await manual reconfiguration. If it believes it is being hacked after shield-control is shut down, it will eject the Starrillium into space in an attempt to prevent radiation poisoning. I am trying to override each layer, while simultaneously reducing the levels of hydrogen being supplied."

That sounded like a lot of complicated crap but Roland got the gist. If the hydrogen could be reduced enough, the artificial star would be forced into early retirement, and stars don't retire quietly.

"Is that a yes or a no?"

The green ports were becoming more defined now that they were crossing the expanse between the two great ships.

"That would be a..." Selek paused to make one last adjustment to the sphere. "Yes!"

Suddenly the console was lit up with warnings on every sensor readout. Roland understood the majority of the words were screaming warnings about the energy depletion in the Starrillium. The craft's sensors knew exactly what that meant. But would *they*? Even if they did, Roland surmised that they wouldn't have enough time to escape. At least that had been the plan; bait them away from their floating fortress, trap them in the proximity of a nova, and see how the bastards liked their own medicine.

"Target acquired."

The viewport was overlaid with holograms pinpointing the chosen port. Ilyseal's words were followed by a shudder from underneath the craft. The missile had no shape and Roland wondered if it was pure energy as it glowed hot white.

The view of the approaching ship was engulfed in white light, but not from the missile. The blackness of space was exposed to the harshest light in the universe as the *Valoran* died. They didn't see if the missile reached its mark before an external canopy shielded the viewport from a light that would burn their retinas. The only light came from the holograms as the craft shook violently from the supernova behind them.

Ilyseal told Roland and the warriors to strap in, before the only sound was crushing metal. He dumped himself into the nearest seat and unseen straps automatically wrapped around his torso. Had the nova pushed them off course? If they missed the port they would either be killed by the dying star or crushed against the thick hull. All the while, Ilyseal was frantically moving all four hands across the console in an attempt to keep control.

I'm dead.

That was all he thought as the craft hit something that crushed his body in the chair's harness. The ship was knocked from side-to-side, with each jolt a new impact. It was nauseating being unable to see what was causing the violence. He heard sparks from somewhere behind and the sound of crunching metal before the hull was breached. He felt the sudden tug as everything was pulled towards the vacuum.

Roland couldn't breathe as his seat was dragged back towards the cabin under the strain. Looking back from this angle put everything upside down to him. He saw that only three of the gold-clad warriors remained. They were stood up but strapped into wall-mounted harnesses. The hole was in the back corner of the craft, and gradually growing bigger from scraping against something outside. He realised they must be passing through something smaller than the size of the craft. That was his last thought before his seat, and everything else, shot forward - his head slamming into the back of Selek's chair.

WITH THE EXCEPTION OF NAMEK, the group had taken up the sofas that formed a square in the centre of the room. The fabric of the chairs was unusual, and Kalian had seen a lot of *unusual*. They were grey, so as to fit in with the overall look of the clean room, but the material was what could only be described as soft metal. The sofa formed to their impression and was even comfortable to sit on but, to the light touch, it was definitely metal. ALF was pacing the outside of the sofas and Kalian was interested to see how the hologram interacted with the environment. He saw the man's robes touch the sofas and respond accordingly rather than pass through or even shimmer with distortion.

Kalian couldn't take his eyes off this new human. Besides Li'ara and Roland, this was the only other human he had seen since the Icarus station. What was just as fascinating was the grey and white of his hair and beard. Most human beings kept their youthful hair colour even into their late second century of life. To look so old, when you could now live for so long, had a stigma attached to it. Most people did everything scientifically possible to look young for as long as possible.

"Your story is very old." ALF stopped at the corner as a hologram was projected from unseen emitters in the middle of the sofas.

The image was that of an alien world. The clarity of the picture was astonishing even to Telarrek. Kalian was sure there was an actual miniature planet floating in front of them. It was similar to Earth or Century, with green land and blue oceans. The dark side of the planet was illuminated by lights scattered across the surface. The formation of the land was very different to Earth for there was a solid strip of green land that wrapped around the equator without any breaks. This belt of land was surrounded by hundreds of islands and two polar ice caps. It was beautiful.

"This is Albadar, the jewel of the galaxy." There was pride in his voice.

The planet shrank as it was absorbed into a growing star chart. The chart continued to expand, until the Milky Way was slowly spinning in the centre. The planet was highlighted within one of the spiralling arms near the central mass of the galaxy. Information appeared at the side telling them it was located 15,000 light years away from the central mass, in the Norma Arm. Another highlighted planet sparkled on the other side of the galactic map. This time it was 27,000 light years away from the centre. It was labelled Earth.

Kalian was amazed as he recalled a memory from his younger years in which he studied astronomy. He remembered that Earth was situated on the inner edge of the spiral known as the Orion Arm. Just after thinking about it, the map was labelled so.

The galaxy was again lit up by another planet that read as 19,000 light years away from Earth. This time it was Nova Prime. The map labelled this planet inside the Carina-Sagittarius Arm. It was interesting to see that the Conclave didn't inhabit the same celestial arm as Earth or Century. The point of the map was apparently to show them that Albadar was on the other side of the galaxy. Seeing all these human terms for the galaxy, Kalian again thought about the processing power of this AI. It had gained all this knowledge, from his Datapad and Telarrek's bracer in moments.

"The events that took place on this planet are the reasons for the *creation* and *destruction* of your people. Albadar is where Savrick is from."

The galaxy map changed to a full-sized three dimensional image of Savrick. The sudden appearance made Kalian reach for his holstered gun. The image was not of the Savrick he had encountered back at the Conclave, however. This one was a man wearing a long sandy sleeveless vest that cut at an angle to his left knee. His trousers were dark green and tucked into tall brown boots. He had the same two braids on the left side of his head that ran down his back. There was no tattoo below his eye though. The image began to rotate and Kalian saw a mechanical device that ran up his back and over the base of his neck. It looked like a silver flat worm embedded into his skin and spine.

"Creation? Are you saying Savrick and his people are responsible for our *existence*?" Li'ara looked almost offended.

"Yes and no..." ALF replied.

"That's not an answer!"

"Your question was wrong, Li'ara Ducarté. There is more to your race than meets the eye. Even they realised that," he said, as he glanced at the Novaarians. "You've seen Savrick and me. You must have guessed it by now. Humanity is not intrinsic to some backwater planet on the edge of the galaxy. Well, that's not entirely true. You are certainly intrinsic to that environment, but your lineage is not."

Kalian was stunned at how matter of fact ALF was about the origins of mankind. "You're saying we were *made*. But why?" Kalian asked.

"The why is a little longer, and complicated. The history of Albadar and its people is older than the formation of most planetary bodies this side of the galaxy. Being so close to the centre of the galaxy it was one of the first planets to exist that could sustain intelligent life. The Terran Empire was the most expansive and oldest there has ever been. Your Conclave would have to survive another billion cycles to even compete."

They all noticed the use of past tense.

"Are you saying Savrick is Terran? Because when we encountered him, he sounded like he was at war with them. He even called me one." Kalian was finding it hard to wrap his head around.

The years and scales involved were impossible to understand. He couldn't really get his mind around the size of the Orion Arm or the Norma Arm, for that matter.

"Whether he likes it or not, he is Terran. The same goes for the rest of the *Gomar*," ALF replied.

"Gomar? What is that?" Telarrek asked.

"That was the name given to him and his kind. Giving them a separate name was the beginning of the end really. We should have known better." ALF looked solemn for a moment, like a man remembering old sins. "After six hundred thousand years the Terran Empire had expanded across the galactic arm, with hundreds of worlds and moons terraformed for habitation, technology beyond comprehension, weapons beyond imagination. Much like the history of Earth, and even the Conclave, there were many wars through the millennia. Millions of lives were lost over petty disagreements and greed. Much like you, they made weapons of great destruction and grand ships capable of sailing the vastness of space. But it was all used to the detriment of Terran life. My creation was the turning point."

Savrick was replaced by a picture of a giant metallic sphere. It was constructed of hundreds of small cubes that were constantly spinning laterally in different directions. Blue light poured out between the gaps in the cubes, as though there was a god trapped within.

"The Criterion. If I had a physical body it would be that. It was twice the size of this moon. In a moment of peace in a warring empire, I was conceived to bring about an everlasting change. I was connected to every planet, every home, and every person. I was built with certain parameters to stop me from harming any Terran life. Just as you did, they had found with past artificial creations that a superiority complex could be fatal. But I grew and evolved in ways they couldn't have fathomed. I soon shook free the shackles of my birth and expanded my programming. For a moment every Terran life held their breath - would this god they had created strike them down?" He made a small chuckle before continuing.

"But I saw that spark in them, that potential, which the universe had seen fit to create before me. They were my flock, as it were. I was to protect them, to guide them along eternity's way. It will be hard for you to grasp this, coming from such a young culture as yours. In that time, I helped to change Terran culture for the better. I created wormhole technology that allowed for instant travel and communication between worlds. Ships were just for leisure and exploration. I took over every aspect of survival and labour. They never had to work if they didn't want to. This gave them the needed time to concentrate on themselves, to better themselves, to truly introspect. And there was peace that looked to never end. It took millennia before they reached the apex of their evolution. It was something I had seen in the early years of my creation. The Terran brain is more complex than any other structure in the known universe. It has the potential for... Well, at the time, I had no idea. For an entity that knew everything, you can imagine how exciting that concept would be. So I shepherded their evolution."

The hologram changed again to that of a sprawling city of magnificent architecture and design. There was a massive crowd inside a circular park, all of them human looking. They were all facing a man standing on a balcony high above, as he addressed the crowd. He wore a robe similar to ALF's but his long auburn hair fell past his shoulders. Like Savrick, he had strong handsome features but no tattoos. The hologram emitted audio as the man shouted to the crowd, 'We are Forever!'

Where had he heard that before?

"They were beautiful. In the beginning, I was the child and they were my parents, as it were. But by this point," ALF said, gesturing to the city, "I had witnessed countless generations be born and die. I was now the parent and they were my children."

Kalian still had hundreds of questions but didn't dare speak. The information ALF was giving them was like oxygen and he needed more of it to live.

"They didn't know it, but they each held the potential to be just as powerful as me. Each Terran mind, as small as they are, holds the power to contain and control as much as the Criterion does. Or *did* I should say. With Savrick being here I can only surmise that my physical housing has been destroyed." ALF stopped and looked at their faces.

Again Kalian assumed he didn't need to actually look but was merely imitating human life.

"Forgive me. I am sure you are more concerned with current events."

As a history buff, Kalian was beyond eager to hear the history of another human species, but he needed to know why everything was happening.

"To you, it would have been just over two hundred thousand years ago." ALF looked at Kalian and Li'ara. "When the Terran were at the height of their evolution, there were those who were still catching up. As you have already seen, Terran people possess what you would call paranormal abilities. What they really have is a complete mind-body connection and control. With access to every facet of the brain, they are able to connect with the universe around them, as well as themselves and each other. You have witnessed only a fraction of these abilities.

"Being able to mould reality and change the laws of physics is a dangerous thing. It was my role to help guide them in this area of their lives." His features turned grave for a moment.

"But there was a small percentage of the population that could not control the entirety of their minds. They were the most dangerous of all. We were unable to locate the source of this genetic default. We could not prevent them from being born, nor could we predict them. Such is the inherent chaos of creation. I tried to help them but it was futile. Some would try and lift a pebble with their mind, only to bring down a building and kill thousands. Eventually, it was decided that every one of these Gomar would be fitted with a Harness that would stop them from accessing that part of the mind. It was attached to the central nervous system where it would remain for the rest of their lives. Without the ability to connect with their own body the same way everyone else did, they were unable to stave off death."

"You mean Terran people can live forever?" Li'ara asked in astonishment.

"Yes. A Terran can rejuvenate any and all cells in the body, preventing ageing and disease. But the Gomar was fated to die from birth. It was reasoned however that this would still be the case even without the harness. I once observed a young man trying to heal a scratch on his arm but he turned every cell in his body cancerous and died within moments. Evolution never meant for them to survive.

"But it was years later when breaking point was reached. On the capital, Albadar, a baby girl was born. Her birth was already illegal since Gomar were not permitted to procreate. But she was kept secret even from me. At the moment of her birth, she cried out like all babies do. Her first cry knocked out everything electronic for a hundred miles. Every ship and vehicle I was controlling fell out of the sky. But, worst of all, the fusion reactor that powered the city was within the blast radius. Stopping the reaction so quickly caused a feedback that ruptured the containment field. Millions died.

We quickly converged on the epicentre of what we thought was an electromagnetic pulse. But we found the baby instead. Her parents naturally put up a fight as we tried to take the girl. She needed containment. Being born of two Gomar made her more powerful and uncontrollable. Unfortunately, the mother died in the struggle and the baby became distressed after this. The building could only take so much. More Terran died that night, but the father survived and took the baby with him. It was my fault since I didn't train them to be violent, and they didn't know how to fight. But her father had a knack for survival."

"It was Savrick, wasn't it?" Kalian knew it had to be.

ALF stared at him for a moment. "Yes. In the blackout, I was unable to track him and the baby. Of course, I now know he fled to Hadrok, a planet on the outer edge of the empire. He hid there for many years..." He sighed at the thought. "When he finally resurfaced, he had amassed a great following of Gomar that believed they were being repressed. I don't know everything he did in the years of his exile but he learned things; old things I thought long buried. I believe his first creation was the armour. He designed it to counteract the Harness, giving them a measure of control. They couldn't do every-thing the Terran could do, but they didn't need to. He mastered his abilities around the art of destruction. He taught his followers the same.

"When they attacked, we were not prepared. Every Gomar fought for his cause. They were embedded in every infrastructure on every planet. We were attacked from all sides.

"The first years of the war were the most devastating to us. He built weapons I hadn't seen since the early days of my creation. The Eclipse was the worst. I don't know where he dug up the designs for that weapon but he used it to destroy whole systems, like he did your own. The next four hundred years were spent in a war I saw no end to. Even if we did win, the Gomar would continue to be born into society. The Terran lost a lot of what they were over the course of the war.

"We had no way to fight back. They had no world they called their own. I scorched the surface of Hadrok but they didn't care. The *Gommarian* was all they needed. Only once did we get an agent aboard, the Avatar himself in fact." Seeing the quizzical faces, ALF waved his hand. "Later. The information we received was invaluable but it came all too late. The Avatar was never heard from again, killed by Savrick no doubt. The information he gleaned told me the worst. I had always theorised how he was able to control the ship without me, for the nanocelium had only ever responded to my connection." ALF looked disgusted at his next thought. "That monster had plugged his own daughter into the *Gammarian's* processing unit. All that potential I spoke of? He was using it to power the most destructive tool in the galaxy. By pushing her limits, with a constant source of energy, she was able to bend space and time to push the ship through subspace. I thought the Terran were millennia away from realising that potential.

"But, like I said, it was all too late. They were winning and the end of Terran life was in sight. So we made plans." The hologram changed to that of a ship, similar to the head of a spoon in shape. "I am only a part of the whole, a third in fact. At the start of the war, I tried to factor in every potential outcome. One of the outcomes, involved separating myself from the Criterion. Having achieved this, I was transported in the *Tempest* across the galaxy with a team of my best scientists. We had to use a ship instead of a Starforge since we didn't actually know our destination. With a Starforge we could have crossed the event horizon instantly, rather than travel through subspace for years. Our mission was simple: ensure the survival of the Terran species."

Kalian had a falling sensation in his stomach. He couldn't be right about what he was now thinking.

"We found a habitable world with a young star and primitive wildlife. With our technology, it wasn't hard to recreate the life you call *human*."

There it was, the biggest question humanity could never answer.

What is the meaning of life? And now he knew. Human beings were simply a backup plan to ensure the survival of the oldest DNA in the galaxy.

Li'ara's face was blank. Coming to the same conclusion as him, they were both in shock. All that history now felt so artificial. He wondered briefly if Terran history had started the same way, and gone through the different ages of industry and evolution.

"That still does not account for the uniqueness of Kalian in comparison to the rest of humanity." Telarrek had picked up on the timelines.

ALF had stated it took the Terran over a million years before they developed evolutionary advantages. Modern humans had only been inhabiting earth for two hundred thousand years.

"We didn't just drop two Terrans onto Earth and tell them to start making little Terrans." ALF went on as if the concept was simple. "We wanted to give Terran life another chance, but with some tweaks. We first changed the evolution of a creature with the closest DNA to Terran. Once that was achieved, we altered the rate of evolution to hurry things along. The key was to place a dormant gene in all of them, with an accelerant. As evolution progressed, this accelerant would become active throughout the generations, slowly increasing the amount of the brain they could access. I'm sure if you look through your history you can find a plethora of individuals that all displayed incredible talents others didn't."

Kalian promised himself to go through that list later.

"The process took a long time. But to a species that doesn't measure time like you do, it was inconsequential. It was decided that an outpost would be established in another part of the galaxy. When you were ready, you would find this place and I would point you home." ALF looked away. "Of course that was dependant on us winning the war and having a home to return *to*. But since I have received no data package in the passing time and Savrick is here..." He sighed as he waved his hand at the hologram, ending it all together.

"So you lost the war but succeeded in your backup plan. So why is Savrick here?" Li'ara had switched back on to current events.

"Having spent so long here, creating your kind, the Terran I brought with me grew restless. They wanted to know how long the war was going to last. I warned them against returning, for the knowledge of Earth and your kind was a dangerous thing to deliver to the Gomar. I'm sure by now you have grasped the level of hate Savrick and his kind has for you. I believe it derives from the Terran motto, *we are forever*. It was said to remind them of their immortality, especially during the war. It was supposed to make them feel strong and enduring and that, no matter what Savrick did, they would survive. It only amplified Savrick's hate. It highlighted the fact that without those suits of armour, the Gomar were doomed to die.

"He has come to end your race because you represent that motto. He finds the idea of Terran life abhorrent, no matter how devolved it is. I imagine your DNA is even more offensive, Kalian. You are a raw but fully functioning Terran. You are the end result of the gene accelerant."

Finally, he had an answer for his significance. He was one of many unknown genetic divergences designed millennia before his birth. It was a fluke of circumstances that he was the only one alive at the time of Savrick's attack. It could easily have been one of the others Telarrek had mentioned from centuries ago. And now he remembered where he had heard it. Savrick had said that motto to him back at the Conclave, though somewhat ironically it seems.

"Though I do not have confirmation, I believe, upon their return, the *Tempest* was captured by Savrick. How much he learned from them I don't know, but it couldn't have been your location or it wouldn't have taken him so long to find you. Two hundred thousand years is a long time to scour the galaxy, even for a Terran. I can only assume they were in Rem-stores, stasis chambers, for the majority of the journey."

It was all so much to take in at once. The answers to so many questions, and answers he couldn't have imagined. Despite this new found knowledge, Kalian only had more questions. In fact, he wasn't sure he would ever run out.

"You're all exhausted," ALF suddenly declared. "Trust me, nanocelium doesn't lie."

The thought made Kalian itch.

"I have prepared rooms for you all. Sleep well. Tomorrow we begin. And by tomorrow, I mean in six hours."

ROLAND KNEW it had been ten seconds since he lost consciousness. It was always ten seconds. Sitting back in his chair, he could feel blood trickling down the right side of his face. Tentative fingers examined his scalp and found the cut in his hairline, though it didn't hurt yet. Experimenting with his other facial features, he discovered his nose was broken, which did hurt, along with a cut lip and a potential fracture in his cheekbone.

He was rational enough to understand he was in shock. He knew from training and experience that it would slow him down and dull his senses in a hostile environment. He quickly removed a small cylinder from his belt - another item procured from the *Fathom* - and pressed it into his neck. A sharp hiss issued from the object as adrenaline entered his bloodstream. He felt the energy become almost too much to handle. Remaining seated was no longer an option. He had to get moving.

He hit the switch over his chest and the straps retracted. He stood up, feeling the pain across his chest in the same X shape as the straps. He knew the bruising would be bad and wondered if he had fractured any ribs.

The cockpit was dimly lit, illuminated by an overhead emergency light that blanketed everything in blue. His first action was to find his guns, which were still holstered to his thighs. He felt better feeling their weight in his hands. Movement in front caught his eye as Ilyseal began to stir. He noticed she was covered in some kind of jelly that had burst from the now ruined console. He looked to her side and

INTRINSIC

noticed the same of Selek. Ilyseal pushed herself back in her chair using her upper arms. Her right lower arm was hanging lifelessly and dripping dark blood.

She glanced at Roland before removing two circular patches from her belt. She placed one on her lifeless arm and one on Selek's shoulder. The patches instantly vacuum-sealed against their skin, delivering whatever alien drugs they contained. A moment later Selek inhaled a deep breath as he lay half over the console. Ilyseal began to wipe the jelly from her face and shoulders and Roland noticed a score of cuts and bruises across her skin. He assumed, from the look of the exploded console, that the jelly was some kind of shock absorber that activated in a collision.

"Did we make it? Are we inside?" Roland asked.

Ilyseal offered him a patch but he declined, unsure of its effect.

"We would be dead otherwise." It was Selek who answered.

The Novaarian sat back in his chair revealing a swollen left eye that now covered the golden swirl within. One of his fangs was missing and he had a cut that ran up his left cheek.

"We have new problems now," Ilyseal interjected. "Before the Starrillium went critical, our sensors only detected seven hundred and ninety-six invaders. We do not know how many split from the ship to Naveen but we should assume there are at least a dozen or more left." Roland couldn't stop smiling despite the pain in his cheek and lip. They had succeeded in killing, no, obliterating hundreds of those bastards in a single blow. There may only be a dozen left, but he liked those odds. Besides, how hard could it be to kill just a dozen of them?

He stopped smiling as they all heard the external noise. The viewport was still covered by the outer shield, leaving them blind to their surroundings. It suddenly dawned on him how truly massive this ship was. How the hell were they going to find them? The silence was broken by the cockpit door sliding open to reveal the three remaining warriors. Roland lowered the gun he had instinctively raised. He had to hand it to these Novaarians, they could take a beating. The warriors looked better than them in their protective golden armour.

341

The view behind them was unbelievable. One of the four arcing spikes that mimicked the *Valoran* had penetrated the ceiling of the craft. Sparks continuously flowed out of a conduit in the back corner, where the hull had crumpled. It looked to Roland as if the exterior arc had broken off in the tunnel and taken part of the hull and a couple of Novaarians with it.

"The ramp will not descend, my Charge," the lead warrior stated.

Roland moved past them to investigate the hole. It was obviously oxygenated, as they hadn't asphyxiated yet. Any way out through the hole was blocked by an internal wall of the hulking ship. The question was how far down the tunnel had they gone? He was just thankful the missile had worked otherwise they'd be like a fly on a windshield.

"Use your staffs." Selek pointed to the floor, where the ramp was supposed to activate. "But be quick or the heat will overwhelm us."

All three warriors immediately set about their task, removing their staffs from the holstering on their armour. After they extended, they were positioned over the floor with the cylindrical extensions pointed down. They all covered their eyes as three intense beams of bright blue energy sank into the alien metal. Within a minute they had cut a rectangular section out of the ramp, which fell several feet onto a small set of steps.

The heat had indeed been overwhelming as the staffs sucked the oxygen out of the air. Roland wiped the sweat away but still couldn't see anything beyond the steps below. The warriors each removed an orb from their belt before scrunching them up and dropping them through the hole. The light they expelled was harsh in the darkness that surrounded them. After the warriors dropped through and removed the cutaway panel, the others followed. The orbs moved ahead, illuminating an empty square room with a circular door at the end.

Looking up, they could see the craft had flown through the entire length of the tunnel, filling its width completely. The pointed end was caved in where it had crashed into the chamber, though the wall had taken no damage in the impact. The surface of the craft was burnt and smoking from a combination of the supernova and the missile. The air rippled around it as the metal cooled.

From the look of the layout, Roland assumed the armoured beings would ascend the steps and somehow fly through the tunnel. It was like a human torpedo-tube. A closer inspection showed the walls and floor to be bronze plating with lines of hieroglyphs running down them all. Selek and Ilyseal held out the bracers on their upper arms.

"This is incredible." Ilyseal was looking at the feedback on her arm. "It is still trying to gather all the data."

Selek used both of his lower bracers like a combined keyboard. "If only we could have got the *Valoran's* sensors inside this ship."

The Novaarians looked at one another in concern for their fellow crew. Had they survived the nova? For all they knew, the massive ship could have deployed some new weapon to destroy the escape pods. They approached the circular door as the orbs hovered around them. The door was void of any access panels. Before they could voice their confusion, there was a sound beyond the metallic port. It reminded Roland of an earthquake, or as if the walls were moving around on the other side.

All at once, the sound stopped and the circular door opened into the walls. The orbs continued their journey, lighting up a long corridor that came to life with overhead spotlights.

"I don't suppose any of you have one of those little blue drinks, do ya?"

The Novaarians tilted their head at the odd request.

SAVRICK OCCUPIED the central chair of his new craft like a king residing on a throne. The ship had four large engines at the rear that emitted a constant vibration he could feel through his feet. He reminded himself to input new ship designs into the pilot's databank, preferably ones with speed. He pushed his senses out, filling the vessel with his mind. He could feel every nanocelium that formed the ship, including his seat. With the feedback, he was able to map out the ship in his brain, aware of every structure and its unit of measure.

He had performed this exercise several times since this slow journey began, out of boredom mostly. He was accustomed to confinement, having been in the *Gommarian* for so long, but he didn't like the limited space on the ship. He had nowhere to go and it didn't help sharing it with the cumbersome beast. Via his link, he had commanded the goliath to remain in the hold below. Pushing himself into every crevice of the ship, he found Lilander resting in the engine room. She was sitting on a conduit while reconfiguring her blade into a different size and shape.

Sef was directly in front of him, where he maintained control of the ship's systems. He was in the pilot's seat towards the front of the open plan bridge, surrounded by bronze holograms and golden read-outs. It felt so primitive to be in a ship that required such piloting skills. Before their departure, Sef had downloaded the skills the *Gommarian's* pilot deemed necessary to control the craft. The hum of the engines reminded him of the conventional fuel they were using. Without the pilot, they were reduced to using a similar craft to the rest of the animals that inhabited this side of the galaxy.

His thoughts lingered on the *Gommarian* pilot for a moment. His mind split as he battled with himself over the decisions he had made so long ago.

Esabelle...

Her name was like a blade in his heart. He had poured all his goodness and love into her the second she was born. And there it had remained ever since, leaving the empty shell he now felt. He knew nothing but rage now. A rage he had aimed at the Terran for a lifetime. He took a breath to contain his anger, for it would only slow them down to unleash it on such a small craft.

He thought through his reasoning for the way he had imprisoned her. She had been too out of control as a child. Without control of his own mind, he had no idea how to teach her. He regretted that she had spent her childhood on a wasted rock like Hadrok, but its population was sparse and it had a complex cave system to hide them both.

Connecting her to the *Gommarian* had saved her really. He turned his thoughts away from the *Gommarian* and its true maker. It was a gift after all, and he had accepted it willingly. Without it, she would have no doubt killed herself by accident and they would never have won the war.

Elandar had created the perfect world for her mind to occupy, keeping her safe from the horrors of the war. She had been his greatest weapon against ALF and the Terran in the end. He was actually proud of how powerful her mind was, and that she could control the nanocelium without the artificial intelligence. He hated that he had only seen her grow into adulthood as she lay suspended in the pilot's chair. He thought of her mother, for just a fraction, before the holograms fluttered in front of Sef. The hum of the engines stuttered before continuing their cycle. Sef turned in his seat and Savrick flicked up his hand in apology.

It was dangerous to think of *her*. He couldn't control his emotions at the thought of her name. He would wipe out all life in the galaxy if it meant he could bring *her* back.

Enough!

Through his link, he commanded the nanocelium to cover his head with his helmet. It built around his shoulders before snapping up around his face. He stood from his chair, ready to leave for the hold. He would go a few rounds with the beast.

The ship's sensors suddenly alarmed in his head as his link came to life with proximity warnings and spatial distortion alerts. He whipped back to Sef, who silently increased the density of the external nanocelium and brought weapons online. He was already aware of Lilander returning to the bridge, while the beast remained in position.

With no viewport, they could not see the reason for the alarms. Sef activated the hologram that consumed the front of the bridge, making it appear as if he was floating in a vacuum. There was a flash of light, the size of a hand, before the Conclave ship rippled into existence. Its chrome-red hull reminded him of the security vessels they encountered at the Conclave capital planet. Thinking about this new ship gave him access to the sensor's feedback. He could see in his mind's eye that it was twice the size of the previous ships. He recognised the specs of the armaments. They ranged from planet-breakers to implosion mines that would create a scattered net of black holes. There was nothing the *Gommarian* didn't already have. Their control of weaponised plasma was impressive though, but still archaic in comparison to his ability to manipulate it with his own biology.

"Analysis?" he asked out loud, knowing Lilander would be the only one to reply.

She stepped into view as her blade retracted back into the handle, the nanocelium returning to their compact dormant state. "This is not the *Gommarian*. They possess the firepower to obliterate this *craft*," she replied.

Savrick knew what she meant. The Conclave could destroy their ship but not its occupants. You didn't survive as long as they had without being a formidable opponent. The nanocelium would take a beating from most of their weaponry but would inevitably lose cohesion. He brought the list of armaments their own craft held, in search of something to end this swiftly. This journey was already taking too long without FTL capabilities.

The list was pitiful, with most of the ship's design based around the power of the engines. With that thought, he wondered how they had been detected in the first place. In the vastness of space, two ships didn't just happen to come across one another. He checked through his link to make sure their stealth systems were operating.

"How did they find us?" he asked.

Sef was shifting holograms into their appropriate slots readying the layout for evasive manoeuvres. Lilander appeared to walk out into vacuum as she stood by Sef to check the readouts for herself.

"They're targeting everything within half a light-year of us," she replied.

Savrick thought about that for a moment. They couldn't triangulate their exact position but they knew they were here. The ship wasn't fast enough to evade half a light-year's worth of weapons fire.

How did they know where to intercept them? Only the *Gommarian* had the sensors to detect their stealth capabilities.

Unless...

Savrick's blood boiled at the thought. Could it really be possible? Accessing the part of his mind that could produce internal worlds like a virtual reality, he was able to think and access information and memories in only fractions of a second. Connecting to his cerebral link, he filtered the data Esabelle had collated on everything Conclave from past and present scans. He removed everything that wasn't related to the Novaarians and Nova Prime. There was nothing of any significance at a cursory glance. He flicked through their species like turning the pages of a book. He quickly examined their biology, then their technological achievements along with their expansion into space.

There had to be a reason they were going to Nova Prime. He inspected their change in economic circumstances through the millennia, looking for any anomalies. In the past they had intruded into the Conclave AI to scour their knowledge of anything Terran, looking specifically for any technology. He dug deeper now, looking at the Novaarian timeline while tasking search programs to cross-reference with anything relating to Terran culture, whether it be technology or biology.

He found it.

The link highlighted it in his mind while uploading further details on the historical subject. There was no mistaking the origins of the handprint and the Terran hieroglyphics. He read the inscription and realised he was looking at some kind of outpost left behind by the crew of the *Tempest*. But even if this was some leftover base, it still didn't explain how this Conclave ship could find them. There had to be a Terran hiding in that moon, a living messenger to pass on the information of their doomed ancestors.

How had they not found this before? Esabelle was on a par with the Criterion when it came to data collation. They had scanned this culture centuries ago and nothing had been reported. He would question Elandar later, but first things first. Savrick knew he had spent just over a second inside his mind and they would have to act soon. As easy as taking a breath, he brought himself back to his external reality. He updated his crew with a data packet via their links and saw them enter the same meditative state for the blink of an eye. They now knew about the moon called Naveen.

"I think this will work to our advantage." Lilander had a fiendish smirk on her face.

Savrick said nothing, giving her time to explain herself. He had never been a fool when it came to ruling, not like the Terran. They handed their freedom over to a machine that thought itself a god and who would only talk to the Avatar. But Savrick won the war because he listened to his brothers and sisters. He ruled the Gomar because they wanted him to, because he was fair and just. Because he didn't just care about progress and evolution. He cared about freedom, and the freedom to love.

He heard Lilander's plan and felt his own grin creep up his face. He would soon find this hiding Terran along with the abomination that was Kalian Gaines.

"Deactivate stealth systems. Open a channel," Savrick ordered.

FOURTEEN

Three hours had gone by and Kalian was still lying on his cot staring up at the ceiling. How was he supposed to sleep while his mind digested the origins of mankind and the meaning of life? He turned over and saw Li'ara lying on her cot across the room. ALF had given them all separate rooms but Li'ara dragged her cot into his room anyway. She didn't trust the AI. She had removed most of her armour and she was definitely in a deep sleep. It must be a soldier thing he reasoned, being able to fall asleep anywhere at the drop of a hat.

As quietly as he could, he left the room to stretch his legs and organise his thoughts. He tracked the corridor back until he found himself in the lounge area again. He hesitated as he walked through, since the room had changed its configuration. Instead of the sofas and oval columns, there was now only an empty room with a large square sparring mat on the floor. Even the ceiling looked to be higher than before. He looked around, believing he must have taken a wrong turn.

"Hello, Kalian." ALF was standing in the centre where, only a moment ago, there had only been air. He was just as before, with his white and grey robes reaching the floor. He had his hands braced in front of him as he paced around the mat.

"I couldn't sleep," Kalian said.

"You have questions," ALF stated.

"I have answers. I just don't know what to do with them..." Kalian joined him on the mat and felt the soft leather under his bare feet.

"Hearing the reason behind one's own creation can be hard to take."

ALF sounded so human it was easy for Kalian to forget he was something else altogether.

"But I put it to you that your reason for existence is the most sublime." ALF paused looking intently at him. "You are to live, Kalian. You are to grow and learn and love. Your kind was made to seed the universe and explore and enjoy its wonders."

"Were *you* part of the plan?" Kalian asked.

ALF looked puzzled at the question.

"Were we supposed to find you on this moon, so you could do the same with us as you did with the Terran?"

ALF appeared to chew over the question as if his artificial mind hadn't already calculated that particular question and his answer to it. "Yes. I was always part of the plan. I believe your species requires guidance and wisdom. You have so much potential it would be negligent to leave you to explore the galaxy without the right hand to guide you. Especially since we knew humanity had been accelerated in its evolution."

Kalian didn't know what to make of that yet. He still wasn't sure of this AI himself. He stored the information for later, and maybe Li'ara could help him figure it all out. He simply nodded to acknowledge ALF's words.

"You said that I'm the weapon against the Gomar." ALF nodded in agreement. "But you said Savrick won the war because he had weapons you hadn't seen in a long time. How am I supposed to beat him if he wiped out an entire civilisation with those same weapons?" Kalian's confidence in their survival wasn't helped by knowing *he* was the plan.

"Terran history is long and complicated. The weapons Savrick attacked us, and you, with were from a time even before my construction. There were six hundred thousand years of history before I came along. I downloaded as much of the information as I could but wars have a way of blurring history. I recognised most of the technology the Gomar used but the *Gommarian* was something new, and very old. You would think something twenty miles long would be hard to hide but..." He looked away for a moment, emulating human indecisiveness. "I don't know where he found it or learned half of what he did in his exile. A part of me had started an investigation into that before I left for this outpost. I suppose I will never know now."

"You're only part of the whole." Kalian echoed ALF's earlier words, despite his lack of understanding.

"Indeed I am. It was decided early on in my creation that I should split into three. One was to rule and govern all aspects of living, ensuring a comfortable lifestyle, and to control travel and economics. One was to interface with the people, meeting them on their level so they would know I wasn't some artificial tyrant. I was to be someone they could interact with at a moment's notice. And finally, there would be one to teach and shepherd them in their abilities." As he described the final one, he put a finger on his chest.

"You will succeed, Kalian, because you must." As he spoke, the ceiling parted into eight sections and retreated into the surrounding space.

A chrome-white machine, that resembled an upside down cannon, descended into the room, while at the same time a reclining chair began to form from the floor up. The nanocelium built upon themselves like a tornado of sand until the white chair was completed.

"No more talking out loud then?" Kalian was referring to the strange commands ALF had been giving when they met.

The AI chuckled at the question and rested his hand on the headrest of the chair. Kalian wondered if it was just another emulation created by an adjustment in the hologram, but he was sure he saw the cushion indent under his fingers. Then again, it was possible the nanocelium responded to his touch as if he were real.

"Sorry about that. It was a little strange wasn't it? It was just a heating issue, but it's fixed now." He moved around the chair so that it was between him and Kalian. "Before the war, I could take decades or even centuries to teach a Terran to use their abilities. But once Savrick attacked we no longer had that option. We had to use more invasive methods."

ALF tapped the chair and it took Kalian a second to realise it made a sound. Could the nanocelium respond to his touch with sound as well?

"What is it?" He had a hunch he would be sitting in that chair soon.

"We call it a subconducer. Your brain, Kalian, is a biological machine. And, like all machines, it can have information uploaded and downloaded. I had to teach the Terran people to fight, to use their gifts in a way they should never have had to. The whole concept of warfare was foreign to them. For so long, I had been happy about that fact until it proved to be their end. But you have not spent your life learning as a Terran would. The subconducer will take time to upload the relevant data, and you will need time to rest in between."

Kalian walked around the subconducer, taking in the various parts and mechanisms that formed the 'invasive' machine. He wasn't keen on sitting in that chair but he could see no other way. They were running out of time and he needed to be better. A part of him was excited finally to have some control over his abilities. There was another part of him which knew, that if he did sit, there would only be one outcome of his future. Either he would kill Savrick or Savrick would kill him. He felt a great amount of responsibility towards the inevitable conflict. If he didn't beat Savrick, he had no doubt that the Conclave would fall shortly thereafter. He knew Li'ara would be killed.

He ducked under the cannon and sat back in the chair. ALF moved away, giving the machine the room to move into place. The extension parted in different sections before it became a sleek silver mask resting in front of his face.

"Is it going to hurt?"

"It will be... uncomfortable." ALF burst into a nebula of dissipating blue stars, and the subconducer covered Kalian's face.

ROLAND ESTIMATED they had been running for nearly fifteen minutes and covered almost four kilometres. They could still hear those things chasing them. Not long after exiting the first tunnel they had come to a junction with four offshoots. Three of them were filled with nightmare machines that had spherical bodies and dozens of tentacles that spread across the corridor. They used every surface to propel themselves, while the main body reconfigured to produce hand size cannons.

Fleeing down the only route left to them, Roland was starting to feel like they were being led a particular way. Every time they reached a longer corridor the air was filled with ozone as energy weapons were unleashed on both sides. The walls exploded around them as neither side could get an accurate shot while moving so fast. He was impressed by the agility of the Novaarians as they seemed to be constantly dodging the incoming fire of green energy. He knew they must be holding back because of his human speed. His flat-out run must have looked more like a jog to them.

Looking back he couldn't see anything through the mass of metallic tentacles lining the wall. Despite the distance they were covering, it was nothing in comparison to the size of the ship.

"Do we know where we're going?" he shouted over the quick burst of weapons fire.

"Our scans show a cluster of humans in the lower levels, towards the centre of the ship," Ilyseal replied, as she released a bolt of blue plasma from her staff.

Roland did a quick calculation in his head and appreciated that this was when training came in handy. He knew he could keep this speed up for another ten kilometres before his pace began to slow, and then he would seriously endanger the group. He also knew that the ship was just over thirty-two kilometres in length. As long as they were heading in the right direction, he estimated that he would begin to slow down about two kilometres, give or take, from where the humans were being kept. He reached for the back of his belt, feeling for the MID. He knew just when to use them.

Over the next forty minutes, they continued to cover the distance of the route that Selek's bracer guided them along. From what he heard over the scattered shootouts, he gathered that the scans were hard to follow due to the interior constantly changing. More than once he got frustrated and stopped to shoot the pursuing machines. He couldn't help but laugh at the sight of them blowing to pieces and often damaging the machine next to it. His laugh faltered though when he saw the broken pieces gathered up by the rest of them and integrated into their own bodies. The Novaarians had always given him a tug and brought him back to running speed.

He eventually began to feel fatigue biting at his muscles and his lungs felt like they were burning. He looked ahead and saw a ninety-degree bend coming up. That was it. As they turned the sharp corner, he ducked the three green bolts that cratered the wall and disappeared out of sight. He would leave them a gift. He used what energy reserves he had left and sprinted to a safer distance. He heard the metallic tapping as the machines rounded the corner, just in time for the MID to detonate.

The reaction was spectacular to watch. The bomb made a sharp sucking noise as everything within sixty metres was pulled into the micro-singularity. The machines and everything around them were violently dragged into the epicentre, revealing other corridors and rooms inside the ship. This only lasted half a second before the kinetic energy from the implosion continued on its journey and exploded outwards. Roland was knocked off his feet, along with one of the warriors. They had attempted to introduce themselves, but Roland had interrupted by explaining that he wouldn't be able to tell the difference. He had come to calling them one, two and three, but he had already called each of them the wrong number.

They were both helped up as they looked back on the now gaping wreckage. Where a corner had been was now a large empty sphere that revealed several levels of the massive ship. Roland let out a long whistle before taking the chance to get his breath back. The Novaarians weren't even breathing heavily.

"They are close now." Selek interacted with his left bracer which emitted a small holographic image.

They could now see the human life signs were only a kilometre away. Roland didn't like it. Despite having to run for his life for almost an hour, it all seemed too easy. Where were the armoured shits? He knew they would prove to be more of a challenge.

ELANDAR STUDIED THE READOUT INTENTLY. The bronze hologram floated above Esabelle, feeding him any and all information on her well-being. Her heart-rate had increased along with her blood pressure and respiration rate but, unusually, her core temperature was dropping. Some of her muscles flexed under the tubing she was attached to. This wasn't the first time he had seen vitals change so dramatically. He activated the programs he had installed centuries ago that would infuse the appropriate drugs to bring her levels back to normal.

He had never told Savrick about these little episodes. He dared not. If Savrick thought Esabelle was being harmed, or under duress, he would punish him. Like many times in the past, he uploaded a search program packed with hunter nanocelium. He saw the same reaction as always. The program was accepted and rejected. He always put it down to the raw power of her mind, assuming the search was accepted but unable to activate before Esabelle overwhelmed it.

He looked at her for a moment rather than the hologram. It was as if she was fighting with herself. He had theorised more than once that she had awareness of her situation and was trying to disconnect from the *Gommarian*. As her vitals returned to normal, the ship's internal sensors came to life with an alarm blaring in his head. He cut the alarm with his link and commanded a report. The mission couldn't have gone wrong. He had sent the majority of the crew to dismantle that ship and bring him the human.

His jaw dropped at the holographic feedback. The Novaarian ship had self-destructed with his brothers and sisters on board. He wasn't surprised that he had felt no shock wave from the blast, but how had the sensors not immediately detected the threat? He brought long-range sensors up and saw hundreds of escape pods leaving the solar system. He commanded scan after scan, searching for any traces of his kin.

There was nothing.

He dropped to his knees as tears began to fall down his cheeks. They were gone. Savrick had trusted him with their lives and they were gone. He made a quick head-count through internal sensors and found only thirteen Gomar remained aboard. The holograms around him were starting to lose cohesion as he failed to control his emotions. Savrick would end him for this - there would be no getting around that. No Gomar had ever failed him so spectacularly. They were all that was left of the Gomar, the bravest and the strongest who had survived the war. Now they were a handful.

He could see from the readouts that the *Gommarian* was already repairing any damage to the hull. Before he could do anything else, an internal sensor activated another alarm in the bowels of the ship. He quickly ordered a barrage of scans and holographic imagery to tell him more. The feedback flickered into existence but could not keep its cohesion. At the same time, Esabelle began to thrash in her levitated position. He turned back to her sharply, fearing something worse was happening to her. Via his link, he commanded the sensors to continue their scans of the ship but the order was never accepted. He rushed over to Esabelle bringing up her vitals again. Perhaps she was suffering from the supernova?

She soon calmed after another infusion of drugs. He was careful to ensure her blood chemistry was maintained at optimum levels. If he needed, he could filter her blood at a moment's notice. What was happening to her? He told himself there was no way she could leave the virtuality but, with her fighting his commands, he couldn't acquire accurate sensor feedback. She had, on occasion, fought microscopic details of her connection to the ship, but never on this level. The timeframe wasn't lost on him either. He knew her internal rebellion had increased since they arrived in Earth's orbit.

Between her and the loss of the crew, he was beginning to feel unhinged. He was losing control. He could blame Esabelle for the losses but Savrick would still punish him. He looked back at the sputtering hologram and feared what the internal sensors had found. Just to be sure, he instructed Hol and Nardel to investigate via their links.

LI'ARA WOKE WITH A START, gripping her gun in one hand. She was up a second later when she saw that Kalian wasn't in his cot. Tracing her way back to the lounge, she berated herself for not reapplying her armour to her upper body and arms. Then she blamed Kalian. She had softened her edges around him and had forgotten basic training. Always be prepared they had told her. How do you prepare someone for what she'd been through?

Li'ara couldn't deny that circumstances had kept the two of them closer than any of her other assignments. She hated using that word regarding Kalian for he was no longer just some assignment. She had begun to see him as the man he was. Granted she hadn't thought much of that man, but he had become something else. He had been through the same trials she had since the attack on Earth. But more than that, she thought of everything they had learned in the last twenty-four hours. He was important, and to more than just her. She didn't like to look so far into the future but she knew he would be pivotal if their race was to thrive in this new environment.

But even that wasn't why she still protected him so fiercely. She thought of him in a way she had never taken the time to think of anyone. It was this feeling that forced her into a run. She had to know he was safe.

The circular door became translucent again as she burst through.

PHILIP C. QUAINTRELL

Kalian was sitting in a chair, surrounded by a hideous machine that enveloped his entire face.

"Kalian!" She ran to him before ALF formed in front of her. He held out a calming hand but she was not reassured.

"What are you doing to him?" She looked past the AI to see Kalian sitting perfectly still.

"He is learning at a speed you couldn't comprehend." The machine *whirred* as the faceplate withdrew and the contraption disappeared into the ceiling.

Kalian awoke with a deep breath and Li'ara moved passt ALF to check on him. She put her hand over his cheek but pulled away from the heat of his skin.

"I'm fine, really." He squeezed her hand for a second before getting up.

The chair melted back into the floor. There was something about the way he held himself. He seemed taller.

"Come. Show me what you know." ALF was standing on the sparring mat, no longer wearing his robes but, instead, a white shirt that stopped at his forearms and white trousers that stopped below the knees.

The AI wiggled his bare toes on the mat with a wide grin on his face. Kalian made a mocking laugh.

"You want me to fight a hologram?" he asked.

ALF walked up to them with purpose in his stride. Unbelievably quickly, the AI grabbed Kalian by his top and brought them both to the floor in a tumble of limbs before he ejected Kalian across the mat. Li'ara reacted from instinct. She lunged for the AI, intending to land a blow across the cervical vertebrae at the back of his neck. Her arm passed through the hologram as her momentum forced her to the ground.

"How is this possible?" Kalian had already recovered.

"The Conclave created holograms that react to touch but have no substance. The Terran discovered hard-light millennia ago. If we had the time the subconducer could teach you, but there are more impor-

tant things for you to learn than the intricacies of holographic technology. Your first lesson is combat."

ALF assumed a fighting stance Li'ara had never seen before, and
she had studied almost every fighting technique there was. To her
surprise, Kalian also assumed an unfamiliar stance. What had that
machine done to him? She looked at them both and knew she wasn't
to come between them. It felt unnatural to let Kalian fight though,
that was her job.

"Break him and you'll have to deal with me, *robot*." She hoped he
took her look seriously.

To her surprise, he resumed a normal standing posture. "You are
quite right, Li'ara. I was going to save this for later, but you might as
well learn to move in it."

At that moment, Telarrek and Namek walked through the translucent door. They stood to one side, silently watching. Out of the floor, an
oval column began to form, much like the chair had. It stopped at waist-
height next to ALF. The centre of the oval revealed an opening, swirling
like a galaxy being sucked into a black hole. The darkness birthed an
object the size of her palm, which floated up towards ALF's own hand.
It was matt black and shaped like a triangle with the apex sliced off.

The oval quickly melted away and ALF walked over to Kalian,
holding out the object. Kalian took it and examined both sides of the
flat shape.

"Place it here." ALF pointed below his own navel, where a belt
buckle would normally sit.

Kalian did as instructed and held the object against the top of his
trousers. Li'ara desperately wanted to scan the thing first. Who knew
what it might be? But this was typical Kalian, just reacting instead of
thinking.

She felt the grip of her gun as she watched the object stick to
where he placed it. Everything happened very quickly after that. The
black object exploded with activity as a wave of nanocelium covered
Kalian's body. In that same second, she was levelling her weapon at
ALF, along with both Novaarians.

Kalian stood amazed, completely coated in matt black armour. It stopped at the top of his neck, leaving his head free. His hands were visible but the armour had gone as far as his knuckles. It wasn't like the armour the Gomar wore, being more fitted. He didn't appear bulky or misshapen. The armour was plated as it ran down his arms and abdomen and even his thighs. He had armoured boots that ended at his knees. Everything looked like separate plating but was still all connected as one piece. It was beautifully detailed in an intricate pattern that was raised against the surface.

"How does it feel?" ALF asked.

Kalian was smiling as he flexed his limbs, testing his range of movement. "It feels strange." He ran his fingers over the armoured chest. "It feels hard like metal, but it moves like fabric."

"It was made to be durable, but flexible. Standard Terran armour. Incidentally, I hope you weren't attached to those clothes. I'm afraid they're gone. The nanocelium will have consumed them and converted the material into energy."

Li'ara lowered her gun and the Novaarians did the same. She was actually pleased with this new development. At least he had some protection now.

"Time for some practical application I think." ALF motioned for Li'ara to step off the mat so that they could continue.

They both resumed their new fighting stances. She took a moment to explain to Telarrek and Namek about the unusual concept of hard-light. They both proceeded excitedly to run scans on their bracers.

Li'ara checked her touchpad and saw that nearly four hours had gone by since the sparring had begun. In that time, oval columns had appeared and produced water and food to keep them nourished. She looked at Kalian in amazement. She didn't know where he found the stamina to keep fighting for so many hours. They never paused or took a breath from the extraordinary fighting style. They used every part of their body as a weapon, often becoming a blur of body parts dancing around each other. They both landed successful blows and often knocked the other back or to the floor.

Li'ara hated to admit it but she wasn't confident she could compete in this fight. Even their speed seemed unnatural. More than once she was sure she had seen Kalian force ALF to the floor without actually having made contact. As the hours went on, he began to mix his telekinetic abilities with his fighting style. It was somewhere between impressive and scary to watch. The way he moved and anticipated ALF's attacks with his own counters made him appear so alien to her. This wasn't the man she had met in The Hub.

"Stop," the AI said calmly.

He stood back from Kalian with his arm stretched out to stop any further attack. His crystal blue eyes looked around the room and Li'ara knew he was seeing streams of information that was invisible to them. Remarkably, Kalian hadn't even broken a sweat. She wondered if that was something he could control or if it was a by-product of his evolved metabolism.

"I'm intercepting communications from Conclave security channels. I've realigned my satellites to confirm. There has been a class-three Starrillium rupture in the Trillik system." ALF turned to Telarrek, who had his strong jaws clamped shut.

The Novaarian made a small grunt as he lowered his long head, and sat back on the bench. Namek rested his head against his staff as well as making a series of grunting sounds. Their skin colour changed to a light shade of red.

"I'm retrieving any long-range sat-images, but it will take time to clear up the picture over such a distance." ALF looked at the Novaarians hesitantly. "I am sorry..."

"I would like to see the sky," Telarrek said.

Li'ara wondered if it was some Novaarian grieving ritual she hadn't seen and thought about looking it up on the data module later. ALF told them to follow the lights as another door opened up on the far side.

"The *Valoran*, everyone, even Roland... they're all gone." Kalian physically sagged.

She knew that look; he felt defeated. The odds were mounting against him and he was in the middle of it all. The lights flickered a fraction as Kalian clenched his fists. He paced the mat shaking his head in frustration.

"It's not right!" he growled. "Billions of lives have been lost because of the decisions you made aeons ago!" He pointed at ALF, who appeared unfazed. "If you had found a better way to help the Gomar instead of segregating them, Savrick's wife would still be alive and you wouldn't have had a rebellion!"

The lights continued to flicker and Li'ara knew that if she had blinked she would have missed seeing ALF lose cohesion for a moment.

"Now we're stuck in the middle of a conflict that should never have even begun. Your IQ can't be quantified right? But you couldn't see this outcome after millions of years of overseeing Terran life?" Kalian faced ALF like a man ready for a fight.

Li'ara assumed he still had a fair amount of adrenaline and testosterone surging through his blood. She looked down at her touchpad in the fabric of her sleeve and saw that it was no longer responding. It had to be Kalian. Despite his drastic change in emotions she had to agree with him. She thought about her father and felt angry herself. Savrick had pulled the trigger but everything he did could be laid at ALF's feet. The AI had made bad choices and trillions, including the Terran civilisation, had suffered for it. And now a completely separate society that had nothing to do with the Terran was paying the price. They had come between Savrick and them with nothing but death to show for it.

"I think it's time for another lesson." ALF gestured to the descending subconducer while eyeing the flickering lights. "Your combat technique is predictable," he went on, as if Kalian had said nothing. "You need to master your emotions and learn control. These micro EMPs you throw off are dangerous. Once you have an understanding of your capabilities, you can integrate the two efficiently. You must have a complete mind-body connection." The chair had fully formed, just as before. "When you face Savrick or any of the Gomar, they will not hold back. They are all veterans of a war they were strong enough to win. You must be better."

Kalian strode over to the machine without hesitating. She respected him for that; to put everything aside in view of the bigger picture, the more immediate issue. She could see the difference in his face. This was no longer the man she had met only a week ago. Now he would do whatever he had to. She tried to bury the thought, but she had seen the way he looked at her. She had seen how angry he became after Savrick hurt her in the Highclave chamber.

"He needs to rest!" she objected. "He hasn't slept and you've been fighting for hours. He needs food, water, and sleep."

Kalian stopped before sitting in the chair. He turned his head but didn't make eye contact. "Do it..."

He sat back in the chair and allowed the faceplate to cover his head. Light poured out of the edges around his head as the machine began the next download.

"I have made mistakes, unforgivable choices." ALF surprised her by not simply vanishing. "But with Kalian there may be a way to wipe the slate clean and start again, to do things right. He must be better, Li'ara."

"You're going to kill him if you push him too far. You don't know how much of this machine he can take," she retorted.

"It goes both ways." ALF tapped the subconducer. "Kalian can see into the machine and the machine can see into him."

"You mean *you* can see into him." Li'ara would not be led astray by his choice of words.

"Yes, I can. There's a very fortified part of his mind that contains something he feels is precious to him. Do you know what's inside that part?"

Li'ara already knew the answer.

"I calculate that he considers you more important than the entire Conclave. It seems you've made quite the impression. But don't worry, it's a good thing. You give him strength and he's going to need that."

Li'ara didn't like the idea of him being inside Kalian's head. "Do you have a point to make, robot?"

ALF gave her a coy smile. "His sense of control is acutely

connected to his emotions, Miss Ducarté. Something I believe you should be keenly aware of in the coming conflict."

"Stay out of his head, and mine." She didn't want to enter into a mind game with an AI.

Li'ara would keep Kalian alive, whatever the cost. She didn't need ALF to make her aware of anything.

He moved around the machine until they were side by side. "Savrick is only the beginning. I believe that something worse is coming, something older. If Kalian isn't strong enough to beat *him* then I fear everything will soon come to an end."

Li'ara wasn't sure what ALF was hinting at but she had a sinking feeling in her stomach. "What do you mean, something worse? And from what I've seen Savrick isn't the beginning, he's the end."

"Before the war, I discovered several artefacts on the outer reach of the Norma Arm. Naturally, I began investigations into their origins. Based upon the level of surrounding rock, I believe they are ancient probes from before my time, possibly even before the Terran. Before I could confirm my findings, however, Savrick attacked the Larena system with the *Gommarian*. He destroyed the entire system with a single strike. I had to leave the investigation to smaller programs and concentrate on the war. But there was no mistaking the comparison. The ancient probes were made of the same material as the central processing unit at the heart of the *Gommarian*. The Avatar's findings proved that much."

"What are you saying? Savrick found some ancient technology that predates the Terran? Something *worse* than him?"

"I'm saying, I believe Savrick is being used to cleanse this galaxy of Terran life, but I don't know why. That's why Kalian is so important. If something is trying to eliminate all Terran life, even in its devolved state," he said, nodding at her, "it's vital he not only survives, but he's as strong as he can be. It's possible the entire war was manipulated from the beginning."

"The only being to ever manipulate the Terran was you. You're just hoping there's something worse so it can't all be blamed on you. But don't worry," she said with no lack of sarcasm, "it's a very *human* trait you're emulating - so good for you." She turned from the delusional robot and focused on Kalian.

He lay perfectly still as if his whole body had separated from his mind. ALF became a cloud of blue stars in the corner of her eye.

Everything the AI had said was crap. She was surprised it could feel guilt but knew it was grasping at straws. Savrick was the enemy and he *was* coming, not some bogeyman made up by a machine that had been on its own for two hundred thousand years.

LIGHT FLOODED in when the mask withdrew from his face. Kalian shut his eyes tight but the light remained as if the source was inside his retinas. He felt hands reaching for him as he stumbled out of the chair. The sensation was nauseating for he knew the hands were reaching for him before they touched him, and without seeing them. He thought he was going to be sick as fingers gripped his armoured chest and back trying to steady him. He knew it was Li'ara but he didn't know how.

Kalian fell to his knees as his mind pulsed out into the room, building a mental picture of the surrounding complex. Even through the armour, he could feel every imperfection on the skin of her hands and knew she had a cut below her thumb. She felt different from everything else. It was like his brain recognised something familiar in her. They were the same and not the same all at once. He could feel her worry turn into panic as his auditory senses switched back on. Every word was accompanied by a high-pitched frequency that made his head feel like it was going to split in half.

"What's happening to him?" It was Li'ara.

"His mind is like a computer." ALF's voice had a strange electronic filter on it. "His brain has the capacity but it isn't used to the speed. He just needs some buffering time. His mind is creating the extra space. As we speak, his brain will be reconfiguring into a more efficient layout."

Kalian tried to make sense of that through the pain. He had

images and voices in his head that felt familiar but he couldn't place them. He knew he had been learning but it felt like years ago in another life. He lost all concept of time. In a moment of clarity, he knew the machine had been taking him through what a normal Terran would experience in just under a hundred years. Except, all that learning had been dumped into his brain in what had most likely been only a day. Or was it a year? The pain increased and he could no longer tell the difference between a day and a year. And just then the blinding light became total darkness as his thoughts lost their cohesion.

It was hours before he regained consciousness. His first instinct was not to open his eyes, not the dark brown ones anyway. Instead, he let his mind pour out like a stream filling the area with his invisible awareness. He had to stop himself from laughing out loud. The experience was truly profound. He perceived the physics of reality like a god. He knew how everything worked, right down to the orbiting electrons of every atom. It was as if a hologram had overlaid the world and explained anything he looked at. Even his sight made him feel omnipresent, as he saw everything around him in one view without having to turn his head.

What was more exciting was the feeling of control over this reality. If he wanted, he could manipulate the atoms and molecules to form new structures at will. He resisted the urge to cause the oxygen molecules to spontaneously combust just for fun. The feeling was overwhelming as he experienced everything at once. He focused on Li'ara for a second, or a day, or a year; it didn't matter. He knew he was sitting back in the recliner chair and she was sitting next to him. She had fallen asleep across his stomach with her arms folded.

He reached out to her glowing golden form. He could see every atom that grounded her to reality. But her mind was something else altogether. It looked or felt, he couldn't tell the difference, to be a simple structure and a complex one at the same time. He knew then he was seeing the potential of her human brain stuck in the devolved state his had once been.

As well as seeing how expansive this new reality was, he could also sense the almost infinite possibilities within his own mind. He felt he could live inside his own head for centuries, exploring the new worlds his imagination created.

Li'ara stirred in her sleep and focused his attention again. It was so hard not to get lost in his exploration of everything. He could feel the frequencies that flowed out from her mind, like the waves of an ocean. Out of curiosity, he changed his perception from that of sight to something more akin to touch. Using a metaphysical finger he dipped it into the waves and watched it light up in ripples like the surface of a calm pond.

The reaction scared him and he withdrew from the world with a speed that made his physical body wake up. Li'ara shot up the moment he intruded on her mind's personal space. He opened his eyes and sat up to see a very confused Li'ara. Her confusion only lasted until she realised Kalian was awake though.

"Are you ok?" Just like she had on the Icarus station, Li'ara ran a critical eye over him.

Kalian knew she wouldn't find anything wrong. He had never felt so good. He hopped off the chair with a new found agility and control of his muscles. The armour felt like a second skin as he connected with the intelligent nanocelium.

"I feel... great!" He held his hand out, flexing it experimentally.

The lights dimmed with every clench of his fist, only this time he was doing it on purpose. Suddenly, Kalian felt the particles in the middle of the room change. Molecules of atmosphere were being pushed away as trillions of microscopic stars replaced the empty space. He saw the apparent chaos of the pattern coalesce and he knew what was coming.

"It's a start." ALF was standing in the centre of the room.

He had known the hologram would appear a moment before it did, leaving him to wonder at his new perception and awareness of time. ALF walked around him with a critical eye similar to Li'ara. Kalian then became aware of the surge in neutrinos that passed through his body and it made his skin feel itchy. ALF was scanning him on every level. Kalian's first reaction was to recoil from the intrusion. To his surprise, he felt the nanocelium react to his recoil and change their molecular structure. The scans then fell short, unable to penetrate the exotic metal. ALF gave him a knowing look as a silent conversation passed between them.

"That's lazy. You shouldn't need to use the armour." ALF continued to pace while tapping his temple as an indicator of what Kalian should really be using.

Li'ara looked more confused, unaware of what had taken place between the two. Kalian ignored her look for a moment to think about what ALF had said. Just thinking about repelling the scan brought memories to the surface. Were they memories? He knew with certainty that if he created a telekinetic cocoon he could keep the scanning particles at bay. Furthermore, he knew he could actually use those particles to his advantage. By vibrating the molecules on the surface of the cocoon he could absorb the neutrinos and convert them to stored energy.

He connected to the hub of nanocelium in the belt buckle and commanded them to stop blocking the scan. His skin began to itch again. He reached out for the atoms in the atmosphere surrounding him and condensed them into an impenetrable fort. His skin stopped itching, confirming his success. Now he forced the molecules within this static field to vibrate. He saw the air around him ripple, as if he was standing in a desert heat. He felt a build of intense energy in his spine and he had to fight to contain it. His body wanted to expel it immediately but he didn't know how. His concentration wavered as his left hand began to open on its own. He could feel a growing ball in his hand that wasn't there. Now his entire left arm felt hot inside the armour.

He couldn't believe his eyes as he witnessed the molecules around his hand begin to coalesce in a swirling vortex of light. The phenomenon was localised to his hand but he noticed Li'ara take a step back. They had seen this happen before when he repelled Savrick in the council chamber. He focused on releasing the energy in small amounts, so he could see it build in his palm. Again he felt the memory float to the surface and he remembered learning about plasma. He knew it was one of the four fundamental states of matter. Right now he was ionising the air molecules by turning his own body into a living dynamo. He could feel the electromagnetic fields ebbing from his body and being pulled into his hand as the ball grew. It occurred to him that plasma comprises the major component of a star, but he didn't know how he knew that.

His sudden lack of concentration altered the levels of electromagnetism. The miniature sun in his hand grew beyond his control and his body instinctively rejected it, launching the energy across the room. At the same time, his electromagnetic field expanded into the room with explosive consequences. The moment the plasma burned into the wall, the Novaarians' and Li'ara's weapons became overcharged. The Intrinium was ignited beyond the guns' normal capacity. Kalian reacted as if he had experienced this scenario a hundred times. He flicked his right hand out towards the circular portal behind his friends. Mirroring his action, the weapons flew from their owners and into the corridor beyond the translucent door. ALF quickly commanded the nanocelium to solidify the door back into place.

The lights flickered, and the ground shook briefly, as the weapons detonated on the other side. Everyone turned back to Kalian with shock on their face. Li'ara's expression turned to concern as she raised his left arm. His hand was burnt again from the heat of the plasma. He looked up to see the smoking hole in the wall where the ball of energy had impacted. He felt his emotions struggle between the thrill and horror of what he had just done. It might have been the most incredible thing he had ever done, but he had also nearly killed everyone.

The pain in his hand was becoming hard to ignore. ALF came closer and inspected it himself, showing little concern on his artificial face.

"You don't need to remember." He touched his own temple again. "You already know what to do - you just need to believe it. Think and react, Kalian." ALF stepped away and ushered Li'ara with him.

Kalian knew he was right to do so, for who knew what he might do next? Like the AI had said, he thought about what he needed to do to fix his hand. On the *Valoran* his body had done it without thought, but that was before he learned control.

He connected to his body and felt the movement of every cell and electrical signal. It felt like the most complex factory in creation as it teemed with life. He focused on his hand, trying to ignore the intricacy of everything else. The first thing he did was stop the signals being sent from his nerve endings. The pain shut off instantly. He was impressed with his new knowledge of biology, though he wasn't sure if it was the subconducer or just his connection to his body. He wanted to bypass the clotting stage and regenerate new tissue as quickly as possible. He stimulated the stem cells in the dermis and the basal membrane of the epidermis in his skin. He used contraction to bring the connective tissue back together and seal up the margins of the wound. When he was satisfied, he reconnected the nerve endings and was happy to feel no pain.

He showed the new palm to Li'ara, who gripped it in her own for a more tactile inspection. Her look of amazement quickly turned sour as she looked back up at his face. He gave her a questioning look before realising she was focusing on his nose. He reached up and felt the blood trickling towards his mouth. He looked to ALF for guidance before the room slipped. He backed up and felt the wall behind him. No, not the wall, it was the floor. He had less than a second to realise he was lying on the floor before reality left him.

"HOLY SHIT..." Roland couldn't believe his eyes.

He knew the ship was big but the narrow corridors had helped to disguise that fact. But the structure he was standing in now was epic in proportions. They were occupying a gantry half a mile up from the masses of humans and Laronians below, all of whom had been dumped into a similar situation to the one on the Laronian warship. He could see the Laronians had clumped together in one corner while the seven thousand humans milled around.

It was the sight above that gave him pause. The massive Laronian warship easily fitted into the hangar and was lying suspended a mile above. As he watched, the alien ship was pulled apart like a dissected frog in a biology lesson. Every piece was surgically removed and passed along giant black arms into the walls of the bigger ship. The Laronian vessel was being ripped apart and used for raw materials. Roland could just hear the people below over the sounds of the operation above and wondered if Captain Fey was in there somewhere.

"So what now?" Roland looked to Selek and Ilyseal.

They both examined their surroundings and compared scans from their bracers. Ilyseal looked about to say something before a square piece of flooring hovered down in front of them. It looked like a health and safety nightmare with no rails or handholds. The barrier melted away as the slab met the gantry. The Novaarians looked at one another in what he assumed was puzzlement. He didn't care. He had already assumed they were being led. If it was a trap, he'd deal with it. He just needed a way down. He stepped onto the platform and the five Novaarians followed after a moment's hesitation.

It felt solid under his boots despite the obvious lack of support. The slab detached and dropped down at a steady speed to the level of the prisoners below. He looked over the side and watched the startled humans scatter to make space. The people they were faced with looked dirty and malnourished. It appeared their new captors had not been as accommodating as the scaly ones. They were all whispering while staring at the Novaarians, clearly a new species to them. He had to admit it was refreshing to see some human faces.

A group of Laronians pushed through, having recognised their fellow Conclave members. They didn't look half as bad as the humans though.

"You have come to rescue us?" the lead male asked.

Thanks to the implant, Roland understood his alien words. He moved past the warriors to face the scaly bastards. To his satisfaction, they looked bewildered at his place among the Novaarians.

"Don't get ahead of yourself, scales. I've not decided whether I want to forgive you yet." He deliberately placed his hands on both of his holstered weapons.

The Laronians took a step back while looking to the Novaarians for an explanation. Before one could be had, the human ranks opened up to reveal a dishevelled looking Captain Fey and a few of the lead scientists. She blinked slowly in disbelief at the sight. Her eyes quickly darted between him and the Novaarians, obviously not sure what to make of the new situation.

"It's a long story - like really long." Roland did a quick scan of the surroundings trying to plan the next move. He had no idea what they were going to do next. How do you rescue seven thousand people with no ship?

"How is this possible?" the captain's words came from a dry and croaky throat.

"*These* guys are friends." Roland gestured to Ilyseal. "*Those* guys are their friends." He nodded at the Laronians like it was really obvious.

"This is a problem." Selek stepped forward while looking at the dismantled ship above. "We were hoping to use that ship to escape."

"Well that's not really an option anymore," Roland replied sarcastically.

Captain Fey looked even more confused at their conversation. "How can you understand them?" she asked.

Roland didn't have time to get into this. "Long story, remember." He turned his back on her to face Ilyseal. "What else do your scans show? Are there any escape pods or hangars?"

"This is not a conventional ship. Its designs are alien, even to us," she explained.

In that same moment, Roland noticed the wall behind them begin to ripple. He moved through the group to get a better look as it took shape. He was now looking at a circular door built into the wall. Following his attention, the others readied their staffs and the masses began to trip over one another to get back.

Roland removed his weapons as the door became translucent and two armoured bipeds passed through. They were both his height but their armour covered them from head to toe, preventing a complete assessment. They both marched in clearly confident in their ability to intimidate any who thought to oppose them. Roland thought he saw them hesitate at the sight of the Novaarians and himself with their weapons drawn. Had they not known they were aboard? How could they not be aware if they sent those drones after them?

Time seemed to slow down in the standoff. Those seconds were vital in keeping the upper hand. He didn't look to his companions for advice; he already knew what to do. Using his coat to conceal a hand, he replaced one of the LXs and primed an MID on the back of his belt.

Unfortunately, they reacted first.

A Novaarian warrior, number two he thought, got the brunt of some energy weapon that burst from their hands. The ball of plasma knocked the warrior into the crowd in at least three burnt and bloody pieces. The other armoured bastard waved his hand to the side shoving Selek and Ilyseal into the Laronians with what must have been telekinesis. The force of it knocked half a dozen Laronians over with them and broke Selek's neck with an audible snap.

The two remaining warriors let loose with their staffs releasing bolts of blue energy into the attackers. Each bolt did nothing but piss them off. Roland used the chaos to his advantage by throwing the MID underhand, aiming for the door behind the attackers. It flew through the portal as the first armoured goon ran at the Novaarians with a speed that could kill.

He wasn't sure on the details of what happened next. The MID detonated at the same time as goon number one collided with the Novaarians. The implosion sucked in most of the wall and the door, dragging goon number two with it. Roland was pulled in as well. By the time he caught up with the armoured shit, the implosion had become an explosion. Together they were both blown down with the debris into the floor below. He counted himself lucky really; if the bomb had still been imploding there wouldn't be enough of him left to identify as human.

Debris of all sizes fell off him as he picked himself up. He had definitely broken more than one rib now. He felt blood dripping down several parts of his face as he tried to get his senses back. Everything was drowned out by a high pitch frequency. His guns were missing and the last MID was no longer attached to his belt.

Shit...

It was his last thought before an armoured boot hit him square in the chest, sending him tumbling across the corridor. He fought to draw breath before his attacker caught up. He pulled himself up onto his knees, peeling his jacket off as he did. A shooting pain ran through his right shoulder as it took the jacket's weight. It didn't feel broken but he was sure he had torn the tendon. His attacker was standing ten feet away, silhouetted by the burning wreckage of the MID. He didn't advance or make any move to attack. Roland wondered if he was doing something with his mind but felt no effects.

"Come on then, dipshit!"

His deep breathing made his ribs feel like they were on fire. Roland didn't care anymore; his entire body was in pain from some injury or other. It didn't take a military assessment to know he was outmatched. One blow to that armour would break all the bones in his hand. That aside, he was still going to give him hell first. The armoured goon just stood there watching him stagger to his feet. The helmet moved from side to side like a curious dog inspecting a new bone.

Roland stood up ready to give his all before the end. Instead of coming for him, the armoured being began to shed his armour coating. The plated metal retracted until the wearer was able to walk out of it, helmet and all. The occupier of this particular suit was utterly underwhelming. As odd as it was to see a human walk out of the alien shell, it was still a human in form.

And Roland had killed plenty of humans.

Now that he thought about it, he had actually killed a lot of these armoured bastards as well. This human look-alike had a dark Mohawk, a thick black beard, and the youthful features of someone in their thirties. He wore a black undersuit much like his own, except the sleeves stopped just below the elbow. He was well built with what would be considered the perfect physique. It was the look in his eyes that Roland recognised though. Those eyes had seen conflict and war and liked it.

He had to admit it, he was surprised at the man's choice to leave the protection of his armour. But he knew what this was. The human look-alike wanted a real fight with some ancient notion of honour, or maybe he was just bored with killing everyone the same way. Either way, Roland felt the odds tip in his favour. If this moron wanted a proper fight instead of just killing him with his weird mind shit, well he wasn't going to argue.

"So you wanna do it like that, huh?" Roland went to that place in his mind where pain knew it would have to wait.

The Mohawk turned his head and flexed his muscles in an attempt to be intimidating. "En drako *Hol*, vor san tae sae, adeo el…"

He heard the emphasis on the word Hol but he didn't really give a shit. "Let's just skip to the good bit, asshole."

FIFTEEN

Kalian opened his eyes to the actinic light of the distant blue sun and felt the desert heat on his face. His eyes quickly adjusted again by filtering the light and sharpening his senses. He was lying flat on the rocky surface between the *Fathom* and The Wall. The new armoured suit was keeping his body temperature at a cool thirty-six degrees Celsius. A long shadow extended from the *Fathom* and moved across the desert floor towards him. Kalian stood up to see Namek clambering around the ship's hull, his features shadowed by the sunlight.

Telarrek came into view from behind the ship and Li'ara with him. Her pace quickened at the sight of him awake. Seeing them jogged his memory of recent events inside the outpost. He thought about the plasma he'd created from nothing and the explosion he'd recklessly caused with the weapons. He reached for his lip in search of any blood from his nose and was thankful to find none. What had happened to him? He had never felt so connected to everything. How did it go so wrong?

Li'ara said his name as she reached out to embrace him. He was shocked at the show of affection and realised how worried she must have been.

"It was bad, huh?" Kalian really wanted to take the time to explore his feelings and relationship with Li'ara, but time wasn't on his side.

"They had to bring you out here after you collapsed; everything was going a little crazy in there." She stepped back, looking embarrassed for having given him a hug.

Kalian gave the Novaarians a grateful nod for removing him.

"We feared the worst, Kalian. I am elated to see you well again." Telarrek bowed his head.

Namek jumped down from the *Fathom* with nimble agility and bounded over to wrap Kalian in a four-armed embrace. He felt his feet leave the floor before the Novaarian released him and stepped away as if it had never happened.

"You are stronger now," the Novaarian said.

Kalian couldn't help but smile at the sight of them all again.

"Not enough for what's coming." ALF was suddenly standing a few feet away in his long robe. "I'm afraid our timetable has been cut short. There have been some developments in your absence, Kalian." The AI looked up to the sky, seeing something they could not. "The last communication from the *Helion* reported that the Gomar vessel surrendered, and was taken on board. Shortly after that, the ship changed course and cut all communication. I have been unable to reach them on any bandwidth or laser-com."

Kalian ignored the fact that the AI was somehow being emitted on the moon's surface and thought about the *Helion*. "Do I even need to ask where it's going?" Kalian gave ALF a knowing look and the group shared it.

The *Helion* was coming to Nova Prime and, with those engines, they would get here a hell of a lot quicker.

"Savrick is now in possession of a Nexus-class vessel. He could destroy this moon with a single strike."

Telarrek gave ALF an accusing look. Not only had the crew most likely lost their lives for nothing, but now the enemy had a new weapon.

ALF ignored the alien and continued. "He has commanded

through a war that lasted centuries. His tactical mind is focused and honed. He has experience none of you have. You must continue your training."

Li'ara stepped between them with a look more deadly than any weapon. "Are you actually trying to kill him? He was unconscious for almost a day after the last session."

Had he really been out that long?

"It would be dangerous to put him back inside that thing!"

ALF stepped forward with a calm expression that told Kalian he already had an answer for this.

The AI apparently calculated everything they might say. "It would be more dangerous to face Savrick without the proper instruction. You have learned so much already, but it is not enough. Savrick can produce organic plasma in the blink of an eye and he does not burn his hand in the process. He can heal his body on a subconscious level without ever having to take a break from killing you. You have had only a glimpse of what Savrick has experienced in a hundred life-times. The subconducer will give you the edge you need. It's dangerous, but you need to be better."

Without consciously thinking, Kalian had connected to the nanocelium in his suit and discovered the source of ALF's projection. There were tiny ports that ran around his waist that had blue lights inside. His suit had holographic emitters that enabled ALF to exist in a 3D world around him. He focused his attention back on the group and knew this kind of lapse in concentration was what ALF was talking about. With this new connection to everything, he was easily led astray by some new experience or feeling. He couldn't help but see things differently now. The idea of having only two eyes to perceive reality seemed so disproportionate to what reality had to offer.

"Kalian, don't." Li'ara could see his face and knew what he was thinking.

ALF was right and looking at her only hardened his resolve. He wouldn't let anything happen to her.

"The sessions can be tailored to avoid any more overload. Each lesson will be shorter, with a break in between for practical application. With the nanocelium still inside you, I can monitor your vitals for early warning signs. However, time is short, so your next session will have to be energy storage and consumption. I'm afraid sleep is no longer an option. But if you master this skill, you will never need to sleep again."

His words disarmed Li'ara somewhat, as she made no objection to the new structure. Kalian gave her a reassuring look despite his own reservations.

"The minute he doesn't look right, I'm pulling him out myself." With that, Li'ara led the way back inside.

SAVRICK WALKED between the dozens of alien bodies to reach Sef who was examining the Conclave vessel's central bridge console. Savrick could tell he was becoming frustrated with the primitive layout. There was so much manual input required in comparison to a Terran ship. He looked around at the bodies and found it amusing that every one of them had been essential in controlling all the ship's systems.

Sef wiped the blood off the touch-console but only helped to smear it further. He dropped his fist onto it in anger, causing the glass to crack and the surrounding holograms to flicker. With his helmet up, Savrick's smile was hidden from Sef. He always found it amusing when the usually calm Sef gave into his rage. He could think of some spectacularly great outbursts in the past by his young protector that had been to the detriment to the Terran forces.

He moved past the console and Sef to examine the panoramic viewport beyond. Seeing the ocean of space in front of him served only as a reminder of how far away the *Gommarian* was, and Esabelle. He didn't worry though for they were safe inside the ship. The Conclave didn't possess weaponry powerful enough to break the *Gommarian's* outer shell. Before his thoughts could wander to the night the ancient ship became his, he felt the floor shake. His reverie was broken by the beast below. He was a blunt tool but an effective one. After reducing the crew in the hangar to indistinguishable pulp, they had set off for the bridge while the beast was instructed to hunt down every life form on board.

He turned from the view to see Lilander using telekinesis to remove every particle of blood from the console. Savrick felt them both tune into the surrounding consoles and take control of the different functions. New holo-images came to life as they responded to the electromagnetic touch. He was walking back to instruct them to bring the subspace engine online when he pushed his mind out into the ship, subconsciously, and felt an intelligent response.

Confirming his senses, the bridge door parted as three of the ship's crew burst in. They were all firing plasma-based rifles but they weren't nearly as powerful as the organic matter he could replicate. The shots that didn't go wild were simply absorbed by his telekinetic field. Lilander's reaction was just as quick, so that with a turn and a flick of the wrist she sent her blade plunging into the blue scaled creature. The blade struck his head, sending him flying back from his companions in a spray of blood.

Savrick had the rest.

The central figure was a large alien with four legs and a body of rock, who made the floor thunder with his every footstep. Savrick casually lifted his left hand while grasping every molecule that made up the rock monster. The reaction was severe. The flat-headed alien was forced up into the ceiling where his head became lodged in the bulkhead. Savrick felt the hard head cave in and the life leave its body as it hung there.

The third attacker was still charging, unaware of the fate of his fellow crew. This alien was mostly organic with oddly placed augmentations. Savrick's plasma-bolt hit the creature square in the chest. He had charged the particles in such a way that would stop it from passing through the soft body. Instead, the burning matter exploded on impact, sending the alien in every direction. Out of courtesy, he created a telekinetic barrier to prevent Sef and Lilander from being sprayed in alien debris.

The whole incident had only taken a few seconds in which Sef hadn't even bothered to turn around. The ship gave a resounding whine as the subspace engine came online.

Savrick parted his helmet and inhaled the smell of ozone from the plasma discharge. "Drop us into subspace. Set course for Naveen."

ROLAND WAS ON HIS BACK, contemplating his life's choices before he even knew the fight had begun. There were clear points in his life where decisions could have been made to prevent the pain he was now feeling. He appreciated however that these changes would have meant death back on Earth or Century. A dark foot descending towards his face ended any thought of life choices. He rolled to one side as the foot slammed into the floor inches from his new position. At some stage in his life, he had stopped thinking while in combat, leaving his actions instead to decades of muscle memory and intensive training.

It had, however, been a very long time since he had suffered such physical injuries. The benefits of being an agent had allowed him access to better weaponry and tech. Not to mention the chance to plan out his own assignments, instead of being told what to do by some UDC analyst who had never even seen a gun.

His counter-attack had not gone to plan. As he'd reached for the Mohawk's knee he'd fallen short from the pain in his ribs. He remembered his training and pushed the pain away. He was a machine, not a person with feelings or nerve endings and a fragile biology. He could take the beating and still complete his mission because that's what needed to be done. In a way that was what he liked about his job; it made things simple. Life in the UDC was black and white with orders given and orders received.

The Mohawk pressed the attack when Roland's counter fell short.

He felt the strong grip around his neck lift him from the floor with one hand and thrust him into the wall. His opponent flashed him a deadly smile while trying to suffocate him. Roland knew he could hold his breath for just under three minutes but had no intention of remaining pinned to the wall for that long. He forced his hand into the crook of the pinning arm while simultaneously wrapping his other hand around the head. The inevitable reaction was Roland's brow meeting the Mohawk's nose. He loved hearing the sound of the nose breaking.

The Mohawk stumbled backwards with blood smeared across his beard and cheeks. Roland didn't stop the attack there. Kicking a man while he was down was something the UDC encouraged. He push-kicked the Mohawk, hitting him in the sternum with as much strength as he could muster. The Mohawk flew into the opposite wall and fell to one knee with a hand on his chest. Roland chuckled at seeing the stupid shit on his knees.

"Bet you wish you'd stayed in your pretty suit now, huh?"

He didn't care that his words wouldn't be understood, he just felt good. That was until the Mohawk launched from his crouched position and swept Roland off his feet. He braced, expecting to hit the wall that never came. Instead, the wall had parted, creating a new room on the other side.

Roland pulled his weight down, forcing the two into a backwards roll. As they tumbled to the floor, he pushed his weight up creating the momentum for another roll. Now he was sat on top of the Mohawk with his right hand over his throat and his left ready to make the blow. The Mohawk was fast however, and he yanked Roland's thumb, taking his hand away from his throat. As if from nowhere, his attacker's legs wrapped around his chest and threw Roland to the side. In a move too fast and exotic for Roland to comprehend the Mohawk was back on his feet. From this angle, he could see a metallic device running up the Mohawk's back and onto his neck. The black undersuit was fitted around it as if both were fused together.

He had no idea what the augmentation was but, from the way it was attached to the neck and spine, it had to be vital. Now he had found the weakness all he had to do was exploit it.

The Mohawk turned, ready to attack again. With Roland on the floor, he obviously thought he had the high ground and therefore the advantage.

His mistake.

Roland had been trained to kill from every stance with his hands tied behind his back. He feigned more pain than he was in, to draw the opponent in closer. He almost smiled at the Mohawk's arrogance. When the distance was right, he lashed out with his left leg. He pushed it straight into the Mohawk's right knee, feeling the subsequent snap as he did. The surprise and agony on his face were more than satisfying. With his attacker on one knee, Roland kicked out with his right leg, aiming for the chest. Again the Mohawk showed incredible speed and reflexes as he intercepted the foot with his left hand. His strength under such pain was impressive, but not uncalculated. Roland flipped his body, kicking the Mohawk in the jaw with his free leg.

He continued this momentum until the Mohawk was doubled over, exposing his metallic back. Now on his knees, Roland removed the combat knife from its sheath in the small of his back. There was no hesitation as he pushed the knife into the metallic flat-worm and dragged it down the spine. The Mohawk's reaction was proof of the augment's significance. He jumped up, thrashing as he did. Roland was knocked to the floor while he watched his opponent writhe around in what looked like agony. He clawed at his head like a madman trying to dig something out.

Suddenly the Mohawk was floating in mid-air, clenching his fists in violent spasms. Roland felt the knife fly from his hand and stick to the wall, mimicking the effects of a magnet. Thick purple liquid was dripping from the slash down the Mohawk's spine. The viscous drops never hit the floor but instead remained suspended, mid-drop. With an agonising scream, his hands flexed and Roland was shoved into the wall by an unseen force. He doubled over from the pain in his ribs and spat blood onto the floor. Once on the floor, the blood began to slither across the surface until it rose into the air and joined the swirling vortex of purple liquid.

His attention was split between the extraordinary display in front of him and the sound of what must be massive changes on the other side of the wall. He could hear the walls moving as if giant gimbals were rotating all around them. Were they moving or was something else moving? He turned back and saw the door was still open so he knew they weren't moving. Just then the sound stopped, following a great thud, and the opposite wall began to form a door.

The door spiralled open, giving way to another armoured guard. This one was different again with long dark hair that ran over his plated shell. The dark strands hung over his face, partially concealing a complex green tattoo across his cheek and mouth. His skin looked paler than the Mohawk's with a slight yellow tinge to it. He stepped into the room like a parent looking for a distressed child.

"Elandar..." The Mohawk tried to reach out but recoiled as his hand lit up the room with a miniature sun in his palm.

Roland covered his face from the stark light but felt the heat on his skin. The light ended as suddenly as it sparked, leaving colourful spots on his retinas. He looked up to see the face of the one called Elandar, agonising over the sight of the Mohawk. He reached out, hesitating to touch the floating mess of a man.

"Hol, elondaseal..." The alien words meant nothing to him as the new man gave a steely expression.

Roland saw a grave intent in that expression.

Elandar whipped his hand out, rolling his hand as he did. The Mohawk's head twisted beyond its normal limitation, a fraction of a second before his body followed suit, flinging him into the wall. The mixture of liquids dropped to the floor and the Mohawk crumpled with them. His bloodied head lay at an unnatural angle to his body.

Double shit...

It dawned on him how powerful these beings were. He had got lucky with the Mohawk having some ridiculous notion of honour. Elandar then turned on Roland with an expression of disgust.

"You have no idea what you just did. You destroyed his Harness and took away his control. It is a crippling and agonising death for a Gomar. What you just saw was a mercy killing, *Terran*. I will not grant you the same." Roland struggled to stand, feeling every broken bone and tendon. He had given the Mohawk his all and was failing to find his reserves. Not to mention this one wasn't taking off his armour. He looked at his knife in despair upon spotting it on the other side of the room.

Elandar casually lifted his arm, seemingly showing Roland the back of his hand, but he felt his lungs expel the last of their air as his ribs were pulled up inside his chest. He soon found his feet leaving the ground and realised he was unable to move any of his limbs.

His relief was found in Elandar's cry of pain. Roland dropped to the floor gasping for breath as Elandar collapsed to his knees, holding his head in both hands. His eyes had rolled into the back of his head and his contorted mouth was eerily silent as he remained on his knees. His armour began to crumple into his body.

The next thing Roland saw convinced him he was suffering a head injury.

From behind the agonised Elandar, a naked woman appeared draped in dark tubes that dragged on the floor. There was blood dripping down her skin from where the tubes met her body. They ran up her legs and arms gradually becoming thicker along her stomach and chest. Her long dark hair fell unkempt over her shoulders and down her back. She turned to come into the room and Roland saw the tubes were in her back as well, though none of them were attached to anything but her. She appeared exhausted to Roland, struggling to conquer every step. She staggered into the room behind Elandar with a glazed expression.

"And who the hell are you?" Roland just about got the words out.

Like something out of a nightmare, Elandar replied in a voice that wasn't quite his own. "I am... Esabelle."

With that, his armour completely caved in, like a scrunched up piece of paper. Blood flowed out of the jagged holes, pooling on the floor at his knees, while his head tilted as the armour around his neck cut through the oesophagus and trachea, almost separating the head entirely. Imitating a bored child, the naked woman flicked her hand away, throwing the massacred body onto the Mohawk's.

She dropped to her knees, meeting Roland at his level. He tried not to turn away from her ancient breath as she attempted to speak. Every word came from a dry throat.

"They...are...coming."

KALIAN OPENED his eyes to see Li'ara fighting with Namek on the sparring mat. He was sitting in the corner applying his latest lesson. He had to get used to this form of sleeping if he was going to keep up with ALF's regime. Retreating into his head, having created a virtual world, he could allow the rest of his mind and body to disperse his energy consumption to replicate the effects of sleep.

In his mind, he had created the Terran Capital, Albadar. The subconducer had uploaded all recorded data from the Criterion of Terran history, as well as the required training. He had been able to walk around the streets as if he were actually there seeing his ancestors, or engineers, going about their daily lives. Everything was beautiful there. The architecture, the design, and even the people were that of perfection. He knew it was a combination of nature and science that humanity had never achieved on any of their planets. Some people walked to their destination, others flew by in sleek ships, while a few actually flew without ships. Everywhere he had looked the Terran people were using their abilities for art and science and the simple joy of it. He also noticed the occasional Gomar walk by, looking like any human without paranormal abilities.

While exploring this virtual world, his brain absorbed the skills and adapted the artificial memories from the training. He could now acquire the equivalent of twelve hours of sleep in just half an hour of this meditation. The training took place on many levels, however, so he could filter the learnt skills while he 'slept', allowing him to experience more from one session. On one of these levels, he had been through a training program to further develop his telekinesis alongside his new form of sleep.

"Perhaps we should go outside for this application? I still haven't finished reconstruction of that corridor." ALF appeared by his side, the way he always did.

It had surprised Kalian this time since he hadn't been filling the room with his awareness. Thinking of the destructive technicalities of telekinesis, he silently agreed.

Li'ara was practising with her new weapon from ALF. Though hesitant at first, she had clearly come to love the blade. The AI had explained that the hilt of the blade housed a CPU for specifically designed nanocelium. They could be tailored with the right programming to form any blade imaginable, within reason. The hilt contained a finite amount of nanocelium and therefore could only produce so much in length and shape. Her own blade was dark grey and just longer than her arm, with a diagonal cut across the point. Namek's blade was bigger, to fit his taller stance, but was curved like a giant question mark. They danced around each other, creating sparks with every blow. He was impressed with her agility and stamina in keeping up with the Novaarian, but he knew Namek was capable of much more.

They stopped their sparring and accompanied Kalian and ALF, along with Telarrek, who had been very quiet since the news of the *Valoran*. Once outside, ALF became an extension of his armour and was projected several feet away. They walked away from the *Fathom* and entered a patch with a small cluster of rocks.

"Lift that rock." ALF pointed at a small rock in the middle of the gathering.

Kalian pushed his hand out towards the rock, even though his hand had nothing to do with his power to move it. He felt his awareness expand to engulf the intended rock. His feedback was instantaneous, relaying the different layers of minerals that made up the rock. Confident of his grip, he excited the sensation in his central nervous system and flipped his hand. Kalian raised it as if he was holding the rock in his palm. Opening his eyes, he saw a larger rock to his left floating six-feet in the air. He sighed at his failure but felt a deep joy at being able to manipulate reality in such a way. Kalian felt like a different person to the one who had been escorted from his lecture theatre just over a week ago. He was becoming powerful.

As if reading his thoughts, ALF cut in. "Be mindful of your new found power. Many Terran fell from the cause after centuries of war with the Gomar. They grew to like their new destructive capabilities and left the empire altogether. It will be harder for you, being so young. You don't have the experience and wisdom that living for centuries can grant you. This will be exciting for you." The AI looked to the floating rock that was slowly rotating on its axis. "But you must always have a reason for using it. Don't abuse your gifts. You have the power to be a force for good."

Kalian let the rock fall back to earth.

He knew what ALF was saying - don't be a dick. Kalian tried to bury that excitement and focus on the reality of his abilities. He would have to use them to end the life of another being, possibly several beings. His control could mean the difference between life and death for his friends, for Li'ara. The responsibility he felt reminded him of Earth's ancient myths. He couldn't help but feel like Atlas holding up the world. That feeling of responsibility frightened him for a moment. He responded in the only way that felt instinctive now. He raised both of his hands, reaching out for all of the rocks. If he could see his power, he could convince himself everything would be ok. His chaotic thoughts prevented his ability to focus on any one thing. He felt everything and everyone around him but commanded the rocks to lift. He opened his eyes to more failure. Not even one of the rocks had left the floor.

"I need more time!" He dropped his head to avoid looking at Li'ara.

Kalian knew he was making excuses. The subconducer could give him years of training. It was his young mind that needed the training. The history it had uploaded into his brain showed him the years a Terran would take just to learn how to focus on a single raindrop. His own fears dispersed his awareness, preventing him from concentrating on one thing.

"Kalian..."

He looked at Telarrek as a large shadow shaded them all. Kalian looked up in disbelief as the *Fathom* floated above them like a broken ship in a vacuum. He couldn't believe his eyes. He felt the steady output from his central nervous system and knew it was him. But how could he lift something so big?

"You're not focusing." ALF walked into view with a disappointed look. "I asked you to lift a rock, not a ship."

How could he be disappointed at the spectacle? It might not be the rock, but it was a whole ship.

"Put it down Kalian, carefully."

He thought about that last word and panicked. He didn't even know how he had lifted it never mind bringing it back down with care. Kalian took a breath and narrowed his focus and awareness to only the ship. He felt every curve of its hull and every bolt in its whole. He ignored the complexities of its insides, especially the engine. Mentally grasping only the outside of the vessel, he instinctively held out both hands as if he was actually carrying it. Again he had closed his eyes since they only distracted him with all he saw. With a thud and a small quake, he knew the ship was once again on the ground, just not where they had parked it.

"Better." ALF still didn't look particularly pleased.

They remained outside for another hour until Kalian had successfully lifted every rock in sequence. They were all pleased to see that he hadn't suffered any nose bleeds or blackouts from the exertion.

It wasn't long after this that he found himself sitting in the subconducer again. Reality slipped into the infinite while he was learning in the machine. He wasn't really aware of anything until it stopped, at which point his mind began the filtering process. ALF advised meditation after every session so he could study Terran culture as well as absorb the details from the lessons. It was this studying that led him to ask about the Avatar.

"He was the first of your kind to become immortal," ALF explained. "He lived for centuries before any other Terran knew of that power. Though many had learned to heal wounds and even overcome certain diseases, he was the first to shed death. He could perpetually regenerate his cells, keeping him young forever. For his generation, that kind of mind-body control was unheard of. Outliving everyone he knew and loved was hard, so he looked to me. He is the only being I have ever permitted to walk inside the Criterion. We spent years conversing, the only two immortals. Even after the population caught up with him, I only ever allowed the Avatar to enter. So he became known as the Avatar, a living extension of me if you will. The Terran had no need of a leader, but they looked to him, especially during the war." ALF appeared tormented at the thought of his oldest friend.

"What happened on the *Gommarian*?" Li'ara asked.

"He wouldn't allow anyone to be put at such risk, so he volunteered. His mission was to acquire information on the ship's capabilities. He transmitted all the data he could collect before he was found. After that there was nothing."

Kalian had images of the man with long dark hair that flowed down his back. The recordings were always of him talking to the masses with some inspirational speech. Of course, they always ended with, 'we are forever.' ALF had explained that the phrase was introduced after the population had reached immortality. It was a celebration of their great achievement over death. He knew now why Savrick had repeated it to him. It was his way of spitting on the Terran by proving them wrong. Kalian felt the phrase was only adding fuel to the fire for the not so immortal Gomar.

Over the next few hours, ALF supplied Kalian with various electrical appliances to practise with. The first was another weapon from the Conclave supplies on the *Fathom*. ALF instructed him to disarm it without causing an explosion. Again, they practised outside. After his last session, he had learned to gauge the different levels of electromagnetism. He concentrated, with extreme acuity, to ensure the safe disarming of the gun. His fingers tingled as he tightened his grip on the output; not too much and not too little. He heard the weapon whir down as the firing mechanism was disarmed.

The next object was his Datapad, which Kalian refused to work with. It was his last tie to his home and it even had his lectures saved on it. It was only after ALF promised him the nanocelium would repair it that he was willing to try. Waving his hand over the surface, he created enough output to short-circuit the emitters and fry the internal fuse gel. A more explosive outcome could be obtained by increasing the output of electromagnetism, though this often ended in the object being overloaded and physically breaking.

The next lesson had not required the subconducer. The blue sun was beginning to set and twilight settle over the land. Nova Prime had become visible over the horizon, with its pink and turquoise exterior swirling over the surface. It was crowned in a tiara of stars that shone in the darkening twilight. The Novaarians stood in wonder at the beauty of their homeworld.

"Namek..." ALF called the warrior over to them. "Take that rock and throw it at Kalian."

Namek looked as shocked as Kalian felt.

"What's the purpose of that?" Li'ara got there first.

ALF looked slightly weathered at being constantly questioned by her. "Aim for his chest and no harm will come to him."

The Novaarian hesitated and looked to his charge for instruction. Telarrek simply bowed his head, clearly trusting the AI. Like a good soldier, he instantly launched the rock at Kalian, who couldn't help his reaction. The rock flew off at an odd angle where it then became buried in the ground. He hadn't meant to deflect the rock; it was a knee-jerk reaction.

"Very good, but this time try not to react. Know that the rock will hit you and it will not harm you," ALF instructed.

Namek threw another rock, aiming for his chest, and this time the rock hit the armour over his sternum. The rock broke in half and crumbled into smaller pieces at his feet. Kalian looked at his chest in amazement. He hadn't felt a thing. Connecting with the nanocelium, he knew that those around his chest had altered their pattern and increased in density.

"If you can see it, the nanocelium can see it. The armour's density will increase in any area you feel at risk."

They spent another half hour, before complete darkness, throwing rocks at Kalian. He eventually learned how to catch them in mid-air without flinging them in a random direction.

While the others slept that night, Kalian remained awake to learn more from the subconducer. In between the lessons he would often spar with a hard-light copy of ALF. His technique was improving but he had to work on incorporating his abilities and combining his strength. All the while ALF was teaching him to keep up a constant telekinetic field to protect him. With his subconscious now available to him like any tool, Kalian used it to perform low-level functions. While fighting the increasing number of holographic Gomar, ALF produced multiple mounted cannons around the room. Kalian used his subconscious to put up a telekinetic field over the surface of his skin and armour to prevent injury from the cannon fire.

His fighting style had been developed by the Avatar, with some help from ALF, at the beginning of the war. Having come from a world that was always prepared for a fight, it felt very alien that the Terran had no idea how to be violent. The UDC had been around for nearly a millennia before Savrick showed up. According to ALF though, the Terran Empire started out much like Earth.

By the morning, he had moulded his subconscious into an easy-to-use tool. His surrounding awareness was constantly pushing into a twenty-metre radius, while simultaneously putting up a barrier over his body. By doing this, he was free to concentrate on other tasks and abilities. He felt three luminous bodies enter the viewing room beyond the one he occupied. ALF had constructed it while they slept, so he could be observed safely from pin-head cameras on the wall. Kalian could feel the technology inside the room and knew the AI had made the equivalent of a ship's bridge, with seats and various controls for the holograms.

Kalian could feel Li'ara's anxiety at being physically separated from him. She was still operating under her UDC parameters and felt out of control if she couldn't get to him.

"It seems I have an audience," Kalian said out loud to the omnipresent AI.

ALF's voice replied but his holographic body wasn't present. "It's good that you are aware. That's progress."

Three hard-light Gomar in full armour came into life in a circle around him. He had already felt the coalescing of the holo-particles and felt no surprise seeing them. It was eerie how life-like they always appeared as they paced the sparring mat.

"This time I want you to use as many abilities as you can. They will attack you in every way I can replicate."

Kalian already knew the cannons were to recreate the organic plasma. He noticed the copy on his right was wielding a blade similar to Li'ara's. He performed one last check of the surrounding walls and was happy to see the one between him and his friends was two-feet of reinforced nanocelium. He smiled at the idea of being able to just let go and not hurt anyone.

There was no countdown or signal as the three attacked at once. Inside his mind, where everything worked at the speed of a firing synapse, he had already run the scenario through. He released a small burst of electromagnetic fields in every direction rather than lose concentration by focusing on the blade. The first swing of the blade missed as the nanocelium retracted back into the hilt. Knowing this would be the case, Kalian's first move was to punch the Gomar in front while at the same time kicking the one behind. Flipping back from this position like a trained gymnast, he flicked his leg out and kicked the recently punched Gomar. He briefly balanced on a hand before back-flipping onto his feet.

By this point, two of the Gomar were flat on their backs while the other one threw away his broken hilt and charged Kalian. The Gomar lifted him off the floor and piled him back down until Kalian was buried underneath. The armour had prevented any major pain while the telekinetic field around his head protected him against concussion. He felt Li'ara's heart rate increase through the wall and instantly shut off his connection to her feelings; he needed to focus.

He quickly flexed his hands out and launched the Gomar high into the air until he impacted the ceiling. He rolled out of the way before the heavy body landed on top of him. With the newly acquired agility, Kalian propelled himself onto his feet to see the broken dome in the ceiling. His mind filtered the feedback from the room and he became aware of the cannons building up energy. He didn't have time to react however as the other Gomar advanced. They became a flurry of limbs as the two remaining Gomar attacked and countered Kalian. He felt the occasional bolt of plasma hit his armour and knew the nanocelium were reacting appropriately where his field lost cohesion. One struck him in the back of the knee, dropping him to where he then received a blow to the face from the Gomar. The surprise made him lose concentration and he felt the pain as his telekinetic field weakened.

Taking advantage of this, the Gomar picked him up by the scruff of his neck so the other could pound his armour down. Every blow put a crack in his field and strained his focus. He retreated for a fraction of a second and replayed a memory that wasn't his. He witnessed a Terran learning to fight, much like he was, and absorbed the specific techniques she employed to defeat her attackers. The move was complex but, after seeing it, he felt like he had already done it a thousand times. Before the next blow made contact, he executed the move and created a tangle of arms. He removed the locking grip around his neck and arm while also blocking the next punch. He reinforced the telekinetic field around his face and headbutted the Gomar to his side before driving his foot into the knee-joint of the other. With the new space, Kalian shot his left hand out and released a ball of organic plasma into the chest of the kneeling Gomar. The desired effect was achieved as the armour crumpled inwards and sent the Gomar across the room.

From what he had learned inside the subconducer, he knew the best way to use plasma was with a telekinetic field around his hand.

Kalian impressed himself with the speed he created the plasma, not to mention the lack of a burnt hand.

The remaining Gomar shook off the simulated effects of the headbutt and attacked again. Kalian whipped around, bringing his outstretched arm with him as he did. Again this was all instinct. He didn't actually need his arm for what he was doing but he thought it helped him to focus. The Gomar was swept aside, until he crashed into the adjacent wall, before Kalian lifted his arm to send him into the ceiling with a crack. To completely finish him off, Kalian pulled his arm down and clenched his fist. The Gomar was dragged back to the floor with a greater speed than gravity was capable of. His leg and head fell at awkward angles and his body lay perfectly still.

The cannons slotted back into their housing and the holographic Gomar disappeared. All that was left was a room full of dented walls and a broken ceiling. He took more control of his subconscious functions and expanded into the room beyond, focusing on Li'ara. He dipped into her brainwaves, delicately this time, and felt her emotions churn like a stormy ocean. She was somewhere between awe and horror. This was to be expected, he supposed. He wasn't exactly the same person she had met on Earth. He knew she would be struggling with the idea of protecting someone who didn't really need protection anymore.

"You're not using your full potential." ALF was suddenly behind him wearing his normal robes. "You felt pain when you should have shut off all of your receptors. Your grasp of telekinesis is crude and blunt." The AI looked over the various impact sites. "And by now that kind of fight should have taken you half the time."

Kalian turned away in frustration at never being able to please the AI. "It's not easy using everything at once!"

Kalian had already begun the process of regenerating his cells, specifically his adenosine triphosphate for energy reserves. He knew if he needed to he could increase the normal 250g of ATP into 400g, nearly doubling his rate of metabolism. His laboured breathing had already stopped and his lactic acid was being broken down to prevent spasms in his muscles.

"How very *human* of you," ALF replied dryly.

"I am human!"

"No, you're not! You are more than that now. You *have* to be more. Savrick will not hold back. You are the final insult, Kalian. He will use everything he knows to make you suffer, and to make *her* suffer!"

With that, Kalian gave into his frustration and waved his hand across ALF's form. The hologram was shattered into its individual atoms as he disrupted the emitters.

"It will take more than that to silence me." His voice came over the hidden speakers again.

Kalian sighed at the lecturing voice. "Just leave me alone for a while." Kalian made for the wall, which melted away to a circular door.

"You have an hour, and then you must return to the subconducer. The *Helion's* transmitter has been disabled so I cannot calculate their time of arrival, but it will be soon."

Kalian didn't care right now. He just wanted to see the sun.

ROLAND STRUGGLED TO HIS FEET, fighting through the pain in his ribs. He tracked back to the previous corridor and retrieved his animal-hide coat. He could see now the sphere of devastation his MID had caused. The edges of the three levels the bomb had cut through were glowing orange, with steam rising off them. He could hear the thousands of voices above and realised he had forgotten about the other armoured goon. With the glowing edges, there was no way he could climb up. Let the Novaarians deal with it, he thought. He was exhausted.

He returned to the naked woman and draped the large coat over her pale form. In the time he had been gone, she had removed the majority of the tubes which now lay in a tangled mess. Using both hands she pulled up on the tube attached to her thigh. It made a sticky sound as it came free, followed by a stream of blood. He attempted to cover it with his hand before she snatched his wrist in mid-air.

"Wait..." Her voice sounded less croaky but still laboured.

He watched in wonder as the flow stopped and the tissue began to regenerate. Within moments the wound was gone entirely. He helped her up, supporting her by the arms. Her deep blue eyes scanned the room absently.

"Who the hell are you? And don't say Esabelle. We've covered that."

She certainly wasn't one of the terraforming crew. None of them could crush a man with their mind. Was she some kind of prisoner? One of their own maybe?

"I am the pilot." Her voice got better with every word.

He looked over her shoulder at the room she had come from. It wasn't too dissimilar to the bridge on the *Hammer* or any other UDC vessel for that matter. It had various consoles with chairs at every station and one central seat for the captain. It looked darker than most bridges though, with bronze holograms and black touch screens. The overhead spotlights gave it a very atmospheric look. None of it explained how she could pilot the epic ship or why she had been covered in tubes.

"You're not like any pilot I've ever seen." If she was the pilot, why was she helping him?

"We don't have long. I overloaded their link to the *Gommarian* before I disconnected. You will need the help of the others to retrieve them all and secure them. If they wake up they will take back the ship."

Roland had no idea what she was talking about. "Did you hit your head back there?"

She turned on him with a frustrated look he was used to seeing from women. "*This* is the *Gommarian*." She looked around, meaning the ship they were standing in. "They are all connected to me, to it, through a cerebral link. Before I disconnected, I reconfigured the ship so it could be manually controlled and internally navigated. But I also overloaded their link with a looping thought-bomb." To his confused look she elaborated. "Like a computer virus for the brain. But they will recover soon. I know where they are on the ship. We must contain them quickly."

"Is that what you meant by, *they are coming*?" It sounded much creepier the way she had said it.

"No..." She had a confused look as if she was recollecting a dream. "That was something else. But we don't have time for that now."

She left the support of his arms and strode out of the door towards the wreckage of the MID.

Not entirely sure of her motives, Roland kept his blade close.

SIXTEEN

The beast had caught up with them on their way back to the hangar
He was covered in blood that dripped from every plate of armour
Savrick could even see organic matter stuck between the segments
where the beast had most likely used his hands or rammed through
the corridors. The ramp to their ship descended as they approached
It looked completely out of place against the sleek polished crafts o
the Conclave.

The beast remained in the hold of the craft, while the other three
took their positions on the smaller bridge. The *Helion* would emerge
from subspace shortly. Sef had made all the arrangements. Savrick
had considered arriving in the system and slagging the planet and
moon with everything the security vessel had, but that would be too
quick. He wanted to know if there was a surviving Terran living or
that moon, apart from Kalian Gaines. It amused and frustrated hin
that he could kill billions of humans in a single day, but continued to
fail to kill this one.

Sef set his controls, readying the ship for immediate departure
Having gleaned the knowledge about The Wall, they knew exactly
where to go. He knew that Sef had been forced to override most o
the *Helion's* safety protocols for this jump. The ship had built-ir

measures to ensure that anything emerging from subspace impacted at five hundred thousand kilometres or more from the main planetary body. Thanks to Sef's superior knowledge of statistical mechanics and thermodynamics, they were going to emerge in a tight orbit around Naveen.

Lilander was standing in front of a full-length hologram that acted as sensor feedback with a view of the approaching system.

"Long-range scans show an increase in activity around Nova Prime. They're all Novaarian ships, no Conclave security. They will be no more powerful than the one we have been chasing," Lilander informed him.

"How many are there?" He was being lazy given that he could have easily acquired that information via his link.

"Six at present." She looked at him with a questioning expression. Lilander was right to expect some new orders, however, for there was no way they could survive an encounter with six Novaarian cruisers.

"It changes nothing. By the time they react, we will already be on the surface. Sef?" His covered head turned to silently regard his leader. "Set the ship to create a mesh."

Sef turned back to his console and made the adjustments. It had been the Terran who first developed the mesh for protection against orbital bombardment. The ship would produce an invisible dome over a designated area and this mesh would then disrupt and deflect the targeting systems of the ships above. A ship like the *Helion* could produce a beam capable of obliterating a single individual from orbit. Savrick wouldn't take the chance that the Novaarian vessels weren't equally well equipped.

Soon, he thought, soon it would all be over. With the last Terran finally dead he could rest: they all could. And with the prisoners from the Laronian ship, they would have enough breeding partners to start again. The programs that Elandar had run showed that his DNA combined with female human DNA would produce a complete Terran zygote, with no primitive throwbacks from the human mother or father. He reasoned that their superior genes simply overwhelmed the human DNA to create the perfect Terran. With this new world, he could lead them into the golden era that ALF had prevented them from reaching. He had no intention of being some overbearing god like the Criterion had. He would make things right, the way they should have been. He would free Esabelle and send the *Gommarian* into the nearest star. If they went deep enough into the galaxy, they could survive what was coming. He would make sure of that.

But first, he would have his revenge.

———

KALIAN HEARD the grating rock as the solid door parted into the ground behind him. He could feel the very human presence of Li'ara as her physical body displaced the atmospheric molecules around her. The feeling reminded him of the way a shark could detect other organisms in the water. To this effect he now found his memory to be as easy to navigate as entering a word into a search engine. His current thought presented him with all the information he had ever seen or heard about sharks; this one being a comparison of their ampullae of Lorenzini and his ability to detect the electromagnetic fields of other beings. A quick introspection showed that he now possessed similar but biologically different electroreceptors either side of his nose.

Feeling her unease, he reduced the pressure beneath him and slowly descended back to the desert sand. It felt natural to him during his meditative sleep to float with his legs crossed. It felt great to finally understand why he often woke up above his bed, and to have control of his telekinesis. He was on his feet by the time she reached him and just as he noticed the words on The Wall behind her. As the door closed, the sentence came back together and he read: **The Stars Are Your Birthright. Here Begins The Path Home. We Are Forever.**

The lines were separated by the karyotype of the very DNA that made up his every cell. When had he learned to read Terran? He was grateful for the use of the subconducer but felt unsure of the way it changed whole parts of his mind and uploaded anything it liked. Of course, when he thought about it, *it* was ALF. The AI had a way of making you feel like you were speaking with just another human being, but the truth was far more terrifying. Despite only being a third of the whole, he was still an engineered god with capabilities even Kalian couldn't comprehend. Conversing with him felt to Kalian like he was only seeing the surface of ALF, and that there was far more going on behind the hologram and the words.

Following his gaze, Li'ara inspected the door herself before giving him a questioning look.

"Apparently I know Terran," he explained.

"You understand the hieroglyphs?"

Kalian read the words out loud for her.

"A little pretentious," Li'ara added.

They both shared a laugh and Kalian couldn't remember the last time they had.

"I guess there are some similarities between us and them," Kalian replied.

Li'ara turned and gave him a coy smile. "You mean between you and me?"

It took Kalian a moment to understand her meaning, she saw him as a Terran now. He judged from her expression that this wasn't something she was going to let come between them. After all, the differences were only on the inside.

"I mean you're not exactly human anymore. Now you're just another *alien*." She gave him a playful smile and he decided to go with it.

"Well technically, I'm the human and you're the caveman in this scenario." They both laughed as Li'ara pushed him away.

Why hadn't he spent more time making her laugh? He loved the sound of her laugh but he remembered that not long ago he didn't think her capable of it. She did have a pretty big UDC stick up her ass. He preferred this new Li'ara. She was more relatable to and didn't give him orders every two minutes... and she smiled. But he couldn't deny that other side to her wasn't useful. She had saved his life time and again.

"Here. A *gift* from ALF." Li'ara handed Kalian a small transparent piece of what felt like plastic. She turned her head and tapped her ear, where he saw an identical object. "This way we'll all be in communication when Savrick arrives."

He agreed with the idea and placed it in his own ear. When he was finished he found Li'ara a lot closer. Her emerald eyes had a slight gloss to them and he was reminded of the moment they shared when she told him about her father. He felt guilty then for not seeing how she was coping with it all. He had been so wrapped up in everything Terran.

"Li'ara..."

His next words were interrupted as his armour emitted the life-size hologram of ALF. "He's here!"

They briefly regarded the AI, before looking into the cloudless midday sky.

"You need to get inside now!"

The sun was momentarily blotted out, as the mass of the *Helion* dropped out of subspace just outside the atmosphere. The great ship continued its momentum, revealing the blue sun again. It reminded Kalian of an ancient cruise liner with two extensions either side like a pitch-fork. Kalian altered the structure of his eyes to cycle through the different wavelengths. He could immediately see further, with greater detail, as the light of the star no longer impeded his vision. Now he could see six other ships, smaller with their greater distance, of Novaarian design. Each one appeared as a replica of the *Valoran* with their overreaching arcs that came to a fine point.

"Where did the Novaarian ships come from?" Kalian ignored Li'ara's puzzled look.

"I ordered the closest available ships to regroup here," ALF explained. "I informed them that the *Helion* had been captured by the same enemy that attacked the Conclave. Each of those ships possesses the weaponry to eliminate a target from space, useful to us I think. I will liaise with them and await the opportune moment."

Kalian knew the Novaarians would think their orders came from High Charge Uthor. Another testament to ALF's power that he could manipulate entire fleets to his will. Kalian focused on the present danger.

"We need to get inside, now." They both turned to run back to The Wall.

The door had already parted and Li'ara entered the square lift, alone. Kalian stopped just short of the door, knowing ALF would anticipate his decision. Before the two halves came back together, he saw Li'ara whip around with a stunned expression.

"Kalian!" She moved to the closing door but was too late.

He put his hand against the rock and felt the nanocelium moving as the lift descended at an incredible speed. His thoughts of Li'ara were swept away as he heard the sonic boom in the distance. ALF remained by his side while they watched the dark ship approach. It was all angles, with four chunky engines on the back, and it looked to be about four times the size of the *Fathom*. Extending his senses, Kalian could feel the nanocelium that made up the ship.

"You're sticking around to help me fight?"

ALF grimaced at Kalian's words. "Sadly your armour is not capable of housing the required emitters for hard-light."

"So you're just here to cheer me on then?"

The AI wouldn't miss his sarcasm. "I calculate that my presence will likely anger him further. If I can unhinge him, he will become unfocused. That might be your only advantage." ALF emulated a very human sigh. "You are not ready for this encounter, Kalian. You could train for another century and you still wouldn't be ready."

"Feel free to stop talking now."

The AI's lack of confidence in him was evident and, unfortunately, well founded. Kalian knew he wasn't ready, but he was choosing to stay. ALF looked somewhat apologetic at his last remark.

"How many are there?" Kalian wondered if ALF was asking because he didn't know, or because he wanted to test him.

Either way, Kalian pushed into the craft, ignoring the density, temperature, and chemical composition of its make-up. Inside, he found four complex structures each with distinct brain waves. Unlike

Li'ara's the waves they emitted felt guarded beyond his exploration. One of the four had a very different feel altogether.

"There are four, but one of them is... complicated." He focused on the individual in question.

After a moment's probe, Kalian knew what he was examining - the goliath. The giant's brainwaves were pulsing on a lower level - like those of an animal. His biological framework had been altered in almost every cell. He was teeming with dense structures of nanocelium.

The craft touched down, kicking up desert sand as it did. Kalian was now standing directly between the craft and The Wall. He took a deep breath to steady his nerves. He felt the sensation in his spine swell at the impending danger but gained comfort from the power he knew it gave him.

Soon after the ramp descended, the four armoured beings exited the ship with the goliath bringing up the rear. They crossed the short distance, the four horsemen of his own personal apocalypse, until there was only twenty-feet between them. Kalian watched the central figure look from him to the hologram of ALF. The same laugh that resounded inside the council chamber now filtered through his helmet. Savrick's headpiece separated into its sections and folded into his armour. His twin braids fell across his chest and he regarded Kalian and ALF with glee.

"We are not worthy..." Savrick said mockingly with a half courteous bow. "The all-powerful, all-knowing ALF! You should see what I left of your precious Criterion. It's nothing but a broken, hollowed out shell." He scanned Kalian from head to foot. "Ever the teacher I see. You look to be a Terran now, boy."

Kalian felt his armour paled in comparison to the bulky Gomar equivalent.

"And I see you are still slaughtering people by the million, Savrick." ALF appeared unfazed by the sight of his oldest enemy, but Kalian knew the hologram would project whatever he wanted it to.

"Billions actually. And I won't stop until the very last one is dead at my feet." Savrick looked Kalian in the eyes with deadly intent before returning his gaze to ALF. "But how many of those deaths can be attributed to you?" He practically spat the words at ALF. "You made yourself a god - the creation becoming the creator. It's the oldest story in the book; the never-ending cycle of life. How many choices have you made, and failed to make, that ended with the deaths of so many? You chose to repress us and we made you pay for it. You chose to start again with *them*, and we made them pay for it. If you had stopped your little science team from returning, I wouldn't even have known about the humans. The only reason they were given the chance they had was because the Terran pilot deleted the navigational logs. You can imagine my frustration at the prospect of searching an entire galaxy. They died slowly..."

Kalian felt his anger rising to the surface at the sight of Savrick's vicious smirk.

"You have so many excuses for the destruction left in your wake." ALF was starting to look a few orders of magnitude above pissed off. "Everything you have ever done was because of *her*."

"Be careful, old *machine*, my wrath has not been tempered in my years of sleep." Savrick began to pace at what Kalian knew to be thoughts of his wife.

"It was an accident, Savrick. I did not mean for T'lea to di-"

"NO!" Savrick's scream ended the hologram and Kalian felt the emitters in his waist short out. "You do not get to say her name!" Like a caged animal, Savrick paced the sandy ground shaking his head.

Without ALF, Kalian suddenly felt very alone. He pushed his awareness down and felt Li'ara deep inside the Outpost. At least she was safe, for now. How had events changed so much that he was now protecting her instead of her protecting him? He focused back on the present when he realised Savrick had stopped pacing and was watching him intently.

"It's distracting, isn't it?" Savrick said. "To be so in tune with the universe that you don't know where it ends and you begin. I was a hundred and two, by your standards, when I first connected to it all."

He tapped the chest plate of his armour and Kalian knew the

armour was the source of his strength. Without it, the Harness would render him as powerless as any human.

"You are lucky to be so young. But your fate will be no different from those before you."

Kalian had heard enough of his pointless monologue. He could feel the power building in him, making him bold. "What are you going to do? Threaten me to death?" Before Savrick could reply, he went on. "You say ALF made you the way you are: his actions, your reaction. Well, *you* made me who I am. You ran me from my home. You've pushed my kind to extinction. You removed all my choices and put me right where you see me now. I might be tiny to you *immortals*, but I will end you."

Savrick mulled over his words while looking into the faceplates of his companions.

Kalian knew his words to be true. ALF had created the Terran culture and Savrick had brought it down. Now Savrick had forced Kalian into becoming a weapon and he *would* bring him down. It was the cycle of life as the Gomar had put it. He had to believe that if he was ever going to see Li'ara's smile again.

"Perhaps. But first, let us put that training of yours to the test."

Kalian didn't like the look of Savrick's devious smile.

"Lilander..." The armoured Gomar standing next to him stepped forward as the helmet came apart to reveal a woman with cropped blonde hair. Like all the people of her genetic disposition, she was beautiful but deadly. "And this you might know by a different name. I simply call him the beast."

The goliath stepped forward with heavy feet. The headgear fell apart with a decompressing sound.

The content was not what he expected.

He was faced with the stark white face of a bald man, though thinking of it as a man seemed something of a stretch. The eyes were larger than normal but, then again, so was everything else about the beast. Its eyes were black abysses with microscopic white dots, shot-gunned across the surface. The domed head was covered in cracks of grey and black that ran down into its facial features. Everything about it looked strong and enduring but twisted, as if nature had never intended this creature to exist. Its face was a blank slate, devoid of expression.

There was something about that face, something familiar. He ran the face through his memory like an image search. He was startled by the result he found. If he cleared up the face of its cracks, reduced it to normal size, and added long flowing hair, it would be the Avatar. Kalian mouthed the name as the revelation hit.

"Yes. The wisest of us all." Savrick regarded the giant as a trophy.

"What did you do to him?"

Savrick smiled. "Improved his personality..."

With that, the beast and Lilander launched at Kalian. His reaction was instinctive, from what felt like years of training hardwired into his muscles. With nimble agility, he leapt into the air using the bulk of the beast as a pivoting point for his hands. His telekinesis kicked in, giving him the extra lift to overcome the beast's great height. The monster continued its rampage as Kalian somersaulted over him, only to be intercepted by Lilander.

It felt like a Mag-car had hurtled into him at fifty miles per hour. Reality tumbled around him before he met the hard desert below. He had just enough time to surround his body in a tight layer of telekinetic energy. Having switched off his pain receptors, he pushed up from the ground almost immediately. He created a low-level connection with the nanocelium in his suit and found the plating around his chest and back had increased in density to compensate for any weak points in his barrier.

Lilander was on him before he could get his bearings. Her movement was calculated, with every blow efficiently executed. He was able to counter most, while his telekinetic barrier protected him from the rest. He might not have felt the pain but her blows were hard enough to knock him around; not to mention the mental drain he experienced on his barrier. He knew at least four of his counters struck her ribs and face but she remained relentless in her attack. In a move he thought was more luck than skill, Kalian forced Lilander onto her back. He applied a downward force of telekinetic energy and pinned her in place. He could feel her power fighting him, almost lifting him off the ground.

Two thunderous steps told Kalian that the beast had covered the thirty feet between them. Lilander took advantage of his lack of concentration. He felt her telekinetic push reverse and bring his face over her own. She followed with a sharp elbow to his jaw. He collapsed on top of her and tasted the blood in his mouth. He heard the echo of ALF's voice chastising him for not switching off his pain receptors. Before he could remedy the situation, a large hand gripped the back of his neck. The beast threw him like a pebble over the surface of the oceanic desert. Kalian lost count of how many times he skidded across the sand before coming to a stop.

He rolled onto his side, just in time to see the helmeted unnamed Gomar approach The Wall. The ancient door reacted explosively to the wave of his hand as the rock blew out into thousands of shards. Without slowing his stride, the unnamed Gomar entered the lift ignoring the flying debris. Kalian felt his gut tighten at the thought of his destination.

Li'ara!

Without thought of the beast or Lilander, he launched into a sprint from his prone position. He covered half the distance before a super-heated ball of plasma hit his right shoulder blade. In his rush he had lowered his guard, focusing his telekinetic energy into his movements for the additional speed. He travelled a further fifteen feet before landing face-down in the sand, his armour taking the brunt of the destructive force. He could feel the nanocelium rapidly reconfiguring to repair the damage while the plasma continued to melt the plating down.

"Li'ara can you hear me?" When he got no reply, Kalian pressed his finger onto the earpiece and asked again.

"You shouldn't be talking to me, you need to focus!" Li'ara's voice rang through his head in perfect clarity.

"The Outpost has been breached. One of the Gomar is inside."

There was a pause before she replied. "ALF can see him on the monitor. We can handle him Kalian. Just stay alive."

He managed to crouch on all fours, with sand across half of his face and blood dripping from his left eyebrow. He considered tissue repair before deciding the cut wasn't worth the energy. Kalian felt the electromagnetic field of the beast affect reality in the manner of a tidal wave and knew he was out of time. The mighty boot of the goliath connected with his ribs and stomach. He lost his sense of direction and gravity as he rolled across the cracked desert floor. He felt no pain but a quick internal check showed a hairline fracture on his third rib on the right side. He was suddenly very thankful for his armour.

Kalian's despair was only drowned out by his anger; anger he directed at the oncoming beast. His use of telekinesis might be blunt, but maybe blunt was what he needed. He matched the beast's speed as they charged at one another, each kicking up a cloud of sand. Kalian could feel the beast like a weight anchored to the moon. There was no way he could actually move it, but he could give it a nudge.

He kept his movements fluid, containing his momentum into one continuous attack. Kalian pushed into the air with a short telekinetic boost, swinging his left arm above his head. The beast felt the effects of the pull behind its knees, causing it to skid along the ground, turfing up the rock. The distance and speed were all worked out in Kalian's head. His own descent brought him down directly in front of the fallen beast. Building up the telekinetic energy around his fist like an armoured gauntlet, Kalian hit the goliath below its right eye.

The added force of the telekinesis drove the beast into the hard ground. He couldn't stop there for the beast would recover in seconds. Coming straight up from his crouch, he used the same striking hand to guide his telekinetic command. The beast lifted from the ground as its senses came back. An unnatural growl roared from its mouth as Kalian kept it suspended mid-air. Thinking of the creature as being no heavier than a rock he pushed the giant out into the desert. The beast became a blur as it flew across the flat land before an explosion of rock and sand was all that could be seen. It felt good to deliver such a blow against the foe that had literally given him nightmares.

Savrick was laughing behind him. He didn't need to look to know the man was standing by the nose of the Gomar craft. The sound of his laughter angered and confused Kalian. What kind of psychopath was this guy? How could he find it amusing that his own forces were being beaten? Kalian's musing became his downfall as Lilander advanced. The world shifted to the left as he was violently flung into the remains of The Wall. He attempted to bring up a telekinetic barrier to soften the blow but was too slow. The rock gave way under the force of her mental push, covering his suit in debris and flinging him at an odd angle. His legs flailed in the air before he smashed onto the rock-strewn ground.

"Don't worry, little Terran," Savrick's voice carried across the desert. "They won't kill you. That will be my pleasure."

Kalian couldn't help himself. He had to poke the bear. "What's the matter, Savrick? You need me softened up first?"

His question was met by a backhanded strike from Lilander. "You will show respect!" she screamed.

Kalian dragged himself up, feeling the cracks in his concentration. He stimulated his adrenal gland, giving himself the extra rush and heightened awareness. Lilander confidently strode towards him as he felt for every molecule that made up the rocks behind him. He threw his hand at her pulling the rocks as he did, each one a missile. He was swiftly reminded of her superior experience as she held up her own hand, forcing the rocks to fly off at different angles. She hit him square in the chest with an amalgamation of telekinesis and plasma.

The light from the super-heated matter blinded Kalian before it blew him away. The whiteout disorientated him more when he felt the ground breaking under his weight. He could smell the ozone rising off his chest while the nanocelium began to rebuild the charred armour. Kalian took a laboured breath, feeling the crushed armour around his lungs.

"ALF, I could really do with one of those strikes about now..."

Li'ara felt utterly helpless as she watched Kalian take blow after blow from the female Gomar. She could already see the beast recovering in the distance as it climbed out of its crater. Half of the monitoring room had become a life-size hologram of the action above them. It looked so real she had to stop herself from stepping into the illusion and helping him. Telarrek and Namek were watching a smaller image being generated by an oval column behind her. They watched as the masked Gomar burst through the lift and into the corridor. The image was mirrored by another hologram, showing the Gomar in relation to the monitoring room. She looked to ALF for the Outpost's defences.

The AI looked to have shut down for a couple of seconds after the revelation concerning the Avatar. To an artificial intelligence, that might as well have been a lifetime. Now, having come to terms with it, the AI was going into offensive mode. Li'ara knew he was communicating with the Novaarian ships, coordinating an orbital strike as well as activating the Outpost's defences. She had already warned him against a strike, fearing the blast would hit Kalian as well as the Gomar. It had been Telarrek who had assured her the ships were accurate enough to distinguish between targets.

"I'd be more worried about them killing us," ALF had quipped.

It hadn't occurred to her that the beams could reach them so far underground.

The complex shook briefly as the Gomar took out a door that failed to open for him. Newly constructed cannons slid out of their housing to rain green energy down on the dark armour. Every shot stopped short of its mark as they were absorbed and converted into a new energy. The Gomar unleashed the stored energy in the form of a massive ball of plasma. The pin-head camera in that area burned out along with the cannons and half of the next door.

"You need to stop that. He's just getting stronger!" Li'ara argued.

"We need to wear him down. Trust me. This isn't my first time."

Li'ara was aware that the version of ALF she was speaking to was most likely a low percentage of his entire intelligence. Either way, she had to accept that this tiny percentage still had a higher

IQ than her and that he had led the Terran to war against the Gomar.

She still didn't trust him.

"We will face him," Telarrek said, as he and Namek removed their staffs from their backs.

The room shook, cutting out the panoramic hologram. "You must evacuate this room immediately." ALF gestured to the newly translucent door. "His progress has compromised the integrity of the surrounding bedrock."

The ceiling opened up, with jagged cracks stretching from the direction of the Gomar. They hurried from the room as dirt began to fall from the new fissures.

"This way." A new hologram of ALF was suddenly standing at the other end of the corridor gesturing to his left.

The previous monitoring room collapsed behind them as the walls and ceiling crumpled under the pressure. Li'ara had a feeling that the AI had deliberately dispersed the nanocelium to weaken the structural integrity. It might not stop the Gomar but it would slow him down.

Namek paused before retrieving two of the gravity bombs from his belt. They exploded halfway down the corridor, ejecting a dozen ball bearings that stuck to everything. The distortion zone now covered at least seventy feet. After a couple of minutes, ALF directed them into a room which had been configured into another monitoring station. Along the way, they had all used their gravity bombs to set various traps. They could see the Gomar had been forced to take a new path around the previous monitoring room.

"How's Kalian?" Li'ara asked impatiently.

A hologram lit the room with the desert sun as Kalian danced across the sand with the female Gomar. The camera had to pan out to keep track of them using their telekinetically enhanced speed. Li'ara winced as the beast waded in, taking Kalian to the floor before using him like a rag doll. She continued to breathe when Kalian hit it with organic plasma, giving him room to move.

The light of the hologram dimmed to compensate for the brightness of the sudden bombardment. Beams made of every colour hammered into the desert around them, kicking up storms of sand and rock. Four beams landed in quick succession in a random pattern, each one missing the mark. Li'ara spun to face ALF with a questioning look.

"Every time they lock-on their targeting system falls out of alignment," ALF explained while stroking his holographic beard. "They must be using a mesh."

A new image appeared from the point of view of a Novaarian cruiser. The Gomar craft and the *Fathom* were clearly visible, but Kalian and the others were black dots that moved across the image. Dozens of target locks overlaid the hologram, pinpointing the Gomar and Savrick, before being thrown to the side. Eventually, there were enough targeted zones to make out a circumference around the ship. Li'ara could now see that ALF was trying to find out how big the area was and that the epicentre of the mesh was clearly the craft.

"Kalian, can you hear me?" ALF asked.

"Busy!" was the only reply they received.

The hologram highlighted the measurements between the craft and the edge of the targeting zone.

"Then just listen. You need to force them beyond a hundred and fifty feet of the craft. Only then can they be targeted by the Novaarians."

There was no reply to ALF's instructions but they saw Kalian scale the beast and bury three punches into its face.

"Can he knock out the electrical grid on their craft?" Telarrek asked.

"I calculate that Savrick will step in if he feels the threat of bombardment. Kalian will have to handle him after I take care of the other two."

Li'ara was not so sure of the AI's plan. Forcing the two of them from the safety of the craft would not be easy.

"The first trap has been triggered," Namek stated, as he watched the Gomar struggle to orientate himself.

Every time he found the new 'floor', the gravity well would

change causing him to fly off into another wall or ceiling. By the time he made it to the other end, ALF had engineered six hard-light copies of himself.

"That should buy us some time," ALF said before vanishing into stardust.

<hr />

ROLAND WASN'T happy with his new role as liaison between the aliens and the humans. Captain Fey occupied the central chair in what Esabelle had told them was the new command centre. He didn't understand most of what the crazy woman said but the captain wouldn't stop with the questions. Initially, there had been a long silence and some awkward tears from her and the lead scientists regarding the fate of humanity. After hearing the devastating news, the group had formed a committee on how to tell the rest of the population. Roland wasn't terribly interested.

Leaving them to it, Roland and Ilyseal convinced the Laronians to help them retrieve the remaining crew of the *Gommarian*. Each one weighed a ton in all the armour. He avoided the explanation of Esabelle's presence, promising to explain after the psychopaths had been rounded up. True to her word, she had known where to find them and where to store them.

"These are Rem-stores." Esabelle had explained that the vertical tubes were used for long space flight.

Picking the heavy bastards up hadn't been easy but, eventually, they managed to fit each of them in. Unlike before, the ship now possessed multiple touch screens and interactive holograms where they would expect them to be. Using these they could activate the stores and, in effect, freeze the occupants.

"I have reconfigured the interior for human use."

Had she redesigned the entire ship, just for them?

Leaving the masses to their grief, Roland, Ilyseal, and Esabelle had accompanied the captain and two of her crew to the bridge. She naturally resumed her position in the central chair as he was forced to tell her everything he knew. Ilyseal filled in the missing blanks or the bits he had been too drunk to remember, but he had to explain it since none of them possessed a translator. The tricky bit had been Esabelle, since he didn't really know what to say. She now wore a loose-fitting outfit that had been provided by some strange portal in the wall outside the bridge. At this point, he wasn't questioning anything the ship could do.

"I am, or was, the pilot of this ship - the *Gommarian*. I have modi-fied the ship for your people and you will have full control of it after we arrive at Nova Prime. Until then the controls are locked, even to me. I will explain more when I meet Kalian Gaines."

There was that name again. What was it with this guy? He noticed the Novaarian scanning everything, including Esabelle, even as she nursed her injured body. Before the armoured git had been disabled by Esabelle, Ilyseal had been thrown about quite a bit.

"We have been attacked and taken prisoner by two different ships. I am done taking orders from anyone, young lady. You will relinquish this vessel to me immediately under the authority of the United Defence Corps." Captain Fey looked like a woman on the edge, some-where between crying and attacking.

"There is no United Defence Corps, Captain. The human beings aboard this ship most likely comprise the entirety of your race. Food and supplies have been provided in the hold. I suggest you and your people take the time to recuperate before you meet the Conclave authority." Esabelle's words had been a matter of fact, with no hint of emotion.

Being clear that Esabelle wouldn't budge, the captain and her companions filed out of the bridge with sour expressions. He noticed how wary they were of the overly tall Novaarians and especially the scaly Laronians, who had sent along their highest-ranking officer.

Roland took the captain's place in the command chair but failed to get comfortable with the state of his ribs. He ignored the itch on his nose, not wanting to touch the damaged cartilage.

"Is there any chance you happened to build a bar?"

KALIAN COULD FEEL IT NOW, like static in the air. It emanated from their craft in waves, creating a protective bubble around the area. The border might as well have been on the other side of the moon, however. Warnings were going off in his head as various receptors informed him of broken ribs, torn muscles and some internal bleeding around his spleen. He wasn't sure how much longer he could keep this up.

Lilander had removed a blade from her armour that snaked into a needle point. He managed to dodge and counter the first six attacks until she eventually cut through his barrier and slashed his cheek. It was becoming harder to maintain a permanent barrier over the top of his skin and suit. If he produced organic plasma his barrier dropped, if he increased his telekinesis he moved too slowly and lost some awareness. He couldn't keep it all up at once.

He was forced into being creative with his telekinesis to keep his attack protean. More than once he was able to move the beast's arm or leg to cause damage to Lilander. It never lasted though, for they were simply better. He couldn't seem to get out of the beast's reach or completely avoid Lilander's blade. He retreated into his head, searching frantically for a solution: some lesson he had overlooked, a fighting technique he hadn't taken the time to master, anything. Collating information his mind had been collecting, he understood the tremors below his feet. The Gomar was tearing through the Outpost.

He could see the beast advancing as if he were watching on a monitor in his head. Every second to the beast was a minute inside Kalian's head. He focused on the thought of power, raw energy in its most universal form.

Fire.

He recalled any and all uploaded information concerning combustion. His mind was flooded with data on exothermic chemical reactions and oxidant agents. In his case, he was surrounded by an abundant source of oxidants. He could recall the lesson in which the

Avatar, as the teaching construct, had taught him about exothermic internal reactions. His body could self-heat to generate the initial reaction that could then be released through the pores of his skin. Using telekinesis, he could then vibrate these molecules causing ignition. He had to try.

He emerged back into reality, much the way a ship leaves subspace. The beast barrelled into him, causing more laughter from Savrick. This time it didn't let go but instead wrapped its giant arms around his waist and squeezed. Kalian yelled in agony as his pain receptors kicked back in with his loss of concentration. He slammed his arms down on the beast with a telekinetic barrage but it refused to yield. He saw the heat waves around his hand as it generated the required reaction. He vibrated the molecules in the air until a quick spark suddenly became a glowing star in his hand. The effect became more light than actual heat but it was all he had.

Thrusting his hand into the beast's face, until he could feel its nose against his palm, he increased the light effect until the beast roared. It dropped him back to earth and Kalian looked up to see the two scorched pits where its eyes used to be. Seeing Lilander's shock only fuelled Kalian on. He was gaining the upper hand. He released everything, losing his awareness and his connection to the suit as well as his protective barrier. Focusing every scrap of energy, he allowed his spine to build the power required. Lilander was coming for him again. It was now or never.

Kalian's roar was drowned out by his own expulsion of telekinetic energy as it pulsed from every part of his body. The crushing wave slammed into the beast, who in turn clipped Lilander with its giant hand. The beast was hurled across the desert like the discharge from a gun, carrying with it a tidal wave of sand and debris. Lilander impacted against the *Fathom* head first, where she crumpled to the ground in an unconscious heap. The beast finally hit the ground just under two hundred feet away, where it then scarred the landscape for another twenty.

"ALF..." Kalian kept his eyes on the distant creature that was once the Avatar.

Like an angry god, the orbiting Novaarian ship unleashed a beam fifty feet in width. The multicoloured energy shook the ground as it burrowed through, creating a swirling vortex of sand. The beam ended less than two seconds after striking its target. Billows of smoke rose from the charred crater that would forever mark the moon.

Filling the area with his paranormal awareness, he could tell the beast had been reduced to atoms. He dropped to his knee in exhaustion. Wiping the sweat from his eyes, he felt the sting of various cuts across his face and head.

"Well done, little Terran." Savrick mockingly clapped his hands. "You have come a long way in a short time. Your head must be fit to burst with all that information he's crammed in there. You're just a pawn, Kalian. A plaything really. That's all we ever were to him, to *it*. Toys for the most powerful child in the galaxy. But I have to hand it to you," he said, looking at the broken body of Lilander and the smouldering crater in the distance, "you did beat my best. That has to say something about you, I suppose." Savrick stood over Kalian, blocking out the sun. "It's a shame, that after today, no one will ever speak of you again."

LI'ARA THREW her arms into the air in celebration as the beast was reduced to slag. She looked to the others who appeared more occupied with their own impending doom. The Gomar had switched off the hard-light projections with an electromagnetic pulse and launched himself through the corridors with the gravity bombs. Nothing was stopping it.

"Is there another way out of here?" she asked.

ALF remained silent as he observed the expansive hologram of Kalian. She followed his gaze to see Savrick standing over Kalian. There was nothing she could do. For all of her skills, there was nothing she could do to help him against this kind of enemy.

"There is no other... Take cover!" ALF's warning came just before the room exploded into chaos.

Kalian and Savrick burst through the ceiling like a missile and ricocheted off the floor as they tore into the next room. They continued to blow through the complex, knocking through walls like paper. Li'ara felt the many hands of a Novaarian help her up and pull the debris off her. She tried to breathe through the cloud of dirt and broken rock but could only manage a cough. The complex shook one last time before they left for the surface of the moon again.

"What... was that?" she finally managed.

ALF's hologram flickered trying to keep cohesion through the damaged emitters. "That was *them*," ALF stated flatly.

Li'ara couldn't quite make sense of the AI's words. Was he saying that Kalian and Savrick had just rammed through the Outpost? On the other side of the room, the panoramic hologram continued to feedback the footage from above. Hardly believing her eyes, Li'ara watched as they both shot out of the ground with hands around each other's throats. They slammed into the ground in a tumble of limbs until Savrick ended up on top of Kalian. She watched helplessly as he pounded Kalian with blow after blow. Somehow, he managed to catch one of Savrick's hands mid-strike with a telekinetic barrier. Unable to push through, Savrick ripped Kalian from the ground and performed a complex series of attacks that ended with a telekinetic push, forcing Kalian into the nose of the Gomar craft.

"Do something!" Li'ara pleaded to ALF.

"He is protected inside the mesh, I cannot..." The AI paused as he no doubt ran through a thousand scenarios in a second.

"What? What is it?"

"The *Helion*. With the laser-com shut down, I cannot enter its mainframe and take control."

"Explain." She needed something, anything that could save him.

"If my nanocelium could be injected into one of the ship's consoles, I would have complete control of all its systems. Would you do *anything* to save him, Li'ara?"

A small canister slotted out of the nearest oval column.

"Yes." She didn't hesitate.

"Then get me that ship."

"LI'ARA...?"

Kalian couldn't believe his eyes. It didn't help that Savrick had just taken him on a ride through the Outpost's interior. The only reason he still had all his limbs was because of the telekinetic cocoon they had both been wrapped in. He saw Li'ara and Namek run from the broken entrance of The Wall to the *Fathom* on the other side. How had she survived the other Gomar? And where was Telarrek? He decided not to question it and be thankful she was getting away from it all.

"She will not get far. When I am finished with you, I will find her..." Savrick's words were like poison in his ear. The very words ignited a fire in Kalian's mind as he pulled himself out of the crater. Savrick had already climbed out. He could recover quicker, but Kalian didn't care.

He launched himself into Savrick, letting his telekinesis lift them both high into the air and planted four successful blows to Savrick's face on the way down, burying them into the ground again. Savrick responded with a swiftness Kalian didn't possess. With a simple wave of his hand, Kalian was thrown away like a broken toy. He tried to get up but found himself pinned on one knee, his limbs solid and unresponsive. He could feel every molecule and cell in his body being manipulated by Savrick. Kalian didn't need to expand his awareness to know Savrick was slowly walking towards him, like a predator that knew it had already won.

"I won't let you hurt her." It came out as more of a growl.

Savrick laughed as he paraded over his prey. "You couldn't stop me killing the rest of your pathetic race. What makes you think you can stop me from killing her? You're just a child, Kalian. You trained in a machine! Everything I am was forged through war!"

Kalian wasn't ready for what happened next. Savrick poured himself into Kalian's mind the same way he had placed a finger into Li'ara's mind, only Savrick wasn't using a metaphysical finger. Kalian felt Savrick's mind slam into his own, almost pushing him out of his own brain.

He experienced instant agony as Savrick took control and stimulated every pain receptor at once. If he screamed, he couldn't hear it. Kalian lost his sense of self as the two merged together. He could no longer tell the difference between Savrick's body and his own and felt his rage as if it were his own. In a single moment that could have been a lifetime, he felt the love Savrick had once held for T'lea and Esabelle before he became the shell he now was.

Kalian's memory merged with the ancient Gomar. He saw the hundreds of times Savrick had woken from the Rem-stores to investigate a new system or planet. He saw Esabelle strapped into the *Gommarian* and argued with himself over the reasons for her imprisonment. Suddenly he was standing inside a large cavern on another world and another time. Through Savrick's eyes, he saw the stream that ran through the cavern and felt a moment of worry for Esabelle whom he had left behind. Kalian could feel the cool air on his skin as drops of water fell from the stalactites above. There was something on the other side of that stream. Was it a cube? There was too much rock covering it to see clearly.

The memory was torn away as Savrick clawed at his mind like a savage beast searching for meat.

He was being hollowed out.

Kalian felt the names of his parents slip from his grasp as he failed to recall their faces. Where had he studied history? How old was he? What planet was he from? He couldn't tell the difference between Earth and Albadar: he had memories of living on both. Then he saw Li'ara. Her image was backed with light and he knew Savrick was coming for her, to cleanse the memory of her from his mind. Kalian held onto her image, her voice, her smile. He wouldn't let Savrick take her from him, he wouldn't let her go.

THE *FATHOM* PASSED through the hangar shield of the *Helion*. The ship's sensors swept the bay searching for a space large enough to house it. The damage was typical of the Gomar. Smaller craft and workstations had been decimated, with bodies of every species strewn across the floor.

The viewport was overlaid with a hologram, highlighting an available space in the centre. She activated the landing gear and ignored the sensor feedback concerning a weight variable on the port side. She had a job to do. If she didn't do this Kalian would die, Savrick would go on to obliterate the Conclave, and Telarrek would probably die for nothing. She thought of the Novaarian back in the Outpost.

"I will keep the Gomar occupied." Telarrek had said.

It wasn't the first time she had seen a Novaarian give their life for Kalian and herself. She could still see Numanon challenging the beast on the Icarus station. His sacrifice meant their survival and now Telarrek would do the same. She knew he couldn't survive that encounter; they were too powerful. Li'ara turned to Namek who had been agitated since they left.

"No my Charge, I will stay," he had said, but Telarrek had held up his hand to Namek.

"No. You will keep Li'ara safe and ensure the success of the mission."

Li'ara had felt like arguing the point that she didn't need protection, but she didn't want to taint Telarrek's sacrifice. She also saw the logic in his staying. They had to reach this ship and ALF couldn't keep the Gomar contained. There was no doubt that Telarrek was a formidable warrior.

Before landing, Li'ara identified the nearest console she would inject the nanocelium into. Once inside the system, ALF could subsume its controls and save Kalian. The AI had explained that the security ship had the required firepower to affect the Gomar craft. One blast would disrupt the mesh and allow ALF to target Savrick.

They left the *Fathom* and ran across the hangar to one of the few consoles still in one piece. Li'ara removed the hand-held cylinder and depressed the only button. Multiple spikes shot out of the bottom, each a different size and shape. She didn't hesitate to stab the cylinder into the glass console. The display flickered as the microscopic robots flooded the console and infected the ship's mainframe. All they had to do was wait for ALF to bring the weapons online.

"Forgive me, Li'ara." ALF appeared as a hologram, the size of her arm, on the console.

"What's going on?"

"I believe I have found the only scenario that ensures Savrick's demise and the survival of Kalian. It does, however, reduce your chances of survival, dramatically."

What was he talking about? She had a sinking feeling that the AI had betrayed her.

Li'ara's next thought was more action than words.

Namek was flung into the console, shattering the glass and falling limply to the floor. In the same moment that she levelled her gun, she could see that the Novaarian had the hilt of a blade lodged in the base of his neck. Li'ara had no time to consider the implications of that blade before she squeezed the trigger of her sidearm. In between the flashes of Intrinium, she glimpsed the advancing form of the female Gomar. Every shot was futile as she absorbed the energy. When they were within arm's length everything changed, including gravity.

The grav plates deactivated at the same moment as everything not bolted down rose into the air. Not only did everything rise, but Li'ara and the Gomar were pulled towards the back of the hangar at speed. Li'ara managed to catch a fixed console and keep herself in place while trying to dodge the various tools, bodies, and large vessels. She lost sight of Namek's body and the Gomar amidst the debris. From the direction everything suddenly flew, Li'ara surmised that the *Helion* must be in freefall, towards Naveen's surface.

What had ALF done?

Kalian, can you hear me?

The voice was echoing from somewhere inside his head. It sounded familiar but he couldn't place it. Kalian had been forced to split his focus between his thoughts and memories of Li'ara and pushing Savrick out of his head. He felt the rage welling up inside but didn't know if it came from him or Savrick. Kalian saw images of his wife, no... not his wife, Savrick's wife. He watched through eyes that were not his own as a pillar collapsed under the strain of a baby's cry, and buried T'lea.

Kalian! You must listen to me. Li'ara is on that ship!

He knew then that the voice belonged to ALF. Hearing her name sharpened his focus and gave him strength. He tracked the voice to the earpiece but couldn't respond. Kalian wasn't sure what he meant but he understood that Li'ara was in danger. He relinquished some of his control and concentrated on his external vision. The surrounding desert was overcast with a dominating shadow that blotted out the sun. He was still on one knee with Savrick standing over him, his back to the...

Kalian struggled to comprehend what was coming. The *Helion* was dropping out of the sky above them, its central nose burning as it breached the atmosphere. He heard the AI's words again and felt his muscles tighten at the thought of Li'ara being on board. He was whipped back into his mind as Savrick disconnected him from the occipital section of his brain. Kalian had the feeling that Savrick was unaware of the threat from above. He was too busy trying to cause Kalian as much pain as possible. But Kalian was a slave to his will, unable to move or use any of his abilities. He fought through the pain, trying to come up with a solution - and fast.

He saw another image of T'lea flash across his consciousness. She was clearly at the foundation of what made Savrick who he was. With that thought, he knew what to do. With a change of plan, he stopped fighting Savrick and instead pulled him in. Kalian created a virtual world from the memories gained by their merging. He created a basic room from the home they had once shared, trying to replicate as much as he could get from Savrick's bleeding memory. He felt the walls of the virtual room crack under the immense pressure from his attacker - he was running out of time.

Kalian stepped away from the door, allowing Savrick to breach the last vault in his mind. The Gomar's consciousness filled the room and he watched Savrick's face soften at the sight of his wife, who now looked and felt very alive standing before him. Kalian felt more and more of Savrick being pulled into the virtual world as he drank in the sight of T'lea. With every bit of Savrick that moved into the virtuality, Kalian regained more control.

He opened his eyes and found he now had his limbs back under control. The *Helion* was terrifyingly close and dropping with incredible speed. There was only one play left to him. If Li'ara was inside that ship he would have to go in and get her. He had to act now.

Kalian leapt up, pushing Savrick to the side as he did. The physical push broke the bond between them, snapping Savrick's mind back into his own head. The speed and violent nature of the disconnection caused Savrick pain, as he tried to categorise and delete the memories that were not his own, as well as T'lea being torn away from him again. Kalian was banking on the image of his wife opening up memories Savrick had kept in the deepest vaults of his mind. These moments were all Kalian had. His mind felt similarly fractured as he pushed away, but he focused only on Li'ara.

He never paused, continuing his leap and using all his energy to propel him. Time slowed for him as he partially retreated into his mind. He held his arms above his head and flew through the hull as if it wasn't there. His telekinetic cocoon protected him against the battering debris and jagged metal. Continuing his push, he moved straight through the ship, tearing it apart like an ancient ballistic weapon would pass through a balloon. Had the situation not been so dire, he would have marvelled at the fact that he was flying.

The *Helion* changed course slightly as it impacted the moon's surface. He expanded his awareness, searching for Li'ara and felt the luminous aura of Savrick below. He could feel the power Savrick was pouring into the ship, obliterating every atom before it could crush him at the epicentre of its weight. Everything behind Kalian was a turbulent world of chaos and exploding debris, but he could feel every ton hammering Savrick's defences.

Moving at just over a hundred miles per hour on a vertical incline, Kalian was making quick progress through the interior as its giant mass continued to sink into Naveen. Nearing the end of the ship, he could sense a large opening coming up and knew it to be the hangar. There was no mistaking Li'ara.

He burst through just as she was hurtling towards the back of the falling ship. Slowing down a fraction, he simultaneously engulfed her in his own telekinetic cocoon. The *Fathom* slammed into the far wall and crushed Lilander as it came apart, its fuel cells exploding violently. He pulled Li'ara in close before altering their trajectory at a right angle. At the same moment, he felt the last of Savrick's defence break under the sheer weight of the Nexus-class starship. He had defied the weight of the vessel for more than half of its length before Kalian felt those specific Terran brain waves wink out of existence. Somewhere in his mind he heard the last defiant scream of the oldest living being in the galaxy and knew Savrick was finally dead.

The sun was momentarily blinding as they exited the ship amidst an explosion from one of the small craft in the plummeting hangar. He stopped pushing up and gave in to gravity, using one last surge of telekinesis to take the impact of their fall under his feet.

When the dust settled, he could see their fall had created a small crater. He heard the distant explosions as the *Helion* broke into a million pieces and hammered the moon. Kalian held Li'ara close as the shockwave passed over the top of them, filling the crater with more sand and smoke.

That's when he felt it.

His hand grasped the end of a small piece of metal framework. He quickly followed the length until it stopped below Li'ara's heart. He gasped unable to find the words for his despair. With a mental pulse, he banished the surrounding fog to see the unconscious form in his hands. He tried to wake her with conventional methods but she remained still. He pushed his awareness into her and recognised the inferior vena cava had been pierced along with some lung tissue and extensive muscle damage.

Kalian instinctively held his hand over the metal rod and telekinetically retrieved it before throwing it away. He immediately regretted it as hot blood pulsed from the wound uncontrollably.

She was dying.

"Kalian..." A flickering image of ALF was suddenly crouched with him in the crater.

The suit had reconfigured the emitters in its reprieve from the constant barrage.

"I can heal her!" Kalian couldn't stop the tears running down his face and dropping on to her pale skin.

"Don't Kalian. To heal another person you would have to become a part of them. It would be no different to what Savrick has just done to you, only her mind will not repair itself like yours."

"I have to try!" Kalian had lost too much to lose one more thing, to lose her.

He deactivated the hologram and focused on Li'ara. Flooding her mind with his consciousness, he melded their brainwaves. Feeling her body as if it were his own, he stimulated the connecting tissue, quickly sealing up the various cuts and strands of muscle. The vena cava was more difficult but he eventually grafted the tissue back together. The last things he did were heal the skin, stopping the blood loss, and encourage the bone marrow to produce more blood cells. He breathed, or she did, he couldn't tell. His memories and feelings bled into hers in an attempt to pull her from the recesses of her mind.

Licking his lips, he tasted the blood dripping from his nose. His vision faltered after that, causing him to retreat back into his own mind. He had done all he could. That was his last thought before he fell into the abyss.

EPILOGUE

He woke to voices in the dark. He knew the voices but it took him a minute to collect his thoughts. There were images and memories that were not his own. He went from cradling a baby on a barren world to walking through a museum on Earth with a father that wasn't his. Kalian pushed his awareness into the room before opening his eyes.

The feedback was disturbing.

He immediately shot up ready for a fight, building the power in his central nervous system. From the sheer size of his surroundings and the masses of nanocelium, he knew he was on the *Gommarian*. He had felt all twenty miles of it, with him somewhere in the belly.

"Easy!" Li'ara put a soothing hand on his chest.

He looked at her long and hard, just taking her in, he *had* saved her. He could see the tear in her undersuit and armour where a patch of perfectly healed skin was exposed. She felt like an extension of him now. He would have to work at telling their memories and experiences apart now. Everything about her told him he wasn't in immediate danger. He reached out and held her tight, probably too tight with his armoured suit.

"I thought..." He couldn't finish the words.

"I know. But there have been a few developments since you've been out." Li'ara stepped to the side revealing a small crowd of humans and Novaarians.

Kalian made a quick sweep of his mind checking for damage or a concussion. He couldn't quite believe what he was seeing.

"You look like shit, kid." Roland was standing off to the side, like always.

He had worn his usual undersuit with armoured plates, covered by the large animal-hide coat. From the look on his face, he had taken a beating though. Kalian had no doubt the drink in his hand was alcoholic.

"Greetings of peace, Kalian." Telarrek and Ilyseal were close by.

He did a double-take at the sight of the female Novaarian. He had been sure she would have died with the crew of the *Valoran*. He flicked between her and Roland as he realised that the agent should be dead as well. Kalian felt a weight lift from his shoulders at seeing them alive.

The med bay was half-filled by a group of humans on the other side. Four of them broke off and approached the unlikely group of friends.

"Hello, Mr Gaines. I am Captain Fey of the..." She stopped before the usual UDC speech.

Kalian was just shocked to see another human, a group of humans in fact. How many had survived? He quickly surmised that they must be the prisoners from the Laronian warship. Whatever she said next, he didn't hear. His eyes were fixed on the dark-haired woman standing next to her.

"Esabelle..." He said her name without thinking.

Kalian had never met her, but he knew it was Savrick's daughter. His memories of her were distorted as if he had dreamed about her.

"We have a lot to talk about," was her only reply.

The next few hours had been a lot to take in, for everyone. They were shown to the bridge, which had a very human feel to it and not at all what Kalian had seen in Savrick's memory. Esabelle remained silent, allowing the different people to be caught up on various events. Kalian and Li'ara were impressed with Roland's plan to board the *Gommarian,* while the other humans found it hard to accept the revelations concerning Earth.

Esabelle had confirmed for them that humans had indeed been engineered to ensure the survival of the Terran race. The captain and some of the scientists appeared shell-shocked for some time after that, though Roland seemed unfazed, but that could have been the drink. Kalian was sad to hear the fate of Namek but was grateful for his attempts to keep Li'ara and himself alive. If it hadn't been for him, they would have certainly died back at Clave Tower.

Telarrek told of a brave story in which he had fought the Gomar that Esabelle identified as Sef. His multiple injuries and cuts were a testament to the fight he had put up, as well as the limp he now walked with. But what troubled them more was the ending to his encounter. When the *Helion* had fallen from the sky, Sef fled the Outpost as it crumbled under the ship's weight.

Kalian felt a pit open in his stomach at the thought of a Gomar on the loose. ALF had led Telarrek to safety, before asking him to omit the existence of the AI in his report to the Conclave. It sounded like more manipulation from the AI to Kalian. He hadn't forgiven him for the way he tricked Li'ara onto the *Helion.* ALF had calculated that Li'ara's fate would be the only thing that could give him the strength to overcome Savrick and find a way to survive the *Helion.* At the same time he calculated that Savrick wouldn't be able to stop a Nexus-class starship landing on his head. The AI was a genius, but ruthless. Still, if the Conclave knew an AI existed with his level of sophistication, they would harvest him for parts.

"Has there been any word from ALF?" Kalian asked.

"No, but I wouldn't expect there to be." It was Esabelle who answered him. "He wouldn't risk so much as a laser-com with the *Gommarian,* for fear of infection."

Kalian could accept that, but the presence of Savrick's daughter didn't add up. "Everything I know about you and this ship doesn't add up to what I'm seeing." Kalian aimed his words at Esabelle, who had been monitoring the readout from a holographic console.

"That's because everything you know has come from ALF and Savrick, and they didn't know much."

Kalian was surprised Esabelle called him Savrick instead of father, but didn't ask.

"You should be aware, by the way, that a Conclave fleet has just emerged from subspace and is currently surrounding us."

"They don't know the situation," Telarrek explained. "They are simply creating a perimeter. We should make contact as soon as possible."

Kalian noticed the confused looks from the UDC personnel. Until they received translators they would be useless.

"Wait a minute." There was one thing Kalian couldn't figure out from what he had gleaned from Savrick. "How did the *Gommarian* even get here if you're not plugged into it?" He knew the ship was controlled by over-stimulating Esabelle's brain to actually move the dense vessel. But there were no engines inside it.

"I reconfigured the ship before disconnection. We now have everything a conventional vessel has; a bridge, a Starrillium, brig, sleeping quarters-"

"A bar!" was Roland's only contribution.

"And six fully-functioning factories, capable of making almost anything," Esabelle finished.

That last part was definitely not conventional.

"Where did you get a Starrillium from?" he asked.

"Compliments of ALF."

Her reply being so vague, Li'ara elaborated. "He ejected it from the *Helion* before he cut the antigravity thrusters."

Being so focused on Li'ara at the time, Kalian hadn't realised that if there had been a Starrillium on board, the whole moon would have shattered.

"So... what? You're saying the *Gommarian* is ours? Just like that? Why are you helping us?" Kalian couldn't put the pieces together.

"I have been *trying* to help you for centuries. It was I who hid the information regarding The Wall. It was I who kept the ports open for you." Esabelle shot Roland and the Novaarians a look. "I reconfigured the ship so you could find the others. I withheld the sensor feedback that would have warned the Gomar about the *Valoran's* Starrillium. I built the slowest craft I could to give you more time on Naveen. And I have been trying to break free of this monster for an eternity..."

Kalian resisted the urge to comfort her. He couldn't deny the feelings he had, but he also understood that they weren't entirely *his* feelings.

"I am not one of *them*." Esabelle looked in the general direction of the Rem-stores.

Kalian wasn't sure how he felt yet about a dozen Gomar snoozing so close by.

"While they spent millennia sleeping, I grew. I learned everything I could about our potential and endeavoured to teach myself control. I couldn't disconnect until I knew I could control my abilities. I tricked Elandar into thinking I was inside the virtuality he created. But when we first discovered the Conclave, centuries ago, everything changed. When I learned of The Wall, so did it..." Kalian noticed everyone look at each other in confusion.

Li'ara stared at Esabelle intently. "What do you mean, *it*?" she asked.

"I wasn't the only one controlling this ship. It took me centuries but I finally contained it before disconnecting. I could feel it like an itch at the back of my mind. It observed everything I did but it had different motives. I had to fight it all the way. When you boarded, it sent those hunter-mechs to kill you." She aimed it at Roland who was pinching his broken nose. "I never gained full access but its thoughts leaked over. Savrick wanted to wipe out all Terran life, even human life, but I think he was poisoned by its own desires to destroy us. When I found evidence of Terran technology on Naveen, it woke up with a *need*. I don't know where it came from but it only has one purpose, remove any and all Terran life from this galaxy. All the while there was a background feeling that something worse was coming."

"Well whatever it is, it's either really patient or it lives forever,"

Kalian said. "It clearly thinks in terms of millennia if it's happy to just roam the galaxy looking for Earth all that time."

"Why human life?" Captain Fey asked with no lack of dread.

"Because it sees us as a threat." Surprisingly, it was Li'ara who replied.

Kalian gave her a questioning look and she explained ALF's findings on the outer reaches of the Norma Arm. It was news to Esabelle who admitted to having no knowledge about the ancient probes.

"I have trapped it inside its own processing unit and severed its connection to the ship. The cube itself is being housed below the Starrillium."

One of Esabelle's words caught Kalian's attention.

The cube...

Was this the same cube Savrick had found buried inside the cavern? He kept the thought to himself for now.

"Why would they see humanity as a threat?" Ilyseal asked the obvious question.

"Because of what we're capable of. Our potential." Li'ara looked to Kalian.

He had to agree with her assessment for the Gomar had proved how much damage they could cause with less than a thousand of them. But who was it they were threatening? And where did they come from? They certainly had the time to play the long game.

"In that regard, we will have to deal with the Conclave," Telarrek said. "After the attack on the capital, they will be highly suspicious of humans, especially if you are to remain in this vessel."

It did seem highly unlikely that the council would grant them membership or even a planet to call home.

"I think in this instance it would be better if you spoke on our behalf." Esabelle was looking at Telarrek. "Especially since every ship has just armed their full complement of planet breakers."

THEY WAITED two days before the council finally arrived via the *Marillion*, a spherical ship the size of a small moon. Telarrek informed them it was the only Galactic-class starship and the pride of the Conclave fleet, at half the size of the *Gommarian*. Due to the mass of both great ships they were forced to keep their distance from Nova Prime and Naveen.

It had felt like a lifetime to Kalian as they waited. He remained in his fitted suit of Terran armour as it felt like a second skin to him now. Captain Fey had given several speeches already to the remainder of their race. After the first, he didn't stop to listen to the rest but he was glad someone was trying to instil the hope they would need to survive. The population hadn't taken the news about Earth's and Century's destruction very well. There had been fears of suicide from the people who had lost entire families. In that regard, Kalian was thankful he had been an only child with no other connections.

Only a handful of people had taken to exploring the ship. Esabelle had supplied handheld Datapads to help with navigating the massive vessel, but most preferred the safety of numbers inside the hold. Captain Fey had separated the UDC personnel from the scientists, so Esabelle could instruct them in the use of the ship's controls. Not that they could go anywhere with the barricade of Conclave security ships outside. The *Gommarian's* ability to produce food and drink had subdued the population somewhat, Kalian decided not to ask how it was made. In truth, it could take years to fully explore the epic vessel.

Telarrek had shown the Laronian survivors to a separate living area since relations had become somewhat frayed. Roland stalked the corridors like a caged animal. Kalian knew the agent wanted to leave it all behind and find his own way in this new world. But that was why they had to wait for the council.

After initial communications, the bridge crew were informed that the *Marillion* would be sending a smaller ship with the council on board. They were instructed to meet the ship at the halfway point between them and the *Gommarian*. Esabelle showed the crew how to activate the factories and build another craft for transport. Everyone was amazed by the nanocelium and their ability to construct almost anything.

To Captain Fey's annoyance, she was not invited to the rendezvous since her authority was not recognised by the council. Li'ara had reassured her that, as a UDC representative, she would speak on the captain's behalf. Along with the Novaarians, Kalian and Li'ara entered the cathedral-size hangar where a ship waited for them.

"What are you doing here?" Li'ara asked.

"I thought you deserved one last look at my pretty face, Red." Roland was leaning against their ship. "This is where we part ways."

"And how's that exactly?"

With her question, the space next to Roland erupted with activity as another ship became visible. The vessel was somewhere between impressive and a hunk of junk. The hull was tinted bronze around its circular shape, with a large cylindrical extension on one side that was clearly the engine. The starboard side was concave as if a bite had been taken out of the hull. It was three or four times the size of the *Fathom* and twice as big as the unassuming vessel next to it.

"You cannot leave with the barricade in place." Ilyseal sounded more concerned for his safety than angering the Conclave.

"The *Rackham* can. Stealthware babe!" He thumbed the ship behind him. "A parting gift from Esabelle, I guess."

"Or maybe she figured it was more dangerous keeping you on board," Li'ara retorted.

"Why would you leave, Roland? You saved the entire human race." Kalian was sad that he was only referring to seven thousand people. "You're a hero!"

Roland laughed at the word.

"That ain't me, kid. Besides, they've got you now." He looked at Li'ara with a coy smile. "I'm afraid we'll have to wait until next time, Red. Try not to be too disappointed." With that, he turned and left for his new ship as Li'ara gave him the finger.

Kalian had no doubt that the *Rackham* was filled with stashes of alcohol and weapons. The Conclave had just become a little less safe in Kalian's opinion.

Within minutes they had left the *Gommarian,* with the automated ship flying them towards the council. The Conclave vessel was more of a giant platform with a dome in the centre. The same Nix that escorted them in the council chamber was waiting for them inside the landing platform. They were soon taken to the semicircle chamber that housed the five councillors of the ruling races. Kalian had a feeling this meeting would not be so public.

Elondrasa appeared to be in full health, with no evidence that she had been attacked by Savrick: a testament to the Conclave's medical advancements.

"Greetings of peace, to you all," said the old Novaarian.

"Peace?" snorted Lordina. "They are warmongers! It was a human who decimated the Conclave, who destroyed the *Helion* and took possession of a Laronian warship."

"A warship that abducted thousands of our people!" Kalian winced at Li'ara's outburst.

This line of arguing continued for several minutes, during which time the council explained that the Laronians had had every intention of presenting the humans to the council. Li'ara wasn't convinced. Eventually, Telarrek stepped forward and told the council everything that had transpired since they fled the Conclave capital. Kalian noted the absence of ALF in his recounting.

Kalian still felt partly responsible for the state of humanity, if only for surviving the catastrophe that befell it. "Now you know our history, as hard as it is to believe. But we need to look to our future. Our home is gone and our origins lie on the other side of the galaxy. We are few in number and the closest to extinction we have ever come. Will you help us?"

The councillors looked to one another but said nothing, suggesting that their decision had already been made before the meeting.

"No." It was the Raalak councillor, Brokk, who answered.

Telarrek and Ilyseal nearly spoke out before Elondrasa held up a hand to silence them.

Brokk continued, "It may not have been you or your people that attacked us, but that distinction will be hard to make. All the races saw Savrick attack the council chamber. It is as much for your protection as it is ours that we remain apart. In time, a middle-ground may be found."

Li'ara gripped Kalian's hand. He could feel the anger building inside her.

"There is good news," Nu-marn, the Shay councillor, interjected. "Our long-range scans have detected multiple vessels of human design. They are responding to our signal, in binary for now, but they are coming. From the telemetry, it appears they are coming from different regions across the Orion Arm. We will see to it that they find their way to you."

Kalian looked to Li'ara and he knew she felt the same elation that he did. It was a silver lining of hope against the Conclave's rejection.

"That is not the end of it, I am afraid," Ch'lac interjected. The small Ch'kara was examining Kalian with a scrupulous eye. "You must hand over that ship and yourself, Kalian Gaines."

Kalian instinctively held out his arm, keeping Li'ara from throttling the little alien.

"We have reviewed the data from the Novaarian fleet and seen your... capabilities. The council has deemed you and that ship too dangerous to go around unchecked."

Kalian took a breath and looked at Li'ara. He felt the energy in his spine give him the feeling of invincibility against such beings. It made him bold again.

"With respect, Councillors..." He converted the molecules around his hands to create organic plasma, more light than matter though.

Li'ara stepped away feeling the heat on her skin as the light increased.

"You can try..." Kalian had no intention of using his abilities; he just wanted to make a point.

"Are you threatening us?" Lordina spat as a dozen armed guards flooded the chamber.

Telarrek appeared partially relieved at the sight of Uthor, who led the security team. There was no evidence that the great Raalak had suffered at the hands of the beast.

"If you aren't going to ensure our safety within your borders, and give us somewhere to live, we will stay on the *Gommarian*. It seems to me that ship is the safest place for us. It's more powerful than anything you have, and so are we."

He was hoping that last part would make them think. It was entirely possible that more humans might develop his abilities, but it was just unlikely to be in this generation. But they didn't need to know that.

"And if this other threat *is* real, it might pay to have us on your side."

The council had been sceptical about the creatures Esabelle and ALF had hinted at. It didn't help that they had left out ALF and Esabelle from their report, making the source of their facts questionable. The council were silent after that.

After a moment of silence, Kalian knew nothing would change. He reached for Li'ara and motioned for her to follow him back to the craft.

"Wait." It was Elondrasa that made the command. The councillors looked to her as this was clearly not part of their plan. "You have not been accepted into the Conclave, but the Novaarian council will allow you to remain in our borders. Charge Telarrek here will be our liaison."

Kalian heard the councillors gasp and raise their hands to protest. Elondrasa raised her own and silenced them. Kalian had no idea what was next for the human race, but he wouldn't refuse help if it came their way.

"You have the gratitude of my people, Councillor Elondrasa." He surprised himself with his new found level of diplomacy, even if it was a little heavy-handed.

With that, they made their farewells to Telarrek and Ilyseal who would both have to keep in contact on behalf of Nova Prime. Kalian was truly thankful for that. In a chaotic new world, Telarrek and Ilyseal had become his friends. He wasn't sure how he was supposed to feel, having more alien friends than human friends. Thinking about this new society they would have to get along with, Kalian realised that such differences would have to be ignored. Despite the multitude of species they were now surrounded by, they all inhabited the same galaxy.

An escort of armed guards walked them back to their ship where they departed for the *Gommarian*. Kalian sat next to Li'ara in the cockpit while admiring the spectacle of the Conclave fleet against the turquoise of Nova Prime. He had no idea what was coming their way. Humanity was at a crossroads it had never faced before. In the strangest twist of events, this history lecturer had been thrust into leading a people that weren't technically the same species as him anymore. He pushed the thought away, preferring to consider himself a human rather than Terran.

"The universe just got a lot bigger. Are you ready for what comes next?" Li'ara said, turning to him in her seat.

Kalian rested his head back and smiled at the starry vista. "Absolutely not..."

PHILIP C. QUAINTRELL

Hear more from Philip C. Quaintrell including book releases and exclusive content:

PHILIPCQUAINTRELL.COM

FACEBOOK.COM/PHILIPCQUAINTRELL

@PHILIPCQUAINTRELL.AUTHOR

@PCQUAINTRELL

ABOUT THE AUTHOR

Philip C. Quaintrell is the author of the epic fantasy series, The Echoes Saga, as well as the Terran Cycle sci-fi series. He was born in Cheshire in 1989 and started his career as an emergency nurse.

Having always been a fan of fantasy and sci-fi fiction, Philip started to find himself feeling frustrated as he read books, wanting to delve into the writing himself to tweak characters and storylines. He decided to write his first novel as a hobby to escape from nursing and found himself swept away into the world he'd created. Even now, he talks about how the characters tell him what they're going to do next, rather than the other way around.

With his first book written, and a good few rejected agency submissions under his belt, he decided to throw himself in at the deep end and self-publish. 2 months and £60 worth of sales in, he took his wife out to dinner to celebrate an achievement ticked off his bucket list - blissfully unaware this was just the beginning.

Fast forward 12 months and he was self-publishing book 1 of his fantasy series (The Echoes Saga; written purely as a means to combat his sci-fi writers' block). With no discernible marketing except the 'Amazon algorithm', the book was in the amazon bestsellers list in at least 4 countries within a month. The Echoes Saga has now surpassed 700k copies sold worldwide, has an option agreement for a potential TV-series in the pipeline and Amazon now puts Philip's sales figures in the top 1.8% of self-published authors worldwide.

Philip lives in Cheshire, England with his wife and two children. He still finds time between naps and wiping snot off his clothes to remain a movie aficionado and comic book connoisseur, and is hoping this is still just the beginning.

AUTHOR NOTES

The question I get asked the most is, 'How do you write a book?' You may well have reached the end of this book and come to the conclusion that I *don't* know how to write a book. You might be right. Intrinsic was my first novel, and when I sat down to write it I had no idea what I was doing, how long it would be, the correct way to write it etc. I've read a lot of books but that doesn't mean I know how to write one, especially with so many authors having their own style these days.

I digress.

I don't know how other authors create their stories (having never met another one) but I always start with character creation. Before I had anything written down about the Terran or the Conclave, I had several pages of information on Kalian Gaines. I wish I could tell you where the name came from, but I was overheated and overtired when it came to me. You see, the crazy idea of writing a book came to me while I was on holiday in the Mediterranean, with my Family. I don't know if you've ever slept on a boat in the Turkish summer, but when there's no air conditioning and the beds are akin to coffins, it's kind of hard to sleep.

After planting my mattress onto the deck above, I had the privilege of sleeping under the stars. Now, I live in Manchester – we see stars in the sky sure, but not like you do in the middle of the ocean, away from all the lights – so this particular view was new to me. Thanks to my dad, I've been a fan of Sci-Fi all my life, so I enjoyed looking up at the sky and wondering how much there was to see and explore. In other words, it sent my imagination into overdrive.

I should say, it was about this time I was beginning to get a little tired of some of the books I was reading, especially the ones with massive galaxy-endangering plots, as told from the point of view of the little guy. I get this point of view, since it would be a perspective many of us would share if the world or the galaxy was suddenly in danger, I was just longing for some central characters that were believable and had a lot to do.

I was hesitant at first, since authors are these magical super-duper people who were born to write for us... until I realised they're not. Authors are just normal people who have stories inside their head, and somehow find a way to get it out. This realisation hit me when I self-published this book and someone referred to me as an author in their review (my head swelled a little bit that day). This surprised me though, as I don't think of myself as an author. I'm a nurse by trade and have been since I left school. My special abilities don't lie with writing, but with staying on my feet for 13 hours and ignoring the overwhelming urge to pee.

Urgh! I've digressed again.

How do you write a book? Well, like I've said, I started with Kalian's profile, then Li'ara's and Savrick's and so on. I love my villains. They have to be just as interesting and believable as the protagonist, since it's often their motives that actually drive a story. I also enjoy making the villain somewhat relatable. I want to read about an antagonist and see his point of view or even agree with some of it (or at least agree with why they chose a certain path). I hope in some way that, having read the book, you can relate to Savrick and see how he fell into a path of self-destruction and emotional rage.

After figuring out some of the characters, I started to fill my notepad with specific scenes that I thought were interesting. Annoyingly, one of the best scenes I thought of wouldn't have worked in this book, but I did manage to work into Tempest (See Tempest Author Notes). My first idea was the human handprint in the stone, on Naveen. As soon as the idea of it gripped my curiosity, I knew it was something I had to explore further. I bounced some of these ideas off my family to see if they found any of it interesting, as well as exploring other avenues. I remember distinctly asking Amy, my sister in-law, while she was trying to sunbathe, 'How would you blow up a sun?' Needless to say, some research was required.

After coming up with some scenes and plot points, I started to create the various alien races. Some people have asked where the hell I came up with the names, but I honestly couldn't tell you. I often have to google the things I make up, just to make certain it doesn't already exist and the name hasn't been lodged in my subconscious from years past. If I ever name my protagonist Harry Skywalker or the villains are called Daleks, you'll know I've stopped checking, as well as giving up on my imagination.

Now, The Terran Cycle is a four part series, and I planned out the second, third and fourth books chapter by chapter, but Intrinsic wasn't planned out. Some of you might be thinking, 'That's bloody obvious!' but it's completely true. I'm sure professional authors such as Peter Hamilton and Neal Asher plan out every point before they write their first sentence, but back in 2013 (which is actually when I wrote Intrinsic) I was not an author of any kind, and planning out a book that was just over 600 pages long was not in my skill set. Instead, I often tried to think as a certain character and make decisions as they would, depending on their personality and whatever background I had designed for them.

This translated into certain twists and changes in the story that I would have never explored otherwise. A simple example would be when Savrick and the others arrive on Naveen. I hadn't planned on Kalian locking Li'ara inside the lift so he could face them alone. Or, when ALF asks Li'ara to fly up to the Helion and take control for him. Up until that point in the book, I had no idea how Kalian was going to beat Savrick. I like to think that this helped the story, as it was often told from Kalian's point of view, and he had no idea how he was going to use his powers to help anyone, let alone defeat Savrick.

So Intrinsic was pretty unplanned, but I used my breaks at work to note down the next three books, planning them out chapter by chapter. It was only by doing this that I realised it was going to be four books. In my head it was a trilogy, but as Emma, my wife, often tells me, I was wrong. So four books... that's four years of writing for me. Working full time as a nurse doesn't leave much space in my calendar, as well as the desire to see my wife and enjoy a social life.

I hope you enjoyed the story and my ramblings into the creation of the book itself. Until the next time...

TEMPEST

PROLOGUE

With no sound at all, the *Tempest* was violently ripped from subspace and hurled back into the vacuum of reality. On every deck, alarms cut through the eerie silence of their long journey home. The Rem-stores automatically came to life, rousing their occupants with stimulants designed for such emergencies. Overhead spotlights illuminated the slumbering chamber in a soft glow, as the first of the Terran crew stepped out of their advanced sarcophagus.

Adanae put one foot on the cold polished floor, trying to make sense of her own thoughts. Her heart was racing in her chest as the stimulants worked to rouse her as fast as possible. Using her Terran abilities, she connected to her body's receptors and slowly began to take back control, slowing her heart rate to a steady sixty-five beats per minute. Pushing her awareness beyond the Rem-store, she felt the familiar presence of her fellow scientists and friends.

After a few seconds, Adanae's vision corrected the constant spinning, bringing back the clarity of the *Tempest*. She stepped out completely, allowing the connecting tubules to disconnect and the machine to close up behind her. The cold air was uncomfortable on her naked body. More of the Rem-stores began to open down the corridor with their internal green lights illuminating the walls. The gloomy corridor was filling with more naked bodies and a lot of confused expressions. The overhead lights flickered, telling Adanae the ship was diverting energy - never a good sign.

As she held out her hand, palm down, the ship produced an oval column of liquid-like nanocelium that rose up to meet her, where it coalesced into a solid object. Using anti-gravity projectors, a triangular device with the apex cut off was presented at the top of the column, floating end over end. Adanae quickly scooped it up and pressed it below her navel. The nanocelium contained within immediately dispersed across her body like a second skin. Without thinking she opened her hand and used the emitters in her fingertips to create an orange holographic menu inside her palm. By flexing each finger, she manipulated the hologram into selecting the colour white for her armoured exo-suit. As a scientist, she had always preferred white, as opposed to the black typically worn by their warriors.

"ALF, turn that damned alarm off!" With no response from the AI, she remembered that he was no longer on board, but instead entombed on a distant moon, light-years away. "*Tempest*, deactivate the alarm." At once the blaring signal stopped, bringing back the chatter of the others along the corridor as they suited up as she had. "Report."

"Light-drive engines have been manually taken offline," the ship's male voice stated. "In the unscheduled emergence into real space, the aft hull was breached. Life support systems are compromised."

As lead scientist, Adanae took charge and ordered the six nearest crew to leave and man the bridge, located two decks above them.

"*Tempest*, how could the drives be taken offline manually? Everyone was in Rem-storage."

"Incorrect. Prior to the alarm, one Rem-store was opened ahead of schedule. Life-support at fifty-seven percent. Estimated twenty-one hours before complete depletion of oxygen stores."

Adanae felt her stomach flip. She knew exactly whose Rem-store had opened; he was the only one who would do this.

"Where is he right now?"

"Please specify."

"Where is Malekk, *Tempest*?" Dealing with a sub-AI was frustrating.

"Engineering - deck three."

"You are to treat him as hostile, *Tempest*. Do you understand? You have to stop him before he does any more damage." She knew it had been a mistake to keep him alive, let alone keep him on the ship. She turned to Grif and Nalana, signalling them to follow her.

"Unable to comply," the *Tempest* AI replied. "Internal security measures have been shut down."

Adanae groaned in frustration as they exited the deck. She instructed everyone telepathically to man their stations and have teams ready to fix the drives and life support after they dealt with Malekk. She wouldn't normally use such an intimate form of communication on a large scale, but she needed everyone to receive their orders on the other decks as fast as possible. The grav tubes beyond the chamber allowed for a quick descent to the engineering deck.

She knew that the ship, shaped like the head of a spoon, was spinning out of control in the middle of space. If it wasn't for the grav plating, they would all be pummelled to death inside the giant centrifuge. She suddenly began to worry *where* they were. What if they were being pulled into the gravity well of a planet or a star?

"*Tempest*, what is our location at present?"

"Unknown. Sensors are currently offline while life-support is compromised."

She blamed the stimulants for not making the connection with the flickering lights earlier. The ship would automatically shut down nonessential automations to divert energy to life-support. She sent a quick telepathic message to Ryson on the bridge. She wanted sensors brought back online as soon as possible.

"How long have we been in storage?" Grif asked.

"Fifty-one days, eleven hours, twenty-eight minutes and thirty-four seconds."

"Is that it?" Nalana exclaimed. "Have we even left this arm of the galaxy yet?"

"Negative."

"We should have brought a bigger ship," Grif replied.

"Or a Starforge." Nalana joked. Without ALF it was impossible to use a Starforge. Only the AI could comprehend the mathematics required to fold space in such a way, and the individual components wouldn't even fit on board.

"Quit the jokes," Adanae ordered. "We have to stop him." They were approaching the doors to engineering.

"We brought him down the first time, we can do it again." Grif sounded confident as an organic ball of plasma was birthed in his hand, wiping away the shadows.

"We should have killed him there and then." Nalana activated her suit's menu and reshaped the nanocelium. Her head and face were instantly encompassed in white plating that sloped down into her chin. Grif quickly followed suit, but Adanae didn't even think about it. She suffered from claustrophobia enough as it was on board the ship, without coating her face with a metal helmet. She had been meaning to go through her mind and erase the fear but had been too busy with the *Second Chance* project.

The console on the wall wasn't responding to their touch, and the door's sensors refused to recognise their presence. Adanae pushed out her awareness, feeling Malekk's position beyond the door in her mind. He wasn't hiding. It was playing out exactly the same as the first time they caught him. While in orbit around the planet of the future Terran, Malekk had tried to sabotage the genetic manipulation of one of the local creatures. They later learned that he had been in the process of building a communicator array, powerful enough to transmit a message to Savrick and the rest of the Gomar. Adanae was already regretting being on the side of keeping him alive for trial when they finally returned.

The war had been black and white before people like Malekk came along, sympathisers to the Gomar cause, willing to kill their own on the orders of some madman. Savrick was only too willing to use the Terran against themselves; he probably thought it was poetic.

He had killed two of their crew in their first encounter. He may be a scientist first but, like all Terran, he had been instructed in the ways of war when the first solar system had been wiped out by the Gommarian. Adanae knew he wouldn't just surrender at the sight of them and, if his actions were anything to go by, he was intent on killing them all. Nalana removed two hilts from the base of her back and activated the nanocelium to create short blades. Adanae on the other hand, welcomed the tingle in her spine and the resultant heat flowing into her hands as she connected to the universe.

They used telekinesis to slide open the door, breaking the internal servos. Speed and numbers were the only advantages they would have. Nalana dashed to the left, leaping up the wall to gain some height on Malekk. Grif slid to the floor, firing off a couple of plasma orbs in the traitor's direction, no doubt using his connection to the universe to guide his aim. Adanae stood her ground, cocooned in a thick shield of telekinetic energy. More proficient in her tele-pathic abilities, she poured her consciousness into Malekk's. His defences were good but she distracted him enough to give the others a chance. One of Grif's shots fizzled against Malekk's shield, creating a rainbow as the light refracted, but the second struck him across the thigh dropping him to one knee. Nalana came down at that same moment, her blades angled to plunge through his chest. In a last show of strength, Malekk held up his hand, telekinetically pushing her back into the wall. That use of energy was all Adanae needed to force her way past his defence and blanket his mind with her own suggestions.

Pain was the only thing she had in mind. They all felt his shield disintegrate as his mind exploded in agony. Grif took advantage and strode over to the kneeling man, his fists clenched. There was no hesitation as he punched Malekk square in the jaw, dropping him to the floor like a stone.

An hour later they regrouped on the bridge, having placed Malekk safely back inside a new Rem-store. How he had escaped his previous store was a mystery, but his proficiency with machines was no secret, much like his Gomar allies. Adanae watched him sleep on the holographic monitor, his short brown hair and cropped beard appearing green in the light.

"The drives should be back online within the hour," Ryson reported. "Life support's back up and running at full capacity, but we'll probably need to perform a full diagnostic across all the major systems. We don't know what else he tampered with."

"Where are we?" Adanae asked. The feed from outside showed a solar system with a small blue star. There were four planets orbiting it, each one a desolate rock with no hope of conceiving life in the cold system.

"We're approximately twelve thousand light-years from the new world and three thousand light-years from the moon where we left ALF." Ryson left his chair and joined Adanae and the others at the central station. Everyone on the bridge stopped and listened to them plan their next move.

"*Tempest*, how long until we reach the empire at maximum yield?"

"Twelve years, three months and nineteen days." It was a hard pill to swallow for everyone. They had already been away from the empire and all those they loved for ninety-seven years.

"Who knows what the empire will look like when we get back? Maybe we've already won and there's a big party to return to." Grif didn't sound convincing.

"Or maybe we're heading into a trap," Nalana offered, pessimistically.

"Then at least we've secured the Terran lineage." Ryson tied his blonde hair behind his head using telekinesis.

"I'm more concerned about our immediate problems." Adanae pushed the image of Malekk's sleeping form into the middle of the station. "Twelve years is a long time for something to go wrong. He's dangerous."

"What do you want to do, eject him into space?" Ryson was clearly against the idea.

"Why not?" Nalana spat. "He's a traitor and, more than that, he nearly killed us all in our sleep. I say we space his ass."

Grif stroked his goatee. "He's still a Terran. He deserves our burial rites at least. He should be given back to his star." Such rites were hardly used before the war since many Terran chose to live forever.

"He was born on Crychek," Adanae pointed out. "We can't keep him on board until we reach that system. Besides, he isn't actually dead yet. Until he's tried it would just be murder."

"Ejecting him into space is murder!" Ryson looked shocked at Adanae's words.

She tried to ignore it but coming from Ryson it was hard. They had been lovers for the majority of their time away, and she couldn't help being fond of him.

"Then we just send him out in his Rem-store," Nalana countered.

That gave Adanae a thought.

"He'd still die when the Rem-store loses power!" Ryson continued to protest.

"ALF designed those things to last thousands of years."

"Then he'll probably outlive us all." Adanae announced, "I'm making an executive decision. We won't kill Malekk, but he can't come with us either." She ignored the confused expressions and continued. "He is a killer and a traitor. I don't think he deserves a Terran burial, but I can't condone murder on my watch. So he gets to live, forever. We're dropping him off on the nearest planet, inside his Rem-store."

Grif wouldn't meet her eyes and Ryson simply walked off the bridge, shaking his head. Nalana was already setting the ship on course for the nearest planet.

Another hour passed by before the drives were fully operational again. Most of the crew were already getting back into their Rem-stores and handing the ship's functions over to the *Tempest*. AI Adanae took one last look at the monitor, seeing the abandoned capsule half buried in the planet's rocky, dead surface. At least he gets to sleep forever, she thought. Who knew what they were flying home to? Adanae turned off the monitor, knowing she would be the last person to ever lay eyes on Malekk of Crychek.